THE
SEA
RISES

THE SEA RISES

The FORM & VOID Trilogy
BOOK III

A·J·SMITH

HEAD
ZEUS

An Ad Astra Book

First published in 2022 by Head of Zeus Ltd,
part of Bloomsbury Publishing Plc

Copyright © A.J. Smith, 2022

The moral right of A.J. Smith to be identified as the author of this
work has been asserted in accordance with the Copyright, Designs
and Patents Act of 1988.

9 7 5 3 1 2 4 6 8

A catalogue record for this book is available from the British Library.

ISBN (HB): 9781786696960
ISBN (XTPB): 9781786696977
ISBN (E): 9781786696953

Typeset by Siliconchips Services Ltd UK

Printed and bound by CPI Group (UK) Ltd, Croydon, CR0 4YY

Head of Zeus Ltd
5–8 Hardwick Street
London EC1R 4RG

WWW.HEADOFZEUS.COM

For Rowan

THE KINGDOM OF THE
FOUR CLAWS

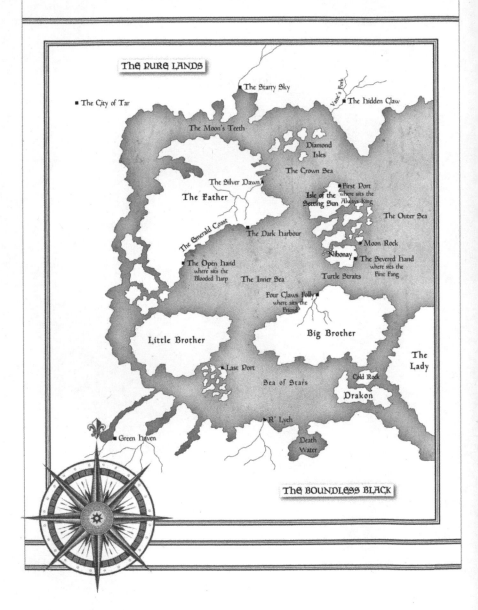

THE PURE LANDS

The Starry Sky

The City of Tar

Vane's Fork

The hidden Claw

The Moon's Teeth

Diamond Isles

The Crown Sea

The Silver Dawn

The Father

Isle of the Setting Sun

First Port
where sits the Always-King

The Outer Sea

The Emerald Coast

The Dark harbour

Moon Rock

The Open hand
where sits the Blooded harp

Nibonay

The Severed hand
where sits the First Fang

The Inner Sea

Turtle Straits

Four Claws Folly
where sits the Friend

Little Brother

Big Brother

The Lady

Last Port

Sea of Stars

Cold Rock

Drakon

R' Lyeh

Green haven

Death Water

THE BOUNDLESS BLACK

THE ISLAND OF
NIBONAY

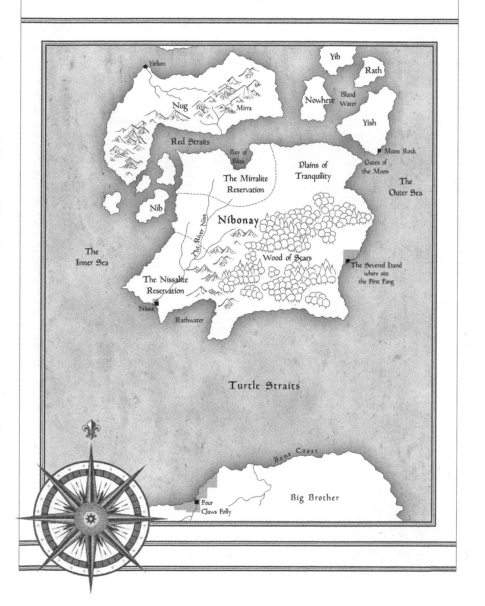

THE HOLD OF THE
SEVERED HAND

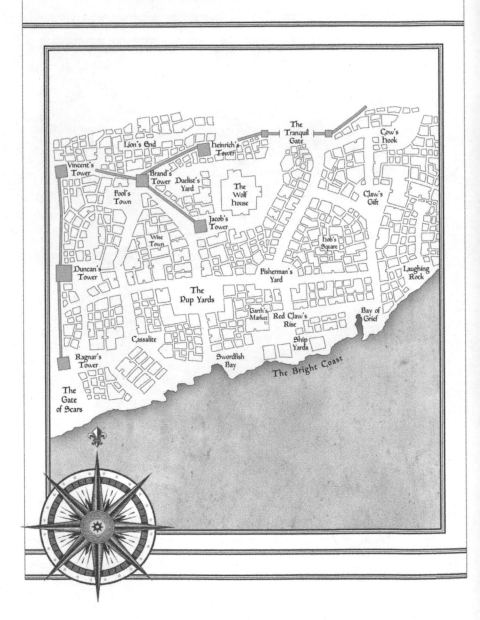

Lion's End

Heinrich's Tower

The Tranquil Gate

Cow's hook

Vincent's Tower

Brand's Tower

Duelist's Yard

The Wolf house

Claw's Gift

Fool's Town

Jacob's Tower

Hob's Square

Wise Town

Duncan's Tower

Fisherman's Yard

Laughing Rock

The Pup Yards

Garth's Market

Red Claw's Rise

Bay of Grief

Cassalite

Ship Yards

Ragnar's Tower

Swordfish Bay

The Bright Coast

The Gate of Scars

PROLOGUE

The water was warm and rolled only gently. As the creature swam nearer to the surface, it covered its eyes in a thin membrane to protect against the glare of the surface world. At this shallow depth, the sea was impossibly blue and crystal clear, and the warmth was gratifying to the creature's old bones. It had not felt warmth for an age and had missed the sensation. It let its gills pulse and ripple in the warm water, sending a delightful tingle across its slender arms and legs. The flared webbing on its hands and feet enabled the creature to glide effortlessly upwards, and the broad, spiny crest down its body and tail gave it tremendous speed, though it was not using its speed to swim directly to the surface. The creature was turning and spiralling in the sea, playfully weaving back and forth just under the water line. It needed time for its large, black eyes to become accustomed to the light, for it could barely remember the last time it had seen the sun.

After a gleeful few hours of playing in the warm water, the creature slowly ascended, weaving upwards with its muscular tail, until its head emerged into the light. Its head was small compared to its large, elegant body, with few facial features other than a pair of circular black eyes and a narrow, wide mouth. The creature *could* be expressive, flaring the light blue crest that began at its forehead and ended at the tip of its tail. It could even smile, should the mood arise. As it was, the creature was pensive, unsure what it would find in the surface world after so long away.

It could tread water indefinitely, turning left and right to get a good view of its surroundings. It feared the view would just be of the open sea, but luckily the creature was not the only thing newly risen from the black depths of the ocean. Rocky pinnacles, covered in seaweed and barnacles, punctuated the water, creating an enormous barrier around a central island. The small landmass was pitted and craggy, with a single peak at its centre, for in the distant past it had been an active volcano. It had languished in a deep ocean trench, only now re-emerging into the clear sky of this world.

The creature smiled, its long, thin mouth covering most of its face. It swished its tail and plunged downwards into a happy somersault, before poking its head back up to the surface world. Long, long ago the island, and the sea-caves beneath it, had been the creature's home. It was excited to return to the beautiful underwater caves, with their brightly coloured fish and vibrant coral.

But its happiness and excitement was short-lived. Nearby, stuck on the newly risen shore of the creature's island, was a strange contraption. It looked as if it was made from pieces of a tree, cut into planks and secured together. Within its concave frame were three babbling animals, encased in fabric, with hairy heads and faces. The creature let forth a startled squeak and ducked back beneath the surface, for fear of being seen as a threat by these strange animals.

The creature silently swam towards the wooden thing, reaching out with its senses to see if it was in danger. It gathered pebbles with a sweep of its webbed hand and allowed itself another small smile. It was nice to feel something other than water.

"By the Bright Lands, what the fuck is that?"

"Calm down, it's just a big fish."

"That is not a fucking fish. It's one of those big frog-things"

The creature wasn't sure what the sounds meant, but the animals in the wooden thing appeared agitated and afraid. Close up, they were quite small, and hefted strange objects of wood and metal. The creature believed they were weapons of some kind, but assessed that the hairy animals were more afraid than *it* was, and probably quite harmless. It wanted to communicate with them, but would need time to understand their sounds. They appeared sophisticated enough to have language, and their forms were familiar. At the very least they had two legs, two arms and a head. Was this what the living world had conjured in the absence of the Ik'thya'nym?

The creature felt an uncomfortable sting at the base of its tail and realized the animals had thrown something at it, using a smaller wooden contraption to propel a splinter at speed. It decided to put a stop to that by emerging onto land.

"Shoot it again."

"It's getting closer."

"What is it? I saw those Sunken Men at the Bay of Bliss, it ain't one of them."

The creature glided into the shallows and stood up, flicking countless centuries of sea water onto the gravelly beach of its island. The sky was endless and intoxicating, and the creature was happy enough to almost ignore the second wooden splinter propelled into its tail. Almost, but not entirely. It turned to the fabric-clad animals, irritated that they'd interrupted its communion with the surface world. It didn't wish to harm them, for it was not a violent creature and didn't like seeing violence in others.

"Again. Shoot it."

One of the animals fumbled in his fabric, trying to pull another splinter from a container hanging around his waist. All three had now stood up and were barely half the height of the creature, though they were solidly built and certainly land animals. It didn't want to scare them, but neither did it want more wooden splinters fired at it.

"Load your fucking crossbow."

"My hands are shaking."

"This island didn't exist a week ago. What's happening?"

The creature stopped fidgeting as it regained comfort in the surface world. The open spaces and changeable winds were wonderful, but had not been felt for a very long time, and the babbling animals were adding an urgency to the situation that was somewhat unwelcome. The creature decided to be gentle. It opened its stance, pulling its long tail from the sea and flaring its pale blue crest. With arms wide and a warm smile on its face, the creature bowed to the animals, trying to convey that it was not a threat.

"What the fuck? What's it doing?"

The creature began to understand the odd utterance. They certainly used separate sounds, almost like words, but strung together with such speed as to make individual meaning hard to discern. They were asking questions, or perhaps just expressing incredulity. It thought it would try to communicate. The creature placed a webbed hand on its head, saying *Ik'thya'nym* to the jittery animals. *Ik'thya'nym.* Then it hunkered down, leaning back on its tail and trying to appear less intimidating. Perhaps they had old stories and the name would be familiar.

One of the animals yelped and hid behind the other two.

"It's talking."

"At least it's not trying to eat us."

"It hasn't got any teeth."

The creature sat on the pebbles, listening carefully to the animals' sounds. They'd stopped trying to hurt it, but were no less questioning. Everything about their body language projected fear and uncertainty, and the creature wished it understood what they were saying. It was supremely perceptive, bordering on the empathic, and could discern intention and character with relative ease, but language still took time. "Ik'thya'nym," it said again, this time with sadness.

One of the animals narrowed its eyes and took a step towards the creature. It waved its hand in the air, before turning back to the other two. "I think it's saying hello."

"Ak," said the creature, smiling again and mimicking the animal's hand-waving.

"Don't get too close to it."

"Relax, it's no Sunken Man. You shot it twice and it's not attacking."

The animal was tentative, but slowly put its fabric-clad feet into the gently lapping wash of the island and approached the creature. Not too close, but close enough to signal a lack of fear. The one that approached was younger than the other two, with less hair and a smoother face.

"Hello," said the animal.

"Ha... lo," replied the creature. "Ak."

"Fuck me, what are you? You don't look like a frog. You're kind of... beautiful."

The animal was trying to express wonder. There was an open friendliness to its face that the creature rather enjoyed. It implied that these animals were far from simple minded and that they perhaps had culture and sophistication. Certainly, for land animals to have turned a tree into a sea-going vessel was impressive, and indicative of some kind of civilization.

Once again, the creature patted itself on the head and said the name of its species. "Ik'thya'nym."

The animal peered at the creature, before mimicking the gesture and saying, "Eastron. Sea Wolf."

PART ONE

Marius Cyclone at the Dark Harbour

1

The cat was black, with a flash of white fur beneath its neck and across its belly. It sat on the windowsill, looking at me and purring. There was an edge of menace to the sound, as if the cat was cross with me. I'd only come to the window intending to close the shutters, but had been stopped in this simple endeavour by a set of glaring green eyes and ruffling whiskers. It became a tense staring contest, though not one I had a chance of winning. The Dark Harbour had many cats, and all were proficient at staring. This particular cat was a fucking grandmaster.

"Don't look at me like that," I muttered. "I'm sorry. I was away longer than I intended. Marta said she'd feed you."

The cat flexed its jaw, exposing sharp fangs and emitting a sharper snarl.

"Okay, you're not cross because you're hungry," I said. "Are you cross that we've not left yet... or are you cross because we're leaving?"

The cat's name was Titus, and he was by far my harshest critic. My wife didn't fully understand why I kept the little bastard around, encumbered as he was with an insatiable desire to scratch virtually everyone who entered his vicinity. Everyone except my daughter and I.

"Please don't be cross," I pleaded. "I couldn't take you to Nowhere, and I *certainly* couldn't take you to the Silver

Parliament... although the thought of appearing through the glass with a big, black cat on my shoulder does hold a certain appeal."

Titus snarled a second time. With a defiant flick of his tail, he stood, and paraded left and right, keeping his eyes on me as he prowled across the windowsill. His glare slowly dug into my soul, judging me and my actions in a way no human being could manage. I'd long suspected that Titus could read my mind, so he was likely catching up on all the stupid shit I'd done since I left the Dark Harbour.

My intentions had been good, if somewhat naive. I'd meet with Prince Oliver, inform him that an ancient, chaotic god was waking up, and secure an alliance with the Winterlords, taking them with us when we fled the realm of form. The reality, that Titus was currently plucking from my mind, was that I'd witnessed two massacres, and inadvertently driven the Winterlord prince insane. The Silver Parliament was gone, as was Snake Guard, and Oliver had become the Waking God's twisted general. Added to these failures was the fact that four void legions were currently marching on my hold, with the unwavering intention of killing every remaining citizen. I was trying to push these details to the back of my mind and focus on the tiny matter of the monsters rising from the sea to devour each and every Eastron I couldn't save. The cat was right to judge me.

There was a knock on the door and Titus fled through the open window, nimbly making his way to the adjacent balcony, where he could point his telepathy at Marta, my seven-year-old daughter.

"I'm on my way," I shouted. "As quickly as I can, whether you keep knocking on my door or not."

I was in my dressing room, belting on black and red armour of hardened steel and boiled leather. In doing so, I felt how thin I was getting. I could feel my ribs, and mused longingly on when I'd last had a good, fatty meal. Unfortunately, my musing was swiftly interrupted by another knock on the door. I'd been back less than a day and had arrived home with three serious wounds, each needing attention before I could get back to work. Now, with considerable expenditure of wyrd, I was fully healed.

I closed the shutters, without allowing sentiment to make me take a final look over the Dark Harbour, and opened the door. Outside was an octagonal sitting-room, with three other doors. Furnishings of dark purple and red gave the space a luxuriant feel and a warm, comforting depth. Jessica, my wife, had an eye for design and had spent many hours, while I was away, turning the Strange Manse into a comfortable home. We'd lived here for fifteen years, since the day I refused my seat at the Silver Parliament and claimed the Dark Harbour for my own.

"Are you well?" asked Esteban Hazat, the man who'd been banging on my door.

"Do I look well?" I replied.

"Not really," said Esteban, with a shake of his head. "But I don't really care if you're well, as long as you're ready."

"I am not well, but I am most certainly ready," I said, smiling at the commander of the twenty-third void legion. "Are they both here?"

"No, Marius, they are not both here," he replied, with an edge of condescension. "Antonia of the Dolcinites is here, but Merlinda of the Tender Strike is not. Word is she refuses to evacuate, and her followers seem to agree. We have three empty transport ships for them, but Merlinda has decreed that they will remain empty. They're staying here, she says."

Esteban was dressed for travel, eschewing his usual plate armour in favour of thick fabric and leather in the same glossy black colour. He was older than me, pushing fifty years of age, and had commanded the urban cohorts of the Dark Harbour for as long as I'd been here. Now, he and all his warriors were coming with me to the island of Nowhere. Assuming I could persuade the remaining citizens to move.

"Very well," I said. "We can deal with Antonia first. Merlinda can wait."

"Not for long she can't," replied Esteban. "The first of your brother's legions will arrive in a day. A few hours after that, the hold will be overrun. One way or another we need to leave before that."

"You're suggesting I leave them?"

"I'm suggesting that Merlinda and the Tender Strike want to stay behind... and we should let them."

"No," I stated, walking past him to the second of the four doors.

Beyond my family's apartments were empty staircases of black wood, set within cavernous halls, and built to deliberately deceive the eye of anyone looking. It was easy to get lost or turned around, without ever finding the door you desired. Even I didn't know every twist and turn of the old labyrinth. There were strange inscriptions and odd quotations, etched into the halls, some of which I'd seen once and never managed to find again. The only permanent inhabitants of the labyrinth were feral cats, nesting in every nook and cranny and said to lead intruders astray. The Lady Dolcinia was fond of cats. She and her husband, Markus Eclipse, had raised the Strange Manse in the twentieth year of the Dark Age. They'd treated with the Sinister Black Cat spirits they'd found here and were given a small army of feline protectors. Unfortunately, I'd learned that this protection applied only tentatively to subsequent elders of the Dark Harbour.

The familiar path, down to the outer circles of the manse, ended in a nondescript door. Esteban followed and we emerged into the audience chamber beyond. The space was modest, but two huge floor to ceiling windows allowed a vast curtain of bright sunlight to give the chamber gravitas.

"My lord Marius," said a robed woman with a deep voice. "We are humble in your presence."

She was one of three Dolcinite Pilgrims waiting for me, each barefoot and robed in black and red. "Antonia," I replied, warmly grasping her hand. "It has been too long." I gritted my teeth and bowed my head. "Your brothers and sisters at Snake Guard did not escape. I'm sorry, but most Outrider Knights have fallen."

She was a young woman, given station by wisdom rather than years. Her eyes pinched slightly at my news, but she maintained her composure, as a good Dolcinite should. She looked past me and bowed at Esteban. "My lord Hazat," she said. "I hope your legions will guard us gently on our voyage to a new world."

"They will be humble," said the commander, "and know of their sins."

"We are eager to leave," said Antonia. "Most of our order are already aboard ship. I must say the provisions you have supplied are far more than we are used to. Tell me, will the Tender Strike be joining us?"

"Not as yet," replied Esteban, drily. "Merlinda does not appear to value her life."

"Let me talk to her," said Antonia. "We are different in many ways, but she must see reason."

"No," I stated. "You have many souls under your care. Let *me* talk to Merlinda. There are thirty ships at anchor, ready to leave. Four of them are for your people, three are for Merlinda's. All will be full before we abandon the Dark Harbour."

"We will endure, Lord Marius," said Antonia. "We will build a new world in the distant void." There was a trusting smile on her face of which I hoped I was worthy.

I clutched her hand again. "Your wisdom will be needed in the years to come, my friend. The Dark Brethren will have much rebuilding to do."

"Marius, time is against us," interrupted Esteban. "The tides won't wait... and neither will your brother. Santago Cyclone is as committed to the Sunken God as Prince Oliver."

"Yes, yes," I replied. "How many warriors do you still have ashore?"

Esteban considered it. "Three, four hundred."

"Right. Do a final sweep, then get everyone aboard ship. Oh, and make sure Jessica and Marta don't wait for me. They should have left already."

"As you say," said the void legionnaire. "Does that mean you're going to see Merlinda alone?"

"No," I stated, giving Antonia a final nod and striding away from the Dolcinite Pilgrims.

Esteban didn't follow, but I could sense his disapproving glare in the back of my head. Though not a Pilgrim, the commander shared their beliefs, that we should all be humble and know of our sins before we judged others. My confidence was often too much for Dolcinites, though they were far too humble to ever call me arrogant. They were loyal only because, fifteen years ago, I'd chosen *them* over the Tender Strike. But they *were* loyal.

Beyond the small audience chamber was a lattice of corridors that, until recently, were adorned with striking images of the sea, the sky and the void, all rendered in beautifully vivid colours and chosen as a counterpoint to the grim, black stone of the Strange Manse. Without the paintings, there was just the stone and the emptiness. So many men, women and children had already left. So many Dark Brethren were already on Nowhere, awaiting my return and our journey into the void. If no other Eastron came with us, at least the people of the Dark Harbour would endure.

The day I met Utha the Ghost was the day my life changed. I was the youngest of the three Cyclone brothers and the least regarded. I'd never excelled in politics or statecraft, nor the highly valued attributes of dominance and cruelty. I was Dark Brethren, but never understood why that meant every other Eastron should hate me. Santago was clever and sadistic, with a mind that could think several steps ahead of his enemies. Trego was bigoted and violent, but ambitious enough to suppress his aggressive impulses. Then there was me, called the Stranger from a young age, purely because I was frequently absent from lessons and family gatherings. Now, Trego was dead, killed on the stone of the Silver Parliament, and Santago was the high priest of the Waking God. All because we'd met Utha the Ghost and he'd shown us who truly ruled this realm of form.

He'd visited the hold of the Open Hand, with an impossibly old Pure One called Ten Cuts. Utha's appearance was striking, with pale skin, white hair and pink eyes, and his power was evident from the moment he walked into Santago's hall. He didn't use wyrd, like the Eastron, but there was a fire in his eyes and a nimbus of energy behind every word he uttered. He told us he'd not been in this realm of form for long and didn't yet understand the Eastron. He told us our world was going to end, that a god, beyond our understanding, was waking up to the south, and would signal the end of our civilization, and that he could help us escape. Then Ten Cuts blew a spirit-whistle, made my two brothers and I see a vision of the sea rising, and each of us went mad.

We went our separate ways, agreeing to come together when we'd processed what we'd seen. And that was the last time I spoke to either of them. I never knew exactly how their minds broke, just that they saw cosmic immensity and could not conceive of defying it. They chose instead to follow it, perhaps believing it was the only rational course of action, or maybe the power was simply too tempting. As for me… my madness slowly coalesced into fear and cowardice, like I'd woken up as a rabbit surrounded by wolves. I didn't want to follow *or* fight, I just wanted to run away. I wanted to run and run, until each step took me over another horizon and I was no longer afraid.

I remembered being chained to a bed in the Strange Manse, howling that we should all kill ourselves before it was too late. After a week of demented hallucinations and nightmares I fear to remember, I awoke. Titus was lying on my naked chest and Jessica, my wife, was asleep in a chair, her hand interlocked with my own. I still wanted to run, but the madness had passed.

There were chains across my arms and legs, with bruises and dried blood wherever they touched my skin. My mind had twisted and turned, until it had shut off half of what I'd seen, allowing the remainder to think clearly. I knew what was waking up, I knew it couldn't be reasoned with or defeated, and I knew we all had to run as far away as we could get.

"Jess," I murmured. "Jess."

"Marius," whispered Jessica, her eyes still closed, as if she were talking to me in her sleep. She was a few years younger than me, in her mid-thirties, but looked younger. She had curly black hair, falling down her back, and clear, light brown skin. She was beautiful by anyone's measure. Her mouth had a natural curl, giving her the appearance of always smiling. Ironically, she was far more miserable than most people I knew, with a cynical view of the world that I'd heavily contributed to.

"Jess," I said.

Her eyes opened and we looked at each other. There had never been much love between us. Just respect and occasional lust. We'd married young, to mollify our families. After our first child was stillborn, we'd started living different lives, coming together only to fuck when the mood took us. Two more failed pregnancies and we decided to remain married to spite the world and anger my brothers, who cared only for the continuation of our bloodline. By the time Marta was born, we realized we'd become friends. We'd been many things over the years, but being parents stopped us caring that we didn't love each other.

"Have you gone mad?" she asked. "Do you still want to kill yourself?"

"Not at the moment," I replied. "But that might change."

"I should probably leave you chained up then," said Jessica.

I nodded, flexing soreness from my neck. "Yes... do that. If I still want to live tomorrow, you can release me. Don't let Marta in here."

"Of course not," she replied. "Tell me what you saw. I've never seen anything do this to you."

Titus flicked his tail, hissed at us both, and leapt to the bare stone floor of the chamber. The cat was probably glad that I was awake and whole, but anything beyond that was an inconvenience, so he chose to leave.

I coughed and screwed up my eyes, keeping the nightmares at bay as best I could. "I saw the thing that will end us," I replied. "We need to run... all of us. All the Eastron. We all need to run or this realm will be our tomb."

She kept hold of my hand and her eyes flickered back and forth. "That's not what Santago says. He sent word two days ago from the Open Hand. He says all Dark Brethren must follow him in turning this realm into something new. Seems he's found religion. Some old god."

"And Trego?" I asked.

"Taken his place as Envoy," she replied, "at the Silver Parliament. He added his name to Santago's decree. He says that we can gain limitless power and dominate all other Eastron. Two-thirds of the Brethren are with them. What do you want to do with *your* third?"

I looked at the stone ceiling, then back at Jessica. As my head turned I realized I was crying, though the tears fell from an expression of resolve, not emotion. "I need to speak to Utha the Ghost," I whispered. "I need to ask him a question. He said he could help us escape, I want to know what he meant. I'm scared, Jess... we should all be scared."

She leaned in and kissed my hand, her eyes moist. "We *are* scared," she replied. "Santago says... if we don't pledge to him and his new god... we'll all be consumed."

"I need to speak to Utha the Ghost," I repeated.

She released me the next day, but I had to kill three people before I could speak to Utha again. I found him by sending hundreds of spirits into the void with a simple message – the Stranger seeks the Ghost. Unfortunately, in my eagerness to find the pale man, I'd alerted Santago to my intentions. He didn't try to *consume* me, but he did send two assassins. At the time, I remember thinking it strange that he'd trust my death to two people, as if it was more of a brotherly slap than a serious attempt on my life. The third person I had to kill was due to Utha's unexpected insistence that we meet in a tavern. It was a strange message to get, mostly because it was delivered by a street urchin on a grubby piece of paper. The lad shoved the message into my hand and ran away, leaving me to wonder if it was too stupid to be a trap. The corpse I had to walk over was a drunk member of Tender Strike who sought to please Merlinda by putting a knife in my ribs, as soon as he saw me walk into the tavern.

"That was the third person I've had to kill while looking for you," I said, approaching the dark corner booth and the pale man sitting within. By the door, two of the tavern's bouncers were silently dealing with the man whose neck I'd just broken.

The pale man stood up opposite me and smiled. Utha the Ghost looked different. It had been six months since I saw him and his nimbus of power was gone, leaving just a man with a striking appearance, as if he'd learned how to blend into the world of the Eastron. He still had white hair, pink eyes and visible red veins across his pale skin, but I struggled to recall the being of immense power who'd shown me the end of the world.

"Good to see you again, Marius," he said, in a strange, clipped accent. "Will you sit? I have a flagon of ale for us."

The flagon was almost empty, as was the mug in front of Utha. He didn't appear drunk, but then he wasn't a man, so perhaps four or five mugs of ale didn't affect him. I sat and poured what was left into a second mug, waving to the barman to bring us another.

"I miss beer," said Utha, swirling his mug. "This is darker and heavier than I like, but it's not bad."

"Beer?" I queried. "That's what you've got to say to me?" I leant over the table, snarling at him. "I haven't slept properly in six fucking months. Behind my eyes I see tentacles, death and the annihilation of the Eastron. Both my brothers want me dead and *I* want to run and hide with every fibre of my being... and it's called stout... you fucking fuck."

The barman placed a second flagon on the table, averting his eyes from me. I was not liked in this part of town, but was far enough from the Glaring that I was in no real danger. I leant back in my chair and filled my mug.

"You dislike me," said Utha. "I'm not surprised. Since we last met, I've learned much about the Eastron. I was wrong to reveal the truth to you and your brothers. You appear to be the strongest of men, but your minds..."

I took a drink and narrowed my eyes at him. "Yes, it's clearly *our* fault. We have weak minds. Who else have you shown?"

"No one," he replied. "Ten Cuts already knew and didn't need to be shown. Since I met you and your brothers, I've been studying the Eastron. Taking my time."

I chuckled. "Seeing whose mind you'll break next?"

He bowed his head. "I'm sorry, Marius. I was ignorant, I showed you too soon. You weren't ready."

I rubbed my eyes and took a deep breath. A piece of me wanted to beat the shit out of him, but a far larger piece still wanted to run away. Looking at the pale man, beyond my anger and confusion, I saw possibly the only chance I had of escaping the end of the world.

"I didn't notice your tattoo," said Utha. "What is it?"

"What?"

"The blue ink on your neck," he replied.

I pulled down the collar of my leather coat, revealing the rampant horse design across my left shoulder and up my neck. "A friend of mine called Quinn did it. He's an Outrider Knight... and please don't change the subject again. Beer... tattoos... how about the weather? Or maybe women?"

He smiled, instantly looking ten years older. His lack of pigment made his age hard to determine, but the creases now visible next to his eyes and mouth showed a man in his middle fifties. "The Stranger seeks the Ghost," he said. "Ask your questions."

"I have two," I replied. "Well, I have two hundred, but two that are stopping me from sleeping. How long do we have and where can we run?"

His smile disappeared and he narrowed his pink eyes. Somewhere, deep within his unnerving stare, was the mighty being I'd first met. Not a man, not a spirit, but something beyond both. "You are sane?" he asked. "Your brothers..."

"I'm sane," I snapped. "I'm fucking scared, and I'm fighting the urge to spend my days screaming and running away, but I'm sane. I certainly don't want to kneel to the Sunken God."

He nodded. "One out of three Cyclone brothers sees the truth."

"Answer my fucking questions."

"A year or two," he said. "It's hard to judge, and you'll see his minions long before he wakes. There's a tomb, far to the south. The Sea Wolves call it the Sunken City, but its true name is R'lyeh. I've only seen it once, just after the Sea Wolf fleet was annihilated."

"The Battle of the Depths?" I asked. "That was... sixty years ago."

"Longer, I think."

"You knew back then, and only told *us* last year?"

"I was busy," stated Utha, "preparing the answer to your second question."

"Where can we run to?" I repeated.

"A void realm," he replied. "*My* void realm. A self-contained world, in the deep void. It was once called the

Shadow Halls, and needed considerable work to make it liveable for the Eastron. There was no point trying to save you, if I couldn't offer a safe haven. It's now a vast and beautiful land – mountains, forests, rivers... it can shelter each and every Eastron who wants to flee before the end of this world."

"Is it ready?" I asked, glancing around the tavern at dozens of care-free Dark Brethren. The citizens of my hold had no idea that a conversation was happening in the corner that would likely change their lives and dictate their future.

"Not yet, but I'm close," said Utha. "There's an island called Nowhere, in the Sea Wolves' territory. There's a void storm on the island."

"The Maelstrom," I replied. "What about it?"

"It's the only place in this realm of form where I can create a doorway to your new home."

"Fuck," I muttered, taking a deep drink of bitter alcohol. "That is a significant complication. Nowhere is a spit from the Severed Hand. Have you *met* the Sea Wolves?"

"I have," he replied, "and I will need your help. Will you help me, Marius? Will you help the Eastron?"

This was it. This was the moment when everything changed. Sitting in a shitty tavern in the Dark Harbour, failing miserably to hide my fear, I was forced to make the most important decision I would ever make. "A last question," I grumbled. "What are you, Utha the Ghost?"

His head bowed and his face fell into a frown. "I fear you won't understand the answer." I saw many layers of knowledge, memory, and deep, deep regret, as if the pale man opposite was struggling to contain his immensity within so simple a form.

"I need to know," I stated. "I *will* help you, but I need to know who you are."

"I'm a shadow giant," he said, "and soon I will be a god."

2

The Dark Harbour was well named. It was a thick horse-shoe of dark buildings and narrow streets, bordering a vast bay called the Sea of Spirits. It had no single harbour, but rather two hundred separate moorings and docks, ranging from those used by fishermen to vast floating platforms, filled with ocean-going galleons. Not a single building in my hold was more than three streets from the open water. I hated that it was now totally empty... well, almost totally. Two pockets of life still existed – one around the main dock, where thirty ships were waiting to leave, and the other around Merlinda's discrete manor house, colloquially called the Glaring, at the northern most point of the hold.

The Tender Strike were almost as old as the Dark Harbour itself. They'd emerged in opposition to the Dolcinite Pilgrims, preaching dominance and sensuality, and had gained much support, as *their* view was far closer to the traditional ethos of the Dark Brethren. Each elder of the hold was forced to make a decision as to which group of Brethren would be in ascendance. When the Strike were dominant, the Dolcinites returned to their abbeys and tended to the populace with no complaints. But when the Pilgrims were chosen, the elder had to cope with defiance, rebellion and occasional riots. As it had been with me when, fifteen years ago, I told Merlinda's predecessor to fuck off. I could possibly have been more polite. We were all Dark Brethren, but our differences were just as pronounced as our similarities.

The Glaring was surrounded by a wide piazza, with numerous covered taverns and joy houses, each pointing inwards, like the spokes of a decadent wheel. If this had been my first visit, I'd have thought that all was well in the hold, for the Tender Strike appeared to be celebrating something. The taverns were full, the joy houses were doing a roaring trade, and the piazza was full of revellers.

I emerged, alone but hooded, from an adjoining street, between two of the quieter buildings that surrounded the Glaring. Behind me, ghosting through the shadows, was my back-up, though they'd remain hidden until needed. The people in the piazza were not fools, despite their refusal to leave. They were guilty only of thinking me a liar. Merlinda Night Eyes didn't believe that Santago had fallen to worship of a malevolent god, nor did she see the wisdom in running away. She'd been taught that any elder of the hold that chose against her people was not to be trusted... so she didn't trust me.

My distinctive black and red armour was hidden beneath the leather of my overcoat and I made sure to walk slowly, so prying eyes couldn't tell I was carrying a sword. Not that they'd care. Most people here were drunk, and a significant portion were singing songs.

The Stranger is a danger, take my wager that he's wrong.
The Stranger is a failure, need a leader who is strong.

I'd heard it before. It had become a rallying cry for those citizens of the Dark Harbour who'd disagree with me if I said the sun was going to rise tomorrow. I tried to sympathize with them, knowing that it wasn't personal, but my patience had reached an end and they needed to make a fucking decision... leave or die, for my brother's legions would kill them without thinking to ask if they liked Marius Cyclone.

I walked from the darkness of the encircling buildings into the light of the piazza, past men and women who were far too busy to notice me. Merlinda had organized this celebration to mock me. She knew that every other citizen of the Dark Harbour had already left, taking their worldly belongings with them, with the last few people waiting for the Tender Strike and their followers. So they were having a party. Logical if you were them, suicidal if you were anyone else.

I was taller than most people here and my stride was less encumbered by liquor, but I managed to cross the piazza without disturbance and approach the Glaring. Merlinda's home was a two storey manor, made of black wood and blacker stone. Around the base, where open doors and awnings allowed access to the ground floor, a thick concentration of revellers blocked my path within.

"Welcome, friend," slurred a young man. "Come drink with us. The Stranger says we'll all be dead soon."

Luckily for me, all these people were drunk. Though my head was bowed, and my face partially concealed by a hood, anyone looking close would recognize me instantly. I glanced either side of the ground floor, reassuring myself that my back-up was moving to the rear of the building.

I took the offered drink, paused for a moment, looking at the brass goblet, then smashed it over the man's head and took a large stride forwards, over the unconscious lump he quickly turned into.

"Why the fuck did you do that?" spat a woman from behind me.

"Don't have time to ask idiots to move," I replied, striding into the Glaring. My actions had started a minor commotion, but I swiftly left it behind and made for the wide staircase.

"Marius the Stranger," said an armed thug, guarding the base of the stairs. He was a big, burly man and clearly sober. "Got time to ask *me* to move?"

"No," I replied, darting forwards and grabbing his throat, then pushing him to the floor. He slapped at my arms, as I flexed my back and dragged the spluttering guard up the first few steps. I barely broke stride, releasing his neck only once I'd stepped past him. He clattered to the wood, clutching his neck, with no obvious desire to follow.

"She won't see you," he coughed.

"That's not up to her," I replied, turning left at the top of the wide staircase.

The first floor of the Glaring contained Merlinda's private rooms. She was open to sharing them, but those with her would not be simple drunken revellers. Those outside just adhered to her doctrine, those within were the inner circle of the Tender Strike. They were unpleasant people, letting whimsy and dominance define them, with no thought to consequences.

"*You're* bold," said a scantily clad woman, reclining amongst other half-naked men and women.

The first floor was open and carpeted, with three doors on each side of a central sitting-room, with these people acting as gate-keepers. There was a large window behind the members of Tender Strike, and I could see two figures nimbly scaling the outside wall. They'd watch and wait, until I needed them.

"Where is Merlinda?" I asked, pushing back my hood to make sure they all knew who I was.

"She is entertaining," replied the woman, leaning forwards from the crowded couch. Her eyes were glazed and it became clear that none of these people intended to leave the hold.

"Shit," said one of the inebriated men, "it's Marius Cyclone. *The Stranger is a danger, take my wager...*"

"Shut up," I barked. "*Where* is she entertaining?"

"Shh," whispered the woman. "Can you hear that? The sound of an empty hold, with no one but the Tender Strike to caress it. Just leave, Marius, we'll be fine without you."

I turned from the canvas of debauchery and drove my boot through the first door on the left. It was an empty bedroom. The second kick revealed two fat women, showing a skinny man who was boss. The last door on the left was a large kitchen, with three startled servants. I marched across the wide sitting-room, shoving two drunken idiots out of the way, before dropping my armoured shoulder into the first door on the right. Five men were sitting around a table within, each sober and armoured, with sheathed straight swords. I lost composure for a moment, as I realized they were void legionnaires, and *not* men under my command.

"You're Lucio Wind Claw's men," I stated, recognizing them as members of the tenth void legion. Lucio, and his sister Alexis, were noble Dark Brethren of the Open Hand, allies of Santago, and fanatical followers of the Sunken God. We'd expected them, but not yet.

"And you're fucking dead," replied the oldest of the five warriors, drawing his sword.

"Probably not," I countered.

Behind the legionnaires, two windows were smashed from the outside and two kukris were thrown. One blade killed a man, impaling him through the back of the neck, and the other dealt a glancing blow to a man's head, sending him to the floor.

Then two Brethren climbed nimbly through the windows. They wore black from head to toe, with covered faces and blades sheathed across their bodies. They were my back-up and were the two finest killers I'd ever met. Asha and Gaius Two Hearts, brother and sister assassins, held a low position, with blades in each hand.

I drew my sword and smiled at the three remaining void legionnaires. "You're early. We weren't expecting your visit for another day. Do you want to surrender? Or do I have to beat information out of the one of you I keep alive?"

"Not necessary," said a sultry voice from behind me.

I turned and saw Merlinda Night Eyes, elder of the Tender Strike, standing in the doorway. She held a thin blanket across her chest, but was otherwise naked, and had obviously been fucking in the very recent past. Her heart-shaped face was flushed and her large, brown eyes were wide, as if highly aroused by the slightest stimulus. Jessica, my wife, fucking hated her, frequently ranting that Merlinda was just an agent of chaos. Unfortunately, she was loved by many hundreds of my people. They were still citizens of the Dark Harbour and, despite their beliefs, they didn't deserve to be left behind.

"Did you welcome these legionnaires?" I asked.

"They got here an hour ago," replied Merlinda, with a euphoric glaze across her eyes. "An advanced guard of the four legions, marching on the Dark Harbour."

"All your people are going to die if you don't come with us," I stated. "These fucking cunts are not your friends. They would welcome a world where the Eastron are slaves to a god. You're still of the Dark Harbour... come with us."

"Marius," said Asha Two Hearts from the window. "Legionnaires approaching. We should leave."

"An advanced guard?" I asked Merlinda. "How many?"

"Perhaps *I* should answer that," said a voice from behind the elder of the Tender Strike. "I *am* their commander after all."

The man had black hair and an angular face. He was half-naked, with Merlinda's sweat glistening across his chest. It was Lucio Wind Claw and he commanded the legions marching on my hold. By any measure, this man was my enemy.

"Five hundred," continued Lucio. "It was a forced march, ahead of the main army. We hoped to find you still here, once I... finished sealing an *alliance* with Merlinda."

I thought quickly, my eyes darting from Lucio Wind Claw to the smashed windows and back again. Behind Merlinda's heavy breathing and the revellers downstairs, I could hear the rhythmic clank of metal. With little hesitation, I killed one of the void legionnaires and signalled for Asha and Gaius to kill the other two.

"Out the window," I said to the two assassins, before turning back to Merlinda and Lucio. "Just tell me one thing... do the Tender Strike follow the Sunken God?"

"Oh, no," she replied, breathlessly. "But the enemy of my enemy is my friend... and you will always be my enemy."

"No sensible Dark Brethren believes your nonsense about a god," added Lucio, a devilish glint in his eye.

I wanted to kill him, but it would mean leaving the room, and I didn't have time. Especially as the clank of metal armour had now reached the base of the wooden stairs. "Tell Santago he can have the Dark Harbour... but he can't have *me* and he can't have my people."

Gaius was the first out of the window, nimbly vaulting to the street, one storey below. Asha paused, waiting for me and keeping an eye on the door. The sound of void legionnaires rushing up the stairs of the Glaring now eclipsed all other sounds.

"Run and hide, Marius," crowed Lucio Wind Claw, as I jumped after Gaius.

Asha followed and the three of us hugged the outside wall. Either side of us there was a low marquee, filled with drunken members of the Tender Strike. We couldn't stay hidden here, but the appearance of a column of void legionnaires was far more distracting than three people jumping out of a window. The plate armoured warriors held broad-bladed spears, with rectangular shields and helmets fashioned into the likeness of an owl. They spread out across the piazza, though didn't actively disrupt the celebrations. Oddly, their arrival caused cheers of glee from Merlinda's followers, as if they'd been waiting for rescue. It didn't make me angry, it just made me sad.

"Follow me," I said. "We need to reach the ships before Lucio gets to them. There aren't enough warriors there to fight these bastards."

I scanned the surrounding buildings and selected the narrowest and darkest alleyway, just as I heard Lucio shout orders to hunt me down. I ran from the Glaring, with Asha and Gaius one step behind.

"There he is!" shouted a voice from behind.

"Cut him off," commanded Lucio from the first-floor window.

I barrelled a drunk out of the way and dodged another two, before reaching the encircling buildings. I didn't want to look behind me, but I knew the best part of two hundred legionnaires would be chasing us. On another night, I may have led the heavily armoured warriors through the narrow back streets of the Dark Harbour, but I couldn't risk that Lucio would just send the majority to the main dock and assault the waiting transports. We had to reach the refugee ships as quickly as possible and cast off.

"Marius, you really can be an idiot," said Gaius, as we darted left and right, manoeuvring through narrow streets, with the roar of pursuit close behind.

"Brother," snapped Asha. "I thought we agreed not to tell him that until we got back."

"Just blurted it out," said Gaius. "Sorry."

"Just run!" I replied, pulling myself around a dark corner and trying to judge the most direct route to the harbour and the waiting ships.

"But you *are* an idiot," said Asha. "What were you thinking, marching in there alone?"

"Why didn't you bring Esteban and a hundred men?" asked Gaius.

"Rather than just us two," added his sister.

"Shut up, both of you."

I found a main street, heading south, and stretched my legs into a sprint, with the Sea of Spirits to my left. The clank of the pursuing void legionnaires travelled far in the empty streets of my hold, and it was clear they couldn't move at any great speed. Nevertheless, whether they chased us or not, they could reach the main harbour in fifteen minutes.

"I think you just like people to be impressed by you," said Gaius, catching up to me.

"It's a character flaw," added Asha, sprinting to my left. "Everyone thinks so."

I didn't engage with them. They were sailors from my warship, the *Dangerous*, currently anchored with the transport ships. Despite their remarkable skill with killing, they were two of the more annoying crew members. They'd spent time with the Sinister Black Cat spirits and, as a result, were loyal but capricious, with little internal monologue and a playful nature.

We reached the end of the main road and a small forest of sails came into view. Of the thirty ships waiting, half were already at anchor in the bay, with the rest in the final stages of loading. I couldn't see how many citizens had yet to board, or how difficult it would be to get the fleet out to sea, but our time was growing short.

We ran past the empty neighbourhoods of my hold, where silence and dust were already reclaiming the streets, and turned towards the last source of light in the Dark Harbour. Around the main harbour, Esteban Hazat and the twenty-third void legion had established a perimeter. There were flaming braziers placed around the harbour and, as twilight fell, the perimeter of fire made me shield my eyes. Unfortunately, when I lowered my hand, I saw a few hundred people, still loitering on the stone of the Dark Harbour. The fleet was not ready to make way, with provisions still being loaded and people still waiting to board their transports.

"That's not ideal," observed Asha.

"I think we'll have to do a bit of fighting," added Gaius. "Lucio will be here before everyone's aboard."

He was right. I scanned the perimeter, looking for my own legionnaires, but barely a handful remained ashore. The last few citizens, yet to leave, were Dolcinite Pilgrims. They'd refused to board until the poorest and most destitute were safe. Antonia, the High Pilgrim, was close by and had seen our approach. She stood with Esteban and the last few members of the twenty-third void legion, organizing the evacuation.

"You two get back to the *Dangerous*," I said to Asha and Gaius. "Get the watch back here."

"That's fifty blades," replied Asha. "Won't do much against five hundred spears."

I glared at her, making it clear that I didn't want to repeat myself. The two of them nodded and ran off, making for the nearest rowing boat. When they'd left, I made for Esteban and Antonia.

"My lord Marius," said the commander of the twenty-third void legion, "what am I to infer by the fact you return at a sprint?" He looked down at my sheathed blade. "Is there blood on that?"

"There is," I replied. "Lucio Wind Claw appears not to care for rest. He's brought five hundred legionnaires on a forced march ahead of Santago and the main army. They chased us from the Glaring. We have ten minutes at most."

"And Merlinda?" asked Antonia.

I shook my head, suddenly angry that I couldn't make the leader of the Tender Strike see reason. "She just... hates me too much."

"That's okay, Marius," offered Esteban, placing a hand on my shoulder, "we all hate you."

"Commander!" said Antonia. "I assure you, Lord Marius, the Dolcinite Pilgrims think most highly of you."

I chuckled at Esteban. "My popularity aside, how long until everyone's at sea? Or at least safe aboard ship?"

He turned to the Dolcinite Pilgrims, patiently awaiting their time to board. "More than ten minutes," he replied.

"Right," I said, thinking quickly, "rally the legionnaires we still have. Get word to the closest warships, I want each of them to send a watch back to solid ground. Lucio has five hundred spears, we need to at least match him with blades. His men will have gone without sleep for the last two days, or they'd never have reached us so quickly. We match them, we buy time. They attack... we'll *hopefully* win. Lucio likes to talk, so I can probably stall him." I turned to Antonia. "Get your followers aboard as quickly as you can and cast off. Lucio has no ship, so ten feet from the harbour might as well be a twenty foot wall."

"As you say," replied Esteban, turning sharply and marching towards his remaining legionnaires.

"At once," replied Antonia, gathering her robe and returning to her brothers and sisters.

I took a deep breath, enjoying the crisp air of the Dark Harbour while I still could. I wanted to shout to the sky that emptying my hold shouldn't be this fucking difficult. Unfortunately, I wasn't an idiot, and had to accept that I had more enemies than friends. Lucio was a hateful bastard, but he'd probably just kill us all. The true torments would come when my brother Santago arrived. *He* didn't just want me dead, he wanted the rebellion I'd started to end in blood and madness. He'd keep me alive and find a way to use me against those who stood against him. Thousands of people, gathered on the island of Nowhere, were at risk if he managed to capture me. And the last few refugee ships would suffer torture and death.

The persistent urge to run away reared its ugly head. Despite my confidence – or arrogance as most saw it – I was constantly fighting the coward within me. Everything I'd done, since the day I met Utha the Ghost, had been about running away. I didn't even understand why I'd chosen to take so many people with me, rather than just abandon everything. Perhaps I simply couldn't conceive of letting so many people die.

I could hear Esteban shouting to the scattered members of his legion. "Twenty-third!" he commanded. "New orders. Hostiles approach. We will meet them at the perimeter." Barely a hundred void legionnaires answered, gathering their helmets and shields, then moving back to the semi-circle of fire.

I let them assemble, and strolled a little way back along the sea front, looking for the first signs of Lucio's warriors. Twilight was taking hold and masks of shadow were forming across every intersection, making it hard to focus. There was no way fully armoured void legionnaires could sneak up on us, and none of the tenth knew the Dark Harbour well enough to outflank us. Once they accepted that they couldn't chase me, they'd just march up the main street, next to the sea front.

3

Three warships, including the *Dangerous*, sent a total of one hundred and fifty blades ashore. With the remaining void legionnaires and a few handfuls of Dolcinites, armed with quarterstaffs, I had three hundred warriors. Antonia had chosen to stay, leaving her brothers and sisters to oversee the final part of our evacuation.

"You didn't plan this very well," said Asha Two Hearts. "We should have left by now." She and her brother stood either side of me, in the centre of a defensive line.

"You'll probably get us all killed," said Gaius.

Esteban had his legionnaires lock their shields in front of us, presenting a solid wall for Lucio's warriors to see. But if they looked closer, around the large, rectangular shields, they'd see a mob of sailors and Pilgrims, individually good at fighting, but not a cohesive force.

"No one likes you, Marius," said Asha.

Twilight was receding into darkness and a column of void legionnaires was marching towards us, along the sea front. Somewhere in the middle of five hundred spears, I could see their heraldry – a woven pennant, showing the haughty Night Wing, with a ring of green energy around its head. It was nice that they'd stopped for a touch of embroidery, once they'd chosen to follow the Sunken God. My own troops no longer used heraldry, for the Night Wing had fallen with the majority of the Dark Brethren, and none of my legion commanders wanted to associate with such a spirit.

I left the Two Hearts twins and paced behind the line of shields, until I stood next to Esteban Hazat. The commander was as tall as me, but had much wider shoulders and a far better posture. *I* tended to slump, whereas Esteban's back was always ramrod straight.

"They're not in a rush," I observed, looking between the wall of shields to the slowly approaching column of legionnaires.

"They rushed to get here," he replied, glaring forwards. "No need to hurry now. You know they're not after the refugees. They're after you."

Antonia appeared behind us, resting on a heavy quarterstaff. "Just a few souls still to board, Lord Marius. Last four ships will be ready to cast off in minutes. We'll have to pack onto the last two."

Three transports and the *Dangerous* were still moored against the main jetty – a prow of stone pointing into the Sea of Spirits. As soon as we were gone, Lucio, Santago and four void legions would occupy my hold. Running from the Sunken God was one thing, but running from these traitorous cunts left a foul taste in my mouth.

"Okay," I muttered, "the refugees may not be their priority, but they won't just let them leave once they've cut me up. If they take one of those ships, they'll easily get to a few more before the fleet leaves the bay."

"Asha would tell you to give yourself up," said Esteban.

"Strange," I replied, "but I appear not to give a fuck what Asha or her brother think. I can probably stall them though."

I left the commander and the Pilgrim, motioning for two legionnaires to part and let me through. Beyond the fires of our defensive line, I could clearly see the front rank of Lucio's men. The clank of their movements was an insistent tempo, getting louder and louder as I walked from our line.

"Lucio Wind Claw," I shouted, alone in front of my three hundred warriors.

The column stopped, holding an impenetrable line no more than twenty feet in front of me. Unlike Esteban's men, they were fully armoured in black plate, with rectangular shields, long spears and owl helmets.

"Marius Cyclone," replied a voice from the rear of the column. "I intend to pierce your body with many blades. I do not wish to hear your poisonous words."

"Then why did you and your men stop? I'm right here." I spread my arms wide and hoped the darkness concealed the fear on my face. "Don't you want to gloat before you kill me? Don't you want my blood and flesh to be your offering? I hear your god likes his slaves to show their devotion. *Fuck him!*"

The tenth void legion, now stationary under their tainted banner, were clearly not just following orders. As I cursed the Sunken God, I saw dozens of men twitch uncomfortably, as if I'd slapped their mothers or insulted their manhood. Most were clearly true believers.

"Your brother *would* very much like to see you again," shouted Lucio, with a barely suppressed growl behind his words.

I took a quick glance back to my own people. The twenty-third maintained a solid wall of shields. Beyond, over the heads of the remaining Dolcinites, was a slow progression of sails, just creeping away from the harbour. I needed more time.

"I don't blame you," I shouted back to Lucio. "You're not a fool, or a wicked man… well, no more so than any Dark Brethren…but you *are* mad. There is no world where the Sunken God allows you a new kingdom. Only madness would drive you to think otherwise."

Lucio was silent for a moment, though I could hear muttered orders being relayed amongst the five hundred warriors of the tenth void legion. I gritted my teeth and slowly grasped the hilt of my straight sword, watching the first few ranks of the tenth begin to fan out, as if slowly surrounding me. Buying time was difficult when your enemy outnumbered you. Lucio was an arrogant cunt, but I couldn't keep him talking forever.

"Are you done talking?" I asked, again glad of the darkness obfuscating my fear. "Does gloating not salt the meat?"

I heard laughter – then the encircling legionnaires sped up, trying to isolate me.

"Marius!" shouted Esteban, throwing a rectangular shield along the ground towards me.

I turned around, sweeping up the shield and drawing my sword in one motion, before summoning a nimbus of crackling white wyrd across my shoulders. I'd been alone, between two forces of void legionnaires, and I'd managed to buy a minute or two, but now I was backing away, with a dozen enemies intent on my death.

The first spear was aimed at my head, and I dodged aside. The second came for my chest, and clanged off the shield. The third met the same fate as the second, but snapped

against steel, sending splinters over its wielder. Then I heard
Esteban roar and Lucio's warriors had something else to
worry about. With Dolcinite Pilgrims hefting quarterstaffs,
and sailors wielding short swords, the twenty-third void
legion advanced. That is to say, the three hundred men and
women who'd chosen to stay behind summoned their wyrd
and ran at the enemy.

I was forced onto the defensive, grabbing the shield with
both hands, focusing my wyrd through it, and pointing it at
any spear point that got too close. Legion shields covered
the user from ankle to chest, allowing me to effectively hide
behind it as I retreated. Even still, I was almost overwhelmed
until Asha and Gaius Two Hearts appeared either side of
me. They threw their kukris, taking two of the tenth at the
neck, before we were joined by the bulk of Esteban's men.
The clash of the two forces filled the width of the street,
from the sea front to the nearest buildings. Lucio's legionnaires
used standard tactics, fighting from behind their shields,
with controlled spear thrusts and minimal wyrd – whereas
my warriors, armed with swords and quarterstaffs, used
considerable spiritual power just to break their opponent's
defences.

I saw Antonia drive her staff into a man's face two, three,
four times, until she'd crushed his skull. I saw Gaius leap over
a shield and drive his short sword into the wielder's back. I
saw sailors from the *Dangerous*, and legionnaires from the
twenty-third, kill and be killed, as blood, steel and shouting
filled the empty hold of the Dark Harbour. Lucio's men
were clearly fatigued from their forced march, but superior
numbers and cohesive tactics would end us well before we
broke their formation.

I joined Esteban, Asha and Antonia in the middle of the melee, quickly joined by Gaius, jostling his way back to our side.

"I'm gonna kill the Stranger," grunted a legionnaire in front of me.

"You're gonna kill nothing," I replied, deflecting his spear and driving my sword into his neck.

"Marius, we need to fall back," said Esteban, clubbing a man off balance with his shield.

"I think he actually wants to die," added Asha Two Hearts. "He's got a martyr complex."

"Don't worry," said Gaius, "I have a plan." The assassin manoeuvred behind me, wrapped his forearm around my neck, and started pulling me backwards, away from the line of combat.

"Get the fuck off me," I barked. "I'm not leaving until everyone else does."

He tightened his hold, stopping just short of choking me. "Shut up, Marius. We're leaving."

I dropped my shield and grabbed his arm, just as we emerged through the back of the melee. The sailors fell back with us, led by Asha, leaving just Esteban's men to hold the line, with the Dolcinites melting backwards from the edges. Lucio's warriors were pushing forwards, funnelling us into a narrow killing zone.

Once clear of the fight, Gaius released me and I saw the last two ships, with hundreds of sailors shouting for us to run away. "Retreat!" I commanded, giving Gaius a nod of thanks. "Everyone, run!"

"To the *Dangerous?*" asked the assassin.

"To the *Dangerous,*" I replied.

My warriors broke, disengaging from the tenth and fleeing back towards the two remaining ships. A dozen or more were cut down as they turned, with the rest joining me in a dead run to the main harbour.

"Marius!" boomed Lucio Wind Claw. "You can't hide from us... you can't hide from the Waking God."

I wasn't trying to fucking hide. I was trying to fucking run. If these weak-willed idiots would just let me, I'd be out of their way in a few weeks. If Santago, Oliver Dawn Claw, and everyone else who had found religion, would just occupy themselves with their twisted worship, they wouldn't have to worry about us. We'd leave this realm of form to whatever mockery of civilization the servants of the Sunken God could conjure. That was all we wanted to do. We wanted to run away... why the fuck wouldn't they just let us run away?

There was no ordered retreat, just the remaining defenders of the Dark Harbour running in haphazard lines to the last transport ship and the *Dangerous*. "Cast off!" I shouted. "Now!"

Gaius and I stopped where the prow of stone met the sea front, and began ushering everyone else past us. Of the three hundred men and women who'd stayed behind, I estimated roughly half were dead, with almost all of Esteban's one hundred and fifty legionnaires having fallen. A few of the most powerful were still covering our retreat, surrounded by the tenth and giving their lives so we could escape.

The last transport ship had a wide gangplank and its crew was practically dragging people aboard, as its moorings were untied and its anchor raised. The *Dangerous* had already slipped its ropes, and was gliding slowly along the docking prow, with fleeing sailors and Dolcinites jumping onto its deck. My younger cousin, Luca Cyclone, called Black Dog, was captain of my warship and I could see him screaming at the crew to assist.

The last few survivors ran past us, with Esteban and Asha bringing up the rear. Lucio's legionnaires were mere steps behind.

"Marius, time to go," said Gaius, grabbing my shoulder.

This time I didn't resist. Once it was clear that the assassin and I were the last two men, I joined him in a sprint to the *Dangerous*. Antonia was last aboard the transport ship and waved across at me, signalling that all surviving souls had left the Dark Harbour. I shoved Gaius ahead of me, just as the warship reached the end of the prow, making sure he jumped first. I paused for an instant, casting a last look across my hold… across my home. My last thought, before I jumped onto my ship, was that I would never again visit the Dark Harbour.

I had the *Dangerous* built shortly after my first child was stillborn. I needed a reason to leave the Strange Manse, and something to think about other than my own misery and the misery of my wife. I'd found a mad old shipwright, drunk in a shitty tavern, and demanded he help me. His name was Alphonse, but he became violent whenever anyone used it, so the local drunks and sailors just called him Salty. He'd trained as a void legionnaire, but was considered unstable, and was thrown out of his cohort within two days of deployment. Even still, before he lost his middle years at the bottom of a bottle, he'd made a name for himself building warships.

At that time, many of my transports were vulnerable to Sea Wolf pirates, and each convoy was given an escort. The seamanship of Ulric Blood's duellists was unparalleled, but it was their ballistae that did the real damage. Salty spent some time as a sailor and witnessed several naval battles along the Emerald Coast. When he returned to the Dark Harbour, having seen how easily the huge steel bolts had holed our ships, he designed a new kind of framing that added weight, but hugely reinforced the hulls of our warships. If he'd not been a violent alcoholic, the man would likely have become a Dark Brethren hero. As it was, ten years and many bottles after his revolutionary design, the *Dangerous* was the last ship he ever built. He called her his masterpiece, then killed himself two days before she was put to sea. Asha and Gaius Two Hearts, and a significant portion of the crew, believed that Salty Alphonse had become a spirit and inhabited the very fabric of his last creation.

"I hate this fucking boat," said Jessica.

"It's a ship, not a boat," I replied.

We were in our cabin, at the stern of the warship, below the stateroom and above the crew quarters. We were changing out of our land clothes, dressing in attire more suitable for a lengthy sea voyage. My long, leather coat was carefully stored, and both of us pulled on loose-fitting trousers and tunics, with heavy leather boots.

"Boat, ship, I hate it," said Jessica. "It's haunted. Marta has nightmares whenever we're aboard."

I finished dressing, steadied myself against a frame on the ceiling, and looked at her. "What do you want me to say? I'm sorry? Because I'm not."

"No," she replied, sneering at me. "I just hate this fucking ship."

I chuckled, reaching a hand up to stroke her cheek. It was the agreed upon signal that we trusted each other, and had been used by both of us to end a thousand arguments. "Where's Titus?" I asked.

"Prowling around the hold, I think. Marta's playing with him. *He* hates this ship as well."

"It's a week to the Red Straits," I said. "You all need to get used to this ship."

"Will they chase us?" she asked, beginning to tie her curly black hair into a ponytail. "Because we've only got five warships... the other twenty-five are packed with innocents."

"Maybe," I replied. "There are ships at the Silver Dawn, if Santago or Oliver Dawn Claw think to use them. I'm hoping they all came over land."

She pushed my hand away and smiled. It was a rare expression and didn't really convey humour. "You hope? Wonderful."

"I didn't really have a choice either way."

She touched my face and nodded at our cabin door. "Go be the Stranger, Marius. They need you more than I do."

I didn't smile back, just belted on my sword and opened the door. "Don't let Titus get Marta in any trouble. He likes playing pranks aboard ship. He thinks it's haunted as well."

She nodded and we turned our backs on each other. Neither of us wanted to admit that we were scared, but we knew each other well enough that we didn't have to.

I exited the cabin and made my way up two flights of stairs to the quarterdeck and the helm. The *Dangerous* had four decks, two holds and a crew of three hundred, though we were currently welcoming an additional hundred guests – mostly Dolcinite Pilgrims. This was no Sea Wolf pirate ship, and the crew quarters were extensive, with small cabins for most of the sailors. As a result, even with so many additional souls, the ship was far from over-crowded.

"Marius," said Sergio Eclipse, called Anvil, quartermaster of my warship. "Our guests are making themselves at home. Lots of the crew gave up their cabins for the Pilgrims. A humble bunch, this lot."

I rolled from the top of the steps, not yet comfortable on the moving deck, and steadied myself against the port railing. The deck of the *Dangerous* was graduated downwards, with each section stepped, from the observation platform at the aft, across the quarterdeck and main deck, to the bow. It made the ship look like a floating wedge. Though I'd grown fond of its lines and strange design, the ship was considered ugly, or even ungainly. Only those who knew its designer could appreciate that its true strength lay below the waterline. Its sharp keel and unique framing gave it a stronger hull than any other ship afloat. It had repelled ballistae, turned battering rams, and even survived an underwater assault from a depth barge.

I nodded at Sergio and made my way to the helm, where Esteban Hazat and Luca Cyclone, called Black Dog, were arguing about something. Luca was the captain and Esteban disliked deferring to anyone but me. The void legionnaire was a larger man than my cousin, but Luca had inherited the infamous Cyclone family trait of being able to glare with his whole body. In *his* case, the glare was accentuated by large, deep brown eyes and a widow's peak that formed his hairline into a spike.

"I assume you're arguing about something productive?" I asked, needing to steady myself against the railing.

"We are not," replied Esteban.

"Yes we fucking are," countered Black Dog.

"It's a question of authority," said Esteban.

"Exactly," said Luca, "you don't have any... not here."

"We can't begin like this," I stated, making them both look at me. "Understand, both of you, that any authority you have, here or elsewhere, is given by me. Esteban, I have given you command of the twenty-third... Luca, I have given you command of the *Dangerous*. That being said, you *will* show each other some fucking respect."

"As you say, Marius," they replied, in unison.

"Now, if you'd be so kind, I would like a report on our situation."

Esteban bowed his head and took a step back, letting Black Dog answer. "Of course, cousin... sorry. All souls are safe, winds are fair, though we can't really use them. We've got a fleet that needs protecting, so it's minimal canvas all the way to the Red Straits. We'll hug the coast for a day or two, then strike out across the Inner Sea. Oh, one other thing – Asha Two Hearts wanted me to tell you that you're a reckless idiot who's gonna get us all killed."

"Wonderful," I replied. "On all counts."

I turned from my cousin and looked back across the transport ships that followed. Thirty vessels and more than twenty thousand Dark Brethren, most of whom were poor families and other non-combatants – the last few people to leave the Dark Harbour. The five warships I had were in two groups, placed at the front and back of the slowly moving fleet, with the *Dangerous* at the vanguard. On our port side

43

was the Emerald Coast and the high, black cliffs of the Night Mountains. To starboard was endless ocean, with nothing between us and Big Brother but the Inner Sea.

"Fucking cat!" snapped a voice from behind me.

I turned and saw Titus, guarding a coiled rope like it was made of gold, and hissing at any sailor who got too close. Marta was skulking by the nearest downward steps, trying to stay hidden while smiling at the grumpy cat.

"You, below deck," I said to Marta, eliciting a pout. "Don't let him get you in trouble." I then marched from the port railing to the coiled rope and the handful of angry sailors. I picked up Titus with one hand and held the hissing cat against my chest. "Shut up, it's me."

I took my cat back to the quarterdeck and Marta quickly disappeared below, likely intending to complain to her mother about how mean I was being. It was odd having my family aboard. I was required to be a husband and father as well as the Stranger. Luckily, it didn't appear to diminish my authority.

"What's the matter?" I asked Titus, scratching behind his ears and receiving a contented purr. "Is it just this ship? It's really not haunted." He flexed his legs and pawed at my face, lightly clawing my cheek. "Okay, not the ship. So, what is it?"

We moved away from everyone else, towards the observation platform at the stern of the ship. Titus wriggled out of my arms and pounced onto the nearest railing. We were close to the highest point of the deck, with a good view fore and aft. The cat flicked his black tail before hissing towards the bow of the *Dangerous*.

"What do you see?"

Titus hissed again, exposing his formidable teeth. I followed his eyes, along the length of the warship, past stowed canvas and dozens of sailors, to the empty water in front of us. Beyond the Dark Harbour, the Emerald Coast trod a gentle north-eastern path, with high cliffs and few coves. The headland, just visible to the east, was the route to the Silver Dawn. It was a path I'd travelled many times, and had been a bustling trade-route until recently. Commerce was one of many things affected by the rising of an old god.

"What do you see?" I asked again, peering at the empty water and barren cliffs. "There's nothing there... oh, fuck."

Around the headland, creeping slowly along the coast, was a warship. Either side of it were other warships, moving south under full sail and cutting across our path. The lead ship flew a familiar banner from its topsail, depicting a rampant eagle in flight. It was a ship of the Winterlords, though the flanking vessels had a lower draft and were clearly of Dark Brethren construction.

"Marius!" shouted Luca Cyclone. "What the fuck is this?"

"It's Prince Oliver Dawn Claw," I replied. "Seems he didn't send everyone over land after all."

PART TWO

Adeline Brand on Nowhere

4

I crouched behind the rock and held my cutlass across my chest. Opposite me, across the steep incline and skulking behind his *own* rock, was Daniel Doesn't Die of the Sundered Wolves. There was a wide path between two sheer walls of rock, leading from the high cliffs of Nowhere to a small, rocky cove. We were at the midpoint of the slope, being careful to remain hidden from those beneath. Above us, armed and ready on the cliff top, were a dozen Sea Wolf duellists, pulsing with wyrd and acting as back-up if Daniel's plan failed. This small island, north of Nibonay, was the last hope of the Eastron and it needed protecting. Tens of thousands of people were already here, awaiting evacuation into the void, with many more on their way.

There was sudden splashing from the cove beneath, and I chanced a look around the rock. With my one arm holding a sword, I needed to keep my footing secure on the loose gravel, or fall down the slope like a fucking idiot. Where the sharp incline met the rocky beach, and the gently rolling tides of the Red Straits caressed the island of Nowhere, were five Sunken Men. They were far smaller than some I'd seen, but still more than twice the size of an Eastron. They'd been seen skulking in the water, investigating for a way inland where the high cliffs didn't provide a natural barrier. All five were draped in seaweed, with seashell adornments sewn into their sickly white and green flesh. The largest was a blubbery fish-man and had a sloping back, ridged with red spines and ending in a muscular tail. Its head was wide and warty, like that of a toad, with large black eyes and a vibrating pink tongue.

I looked across at Daniel. He was not as fit as me and was obviously out of breath after our climb down the slope. It was strange that a man who couldn't die was wheezing against a rock and holding his chest. It was clear that he'd spent little of his long life exercising. I tapped my cutlass against the rock, just loud enough for him to hear, and mouthed the words *do it!*

He held up a hand, as if asking me to wait, before delving into a canvas bag. From this he produced two small packages, wrapped in paper and trailing long fuses. He placed one at his feet and motioned to throw me the other. Sheathing my cutlass, I braced my shoulder against the rock, before nodding at him. He lobbed the other package across the steep incline and I managed to grab it in one hand at the second attempt. Daniel winced at my fumble, followed by an awkward smile when I hung on.

We both glanced back towards the emerging Sunken Men, but there was no indication they'd seen or heard us. In fact, the grotesque creatures appeared to be communicating amongst themselves, with their mouths popping and their brightly coloured crests flaring. I imagined they were confirming to each other that they'd found a way to sneak onto the island of Nowhere.

I watched Daniel place the first package at the base of the rocks, making sure the fuse ran back up the slope, in the direction we'd be leaving. I mimicked his movements, being careful not to pierce the package, while trying to keep an eye on the Sunken Men. It was tricky with only one arm, but we managed to set the two charges of black dust and begin our crawl, back up the sharp incline, to the cliff top. We stopped at the end of our fuses and locked eyes. Once the packages were lit, we'd have to move quickly, or we'd bring the cliff down on *us*, as well as the Sunken Men.

The Sundered Wolf held up three fingers and began a countdown. I pushed a small flame of wyrd into my fingertip and, when Daniel counted *one*, I touched the end of the fuse. He'd done the same and a quiet fizzing sound emanated from both packages. I was a one-armed woman and he was a deeply unfit man, but we each hauled ourselves back up the incline as fast as we could.

Above us, trailing through the loose gravel of the cliff, were two knotted ropes, and holding them, secure behind the precipice, were Siggy Blackeye and Kieran Greenfire. The master and mistress of *Halfdan's Revenge* had insisted on coming with me. Apparently, I tended to be impulsive and needed trusted people to tell me when I was wrong. It was probably a fair assessment.

Daniel and I hefted ourselves up to the cliff top, struggling with our weaknesses as best we were able. *He* wheezed at the exertion, *I* fumbled with the rope, using my thighs to off-set having only one arm, but we got clear of the burning fuses and the packages of black dust. Siggy grasped my hand, and Kieran grasped Daniel's, just as the black dust detonated. The two outcroppings of rock burst outwards, filling the air with rock and dust, and my ears with a sharp ringing sound.

We all fell to the rugged cliff top, pulling ourselves away from the crumbling precipice, with the rest of my duellists assisting. After a moment, the dust cleared and I fiddled with my ears, cracking my jaw and trying to regain my hearing. "That seemed effective," I said.

"Let's check they're dead first," replied Daniel, speaking between deep, laboured breaths.

"Much as I like seeing dead Sunken Men," I said, "the point is to block the pass and close another route inland."

"This will be the fourth," offered Siggy – a stern duellist, with red hair and several scars across her cheeks and neck. "Unless the froggy bastards learn how to climb sheer cliffs, they'll have to come at us through Duncan's Fall."

I took a tentative step back towards the cliff top and peered down. Where there had been a steep pass from the cove to the cliff, there was now a wall of rubble, rising almost vertically from the water. Three of the Sunken Men were certainly dead, with pieces of their grotesque bodies poking out from under the larger rocks. The other two were either buried under rubble or had fled into the sea. Either way this was no longer a viable way inland.

"Job done," I stated.

"Fuck," said Kieran Greenfire – a short Sea Wolf with a shaven head. "Does that mean we have to go back to Cold Point?"

"Afraid so," I replied. "Unless any of us can conjure a reason to return to the *Revenge*. We can't keep avoiding the Dark Brethren. We're allies now, remember?"

"Fuck," repeated the diminutive quartermaster.

There were thousands of Wolves on Nowhere – those who sail, those who kneel and those who were sundered – and the vast majority had stayed away from Cold Point, the hold of Xavyer Ice, called the Grim Wolf. It was a miserable, grey fortress, currently occupied by Marius Cyclone's void legionnaires, awaiting the arrival of their master and the last refugees from the Dark Harbour. I tried to think of them as allies, I really did, but one hundred and fifty years of hating Dark Brethren was difficult to shake. As a precautionary measure, I'd made sure my people were billeted on the southern plains, between the hold and Duncan's Fall. It allowed us access to our ships and stopped my duellists picking fights with random void legionnaires. We were pledged to flee with them into the far void, but Sea Wolves were violent and proud, and each warrior had some kind of vendetta against the Brethren.

"Adeline, look yonder," said Siggy.

I turned from the cliff. Daniel and the others were swearing amongst themselves at the sight of approaching void legionnaires. It was all muttered and spiteful, but no one reached for a blade or summoned their wyrd. If anything, the cursing was out of frustration, as if things had been simpler when we just attacked each other on sight.

"We're busy. What do you want?" I asked.

It was a cohort of twenty Dark Brethren warriors, clad in black steel armour, with large shields and long spears. They were good fighters, with excellent training, but lacked the savagery and strength of the Sea Wolves.

"You've been busy for a week or so," replied their commander, a young legionnaire called Andre. I'd not caught his full-name, and knew only that he'd been tasked with keeping an eye on me.

I moved across the cliff top to greet him, with Kieran and Siggy flanking me. "Don't you get annoyed, following me all over this island?"

"It's my duty," he replied. "Lord Death Spell is concerned that you should feel welcome here."

The Sea Wolf duellists at my back all laughed. "So, this is some form of hospitality?" I asked, grinning at the legionnaire. "Tell Jessimion Death Spell that I will be returning to his council chamber directly."

"And I am here to escort you," replied Andre. "A matter has arisen and your words are needed, my lady First Fang."

I hadn't been to the island of Nowhere since I was a young girl, and it had changed significantly. Cold Point, the fortress of the Grim Wolf and his People of Ice, had always been near impenetrable, but now, with two Dark Brethren void legions guarding the beach at Duncan's Fall and *our* efforts to destroy any pass down to the sea, we'd turned the entire island into a fortress. Where cliffs provided no natural defence, huge barricades had been erected, with artillery pointing into the Red Straits. Many thousands of Eastron were slowly being moved within the perimeter, ready to take their families and worldly belongings through the calmed Maelstrom, into the distant void. It made me sad to think that every Eastron, those not pledged to serve the Sunken God, was skulking on a small island off Nibonay. Even my people and I had pledged to escape this realm of form and build a new life somewhere far away.

But our time was short and much still needed to be done. We'd seen the face of the enemy and lost many thousands of Eastron to his minions. He was coming, he was waking... and his eye was already fixed upon this small island.

Andre and his cohort escorted us from the eastern cliffs to Cold Point, across the congested plains of Nowhere. Closest to the grey, stone hold were Dark Brethren families from the Dark Harbour, clustered in small encampments. They were just a fraction of the Eastron, crowded into every nook and cranny of the rugged landscape, where a small, canvas town of refugees was patiently waiting its turn to move through Utha's Gate. Kneeling Wolves, Sundered Wolves, Sea Wolves and Dark Brethren.

The only camp of Eastron not represented on the island of Nowhere was the Winterlords, for they had chosen a different path. Whether through ignorance or intent, Prince Oliver Dawn Claw's people had sided with him and the Sunken God. They had always been our leaders, and the noblest of the Eastron, commanding respect from all, even the Sea Wolves.

We were led from the plains to the main gate of Cold Point. Three rivers plunged towards the hold, each meeting a sluice gate and a high arched entranceway. It was a strange place, and nothing like the Severed Hand. It had dozens of high walls, criss-crossing the interior streets and creating small forts at every intersection. Nothing was ramshackle or in need of repair. Even simple doors were framed in iron and flush to the granite walls when closed. Every street, every turning, every crossroads could be locked up and defended. It was a hold designed to make an attacker bleed. Legends of its creation differed, but all agreed that its raising had been a response to Sea Wolf aggression. The irony was not lost on me.

"Adeline Brand, welcome back," said Xavyer Ice, called the Grim Wolf. "Anyone would think your people didn't like my hold." The elder of Cold Point approached from the base of the largest tower, his piercing blue eyes and rugged, bearded face twisted in sarcasm.

In the central square, we were overlooked by a hundred men and women of Ice, covering the adjoining streets with longbows. Closer to the outer walls were hundreds more, as if the People of Ice expected an imminent attack.

"Don't take it personally, Xavyer," I replied. "It's your Dark Brethren friends who give us pause."

"They're *your* friends too," said the Grim Wolf, eliciting a chuckle from Siggy Blackeye.

I didn't laugh, but allowed myself a smile. "Yes, we're to build a new world together... but Sea Wolves bear grudges. No sense in starting unnecessary fights over pointless shit. Now, what does Jessimion Death Spell want?"

The burly man of Ice shook his head, as if in frustration. "Adeline, it's not what *he* wants, it's what the council wants... the council of which *you* are also a part. Though you've not yet thought to attend."

"Been busy," I replied, "making sure we're all safe on this island. I told Death Spell I'd attend when Marius Cyclone gets back. Is he back?"

The Grim Wolf shook his head, before turning and sweeping an arm back into the tower. "After you, my lady First Fang."

I paused, turning to address my companions. "Kieran, Siggy, stay down here. Daniel, you're with me."

"Try not to punch anyone," replied Kieran.

I grinned, before striding into the wide granite tower, with the Grim Wolf and the man who couldn't die following me. The inside was much like the outside – grey and cold, with defence far more important than comfort. The People of Ice had framed their lives around a persistent hatred of the Sea Wolves, with the belief that we'd take everything from them at a moment's notice. They'd sacrificed comfort for security, apparently unaware that most Sea Wolves didn't give a shit about them. Neither Ulric Blood nor his father, the Bloody Fang, had turned their eye to Nowhere, as if the People of Ice were well beaten and not worthy of attention. If only we'd known how important the island of Nowhere would become.

We walked up a steep, spiral staircase, snaking around the edge of the interior, and emerged into the wide council chamber above. The tower had been unoccupied and had no frippery around its circular stone table. There were no windows, but smouldering braziers encircled the space, casting a flickering light across the dusty grey stone and half a dozen faces. Two Dark Brethren were here – Santos Spirit Killer and Jessimion Death Spell, each commanding one of Marius Cyclone's legions and charged with the defence of Nowhere. Either side of them were the leaders of the other Eastron camps – Eva Rage Breaker, representing the Sundered Wolves, and Oswald Leaf of the Kneeling Wolves. The only Sea Wolf, languishing here at my insistence, was Wilhelm Greenfire, the High Captain. Of the three remaining seats, one was taken by Xavyer Ice, one was reserved for me, and one was occupied by a strange, pale man with white hair and pink eyes.

Before I could enact a formal greeting of some kind, I was enveloped in a warm hug by Tasha Strong, the Kneeling Wolf cook who'd been loitering behind Eva. "Are you finished blowing up cliffs?" she asked, inspecting me. "You're not eating properly. I told you, you need to take care of yourself."

I returned the hug. I'd kept her away from our work on the perimeter of Nowhere, hoping she'd be alive to help me once we passed through Utha's Gate. She'd proven adept at quietening my mind and I valued her friendship far too much to risk her life.

"I'm eating," I replied. "Not well... but I am eating."

"Adeline," she said, raising her eyebrows, "you're First Fang. The least you can allow yourself is a good fish-pie once a week."

"Please," grunted Jessimion Death Spell, his smug face turned towards Tasha, as if she were an irritant. "This is not the time to review your dietary requirements."

I grinned at Tasha and stepped past her, to the edge of the circular table. "I believe in being honest," I said. "It can establish a rapport amongst the worst of enemies, once everyone knows where they stand. With that in mind, it's important you know something, Death Spell. I think you are an enormous piece of shit and I dislike you intensely... but I accept that you're necessary. I've done you the courtesy of keeping my people away from yours, and I am pledged to flee this realm of form, so what the fuck do you want? We have things to do."

Jessimion Death Spell was a typical void legionnaire. His hair was black and shaven close, his face was hairless and looked as if it didn't know how to smile. "We need your ships and your expertise at sea," said the commander of the third void legion. "A matter has arisen that we are not equipped to deal with."

"It's important, Adeline," said Eva Rage Breaker, the elder of the Sundered Wolves. She was a matronly old woman, with an unnerving ability to use her wyrd to calm anyone close to her. "You're the best sailors we have."

"*You* I like," I replied, "but don't use your wyrd. Sometimes I need to be angry. Sometimes it sharpens my mind. Now... tell me why you've summoned me and use plain language. You need our ships?"

Those around the circular table shared a complex web of glances and narrow eyes, conveying too many emotions for me to process. The two Dark Brethren commanders remained professional, but their scorn was evident. Eva and the Grim Wolf wore friendlier faces, and Wilhelm Greenfire, sitting closest, stood from the table and approached me.

"Adeline," began the High Captain, "a small fleet of ships is holding position north of Blood Water. In the channel between Rath and Yib."

"They're Winterlords," added Death Spell, "from First Port."

"Hmm," I grunted, suddenly intrigued. "Their intentions?"

"Unknown," said the High Captain. "But we should be in force when we find out."

"Hmm," I said again. I'd never admit it in front of the Dark Brethren, but the mere possibility of a jaunt away from Nowhere, no matter how brief, was reason enough to meet the Winterlords. "Very well. How many ships do they have?"

"Twenty that we've seen," said Wilhelm. "Ironclads. Heavily armoured, but slow as my dear departed mother."

"Are the Winterlords known for their seamanship? Are they dangerous?" asked Eva Rage Breaker. She and her people, the Sundered Wolves, had only recently returned to the Kingdom of the Four Claws and would likely have never met a Winterlord.

"No and yes," I replied. "Their wyrd is strong." I glanced at Wilhelm, then at Death Spell, finding myself in the odd position of having to explain the Winterlords to an outsider. "I can't summarize our history for you, but they've always been our leaders. They're the most powerful Eastron."

"So, you will sail to meet them?" asked Jessimion Death Spell. "And assess their intentions?"

"Sea Wolves are more used to fighting Dark Brethren galleys," I replied. "Ironclads provide a different challenge. But, yes, we'll sail to meet them. Wilhelm, get back to the *Never*. Ozzie, try and find Charlie Vane, we'll need the *Lucretia*. I can deploy ten fast warships and we'll leave at once."

"Wait," said the Grim Wolf. "That is not all. There *is* one Winterlord on Nowhere. Well... not exactly *on* Nowhere."

"Who?" I asked.

"Elizabeth Defiant," he replied. "She was an Envoy of the Silver Parliament. You should take her with you."

I frowned at him. "Why was I not told about this? When did she arrive and where is she?"

"She arrived a few days ago, with someone else," continued the Grim Wolf, "and *he* was most insistent that they both be left in peace. They've already passed through Utha's Gate."

"The man left his falchion behind," said Eva Rage Breaker, producing a dark leather scabbard containing a heavy bladed sword. I recognized it instantly.

"Rys Coldfire," I stated, "called the Wolf's Bastard." I gulped and looked at the floor, trying to find meaning in dusty stone slabs. "He's my friend. I thought he was dead. Now you tell me he's gone into the void realm with a Winterlord? Doesn't sound like the man I knew."

"Nevertheless," said the Grim Wolf, "that's where he has gone. You have our leave to pass through Utha's Gate and retrieve the Winterlord Envoy..." He paused. "What you do with the Wolf's Bastard is your own affair."

Throughout the exchange, the pale man said nothing. He sat next to Eva Rage Breaker, but didn't react to our conversation and was not acknowledged by the other members of Death Spell's council. Yet, just before we left the chamber, my eyes were drawn to him, as if he'd been invisible up to that point. "The Dreaming God dreams no longer," he said. "He wakes... and he is coming."

Utha's Gate, the doorway to our new home, was in the centre of the island, an hour's walk from Cold Point. The gate itself was modest – two pillars of rock, bending towards each other, not quite meeting in an archway, framed a shimmering wall of blue light. Above it, dominating the rugged landscape, was a vast pillar of white light, where a void storm had once been. Once the Maelstrom had calmed, a stable bridge had been created, leading to a distant realm.

All around the gate, camped in organized lines across the rocky land, people were sheltering. Families were the priority and hundreds of children played between the tents and rock formations, serving as a reminder that the Eastron would endure. Most people here were Brethren and citizens of the Dark Harbour, and had been the first to arrive – but, just joining the queue, between Utha's Gate and Cold Point, were Sea Wolf families from the Severed Hand and Sundered Wolf families from the Starry Sky. They could only travel through the gate in small numbers, with an agonizing wait of over an hour before the next group could leave. Thousands were already there, but a hundred thousand or more were still on the island of Nowhere, patiently waiting their turn.

"What's it like?" asked Tasha Strong, walking next to me. "The void realm? Our new home. I've only heard stories."

"What do the stories say?" I asked, trying to hide my trepidation at passing through Utha's Gate.

"Mountains," replied the Kneeling Wolf. "Two lines of mountains, covered in dark green woods, and a wide river, cutting through the valley. But most people talk about the sky. It's blue, just like ours... and the sun is made of wyrd."

"A perfect home," I said, drily. "As long as that river leads to some kind of ocean."

Only Tasha had come with me. Siggy and Kieran had returned to *Halfdan's Revenge*, preparing her to make sail. Daniel Doesn't Die had gone with them, to oversee deployment of the black dust. The substance gave our warship a huge advantage in combat, but was treated carefully at all times. Daniel insisted that he alone manage the cargo, refusing to give any to the Dark Brethren. For this and many other reasons I was eager to return to the *Revenge*. Paramount amongst my reasons was fear of passing through Utha's Gate.

I was no stranger to the glass. I'd spent my life travelling between the realms of form and void, but this was different. This wasn't just breaking the glass; this was walking through a door to the far void, and a new world, designed for my people.

"In your own time," prompted a woman of Ice, standing by the gate. "It can be jarring. There be a bridge of shadows, a short walk, and another gate."

Tasha realized I was just staring at the wall of gently undulating blue light, and she took my arm, leading me forwards. Neither of us had been through before, but Tasha was far less concerned by the enormity of what we were about to do. "Deep breath," she said, cheerfully.

We stepped through Utha's Gate and everything changed. Ordinarily, when you broke the glass, the void you entered was a reflection of the realm you'd stepped from, with identifiable natural features and the occasional shell of a manmade structure. Even when we'd sailed *Halfdan's Revenge* through the glass on the back of a phoenix spirit, we'd seen recognizable land far below us. Utha's Gate showed me something else. It was the void, but it was far, far away from where we'd stepped through, and there was no recognizable land, as if we were walking through the night sky itself.

"A *bridge of shadows* doesn't do it justice," said Tasha, in awe of the spectacle before us.

"I've seen a lot of shit... but I've not seen this."

We were looking at a beautiful black sky, with sparkling points of light, and colourful lines of energy. Everything was impossibly far away, and looking too long at any point made my eyes water, as if there were infinite depths for me to fall into. Ahead of us, the bridge of shadows was crystalline black, with more points of light embedded in the ornate twists and turns of the railings. The sky and the bridge were both black, but there was more than enough light to clearly see where we were going.

We began walking along the bridge, away from Utha's Gate. It was wide enough for a column of ten people or more, and I imagined the many thousands of Eastron who'd already walked across the bridge, and how it would have affected them. Certainly, the further *I* travelled from my own realm of form the more unreal I felt.

The second gate, from the bridge to the void realm, appeared to be made of black wood. There was no door frame or hinges, but two huge doors opened outwards, framing another wall of crackling blue energy.

"Shall we visit our new home?" I asked, mustering a smile.

5

The stories told by the few Eastron who'd returned from our new home *were* accurate, but they did no justice to the immense spectacle beyond the second gate. It was still the void, but like nothing through the glass I'd ever seen... like nothing I'd ever dreamt of. I'd never been to a void realm. I'd never seen a blue sky beyond the glass, nor a yellow sun. There were no spirits here, nor the usual tides of the void, and the casual eye would think us still in the realm of form. Even a cynical bitch like me, with all I'd endured to protect my people, felt a twinge of hope when I first saw the vast, rugged country of our new home.

The mountains first drew my eyes. Two parallel lines of snowy peaks, far larger than anything on Nibonay, Yish or Nowhere, stretched as far as I could see, tapering downwards in a series of lush, green valleys, with a river bisecting each. At the lowest point, the rivers were wide and fast flowing, making it apparent that somewhere there was an ocean.

Tasha and I stood on the only stone structure within view – a huge citadel, simply called the Shadow for the way the sunlight cast unnatural angles upon its black surface. It was vast, though mostly uninhabited, and was being used as a secure storage depot for the necessary supplies being brought through Utha's Gate. I'd heard tell of it, but the reality was far more bizarre. In the realm of form, shadows didn't behave like this. Here, they appeared to be fighting back against any sliver of light that dared to get too close to the citadel. Elsewhere, the land was bathed in warm sunlight.

We both jumped, as the gate behind us slammed shut. It would be another hour until it could be opened again.

"People down there," said Tasha. "Along the river... look."

I stepped from the gate. We were on one of many terraces overlooking the valley, and I approached an ornate, black railing. Beneath us, where a line of rocks formed rapids in the river, were waterwheels, and around them were dozens of Eastron, using the energy of the wheels to drive saws and hammers. The saws prepared planks of wood and the hammers shaped metal. Lumber mills and forges filled the left bank of the wide river, and beyond that were structures – perhaps houses, perhaps meeting halls, but all wooden and of solid construction. They even had chimneys, with smoke rising from newly built hearths.

"Our new home," said Tasha. "I like it."

I closed my eyes and took a deep breath of crisp, clean air. I was a little overwhelmed. This was where I was running to. This was our safe haven in the void, far from the reach of the Sunken God and his fucking frogs. If the Eastron were to survive, grow and flourish anew, it would be here. As I looked, taking in the pristine land, one word kept swirling through my head. Peace. It was peaceful. It might have been the most peaceful land I'd ever visited.

"Ahoy there, Sea Wolf," said a cheerful voice from nearby. "You are not who we were expecting." He was a young Dark Brethren, likely a void legionnaire, but he wore no armour and held no weapon. He approached from the terrace, with a small group of similarly attired men.

"Who were you expecting?" I replied.

The young man smiled and retrieved a pile of scrolls from another man. Folding over a few pages, he ran a finger down the parchment. "Erm, looks like the start of our livestock was expected through." He smiled again. "We have a few pigs and chickens, but we've been clearing a pasture for cattle. Are you, by any chance, a skilled cattlewoman? Sent ahead of the first herd?"

Tasha giggled.

"Give me your name, sir?" I asked, suppressing a laugh of my own.

He placed a hand on his chest. "I am Jacob Hazat, pleased to meet you."

"I'm Adeline Brand," I replied, "First Fang of the wolves who sail, the wolves who kneel, and the wolves who are sundered."

"She is," agreed Tasha, with a nod.

His eyes nearly burst from his skull in surprise. Those with him flailed for a moment before each bowed in respect. "Heartfelt apologies, my lady," said Jacob. "I did not know your face. It is a great honour. We know of your deeds and have been told you are now one of our closest allies."

"Adeline," said Tasha, excitedly, "they've heard of your deeds."

I frowned. "What deeds?"

"Well," began Jacob, clearly intimidated by me, "you led the defence of the Severed Hand. You killed an enormous Sunken Man at the Bay of Bliss and... you are the only Eastron to have defeated their depth barges in battle. It's also said that you sailed a warship through the void on the back of a mighty phoenix and found a lost hold of Eastron."

"Is that true?" asked one of the other Dark Brethren.

"I suppose... yes, that's all true."

"You're blushing, Adeline," observed Tasha.

"Shut up," I muttered.

"Apologies, my lady," said Jacob Hazat. "We meant only to honour you, not to cause discomfort. Now, what brings you through Utha's Gate? We are charged with assisting any and all arrivals."

Beyond the void legionnaires I could now see along the terrace, where huge wooden cranes and gantries moved supplies from the gate to the valley below. A hundred more Dark Brethren worked happily to provide the waiting craftsmen with everything they needed. It was the beginning of something, and there was an air of joyful anticipation to those at work. Again, the word *peace* entered my mind.

"My lady?" prompted Jacob, after a moment of silence.

"Erm," said Tasha, when it became clear I was lost in thought. "We are here to find some people and bring them back. They're needed in the realm of form."

"Of course," replied Jacob. "We have extensive records. Who do you wish to find?"

"Rys Coldfire," I replied, "and Elizabeth Defiant."

"Ah, yes," said Jacob, no longer smiling. "That was a particularly memorable day. They came through last week. The first Sea Wolf and the first Winterlord to join us."

"I assume Rys was less than polite?" I asked.

He considered it. "I'd describe him as stern," replied Jacob, his smile slowly returning. "Though Lady Elizabeth was most gracious. I'll take you to them, my lady."

★

The true scale of our new home was only evident once we left the Shadow. With the citadel at our back, Tasha and I were led along the wide, fast-flowing river, past hundreds of Eastron at labour, and into the thick forest on the eastern bank. The structures I'd seen from above were but a fraction of the buildings at ground level. A settlement had been built, formed in a horseshoe around the waterwheels. Further along the river were more settlements, and under the canopy of the forest were small lumber mills and modest farms. Land had been tilled and crops had been grown, awaiting the thousands who would steadily arrive over the coming weeks.

The cottage emerged from between tall trees. It was set back from the nearest other building, with a narrow dirt road snaking down towards a tributary of the main river. Small birds chirped their way from one branch to another, as if announcing our presence to the cottage's inhabitants.

"We'll leave you here," said Jacob Hazat. "Master Coldfire likes his privacy. We'll wait at the top of the path when you're ready to return to Utha's Gate."

Tasha shook his hand warmly. "Thank you. May I say, you're very polite and friendly."

"For a void legionnaire," I added.

The perpetually smiling young Dark Brethren returned the handshake. "It's this place," he replied, "it somehow... softens the mind."

"Hmm," I grunted, still trying to process the spectacle of our new home. The idea that it could suppress my anger was an internal debate for another day. "Thank you, Jacob."

Tasha and I left the void legionnaires and strolled down the path, trying to take in as much of the beautiful, virgin land as possible.

"Where do you think the birds come from?" I mused. "They're not spirits."

Tasha looked up at the chirping creatures. "Maybe someone brought *them* through as well. Makes it seem more like home."

At the bottom of the path, where the trees thinned out, was a small field next to the river. The cottage itself was only half built, with a supply of freshly cut logs piled nearby. There was framing for two storeys, though only a portion of the roof and floor had been constructed. When finished, it would be a delightful, river-side cabin. Where the front door would be, fenced in either side of a gravel pathway, was a small garden, with furrows dug in the dark earth. Here a woman crouched over in the dirt, holding a trowel and sprinkling seeds.

"Excuse the interruption," I said.

The woman jumped and stood up. "Oh, you startled me," she said, before facing us, wiping dirt from her hands and smiling. She was a Winterlord of fifty years or more, with greying blonde hair and pale skin. She was slender and possessed a striking, mature beauty.

"You are Elizabeth Defiant?" I asked.

"I am," she replied. "Originally of First Port, latterly of the Silver Dawn. Now... I live here. And what are your names?"

"I'm Adeline Brand. This is Tasha Strong."

The answer startled her, but not so much as to diminish her composure. Winterlords always made me a little twitchy. There was something in their demeanour that made the lowliest amongst them appear noble. My brother Arthur used to joke that every boy of the Winterlords thought himself a prince, and every girl a princess. Even the harmless woman before me, with dirt on her hands and knees, had the bearing of royalty.

"You're here for Rys," said Elizabeth Defiant. "He said you might come. That your bond was strong."

"Are you his woman now?" I asked. "For that is an odd pairing."

"Adeline, manners," chided Tasha.

Elizabeth smiled at me, though she was far less open and trusting than Jacob Hazat and his void legionnaires. She had intelligent eyes and looked at me as if conducting an assessment. "I was an Envoy of the Silver Parliament," she said. "I'm immune to most comments on my character, and that was barely more than an observation. Even still… no, I am not his woman. We are friends. He appears to have no interest in anything else. We enjoy having conversations."

"Sorry," I said, suddenly uncomfortable at my rudeness. "But I'm afraid I need you to come back with me."

"Indeed," she replied. "But our house is not yet built. Nor is my writing desk finished. I've requested quill and parchment, and I plan to chronicle the decline and fall of the Kingdom of the Four Claws. This new world may have few Winterlords, but it will still need books."

"That's the thing, you see," said Tasha. "We may be able to ally with more Winterlords."

I glanced back at her. "We don't know if they're allies or enemies," I added, "but they *are* one or the other, and they've sailed into Blood Water. Twenty ironclads from First Port. I am to go and meet them and I want you to come with me."

"And Rys?"

"That's up to him," I replied. "I am the First Fang of the Sea Wolves, but I would never tell that man what to do."

She pouted and bowed her head. "When he said you might come after us, I asked him to describe you. Do you know what he said?"

I frowned and shook my head.

"He didn't mention the one arm," she continued. "He didn't mention your height, your black hair, or your brown eyes. He said only that I should imagine the kind of woman who would stand her ground as a tidal wave approached. The kind of woman who could quieten a tornado with her glare."

"Have you heard of her deeds?" asked Tasha, making me blush.

Elizabeth narrowed her eyes, but managed a thin smile at the Kneeling Wolf. "Only what Rys has told me. And a few rumours from the Brethren who guard this place. They're quite taken with you, Adeline."

I wasn't used to being addressed so informally by people I'd just met, and was a little suspicious of unexpected compliments, but I chose not to question her. It was strange meeting Eastron who'd only heard our story second-hand. Most of my companions had been with me at the Bay of Bliss, the Starry Sky and the Bone Coast. They'd experienced the decimation of the Sea Wolves first hand and knew better than to throw around undeserved compliments when so many of our people were dead.

"Okay, okay," I said, "enough about my deeds and terrifying glare. Elizabeth, you need to come back with us."

"I don't *need* to do anything," she replied. "But I will return with you, for the sake of the Winterlords. Of course, you'll have to convince Rys... and I won't be going back without him."

"Where is he?" I asked. "Gardening, like you?"

"No, he's fishing, a little way down the river. Follow me."

Rys Coldfire, called the Wolf's Bastard, the most dangerous man I'd ever met, was fucking fishing. He was perched on a stool, a few paces from the cottage, wearing thin canvas clothing, his bare feet submerged in shallow water. At his side was a wicker basket, with a handful of freshly caught fish. It was unlikely that an Eastron had thought to stock the river with trout, so my earlier musing about the birds resurfaced.

"Rys, we have visitors," said Elizabeth, making him lower his fishing rod and bow his head. He didn't turn around and clearly knew who these visitors were.

"Hello, Addie," he said. "How have you been?" He only turned to face me once he'd finished speaking. His hair was longer than I remembered and swept back past his ears, and a thin beard framed his angular jaw.

"Well enough," I replied. "I'm still alive, so I fare better than most Sea Wolves."

He gritted his teeth and stood from his stool. Slowly, one step at a time, he approached. He wore no armour and wielded no falchion, but his strength was undiminished. He stopped in front of me, sparing a sideways glance at Tasha, before he and I grabbed each other in a tight embrace. He was one of the few people I truly trusted. I'd known him my entire life, always aspired to be like him and sought his approval. The strength in our embrace was mutual, and I thought that the Wolf's Bastard might actually have missed me.

When we parted, I saw a single tear in his eye. "It's good to see you, Addie."

"You too," I replied. "I thought you'd died at the Silver Dawn. But why didn't you rejoin me?"

He stepped back and wiped the tear from his eye. "I didn't rejoin you because..." He was wrestling with something, perhaps trying to find the right words. "Imagine you know exactly who you are. You scratch the last slivers of your power to stay alive and return to what you know. But, when you return, nothing is as you remember."

"A lot has happened since you and Lagertha left the Severed Hand."

He nodded. "I know."

"So you went fishing?" I asked.

"I like fishing," he replied. "I rarely got the chance at the Severed Hand. But not just fishing. I'm building a house and starting a new life... in peace. Isn't that what we're all doing?"

"Eventually," I said. "But there are thousands of vulnerable people on Nowhere who still need protecting."

"I'm going back with her," offered Elizabeth Defiant. "There are Winterlords I need to speak to. That kind of interaction requires a certain... formality." She stood close to him, holding his hand. "They still need you, Rys, with or without your falchion."

There was a moment of silence as Rys and Elizabeth shared silent thoughts, allowing Tasha and I to gaze across the landscape. The low riverbank, the distant mountains and thick forests of green and brown, all of it was so very peaceful that it almost made me forget the strife still felt in the realm of form. I empathized with Rys, and was strangely jealous of the peace he'd found here. I had no interest in fishing, nor in house building, and worried that I too was just a killer, but spending time beyond Utha's Gate made me wonder if there was something more.

"Very well," said Rys, suddenly. "I still trust you, Addie, but I must ask – are you no longer the Alpha Wolf?"

I sighed. The Wolf's Bastard had left me when the Old Bitch of the Sea still controlled many of my actions. The Adeline Brand he remembered was a different woman, infused by the spirit totem of the Sea Wolves. "It's not a name I enjoy," I replied. "These days I prefer being called the First Fang."

He let forth a grunt of mirth. "You? First Fang?" The grunt flowed into a broad smile. "I can think of no Sea Wolf more worthy. I'll come back with you, if you'll have me."

We embraced a second time. He was far from the only Eastron I trusted, but his renewed friendship felt like a fresh suit of armour, gifting me certainty and confidence. The Sunken God was coming, and having the Wolf's Bastard at my side when he arrived could only give me strength.

"I fear for the enemy," said Elizabeth Defiant. "With you two, standing side by side, the Waking God himself may flee from Nowhere in terror."

"He's coming," I replied, parting from my old friend. "I don't know when, but he's awake."

We walked back through the gate together, but somehow *I* arrived somewhere else. It was as if some power grabbed me as I left the void realm, pulling me to a different destination. Utha's Gate behaved nothing like a conventional break in the glass.

Where the fuck was I? I heard a whistle, but I couldn't be sure. I thought I saw a pale man, but he may have been a dream. Everything may have been a dream, but I didn't think so. I believed I was awake, though I did not feel like a whole person. I felt as if my mind was distant from my body, experiencing something the rest of me was not allowed to see.

"Hello, Adeline Brand," said a young voice from faraway. "Take your time, you'll regain your senses."

"Where am I?" I asked, thinking I recognized the voice.

"You're in a pocket realm of the void," was the reply. "I apologize for diverting you from your journey back to Nowhere. Think of this as a balcony, overlooking something in the realm of form."

As soon as the word was said, I was standing on a balcony. I was whole and aware, though my wyrd tingled, as if the air itself was charged in some way. In front of me, standing next to a black stone railing, was Duncan Greenfire, called Sharp Tongue. He was the High Captain's son and Kieran's younger brother, but we all believed him to be dead. He'd detonated his uncommonly powerful wyrd on Nowhere, killing hundreds of Eastron and giving a name to the cove of Duncan's Fall. I'd seen him grow up at the Severed Hand and Moon Rock, but not thought I'd ever see him again.

"Are you real?" I asked. "Last time I saw you, you saved Prince Oliver's life. A lot has happened since then."

All Greenfires were short, but Duncan was smaller even than his diminutive brother. He'd survived the Sea Wolf rite of passage, dragging himself out of the Bay of Bliss on his seventeenth birthday, and had gained station as a Sea Wolf only because his wyrd was powerful and chaotic.

"Am I real?" mused Duncan, as if I'd posed a deep, philosophical question. "Perhaps you should come and join me by the balcony. You need to see something – a reality you've glimpsed, but not yet seen."

I was dressed in plain fabrics, with no armour or weaponry. My long, black hair was untied and far cleaner than I usually kept it. Then I looked to my left and saw my missing arm had returned. Wherever I was, I had two arms, as if the chaos spawn had never bitten one off. "Whose power is this?" I asked. "Yours?"

"No," replied Duncan. "But it is mine to use. Come. See."

I joined him at the railing, placing both my hands against the cold stone. Below was an ocean, viewed from far above, with a distant coastline at the edge of my vision. It was cold and the tides were high, though the landscape was not one I recognized. "What sea is this?" I asked.

"The Sea of Stars," replied Duncan. "Far to the south."

As I looked over the railing, the distant horizon came into focus, almost as if we were travelling closer to the coastline. Above the crashing waves were high cliffs, rising as a sheer wall from the sea, with a series of pinnacles clustered together and forming a circular bay.

"Look closer," said Duncan. "Your mind is protected, so you can look freely. Others have not been so lucky."

I peered forwards, over the balcony, and my sight travelled closer to the coastline and the circular bay. The things I'd thought were rocky pinnacles were in fact buildings, each hundreds of feet tall. They were black, irregular towers with no windows or doors, but clearly of deliberate construction. All around them, like shrubs sprouting from the trunks of enormous trees, were numerous other buildings, creating an immense, circular monument, just above the water line. Everything was green and mouldy, covered in seaweed and stagnant water, as if newly risen from the depths of the ocean. In the centre, dominating the bizarre stone settlement, were dozens of huge rectangular structures, like standing coffins, encircling a single edifice, almost too big to comprehend.

"The Sea Wolves call this place the Sunken City," said Duncan, "though its true name is hard for Eastron to pronounce."

"The Battle of the Depths happened here," I replied. "A hundred thousand Sea Wolves died in these waters."

"Indeed," he replied. "And if this city's principal inhabitant reaches Utha's Gate, thousands more will die."

I looked at the young man. He was mostly as I remembered, but the scared little boy had gone from his eyes and he spoke with authority. Around his throat was a necklace of thorns that appeared to twist and writhe against his skin, causing small pinpricks of blood to appear and disappear across his neck.

"The void realm," I stated. "We're safe there."

"Not until the doorway is closed," said Duncan. "Like any creature of this realm of form, the Waking God can pass through the gate. He knows what we're doing and he *will* try to stop us. Something about the Inner Sea gives him pause, but that will not hold him for long."

Having your worst fears confirmed was not an enjoyable experience. I'd been saying this since I arrived on Nowhere, and been constantly frustrated that no one else took it as seriously as me.

"The place looks empty," I said, peering down at the city that had been witness to the Sea Wolf's greatest defeat.

"Because I've not yet revealed the inhabitants," replied Duncan. "It is an unnerving sight, even with the protection I have placed around your mind."

"I've seen Sunken Men," I said. "I've seen depth barges, vile frogspawn that consumes everything, *and* whips… and I've killed many."

"Very well," he said. "Look."

Gradually, my view changed. First appeared depth barges, thick as ants, clustered around the seaward perimeter of the city. Then Sunken Men, of every imaginable size, crawling over the black, stone structures, trailing slime and seaweed in their wake. In the middle, standing by three of the larger stone coffins, were the immense whips I'd seen along the Bone Coast, each large enough to crush a warship with a single hand. They were unique mockeries of fish, frog and man, smashed together like the drawings of a madman, with oozing puddles of frogspawn excreting from their bodies.

"I see him," I whispered, looking beyond the three largest creatures I'd ever seen, to the even greater monstrosity beyond. From the central building, around which the whips knelt in twisted worship, strode a single being, larger and more powerful than my worst nightmare could conjure. I closed my eyes and turned away.

"Take your time," said Duncan. "He'll still be there when you open your eyes."

"Is this real?" I asked again, keeping my eyes shut. "I mean, is this happening now?"

"Two days ago," he replied. "Two days before you travelled through Utha's Gate."

I screwed up my face, not wanting to look at the Sunken God. I wondered what I could gain from seeing his face. What insight or knowledge I could glean from looking at him in the flesh. I kept my eyes tight shut. "I don't need to see him," I stated. "It will change nothing. I know everything I need to know about the enemy."

"I hope you're right," said Duncan.

"Send me back," I said. "I'm needed on Nowhere."

6

The transition back to the realm of form was just as jarring as the journey to the void realm had been. Duncan, or whoever's power he was using, appeared to have a way to bypass the traditional barrier between worlds. The tremendous, churning energy of the Maelstrom, quietened or not, displaced everything I thought I knew about the glass. Being dragged around to pocket realms and the like would take some getting used to.

Neither Tasha, Rys nor Elizabeth enquired as to where I'd been, giving me the impression that my visit to Duncan's balcony had taken no actual time. To their senses, I'd left the void realm with them, travelled across the shadow bridge, and returned to Nowhere without incident. Once back, I quickly returned to the business at hand. The four of us travelled to Cold Point, where I left Tasha, then onward to Duncan's Fall, with no talk of what I'd seen. The talk was of how many warships we had to meet the twenty Winterlord ironclads, and all the hundreds of things that could go wrong with such a confrontation.

By the time we boarded *Halfdan's Revenge* and sailed as part of a small fleet into the Red Straits, I had more than enough reasons to worry. There were ten fast warships, sailing into Blood Water, intending to face down twenty Winterlord ironclads. All things considered, after a positive start, it was turning into a terribly depressing day. I'd seen the peace of our new home, then had it smashed to pieces by the terror of what was coming for us. I'd not even had time to reiterate to the council of Nowhere how much danger we were in before boarding *Halfdan's Revenge*. Perhaps things would change when Marius Cyclone returned. By all accounts, the Stranger knew the face of the enemy better than anyone.

"Adeline," said Tynian Driftwood, the peg-leg captain of the *Revenge*, "you're staring into empty space again. I'm sure it's fascinating, but we're getting close to the Winterlords."

I stopped staring into empty space and took in my surroundings. To port was Captain Charlie Vane, called the War Rat, and the *Lucretia* – a swift Kneeling Wolf vessel, filled to the brim with grubby faced killers. To starboard was Wilhelm Greenfire, the High Captain, and the *Never* – a robust Sea Wolf warship with two ballistae decks and a fearsome ram. They flanked *Halfdan's Revenge*, the largest and fastest ship we had, with two hundred warriors and ballistae loaded with explosive black dust. We also had a serrated metal battering ram, named the Fair Lady. Behind us were seven more Sea Wolf warships, similarly equipped for combat. By anyone's measure, it was a fearsome fleet.

"Adeline," repeated Captain Driftwood. "They're signalling. At least we use the same flag codes."

I returned to the helm. Across the main deck, Siggy and Kieran were shouting their way from one side of the ship to the other, preparing us for a potential battle. Below deck, I could hear Daniel Doesn't Die commanding the ballistae crews in the proper usage of the black dust; and at the bow of the ship, removed from any activity, stood Rys Coldfire and Elizabeth Defiant.

"What are the Winterlords saying?" I asked, joining Driftwood at the helm.

"Parlay," he replied. "Broadly speaking. Their language is slightly more florid than we're used to, but their flags say something about a peaceful meeting of honourable equals. They're lowering a platform and launching boats, so we can meet halfway between us."

"Who's there?" I asked. "Who are we speaking to?"

The gruff, bearded captain screwed up his face and looked forward, to where Elizabeth Defiant stood. "Not sure, but perhaps *she* knows."

I nodded. "Deploy the fleet, present a broadside. Signal back that we'll meet them on their platform in peace. Use as few words as possible."

The captain smiled. "Aye, my lady First Fang." He turned to the main deck. "Kieran! Signal one word back to these Winterlords. Tell them... *okay*."

A welcome ripple of humour flowed across the deck. These men and women had fought depth barges and sailed through the void, but still they feared the legendary might of the Winterlords, their strong wyrd, and their armoured tubs. I wanted to share their mirth, but my responsibility was now more than that of a simple duellist. I had to consider the things that no one else did. We had the advantage in seamanship and artillery, but it would be no simple victory against so mighty a foe.

"Siggy," I shouted, "get Elizabeth up here."

The mistress of the boat nodded and rushed past a dozen sailors to the bow. After a moment of no doubt one-sided conversation, the Winterlord Envoy left the railing and made her way to the quarterdeck. She was clearly uncomfortable aboard ship and needed Rys's help to stay upright on the deck. The Wolf's Bastard had donned no armour and had not reclaimed his falchion. Even so, he was the most intimidating Sea Wolf aboard *Halfdan's Revenge*.

"The sea air is most refreshing," said Elizabeth, as she gingerly pulled herself up the steps to the quarterdeck. "Though your vessels are less... stable than those I'm used to."

"Your tubs are built for stability," said Driftwood. "Ours are built for speed, Lady Elizabeth."

"Thank you, captain," she replied, maintaining her formality. "Now, do you have a looking-glass for me?" She daintily reached a hand forwards.

Driftwood plonked a leather-bound looking-glass in her palm, making her wince slightly as his large, hairy hand brushed her own. "Have a look," said the captain. "Your banners don't mean much to us."

"Hmm," she replied, frowning at the big, bearded Sea Wolf. "Give me a moment."

Kieran Greenfire and I locked eyes and shared a discreet chuckle. Elizabeth and Tynian Driftwood could not be more different, almost as if they came from opposite ends of the Eastron spectrum. Then Rys cleared his throat and silenced both our chuckles.

The Winterlord Envoy took her time, using the glass to scan the twenty ironclad ships. They were at anchor in the opposite channel, between the islands of Yib and Rath. They were stationary, in lines of three or four, with the four largest at the vanguard, covering the entrance to Blood Water. It was unlikely Elizabeth would recognize how poor their formation was, nor how dangerously clustered they were. Even if they *wanted* to reform their lines, such heavy vessels would take an age to make way, and my own fleet could pepper them at will. The Winterlord ironclads used massive catapults but, even when charged with wyrd, the boulders they fired were next to useless against moving ships.

"The middle ship," observed Elizabeth, still squinting through the glass. "The one floating the platform and launching the boats. I believe it's called the *Blade of Dawn*, though its banner has changed. The captain is – now, let me think – Tristan Sky, yes, that's right. A terribly ambitious young knight."

"What's wrong with the banner?" I asked.

"Well," she began, as if addressing children in a school room, "the eagle banner of my people is employed in a number of different ways. Claws bared and in flight for the house of Dawn Claw. Standing proud, with wings gathered, for Falcon's Watch and our knights. Most commonly seen is an elegant silver eagle in peaceful flight, used by all other official Winterlord vessels. All three variants are placed on a field of gold. It appears Captain Sky, and most of his fleet, have placed *their* banners on a field of dark green."

"Signalling again," said Kieran Greenfire, observing through a second looking-glass. "They're grateful that we accept parlay and..." he turned back to face me, "They welcome you to meet them halfway. *You*, by name."

"There's certainly some royalty there," continued Elizabeth Defiant, not taking her eye from the glass. "I think it's Natasha Dawn Claw, now the queen-mother. The Shining Sword's widow. I believe she's an honourable woman, Adeline. By reputation at least."

Our sails were trimmed and *Halfdan's Revenge* came to a gradual stop, her broadside facing the *Blade of Dawn*. The rest of my fleet formed a flanking line, pointing a considerable amount of artillery at the Winterlords. I had half their ships, but our skill, and *their* evident stupidity, kept the odds even. Even still, I didn't want to cross swords with the Winterlords. "Fuck," I spat, "I have to go and meet them, don't I?"

"Looks like it," said Driftwood. "I should stay here. I've only got one leg – I'd probably slow you down."

"Elizabeth and I will join you," said Rys Coldfire.

"Yes, you bloody will," I replied. "Siggy, you're coming too. Someone go and tell Daniel that I want him as well."

"This is the man who can't die?" asked Rys. "Interesting."

The Winterlord ironclads didn't move, even as my ten warships took up ideal firing positions and opened their ballistae ports. We couldn't penetrate their metal hulls, but we could deliver enough fire and destruction to their decks and masts to cause panic, and burn a few of their lumbering tubs before they could respond. With the black dust aboard the *Revenge*, we may even sink one or two.

I launched two longboats to greet them, with ten sailors pulling from the *Revenge* to the waiting parlay. Elizabeth and Rys accompanied me on the lead boat, with Siggy and Daniel on the following vessel. With two obvious exceptions, we were all armed and armoured, ready to fight our way back to the ship if required, though I hoped that the presence of the Envoy would work in our favour. Perhaps the Winterlords could even be persuaded to abandon Prince Oliver Dawn Claw and flee this realm of form with the rest of the Eastron.

I didn't yet know how far towards the Sunken God they'd fallen.

The large platform they'd floated was a strange innovation, lashed between three large rowing boats, and bobbing gently on the calm sea. It remained static, at the midpoint between our two fleets, and was large enough for the Winterlord sailors to erect a large awning and fill it with table and chairs. There were a dozen Winterlords across the ships, four of whom did not appear to be normal sailors. There was an old woman and a man with a burned face, neither of them dressed like sailors or warriors. Two more, holding high plumed helmets, cast into the likeness of eagle's wings, appeared to hold command positions, giving orders to the lesser sailors.

"Name them," I said to Elizabeth, as our boat glided closer.

"Yes, yes, okay," she replied, "just let me get my footing." She leant on Rys and positioned herself at the bow of the vessel, over my left shoulder. "The elegant woman in the inappropriate dress is Natasha Dawn Claw. I don't recall the scarred man's name, but I believe he's the senior spirit-master of First Port. The other two are Captain Tristan Sky and, I think, a senior knight of Falcon's Watch."

I knew little of their rituals, ranks and formalities, but that all sounded rather impressive, as if this was indeed the leadership of their people, come to parlay with the Eastron of Nowhere. None of my people would admit it, but the sight of the senior Winterlords sent a shiver of awe across our two rowing boats. They were taller and stronger than the rest of us, and possessed the mightiest wyrd. From our first days in the Kingdom of the Four Claws they had been our leaders.

"Natasha is Prince Oliver's mother," said Elizabeth. "I assume she'll know what became of the prince. He was one of my students, you know? A kind-hearted young man... once. He enjoyed reading."

"Throw your oars," I commanded. "Bring us alongside."

It was notable that those opposite us were also well armed – all except Natasha Dawn Claw and the scarred spirit-master. The sailors had sheathed short swords and the two knights had broadswords. As our boats gently bumped against the floating platform, a tense silence filled the fresh air of Blood Water. The Sea Wolf sailors almost universally looked down at the wood of their rowing boats, while the Winterlords appeared to assess us in a variety of frowns, smirks and raised eyebrows.

"Adeline Brand," said the older and larger of the two knights – a clean-cut and imposing warrior with a thin mouth and pointed nose. "Please join us in peace. My name is Gustav High Heart. I have the honour to be the new commander of Falcon's Watch, the guardians of the Forever King." He swept his hand to the other Winterlords, circling the table, as if he was about to introduce them, but his words were interrupted by the scarred spirit-master.

"What is the Defiant doing here?" asked the burned man. "She is in exile."

"From First Port," replied Rys, being the first of us to stride from the rowing boat to the floating platform. "But she is not *at* First Port." He turned and tenderly helped Elizabeth from the boat.

"And she is our friend," I added, hopping up to stand by the Wolf's Bastard.

Daniel and Siggy joined us, leaving the remaining Sea Wolf sailors to tie off our rowing boats. The platform tilted, with a small slick of water pulsing up from one of the corners, before it settled. The two groups stood opposite each other, until Rys snorted and was the first to take a seat. Slowly, before more formal introductions could be offered, everyone else joined him around the floating table.

"I am Natasha Dawn Claw," said the elegant woman. "You and I have met before, Lady Brand, when my son and I came to petition Ulric Blood for an alliance."

I nodded. "I remember. Duncan Greenfire saved his life. You'll be pleased to know the young man has prospered since then. Will you introduce these other two men? Or will they speak for themselves?"

She emitted a restrained sound that may have been a giggle, or some other sound of amusement. "I will usurp the honour from Gustav," she replied. "This is Alaric Sees the Setting Sun, high spirit-master of First Point." She cast a demure hand towards the man with the burned face. "And this is Captain Tristan Sky of the *Blade of Dawn*, our flagship." The captain was a handsome young man, with broad shoulders and an oddly angelic face.

I smiled, finding gallows humour in how uncomfortable I felt amongst these people. "A pleasure to meet you all," I replied. "You know Lady Elizabeth. These two are Siggy Blackeye and Rys Coldfire, called the Wolf's Bastard. The man on the end is Daniel of the Sundered Wolves. And I'm Adeline Brand, First Fang of the wolves who sail, the wolves who kneel and the wolves who are sundered."

I tried to assess their reactions, but there were too many to adequately process. Alaric, the burned man, kept his glare on Elizabeth and appeared not to care who the rest of us were. Gustav, the imposing commander of Falcon's Watch, had clearly heard of the Wolf's Bastard and thrust out his chin at the legendary Sea Wolf duellist. As for Captain Tristan Sky and Natasha Dawn Claw, they largely kept their composure, with just a raised eyebrow at my new title and mention of the Sundered Wolves.

I leant back in the chair, running my hand along the rich mahogany. It was a fine piece of furniture, wasted on a floating parlay platform. "So," I said, "what shall we talk about?"

Despite her mighty company, it was clear that Oliver's mother held seniority. The captain of their flagship, the commander of their elite warriors, and their spiritual leader, all glanced at the woman.

"We are here in peace," said Natasha Dawn Claw, "and with a simple question. What are your intentions on Nowhere? We have heard talk of an, almost unbelievable, alliance between Marius the Stranger and the First Fang."

"And there is other talk," said Alaric, in a raspy voice. "Talk of a doorway to a distant void realm, and a plot to betray the Kingdom of the Four Claws."

I frowned. This was not what I wanted to talk about, nor did it tell me if these people were truly my enemies.

"There is a dark green field on your banners," said Daniel Doesn't Die, leaning forwards and crossing his arms on the table. "What does that mean?"

"You are a Sundered Wolf," said Alaric. "You have relinquished your voice in this kingdom. Please be silent."

"Fuck off!" growled Rys Coldfire.

"We will maintain decorum," snapped Natasha Dawn Claw. "We are all bound by honour to talk in peace."

"Peace," I said. "What does peace mean to you? To us it means leaving this realm of form through Utha's Gate, saving as many Eastron as we can, and confounding the

Sunken God. If it means something else to you, speak it now!"

Behind me, the sailors of *Halfdan's Revenge* held the hilts of their cutlasses, sensing my tone and, despite their fear of the Winterlords, preparing to move if I commanded. Siggy Blackeye, seated to my left, pushed a subtle layer of wyrd into her sword arm and tickled the handle of her basket-hilted blade. Rys barely reacted but, even without a sword, he was a killer with few equals.

"Please," said Natasha, "peace means we are friends, at least for now."

"The green banner," repeated Daniel, tilting his face upwards and locking eyes with Alaric Sees the Setting Sun. "That banner has not changed for more than a hundred and fifty years. Why now?"

"Answer him," said Natasha, wagging a finger at the scarred spirit-master. "We must repay the First Fang's bluntness with our own."

"Very well," said Alaric. "It's quite simple really. Oliver Dawn Claw, the Forever King, demands your allegiance. The Green Dawn Claw is his new totem spirit – and the new totem spirit of the Winterlords. In time it will reign over all of us."

I glanced left, locking eyes with Siggy, then right, locking eyes with Rys. I conveyed a subtle shake of the head to both. This parlay was not going to end well. In fact, as I looked into the faces of the burned man and old woman, I suspected it would end in blood. However, there was no need to rush the parlay, and I'd heard things I wanted clarifying.

"Okay," I said. "The Green Dawn Claw and the Forever King. I understood the Silver Parliament was dissolved before Oliver could gain their pillar of rule."

"It was," said Elizabeth Defiant. "Rys and I were there. We barely escaped. Alexis Wind Claw had a hundred Winterlords killed. *She* is our enemy. The enemy of all Eastron. Her and her Sunken God."

"Indeed," said Natasha Dawn Claw. "We follow no Sunken God. We follow the newly found strength of my son, King Oliver Dawn Claw. He and the great eagle of the Winterlords have changed and we are sworn to follow them. There will be a new Kingdom of the Four Claws."

"Tell me," said Rys Coldfire, straightening in his chair. "What happened to Prince Oliver at Snake Guard?"

"*King* Oliver!" announced Natasha. "He saw this rising god and was mighty enough to take his power. The Green Dawn Claw visited us at First Port and showed us what true strength was. Our kingdom will be rebuilt... and will be so much more magnificent."

The table was silent for a moment, with the floating platform barely moving. The four Winterlords opposite us adopted strangely serene expressions. Even the grotesque face of Alaric Sees the Setting Sun was suddenly calm. Then I saw a shape above them. It was as if something was in the void, beating its huge wings against the glass. The outline of an enormous eagle, wreathed in rotten green wyrd, was pulsing behind each of them. All of us had seen the wyrd of the Sunken God and the Dawn Claw was infected with the worst of it. All at once my companions and I realized the Winterlords had fallen.

"What's happened to you?" asked Elizabeth Defiant, suddenly afraid. "You follow the twisted ways of the Sunken God. Your totem is corrupted. You *must* see that. Please. Where is Oliver? I could reason with him."

"Enough of this," stated the Wolf's Bastard, sending a rush of wyrd into both his hands and clamping them onto the edge of the table. With a single movement, he flung it upwards, into the faces of those opposite.

Of the four opposing Winterlords, two – the spirit-master and the woman – were flung into the water by the tumbling wooden table. The two knights, using their own formidable wyrd, were able to deflect enough of the impact to remain standing. Their sailors drew short swords, mine drew cutlasses, and suddenly it was a fight.

"Back to the *Revenge*," I barked, drawing my sword and summoning a shirt of light blue wyrd.

"Take them alive," ordered Gustav High Heart, the knight of Falcon's Watch, suddenly glowing with his own golden wyrd.

Elizabeth Defiant cowered and Daniel Doesn't Die stayed still, but everyone else prepared to fight. We were outnumbered, but not by much. The concern I saw in Siggy's face, shared by most of the Sea Wolf sailors, was that none of us had ever fought Winterlords. Luckily, Rys didn't seem to care. The Wolf's Bastard swept an arm backwards, shepherding Elizabeth to the relative safety of the rowing boat, before picking up the chair he was sitting on and smashing it over Gustav's head. Sailors on both sides began a flailing contest from their boats – delivering cuts, but little more – as the sudden movement caused everything to buck and sway on the water. Siggy and I moved to engage Captain Tristan Sky, but our footing was far from stable.

"Just restrain them!" shouted the young Winterlord knight, showing their evident confidence when fighting lowly Sea Wolves.

On the far side of the floating platform, Natasha Dawn Claw and Alaric Sees the Setting Sun were being helped from the water and into one of their boats. On our side, the rowing boats were trying to push off and get some distance from the Winterlords' short swords. To my right, Rys clinched with Gustav, nullifying his sword and forcing him to wrestle. The Wolf's Bastard was the smaller man, but far less encumbered by armour, and he managed to throw the commander to the tilting platform.

Siggy and I attacked together, going high and low at the captain. Everything was off balance and the three of us bumped into each other when the platform surged. There was a tangle of blades, legs and swearing, as we tumbled to the wooden floor. It was impossible to see what was going on and sea water was now flowing over everything. We had to get back to the *Revenge*, somehow retreat and find a way to deal with another fucking enemy.

"Time to go," announced Daniel, grabbing me by the arm and Siggy by the shoulder. "You can't beat them like this."

I drove my elbow into Tristan Sky's chest and pushed away from him, regaining my footing on the swaying platform. Siggy dug her teeth into his hand, causing a pained howl, before rolling towards Daniel. The captain was suddenly able to wildly swing his broadsword, cutting my thigh, glancing across Siggy's back, and stopping with a squelch in Daniel's neck. The Sundered Wolf didn't make a sound as he died, but his eyes went wide and his blood flowed into a mantle of red across his chest.

I grabbed Siggy and the two of us fell backwards, landing next to Elizabeth Defiant on the rowing boat. Rys Coldfire finished choking Gustav High Heart into unconsciousness and darted away, using his prodigious wyrd to stay upright on the tilting surface. He dropped his shoulder into the slowly toppling body of Daniel, pushing him off Tristan's blade. The bleeding corpse landed on me, his limp arms and staring eyes all I could see for a moment. Then Rys leapt over us and our boats separated from the platform. The rest of my sailors had minor cuts, but none were dead, and we slowly glided beyond the reach of the Winterlords.

I wiped Daniel's blood from my face and pushed his corpse to the wooden deck, knowing it wouldn't stay a corpse for long. Then I used my cutlass to help me stand and, breathing heavily, faced the Winterlords. Gustav, the commander of Falcon's Watch, was rubbing his throat and slowly standing up. Tristan Sky, captain of the *Blade of Dawn*, joined him, though he was flustered and his hand was covered in blood.

"At least we know where we stand," I shouted, as my sailors sat on their oars and we moved back to the fleet. "We want to save the Eastron. You want us all to kneel. Your totem and your prince have fallen and you refuse to see it." I looked back at *Halfdan's Revenge* and the fearsome broadside facing the cumbersome Winterlord ironclads. "I will now destroy your fleet... and kill every last one of you."

PART THREE

Marius Cyclone on the Inner Sea

7

My people didn't follow me because of my rapier wit and charm. Nor did they obey my orders out of a sense of duty or loyalty. They were loyal, certainly, but the Brethren of the Dark Harbour followed me because they'd seen things other Eastron had not. It was strange for people to flock to a leader who wanted to run away, but it was exactly what they wanted and appeared at exactly the right time. Any hope Santago had of turning my people against me, and corrupting them into worship of the Sunken God, had ended when he sent the Twitching Whip into the Sea of Spirits to attack the Dark Harbour.

Two weeks after meeting Utha, just before I began the evacuation of my hold, I received a final message from Santago. There was a second scrawl at the bottom of the message that may have been Trego's signature, but all accounts indicated that our middle brother had suffered a complete mental collapse. He'd been given into the care of Alexis Wind Claw and propped up at the Silver Parliament, little more than a mannequin who simply did what he was told. His signature meant little, but it gave our eldest brother added authority to demand my surrender. I'd resisted a childish impulse to tell him to go and fuck himself, and simply ignored the message. His response to being ignored had nearly destroyed my hold.

I'd already decided to run, and was deeply immersed in the painful process of convincing my people to join me. The Dolcinites would follow me no matter what, and the Strike would defy me no matter what, but it was everyone else I had to convince. I commanded legions, and my three commanders needed the most convincing. Jessimion Death Spell, Inigo Night Walker and Esteban Hazat were each responsible for five thousand warriors – the void legionnaires of the Dark Harbour – and they would not flee into the void on my word alone. In a strange twist of fate, it was my brother Santago's actions that convinced them.

On a warm summer evening, with the sun slowly disappearing over the horizon, a huge creature attacked the Dark Harbour. In his final message, my brother was nice enough to send me a cryptic warning, but hearing that *the Twitching Whip will be calling*, was not language I understood at the time. Not until a huge wave broke from the calm sea. Everyone saw it, even Merlinda and the Tender Strike. The Sea of Spirits could be seen from almost every building in my hold, and every window was full of terrified onlookers.

First there was a hand – enormous and scaly, with webbed digits and cruel claws. Then an arm – sinewy, with translucent green skin stretched around red spines. Before its head emerged, the hand groped inland, as if trying to pull itself upwards. It smashed through a line of stone houses, before gaining purchase on the largest of the seaward docks. Dozens ran screaming and dozens more died, before I could get Esteban and his men to the sea front. All we saw when we got there was a head emerging from the Sea of Spirits. The hand and the arm had focused our attention, but they faded into the background when the thing pulled itself from the water. Three ridges of spines swept backwards from its forehead, each crested with the same red colour. As the churning water parted, angular eyes and pulsing gills emerged.

The Twitching Whip was the biggest creature I had ever seen. Even in my fevered dreams of the Sunken God, I'd never conjured such an immense beast. Esteban and I had a thousand warriors, facing the harbour, but each and every one of us questioned our very reality as we saw the thing rise from the sea. How could such a creature exist? Suddenly, my talk of a waking god was no longer so far-fetched. I'd warned everyone of this, over and over again, but I was as startled as them as I saw the monster before me. I'd gained no victory by being right. I didn't feel smug or justified, I just felt fear... I just wanted to run away.

Hundreds of us died, fighting the thing. Normal citizens of the hold, void legionnaires, sailors, men and women who wanted nothing more than to protect their families and their homes. As the creature tried to pull itself from the sea, I remember feeling ashamed. I was a coward, driven on only by those around me. Even as I hacked at the slimy green skin before me, I wanted to run from it. It was only the sacrifice of my people that stopped me. Dark Brethren rushed from every house and every street, wielding any weapons they could find, until the Twitching Whip had no space to move without meeting the edge of a blade or the point of a sharp stick.

It was impossible to tell if we'd killed it. All that could be seen, when I pulled my eyes from the deep trench of flesh I'd cut, was a toppling mass of green, as the beast fell back into the Sea of Spirits. People stood on every angle of the seaward dock and all along the seafront. A thousand or more stood amongst the mutilated bodies and chunks of the creature's flesh, watching bubbles form and pop on the surface of the water.

I never knew what Santago was thinking. Was he just trying to scare us? Perhaps kill enough citizens that the remainder would fall in line? Or maybe he was just playing with his new toy, slapping his youngest brother in the face with the power given to him by the Sunken God? Whatever his intentions, he galvanized the people of the Dark Harbour in a way I could never have done. Now most of us had abandoned our hold, with the last few at sea, leaving the Dark Harbour forever.

I only had five warships. Ahead of the *Dangerous*, blocking our path along the Emerald Coast, were ten Dark Brethren vessels and a single Winterlord ironclad, flying the banner of Prince Oliver Dawn Claw – a rampant silver eagle in flight, upon a dark green field. They were under sail and cutting south across our path. We had an hour at the most before they'd intercept the head of our fleet. Behind the *Dangerous* were twenty-five other ships, packed with the last few refugees from the Dark Harbour. I couldn't afford to lose a single ship, nor would I allow any more of my people to die or be taken prisoner. I had to think fast.

"Trim sails," commanded Luca Cyclone, called Black Dog, the captain of my ship. "Slow us down and signal the fleet to do the same. Buy us some time."

Sailors pulled their eyes from the approaching vessels and hastened to their work. Warning bells were rung and the fleet deployed, fanning out and slowing down at our command. My other four warships, flanking the more vulnerable transports, moved to join us at the vanguard of the fleet.

"Marius," shouted Luca, "what are your orders?"

Esteban Hazat, commander of the twenty-third void legion, was summoning his warriors from below deck, causing a loud, metallic clatter to travel across the sloping deck.

I stayed on the observation platform at the stern of the ship, staring ahead at the huge Winterlord vessel. Sluggish but heavily armoured, it was likely filled with three or four times as many warriors as I had aboard the *Dangerous*. The smaller Brethren ships were faster, but keeping pace with the ironclad, as if they were a pack of wolves following their alpha. They weaved left and right, covering any trajectory we might use to sail past them. I looked up at the sails. The wind was in their favour. We could slow down, but we couldn't take the weather gauge, meaning they'd always have control of the engagement.

"Marius!" roared Luca a second time.

Titus, my defiant cat, hissed at me and pounced back to the observation platform. The large, black and white animal quickly disappeared down the nearest set of steps, displacing two void legionnaires, fumbling with their shields. I watched him disappear, before striding down to join Luca on the quarterdeck.

"We can't fight them," I said.

"Obviously," replied my cousin.

"We can't run," I said.

"Clearly," he replied. "They have the weather gauge, they'd board us at their leisure. So, what can we do?"

"He doesn't know," said Asha Two Hearts, appearing next to me. "He's going to get us all killed. He's just trying to look clever." She and her brother, Gaius, had a habit of silently approaching whenever the opportunity to insult me reared its head. Of late there had been many opportunities.

"I'm thinking," I stated. "Allow me a moment."

What the fuck could I do? I was a good sailor, with extensive knowledge of battle tactics, but certainly not skilled enough to be victorious in such a one-sided battle. Even with Black Dog's help, I could see no tricks or manoeuvres that would outwit the approaching warships. I considered the possibility that we were thoroughly fucked… but then something occurred to me and I turned back to the Dark Brethren vessels, flanking the ironclad.

"They're not after the fleet," I said. "If Santago's there… they're after me."

"So?" queried Luca. "They get *you*, they get all of us."

"Not necessarily," I replied. "I have an idea."

Esteban, now wearing black plate armour, rushed back to the quarterdeck. "What are we doing?" demanded the void legionnaire. "I only have fifty warriors aboard."

"Apparently," said Asha, "the Stranger has an idea."

They all looked at me, as did the dozen closest members of the crew. If Titus were here, he'd be hissing in my direction. The problem with cultivating a reputation for being cleverer than everyone else, was that you occasionally had to prove it.

"We split them up," I said. "Send the fleet south, into the Inner Sea, and keep all four warships in a perimeter."

"They'll be crawling," said Luca. "Even under full sail. Those bastards will easily overtake them."

"*If* they pursue," I countered. "We take the *Dangerous* east, well away from the fleet. We can push through the smaller tubs at the southern edge of their line and keep the wind. If Santago's there, he'll know this ship is mine. At least half of them will come after us... I'm betting the majority will. They might send a few ships after the fleet, but that gives them a chance. They still have four warships to protect them and near a thousand legionnaires... and they'll defend the refugees with everything they've got."

I saw a lot of frowns and a few open mouths, as everyone who'd heard tried to process my words.

"A gamble," said Esteban, "that they want you more than they want those refugees."

I nodded at the commander. "Most of our people are already on Nowhere. Do you think Santago and Oliver Dawn Claw really give a shit about a few more? They're not here for the Dolcinite Pilgrims and the poor of the Dark Harbour. They're here for me. That gives all of us a chance."

"Interesting," said Luca.

"Arrogant," said Asha.

I took a deep breath. I rarely exerted my full authority over my people, preferring to think that they followed me out of loyalty and good sense. On this occasion, with time a defining factor, I decided to shout. "This is not a fucking suggestion – these are orders! You will signal the fleet and send them south. They are to travel for a day before bearing east towards the Red Straits and Nowhere, with the warships in close guard. The *Dangerous* will lay on all sail and push through the enemy line, along the Emerald Coast. Asha, would you be so kind as to get all the warriors we have up on deck and, err, politely enquire of the Dolcinites if they would take up arms in defence of the ship? Do it, now!"

My voice carried far and a few dozen of the crew moved, without thinking, to obey my orders and pass the word. Those closest were a little slower, but even Luca Cyclone and Asha Two Hearts offered no disagreement. Even if I was wrong, they had nothing to lose. I really hoped I wasn't wrong.

"So," said Esteban, the only person to stay close to me, "*we* die instead of the fleet. Good plan. Is this an honourable sacrifice of some kind? Because I'm not sure what that would accomplish, my lord."

"Neither am I," I replied, my mind still racing. "I'm dealing with the first problem... I'm sure others will arise shortly, and I will deal with them then."

Communicating with the fleet happened quickly, in a dance of bells, coloured flags and shouting. The other warships moved first, shepherding the slower transports as they turned against the wind and pushed south from the Emerald Coast. Canvas was unfurled and feverish activity covered every deck, but the ships slowed significantly. If I was wrong and more than half of the ten enemy vessels pursued them, the refugees would be quickly overwhelmed and boarded.

The *Dangerous* surged forwards as the quartermaster, Sergio Eclipse, called Anvil, commanded we lay on all sail. With a huge, white blanket of canvas, bulging down the length of the ship, we jumped away from the turning fleet of refugees and towards the expanding line of oncoming warships. Esteban's legionnaires had split into two groups and held position along each railing. Alone, there weren't enough of them to effectively repel boarders, but with Asha and Gaius Two Hearts commanding two further companies of warriors – mostly Dolcinites, armed with maces and quarterstaffs – we would give any force boarding us a serious fight.

I moved to the helm, looking over Luca's shoulder. "Find a weak point in their line, cousin, and break it."

"Difficult," he replied.

"The furthest point from the ironclad," I said. "The small ships at the edges will have no artillery to worry us. They're not Sea Wolf pirate ships; they rely on boarding. Hopefully the *Dangerous* can cripple one or two of them."

Esteban grumbled as he looked over the small Dark Brethren cutters at the edges of their lines. "Those are troop ships, Marius. They'll have ropes, hooks, ladders, crossbows... anything to latch onto us."

I let his words hang in the air, and took a few strides to the port railing. We were towards the rear of the fast moving wedge, with four stepped sections of the deck in front of us. The framing of the *Dangerous* gave her the strongest hull afloat, and at speed she was devastating – but neither I, nor Salty Alphonse, would have thought to test her strength by ramming through a line of Brethren warships.

"We're at full sail, Marius," shouted Luca, needing to raise his voice to be heard above the sound of crashing waves. "They're getting awfully close."

I looked forward along the port side, then back at the slowly manoeuvring refugee fleet. We'd left them behind and were now a lone ship, plunging at speed along the Emerald Coast. I imagined confusion was flowing over Santago and Oliver's warships, as they tried to fathom what I was doing by splitting the fleet and charging straight for them. If I was right, my brother would quickly decide that I was the greater prize.

"Three points to starboard," commanded Luca. "Point us at the last two cutters... and secure the deck for impact."

We veered across the line of warships, changing our point of sail from the huge Winterlord ironclad to the edge of their line, furthest from the coast. There was barely a gap between the last two cutters, and only a madman with an unusually resilient warship would think to smash into them under full sail.

"You're insane, Marius," shouted Asha.

"Everyone thinks so," agreed Gaius.

"Shut up," I replied, "and hang onto something."

It all happened in slow motion. I wrapped both arms around the port railing and was close enough to the enemy to see their faces. Void legionnaires, thousands of them, spread across ten ships. The draft of the ironclad was too high for me to see much, but at the stern was an enormous, bloated man in green-tinged, silvery armour. Prince Oliver Dawn Claw was only visible for a second, but he looked even more grotesque than when I'd last seen him – bald, with red veins across his skin. I couldn't tell if he saw me, or if Santago was with him.

"Brace!" commanded Luca, as we plunged the last few feet towards the enemy line.

Everything turned upside down. Wood, water and a deafening crack, then shouting and screaming. An enormous bow-wave crashed over everything, forcing me to close my eyes and curl into a ball on the quarterdeck. We'd smashed into the small gap between the cutters and, for a moment, it was impossible to tell who'd come off worse. The deck of the *Dangerous* was filled with tumbling sailors, braced legionnaires and cowering Pilgrims, but we weathered the initial impact.

I pulled myself up the port railing, blinking sea water from my eyes, and trying to see what had happened. Below us, on both sides, were listing ships. The last two cutters in their line had both turned inwards at the immense impact. Closest to me, on the port side, the troop ship appeared stricken, with a gaping hole along the side of its hull. The *Dangerous* had sliced through the wood, exposing two decks to the sea and forcing the tightly packed warriors aboard to fling themselves into the water. I rushed to the other side, where the second cutter was quickly righting itself. We'd bumped it out of the way, destroying its foresail, but it was still seaworthy, and the troops aboard had survived the impact.

As for my own ship, she was surging back and forth against the bow-wave, and a wrecked section of rigging and canvas was hanging from the mainmast, but she appeared otherwise unscathed. We were still at full sail and the bulging canvas pushed us on, through the gap we'd created.

"Starboard railing!" shouted Luca Cyclone from the helm. "Defend the ship!"

Grappling hooks and rigging were being flung upwards from the second cutter. With the port railing likely secure, Esteban directed his few legionnaires to the starboard. Asha and Gaius joined him, forming a line of Dolcinites next to the railing. From the low troop ship, spear tops and owl helms became visible – then crossbowmen appeared across the railing, firing onto our deck and killing a dozen of my warriors in a single volley.

I swore and moved to join Esteban, bringing Luca with me as I passed the helm. The *Dangerous* didn't stop, even as a significant portion of the enemy fleet tried to turn against the wind. We'd smashed through their line and they'd need time to manoeuvre around and pursue us. By then, the weather gauge would be in *our* favour... but only if we could repel the boarders. They swarmed across the starboard railing, using spears and crossbows to drive back the defenders. I knew they were the priority, but I kept an eye on the enemy fleet, hoping they'd follow and I'd be proven right. A skirmish on our deck, unless we were completely overwhelmed, was of secondary concern to making sure we were being chased by Santago and Prince Oliver.

A Dolcinite corpse landed at my feet, his neck pierced by a crossbow bolt. A void legionnaire next to him flew backwards, his breastplate buckled by a powerful spear thrust. There was now a line of enemies on our deck, with more coming behind. Their troop ship was being carried along by the *Dangerous*, fastened with ropes, hooks and rigging, as the wind once again filled our sails and pushed us to the east.

"Asha!" I shouted. "Cut their ropes, we'll leave the troop ship behind."

She and her brother were busy slicing throats, cutting tendons, and finding tiny holes in the opposition's black armour. At my command, with only a slight stare of annoyance, she disengaged, leading a gang of sailors to outflank the enemy and cut their ship loose. I joined her from the opposite flank, as we tried to isolate those who'd already boarded and stop any more from leaving the troop ship.

The *Revenge* was picking up speed again, quickly putting ocean between us and the enemy fleet. The Dark Brethren cutter, clinging to our starboard hull, was rolling and turning as it was swept along on the strength of our sails. At least a hundred more legionnaires waited aboard, pushing and shoving to board us, before their own ship was stricken. Its masts had already buckled and broken, and its hull was in danger of splintering.

I severed a taut rope, sending two warriors into the sea. Next to me, a sailor chopped through two more ropes, releasing a section of rigging that kept the two ships tethered. A dozen warriors from the troop ship plunged into the ocean, as Asha Two Hearts threw off every grappling hook and rope she could find. Between our two groups, we cleaved a line behind those who'd boarded us, and released the cutter to flail behind, its sails broken and its troops tumbling into the sea. The fifty or so warriors who remained on our deck suddenly paused, realizing they were trapped and outnumbered, with no chance of reinforcements.

"Hold!" I commanded, wanting to give them the chance to surrender. Brethren fighting Brethren was not uncommon, but I couldn't believe each of them was as devoted to the Sunken God as my brother.

Esteban, Gaius Two Hearts and the few remaining members of the twenty-third void legion, held their position, forming a defensive line and isolating the enemy in a small portion of the main deck. Asha and I formed a second line behind them, but no one attacked. "Surrender," I demanded. "You won't get a second chance."

A handful screeched fanatically and rushed to their deaths, but most threw down their spears. "Right," I began, sheathing my sword, "the rest of you get overboard while you can still swim back to your fleet. We haven't got space for prisoners. Leave with your lives."

"You heard him," boomed Esteban Hazat, shepherding the vanquished warriors to the starboard railing, where they were politely helped overboard by Dolcinite Pilgrims.

Luca went back to the helm and sailors returned aloft, making sure the *Dangerous* kept her line east. "We're clear of the fleet, Marius," said my cousin.

"And you were right," added Esteban. "Eight of the ten ships are turning to pursue us. The other two must just be following the refugees, but they won't be able to trouble them." The commander approached me, clearly wanting to talk with more privacy. "First problem solved, my lord. Now what the fuck do we do? Seven Brethren ships and a Winterlord ironclad. That is a lot of ships against little old us."

I kept my eyes on the fleet deployment behind us. "But I was right," I replied, smiling at him.

8

The three of them looked at me, using a variety of glares, shakes of the head and clenched jaws. A woman, a girl and a big, black and white cat. Jessica, my wife, was not happy that we'd left the fleet behind, and she was positively livid that we were being chased by eight warships. Her anger had infected Marta, our seven-year-old daughter, though I suspected Titus was just joining in because he enjoyed glaring at me.

"I had no choice," I said, as if addressing a courtroom. "If we'd not split the fleet, we'd all be dead."

"Oliver Dawn Claw *and* Santago?" she asked, as if it would completely explain why she was cross. "We can't win against that."

Titus hissed, prancing across to sit in Marta's lap, flicking his tail at me as he moved.

"No, we can't win," I conceded. "Unless something remarkable happens with the wind or the sea, they'll overtake us – perhaps half a day before we reach the Red Straits."

"If only Salty Alphonse had built this bloody ship for speed, not strength." She gave Marta a kiss on the cheek and ushered her out of our chamber.

"I'm cross too," said my daughter, before she and Titus left to cause trouble in the hold. I'd never tell her, but her disapproval cut more than either my wife's or my cat's.

I sat next to Jessica, intertwining our fingers. Once Marta had closed the door, my wife gave me the smallest of smiles.

"Esteban keeps asking me what we're going to do," I said. "I don't have an answer for him. Luca keeps giving me updates about the wind, the tides, the sails, the state of the crew, as if any minute I'll give him new orders that'll change everything. Then there're the Dolcinites – I can't walk past one without them blessing me and praising my bravery."

"What about the Two Hearts twins?" she asked. "I bet they're on your side."

I laughed. "Well, Asha thinks I'm suffering from a mental illness, and Gaius thinks I've been possessed by the spirit of Salty Alphonse. *Both* of them think I'm going to get us all killed."

"Well you are, aren't you?" she replied, clutching my hand.

I nodded. "Probably, yes. But the refugee fleet will survive, and tens of thousands more on Nowhere have a chance at a new life. I suppose the *Dangerous* and our lives is a small price to pay."

Jessica took a deep breath and shifted her weight. "You're right, but that's a hard thing to sell – *you're going to die tomorrow, but a lot of people are still alive because of you.*"

"But that's the reality," I said. "Tomorrow morning, we'll be in range of their forward ballistae. A few hours after that, their fastest warships will be able to overtake us. It'll all be very slow. With the weather gauge, Santago knows he can take his time. They'll surround us, probably cripple us, and wait for Prince Oliver and the ironclad to catch up. After that, I don't know, but they've got enough warriors to make any defence we mount pretty meaningless."

"It looks like we won't get to walk through Utha's Gate after all," she replied. "I was looking forward to a new house – something less macabre than the Strange Manse." She paused and kissed me. "What about Marta?"

"I don't know," I repeated. "Santago won't kill *me* straightaway. Perhaps he's deranged enough to keep you and Marta alive, just to torment me. And I have no earthly idea what the thing that used to be Oliver Dawn Claw will do. If you can spare Marta from pain…"

There was a tear, slowly forming in her left eye. "I thought we might actually escape," she whispered. "It looked like we would for a long time." She wiped the tear away and kissed me again. "What are you going to tell the crew?"

"A lot of them already know we're fucked, they're just trying not to talk about it. The others still have hope that the Stranger will produce some miracle to get us out of this. Esteban still has faith in me."

"There are four hundred Dark Brethren on this boat," she said.

"Ship," I corrected.

Jessica took a deep breath, as if stopping herself from slapping me. "There are four hundred Brethren aboard this fucking ship. What I was going to say is that *all* of them still have faith in you. Especially your daughter."

I gulped and turned away. After everything I'd done, I still felt like a fraud. I'd been the disregarded, younger brother;

I'd defied everyone and everything to try and save my people, and nearly died a dozen times because of it. Whatever fate had in store for the *Dangerous*, I knew that the Eastron would endure. But I feared it had all been luck. If shown the same reality and given the same choice, would not a Winterlord or a Sea Wolf have done the same thing as me?

"Stop brooding," said Jessica.

"I can't brood on the quarterdeck," I replied, nodding up to the ceiling of our cabin. "People would ask questions."

"You're not a good husband, Marius," she said, stroking my face. "You're not a good father, and I'd never call you a good man... but you *are* a good leader, and you made the right decision in defying your brothers and this Sunken God." She grabbed my head and turned me back to face her. Before she spoke again, I realized I was crying. "I know you hate compliments, but your actions will save the lives of thousands of Eastron." She smiled and gently kissed me, running a hand down the back of my neck. "Marius Cyclone and the Stranger... we needed both of you."

I was about to return her kiss, or maybe say something profound, when a chain of bells was rung from the deck above. It started as a single bell, probably from the crow's nest, then became a cacophony from fore and aft, as whatever had been seen was picked up by the deck watch. It was a strange rhythm, not the usual tempo of any warning signal, and suggested confusion from those above.

"I think the open sea is causing panic," I said, drily. "I should go up on deck."

"You should," she replied, releasing my hand. "Let me know when I should kill myself and our daughter... if things look especially bad."

"Fuck!" I grunted, throwing back my head. "Say something *more* depressing, please!"

She shrugged her shoulders. "Titus will probably get away."

I smiled, took a deep breath, and stood from our bed. I left the cabin, almost treading on Titus as I did so, and made my way to the quarterdeck. The ringing started again. This time, it was a single sound from the bow, accompanied by a shout... *Land sighted.* I stopped midway up the steps. The shout made no sense. We'd left the Emerald Coast behind and were in open water, between the Father and Nibonay, and the Inner Sea had no islands.

I rushed up the last few steps and moved to the helm. "What is it? What land?"

"Directly in our path," said a confused Luca Cyclone, passing a looking-glass.

I put the glass to my eye and looked forward. *Halfdan's Revenge* was cutting through the ocean with tremendous speed, trying to squeeze every ounce of distance over the pursuing ships. I had to grasp a railing to steady myself and see what was causing the confusion. Over the heads of a hundred staring sailors, legionnaires and Pilgrims, I saw a distant island, surrounded by grey pillars of rock. The island had a single peak with a flat summit, as if it had once been a volcano, and the pillars were covered in barnacles and seaweed. I removed the looking-glass, blinked rapidly, then looked again. I saw the same thing – an island that shouldn't be there.

I took a moment, before turning around and using the glass in the opposite direction. Behind the *Dangerous* was a line of fast warships under full sail. I couldn't see the ironclad, but the rest were slowly gaining on us. They'd spy the island in less than an hour.

"That island was not there a week ago," said Luca.

"The sea rises," I replied, feeling an ominous chill travel down my spine.

Esteban Hazat, now without his armour, joined us at the helm. The commander of the twenty-third void legion knew, more than anyone else, that we would probably all die tomorrow morning. "I am not a knowledgeable sailor, but I was under the impression that the Inner Sea had no such islands."

Again, I was forced to think quickly. Nothing good had yet come from the sea rising, but in the context of our current situation, I was forced to consider that anything new could be a potential advantage. The island was likely crawling with Sunken Men and depth barges, but all we had to fear from them was death, and Santago wouldn't give us a better offer. At least the servants of the Sunken God would kill us quickly. And then there was the slight chance that the island meant something else.

"Marius, it's getting dark," said Luca. "We have seven or eight hours until they overtake us."

"Don't change course," I said. "Those pinnacles are like a circle around the island. Take us within the circle and drop anchor. The condemned can be bold. Let's see what Santago does."

"Aye," replied Luca, fighting through his confusion. "Anvil, keep us on course. Trim sails and make for that island. Take soundings and don't let us run aground. We're anchoring off the coast."

Sergio Eclipse, the quartermaster, was at the bow, answering a hundred questions about why an island had suddenly appeared in the Inner Sea. It took a second command from Luca to get him to carry out his captain's orders and rally the crew back to work. Sailors went aloft and trimmed all but the mainsail, gradually slowing us down.

"So, do you want to die with land under your feet?" quipped Esteban. "You know that island probably isn't friendly."

"We're dead either way," I stated. "At least this is new. Given our situation, new could be good."

"And it could be a worse way to die," he replied. "No matter, I've made my peace with this world, and it appears I won't see another."

I put a hand on his shoulder. "I'm not giving my life away, nor the lives of any soul aboard this ship. If anyone or anything wants our lives, they'll have to *take* them." I frowned. "But we can't win."

"I know," replied Esteban. "So do my legionnaires. At least this new island is a distraction for those of us not so realistically morbid in their thinking."

"Good point," I said. "Now, shall we see if it has something other than death to offer us?"

The *Dangerous* was still moving quickly, with the crashing of waves audible above our chatter. Ahead, the circle of pinnacles rose high above the churning ocean, twice as tall as our mainmast. We were headed towards a gap between two of them, just wide enough for us to pass. As we approached I tried to judge whether or not there was a gap wide enough for Prince Oliver's ironclad to pursue us. It was hard to gauge, for the pinnacles were placed in no regular order and were not of uniform size. But it would certainly cause the pursuing fleet to break up. "What the fuck is this?" I muttered to myself, as confused as my crew.

Everyone watched in awe, as the *Dangerous* glided past the pinnacles. They were craggy and pointed, with a glistening mosaic of green seaweed and silvery barnacles covering much of their surface. White sea-birds squawked and leapt from the formations, gliding away from us on the brisk wind. The air was calm and the scene all around us was peaceful, as if painted by a skilled artist. I'd seen the emanations of the Sunken God and this felt different. It was strangely beautiful.

"Nice and slow," commanded Luca, as we passed the circle of pinnacles and approached the volcanic island. "Cut the mainsail. Prepare to drop the anchor."

Anvil, the quartermaster, was taking soundings of the ocean as we moved, and every shouted report was of adequate depth for our passage. The pinnacles were like the peaks of underwater mountains, just poking through the surface, though the island itself was far larger, big enough for a decent sized settlement to be built at the base of the volcano.

"Getting shallow," said Anvil, shouting to both Luca and the sailors clustered around the anchor. He looked up, judging the wind. "Captain, pull us a little to port, then drop the anchor."

The helm was turned and the coiled chain, securing the anchor, was released with a rhythmic clank. The *Dangerous* slowly came to a stop, three or four ship lengths from a gravelly beach.

I joined a mob of sailors, Pilgrims and legionnaires, staring in wonder at the new landscape. The sea was indeed rising, and it had thrown forth more than just the Sunken Men. This had none of the rotten energy we'd come to expect, nor was it dark and foreboding. On the contrary, the island we faced was both peaceful and beautiful, as if the best parts of this realm of form had assembled to welcome us. The volcano was ringed with lines of seaweed, drying into a pleasing bright green colour under the open sky. Beyond the gravel of the beach the flat, dark earth was peppered with smooth rocks. In time, the island would be fertile indeed, as if the deep ocean water had somehow preserved it. Further inland, amidst foothills and brightly coloured coral, there were wide caves and elegant parapets, each accentuating the majesty of the central peak.

Then I saw something move in the shallow water. "There's something there," I said. "Under the surface."

"Stand ready," commanded Esteban, narrowing his eyes at the calm waters and the gravelly beach. The order *was* answered, but the forty or so void legionnaires conducted their duty at a slow pace, as if reluctant to draw arms in sight of the peaceful island.

I looked again and saw a long, sinewy shape, undulating across my field of vision. It moved quickly, slithering through the water at great speed. Then I saw another, until half a dozen similar shapes could be seen swimming around the *Dangerous*. They weren't Sunken Men. Their movements were elegant and smooth, as if the water parted at their approach, allowing them to travel through the ocean as easily as the tides.

"They're circling the ship," shouted the lookout. "Maybe ten of them."

Weapons appeared amongst the crew – short swords, crossbows and hand-axes. The twenty-third had short spears and directed them to the railing, either side of the quarterdeck.

"Keep calm," I ordered, making sure my voice was heard by all. "Lower your weapons, but keep your eyes sharp. I don't think there's a fight here, but there's still one behind us. I want to know what Santago does with his fleet. Let me deal with whatever's in the water."

"Marius," grunted Asha Two Hearts, "there's a rowing boat over there, on the beach – and a man waving his arms at us."

She was right. Around the coast, resting high up on the gravel beach, as if left there by the tide, was a fishing boat. I raised the looking-glass to my eye and squinted. There I saw a young man in ship leathers, with a cutlass at his waist. He was a Sea Wolf, with arms raised above his head, signalling us. It was far from the strangest thing within view, but was unexpected nonetheless. When it became obvious to the young man that we'd seen him, his arm waving changed. He now appeared to be beckoning forwards, as if inviting us to join him on the beach.

I lowered the glass and looked back to the rippling shapes encircling the *Dangerous*. If the young Sea Wolf was drawing us into a trap, it was a bloody obvious one. I considered a double, triple or quadruple bluff, before deciding that I was being an idiot, and had little choice but to further investigate the island.

"Drop a launch," I commanded. "I'm going ashore."

With a few exceptions, everyone on deck was keeping half their awareness on the large creatures swimming around us. Jessica and Marta were huddled on the observation deck at the aft, pointing excitedly whenever a shape darted past. Closer to me, Asha and Gaius Two Hearts were grinning broadly, mimicking the shapes' movements with their arms. All across the deck, the mood was changed. An hour ago, we'd all been processing our imminent deaths. Now, the magical new island had calmed the most stubborn of minds.

"I'm coming too," said Esteban, as sailors moved to winch a rowing boat into the calm ocean. "I don't trust this place."

I smiled at him. "Me neither, but my wyrd isn't tingling, and those are not Sunken Men."

"And we have nothing to lose," he said.

"And we have nothing to lose," I replied, before turning to the Two Hearts twins. "You two are coming with me. Keep your eyes open and your blades to hand."

They grumbled to each other, making jokes about how stupid I was and confirming the status of an existing wager. Apparently they'd laid money as to how long they had to live. Luckily for me, they'd not yet progressed to ignoring my orders, and made their way to the launch, just as it struck the water.

Everyone looked down, afraid that the disturbance would rile the circling creatures. Strangely, all the new ripples caused was an alteration in their path, causing them to dive and somersault under the hull of the boat, as if they were playing in the water.

Two Dolcinite Pilgrims insisted on acting as oarsmen, and followed Asha and Gaius down to the launch, with Esteban and I bringing up the rear. Pushing away from the *Dangerous*, we made our way ashore, the oars tickling through the calm water.

Several of the underwater shapes left the warship and swam to track our movements. One in particular, larger than the others, swam in shallow twists and turns under the launch, letting its light green fins break the surface as it moved. When we were halfway between the warship and the beach, the creature darted away and pulsed its long body, breaking the surface in a spectacular spray of water. It propelled itself twenty feet above the surface, letting forth a playful chirping sound, before doing a somersault over the rowing boat and diving back into the ocean. It was only visible for a few seconds, but it silenced any chatter from the *Dangerous*, and made me gasp in amazement. The creature had a long, sinewy body, with webbed hands and feet held tightly against its flanks. A broad, spiny crest ran from its circular head to the tip of its muscular tail, and fluttered in the air, like a tingle of excitement. Its small face was surprisingly expressive, with a pair of large, black eyes and a long, narrow mouth.

"Don't worry!" shouted the Sea Wolf, from the beach. "He's just excited."

"I don't like Sea Wolves," said Asha Two Hearts.

"Or strange new sea creatures," added Gaius.

"But they are not servants of the Sunken God," said Esteban.

The two Pilgrims spent a moment leaning on their oars, letting the boat glide towards the beach, before pulling us the last few boat lengths. We struck gravel and everyone jumped into the shallows and pulled the boat a little way up the beach. The twins kept their hands poised on a variety of weapons – but the Pilgrims, and Esteban and I, kept our palms empty and our arms wide.

For a change, I wasn't required to have all the answers. An island had appeared in the Inner Sea and, behind us, half a dozen beautifully elegant sea creatures were slowly rising from the shallow water, their slender arms spread wide, mimicking our own gesture of peace. Even Marius Cyclone, called the Stranger, couldn't be expected to have a strategy for such an occurrence.

"Welcome," said the Sea Wolf, a young man with patchy stubble and a warm smile. "I wasn't expecting Dark Brethren. We thought the Sea Wolves would find us first."

I walked to meet him. The fishing boat had clearly been here for a while, but there was no tackle or equipment within. It would have needed a crew of at least four people to get this far from Nibonay, but only the smiling young man was present. He was no duellist, and I sensed only a moderate amount of wyrd. He was merely a fisherman who'd run aground on the strange new island.

"I'm Brindon Grief," said the Sea Wolf. "You're in no danger here."

"I'm Marius Cyclone, called the Stranger."

He knew the name and took an involuntary step backwards. Unfortunately, due to my ships being arrogant enough to fight back against their pirates, I was universally hated amongst the Sea Wolves. Even Adeline Brand, their talismanic leader, had basically told me to fuck off.

"You're in no danger either," said Esteban Hazat. "We are fleeing an enemy and happened upon this island. We are outnumbered and sure to be killed by the time the sun has risen."

"Killed?"

The voice came from behind us. It was deep and clearly enunciated, as if the speaker was being careful to pronounce the word correctly. We all turned from the Sea Wolf. Standing in the shallows, one of its hands fiddling with the oars of our launch, was a creature, twelve feet tall, with mottled light green skin. It was vaguely humanoid, with long limbs and a thick tail. But its extremities were gathered together, presenting a slim profile. Its head was small in comparison to its body, with few features but wide, black eyes and an expressive mouth. It appeared to be smiling.

"What the fuck are you?" I asked, maintaining my composure as those around me formed a line and tried not to panic.

It shook sea water from its body and slowly sat cross-legged in the wash. Its eyes pulsed, and blinked several times, though its wide mouth kept smiling. "Ik'thya'nym," said the creature.

"That's what they're called," said Brindon Grief. "Don't worry, they're peaceful. They eat plants and want to know about the Eastron."

"They speak our language?" I asked, not averting my gaze from the creature.

"That one does," he replied. "The rest understand more than they can speak. But they learn quick. Really quick. Do you want to know his name?"

I turned to glare at Brindon Grief. It wasn't one of my more aggressive glares, but successfully conveyed my incredulity that they had names.

"He's called Hin'bak'ish," said the young Sea Wolf. "He likes to be called Kish. He's very friendly."

"Kish," said the creature, his smile broadening. He crept forwards, trying to mitigate his height, clearly sensing that my companions were afraid. "You are Marius. We will be friends."

9

There were more than a hundred of the Ik'thya'nym swimming around the island, within the ring of pinnacles. They danced in the water, circling and diving, but doing nothing to interfere with my ship or her crew. A few more boats were launched, letting more of my people stretch their legs on solid ground, but most stayed aboard the *Dangerous*, keeping a close eye on the pursuing fleet. The eight ships arrived an hour after us, but stayed beyond the pinnacles, as if their situation allowed less risk-taking than mine. Santago's cutters kept a vigilant pattern of sail around the island, apparently content to keep us isolated, though they sent frequent signals calling for my surrender.

The six of us who'd initially come ashore were guided further inland by Brindon Grief, with Kish slinking along behind us. Asha and Gaius barely took their eyes from the creature, whereas the Dolcinites and Esteban tried desperately not to look at it. Strangely, none of us were worried that the fleet would attack in our absence. Neither the Sea Wolf, nor any of the Ik'thya'nym, had given us reassurances of our safety, but still we weren't worried.

Brindon led us past beautiful coral formations, splayed out like flower petals, and towards a cave entrance. It was a narrow slice in the volcanic rock face, wide enough only for single-file. The Sea Wolf, still smiling, walked in first, beckoning us to follow.

"Inside, inside," said Kish, making the Two Hearts twins whimper and reach for their blades. They clutched the hilts of various sharp implements, as if they needed a comfort blanket of some kind.

"It learned to speak from a fucking Sea Wolf," said Gaius.

"Must have a limited vocabulary," added Asha.

"Relax," I said. "We expected to be dead around now. We're alive, enjoy it."

Brindon Grief heard what we said, but the young sailor maintained his smile. Perhaps he was the first Sea Wolf not to have an irrational desire to attack people, or perhaps the island and the Ik'thya'nym had affected his mind. He looked past us to Kish, who had been only a few feet behind. Now, with the evident alarm of the twins, the gangly creature backed away and hunkered down, significantly diminishing his height.

"He knows you're scared of him," said Brindon. "I was fucking terrified when I first saw him. A mate of mine shot him twice with a crossbow."

"How long have you been here?" I asked, giving Asha and Gaius a chance to calm down.

"A week and a half," he said. "We were fishing. Supplies on Nowhere are getting thin, so we came to the deep water. Lots of mouths to feed."

"Nowhere?" I replied. "The Sea Wolves are on Nowhere? Has Adeline Brand changed her mind?"

He screwed up his face and I saw a simple man, a little overwhelmed by his situation. "I follow Adeline Brand, yes.

I've heard of *you*, of course. You command the legions on Nowhere – Jessimion Death Spell and Santos Spirit Killer work for you. But everything's upside down at the moment. All I know is we're fleeing into the void."

I smiled, my first since we'd arrived at the strange new island. "I'm very glad to hear that. I feared you'd be left behind, or die in a futile battle."

Esteban grunted, as if reminding me to see the big picture. "Marius, we are still being hounded by eight warships. We've not escaped. *This* is a new problem."

"Yes, of course," I replied, my smile turning back to a glare. "Brindon, can your friends help us?"

"I don't know," said the Sea Wolf, turning back towards the cave. "Come inside."

The two Pilgrims made sure to encourage Asha and Gaius to join us, and we entered the narrow cave entrance. Kish gathered his long limbs and slunk along behind us, effortlessly fitting through the gap. Within, the cave opened out into a large, circular chamber. It was domed, with a pool of still water dominating the rocky ground. In the middle of the pool was an oddly angled gemstone of some kind, refracting light at impossible angles. More jewels of light emanated from crystalline formations around the walls, and floating patches of bioluminescent algae made the cave far brighter than the twilight outside. As my eyes acclimatized to the new light, I saw a single feature in the chamber. On the opposite wall, etched into the stone, was a huge face. It was round, and reminiscent of the Ik'thya'nym, but had two frills carved either side of the face and its large eyes were slightly more angular. It wore a benevolent expression, with a subtle smile on its wide mouth.

Brindon Grief led us around the pool, giving Kish enough space to rise to his full height behind us. The tall creature could clearly be imposing if he wished, but chose to keep his body as slim as possible, even as he strode around the pool. Bowing towards the strange jewel in the water, he approached the carved face.

"Nym'zu," said Kish, gently stroking a webbed hand down the large face. As he touched the carving, the angled gemstone in the water began to glow a warm red colour.

Kish then gestured to the opposite wall, pointing above the cave entrance. "Klu'zu."

I turned, just as a patch of crystalline rock illuminated a second carving behind us. This one was not peaceful or friendly. It was a fearsome visage, with sharp, glaring eyes. The bottom of the face was covered in a beard of thick tentacles, where a nose, mouth and chin should be. There was a malevolence to the face, beyond what a mere stone etching should be able to convey.

"Is that the Sunken God?" I asked, pulling my eyes from the carving and facing Kish. "You understand me, don't you?"

He blinked his large black eyes. "Klu'zu," he repeated. "*God* is word without true meaning." His words were clear, though spoken slowly and deliberately.

"I asked him the same thing," said Brindon. "They don't know what gods are. The word has no meaning to them."

Kish waved his hand and the vile carving was again hidden in darkness, though the strange jewel in the water appeared to vibrate. "Ya'lan'ah'loth," said the creature. "They are both Ya'lan'ah'loth. Beneath time. Above reality. Ya'lan'ah'loth are parents of form. Nym'zu mother to Ik'thya'nym… Klu'zu father to Zul'zya'zyn."

131

I took a deep breath. I knew the name of the Sunken God and his Sunken Men. For the first time in weeks I thought of Utha the Ghost, and wished the pale man was here to give me some context.

"How does this help us?" demanded Esteban Hazat. "This realm of form can fuck off, along with the Sunken God *and* his fucking sister. Are we any closer to escaping Santago and Oliver Dawn Claw? Or are we going to die here, instead of at sea?"

Kish chirped, his wide mouth rippling in concern. He pulled his long body into a crouch, blinking at Esteban across the circular cave. The creature dangled a hand into the pool of water and absently tickled the surface, as if unsure how to respond.

"Swearing," said Brindon Grief. "He doesn't understand it. He only sees the anger."

Kish shrank even smaller, managing to pull his body into a ball, with only his mournful face and the tip of his tail pointing forwards. Brindon moved around the pool of water and stroked his hand across Kish's head, as if mollifying an agitated puppy. The Ik'thya'nym chirped contentedly and leant into Brindon's hand.

"It calms him down," said the Sea Wolf. "When he gets confused by us. Think about it, he's been asleep under the ocean for..."

"How long?" I asked, addressing the question to both of them.

"I've not been able to get a good answer to that," said Brindon. "I think they're immortal. He keeps talking about ages and cycles of the world. Time don't seem to mean much to him."

"Ages," agreed Kish. "*Time* what you call cycles." He flapped his hand, as if trying to find the right words. "World moves in ages. Sea rises when age ends. Old world wakes up."

"And us?" I asked. "What happens to mortals when ages end? When our cycle is done?"

"You end," replied the Ik'thya'nym. "Like endless others before Eastron."

Esteban's face twitched, and the twins grumbled, shuffling their feet in anger at what they were hearing. I decided that I should probably take charge of the situation. I really wanted to just be another startled Eastron, gathered with my peers and unable to comprehend what was happening. Unfortunately, I was cursed to be Marius Cyclone.

"Right," I stated, loudly. "I will do the talking from now on. People – and Ik'thya'nym – will only speak in answer to questions I ask. Is this clear? You can just nod."

The two Dolcinites nodded first, quickly followed by Esteban and the Sea Wolf. The twins took their time, but were confused enough to comply. Lastly, after casting his black eyes across all of our faces, Kish nodded his head. The Ik'thya'nym was peaceful, and clearly perceptive, but he was like nothing I'd ever known. How could I relate to such an ancient creature? Though his aura was somewhat mitigated by him letting the Sea Wolf stroke his head.

"We are being chased. We will shortly be dead, unless we can get to Nowhere ahead of those chasing us. You." I gestured to Kish. "Will you help us? *Can* you help us?"

The creature stood from Brindon, unfurling his long limbs and suddenly becoming twelve feet tall again. "Some of you hate others of you," intoned Kish. "I will help. Will tell

Vil'arn'azi." His long, thin mouth was bizarrely malleable and rippled into a satisfied smile. "Will talk to Brindon. He translate."

I found a large, flat rock and sat on it, looking out to sea. It was dark now, but a full-moon and a hundred lanterns illuminated a good portion of the sea. The *Dangerous* had stowed her sails, and repairs to her hull were well underway. Luca's crew, and most of the legionnaires, remained aboard, whilst the Dolcinite Pilgrims had come ashore and were conversing with the Ik'thya'nym. Kish's people were smaller, but just as impressive, and just as eager to talk with Eastron. They understood less of our language, but after a week and a half of talking to a Sea Wolf, their comprehension was still remarkable.

Brindon and Kish were still in the cave, trying to frame the creature's help into a form I'd understand, and we were forced to wait. I made sure looking-glasses were always pointed outwards, towards the pinnacles, but Santago and Oliver appeared content to remain in the open sea, circling the island. Even at their distance, they'd be able to see the Ik'thya'nym, and it amused me to wonder what my brother was thinking. Even before he devoted his wyrd to the Sunken God, Santago was intractable and arrogant, especially about the Dark Brethren and the Eastron.

"I don't want you to die," said Marta. Somehow, she and Titus had made their way ashore, and the cat had found a marvellous vantage point from which to glare at me.

"Come here," I said to my daughter.

She sat next to me, and we shared a hug. Jessica didn't think I was a good father, and she was probably right, but Marta and I still adored each other.

"I don't want Mother to die either," she said.

"You shouldn't be thinking about that," I replied, gently. "You should be thinking about the new house we're going to build."

Titus hissed at me. "He doesn't want to die either," said Marta.

"Look, you! No matter what happens to me or your mother, we will always keep you safe. If they kill me, my ghost will be at your side forever. You are the best thing about me. Never forget that."

Titus flicked his tail into the air, as if he was happy. His front paws padded on the rocks. Close by, one of the smaller Ik'thya'nym was staring at the cat, its webbed hands stroking the air, as if it wanted to reach for the small animal.

"Don't," said Marta. "He'll bite you."

It appeared to understand her, and hunkered down on the rocks, before springing backwards and inspecting two Dolcinites, standing near the cave entrance. Titus wrinkled up his face and jumped into my daughter's lap. He sensed the warmth between us and wanted to be a part of it. He flexed his claws against Marta's thigh, before nuzzling into my chest and curling up.

There was a chirp from behind, making all three of us sit up and turn. Brindon Grief was standing there, with Kish behind him. The Ik'thya'nym appeared more relaxed, standing at his full height and letting his long limbs hang naturally. His large eyes managed to convey significant emotion, despite being pitch black, and the creature looked happy. He gazed across the rocky beach, where dozens of his people were interacting as best they could with Dark Brethren sailors and Pilgrims. Fires had been lit across the beach and globes of vivid light dispelled the darkness at regular intervals.

Then Titus hissed and startled the Ik'thya'nym. "What is this?" asked Kish. "Small, hairy Eastron?"

"He's a cat," replied Marta.

"A domesticated animal," I added. "Sort of."

Titus leapt from my lap and strolled confidently towards the tall creature. Brindon stepped aside and let Kish crane his body in half to gracefully lean down and face the large black and white cat. It was a tense meeting of minds, as Titus looked up into the eyes of the Ik'thya'nym. I wondered if his telepathy extended to ageless creatures from the deep ocean, or if he was just better at hiding his confusion than us simple humans.

"I like the cat," said Kish, his wide, thin mouth forming into a friendly smile. "Small and fluffy."

Titus sat back and flexed his jaw, exposing vicious teeth, before reaching up with a paw and padding at Kish's cheek. The Ik'thya'nym chirped and I saw a shiver of enjoyment travel down his long back, making his thick tail flick in the air.

My perpetual frown softened just a little and I shared a smile with Marta. "He likes you," I said. "You're in an elite group of three."

Titus backed away, keeping his glare on Kish, before turning and bounding back to Marta's lap. He gave a protective hiss, then curled up against my daughter, leaving only his eyes visible.

"Take him back to the ship," I whispered.

"Don't die while we're gone," she replied, picking up the cat and moving quickly down the beach.

"Do you have something to tell me?" I asked, directing the question at the young Sea Wolf. "We're glad of the break from sea travel, but we can't stay here forever. He offered help."

"He'll give it," replied Brindon. "But I'm not sure it's what you're expecting. They're peaceful creatures, my lord Stranger. They *understand* violence – weapons, wars, destruction, all that stuff – but it's just not part of their character."

"So?" I prompted, suspiciously. "What form will this help take?"

"Peace," offered Kish, spreading his arms wide as if presenting me with a magnificent prize.

"Erm," spluttered the Sea Wolf, evidently trying to frame troublesome words. "I think what he intends is to invite your pursuers here and… find peace between you. I think they're afraid of violence. The little ones more than Kish, but they run away whenever anyone gets too angry He kept saying *when enemies are talking, they're not fighting.*"

"Enemies talking," agreed Kish, "not fighting."

"I don't understand everything," said Brindon. "He mentioned a friend – I think it's another Ik'thya'nym, called Vil'arn'azi. But I don't know what he was trying to say."

I sighed, musing momentarily on what help I'd expected from the Ik'thya'nym. I'd conjured no image of them wielding weapons and joining us in battle, but I thought they'd at least escort us a distance, stating enough of a presence to deter Santago's warships.

I rubbed a hand down my face. "I doubt your grasp of our language has extended to such phrases, but you can go and fuck yourself if you think I won't kill my brother on sight."

Kish's eyes and mouth flicked through a dozen contrasting expressions as he tried to untangle my words. He was certainly familiar with cursing, and balked a little at the word *fuck*, but he didn't shrink away or huddle up. "Don't be angry," said the Ik'thya'nym. "Peace should not make you angry."

Oddly, his words did make me fucking angry. "You, Sea Wolf, does he understand that we're running for our lives from the servants of the Sunken God? That small Eastron with the cat was my daughter." I stood and pointed out to sea. "Klu'zu has stuck his talons into thousands of Eastron, and killed thousands more. The few of us still alive and unbound are fleeing into the void. If there was ever a path to peace, we flew past it long ago."

"Please," said Brindon Grief. His young face was red, with veins of stress appearing on his forehead. "I don't think you'll get much else from them."

I sat back down on the rock and took a moment to think, keeping my eyes away from the twelve-feet-tall sea creature. Peace talks with my brother? What a fucking surreal idea, with the bloated image of Oliver Dawn Claw acting as a horrific counterpoint. If the parlay was offered, they would surely take it, if only to punch me in the face with their smugness. If there was a way to manipulate the situation to my advantage, I feared I wasn't clever enough to see it, and I now understood that the Ik'thya'nym were pacifists. Our thought processes were so different, and I wondered if they'd just let us die, without fully grasping what was happening.

They were afraid of violence, and might just chirp and run away if a sword was drawn.

"Oh, fuck me," I muttered, suddenly aware that I should probably get some sleep before the sun appeared. It had been dark since we exited the cave, and the *Dangerous* would soon ring a bell to signal the second night-watch. Everyone else would likely have snatched an hour or two of sleep by now.

"Lord Stranger," murmured Brindon. "You should probably invite them to parlay. Maybe just five or ten of them, to keep things safe and peaceful."

"If you don't mind," I grumbled, "I think I'll return to my ship and sleep for a couple of hours. I'll rise with the sun – and hopefully by then I'll have a clear idea about how I'm going to solve this particular problem."

I certainly slept, but as the bells rang for the morning watch, I felt as if I'd spent more time staring at the vaulted ceiling of my cabin. Jessica and Marta were elsewhere, helping the Dolcinites with the arduous task of feeding four hundred refugees. I was wide awake when the bells rang, and only paused for a moment or two before rising.

I'd not thought to get undressed before I fell into bed, so just needed a moment to splash water on my face. As I did so, swilling out my mouth, I glanced up at my leather coat, hanging on the back of the door. I rarely wore it at sea, when I was amongst friends, but at most other times it was like a second skin. It covered both the blue tattoo on my neck and my sword. If I was to sit at a parlay table with my brother, I felt the coat was appropriate.

I'd still not fathomed a way to turn the meeting to my advantage, but I did have an option. It was another gamble, and would only work if Santago and Oliver had the tiniest amount of honour left within them. I'd pursued and discounted a hundred other options, and I felt I'd at least found a solution to the next problem, however risky.

There was a bang on the door. "Marius, get up!" shouted Esteban. "People keep asking questions, and I keep saying *you'll* need to answer. It's time you come and answer some of them."

I burped loudly and took a stride to my bed-pan. "I'm just having a piss," I replied. "I hope those questions will wait."

He laughed as I sighed and tilted my head backwards, relieving myself into the brass receptacle.

"Hurry up," said Esteban. "We can't stay here forever, and those eights ships aren't going anywhere. The ironclad has been front and centre since dawn."

"Still pissing," I replied.

"Marius!"

I finished, with a slight shiver, before donning my coat, belting on my straight sword, and opening the cabin door. I faced Esteban, seeing dozens of others trying to pretend they weren't listening.

"The sea creatures?" queried the commander of the twenty-third void legion. "Kish said they'd help."

I took a deep breath. "Signal the ironclad."

He frowned, noting my coat. "Signal them what?"

"A parlay," I replied. "The Ik'thya'nym will let ten of them come ashore in peace. Santago and Oliver must be amongst them."

A few of the nearby sailors gasped, and a few more disappeared into the ship, likely to tell others that the Stranger had made a decision.

Esteban just stared at me. "The sea creatures won't fight for us, will they?"

"No," I stated. "I don't even think they'd defend us. Santago and his warships could sail right through the pinnacles and kill us all, if only he knew. It's just fear of what's in the water that's keeping them back. But they don't need to fear."

"We're fucked, aren't we?" grunted Esteban, making sure that any further words were just between he and I.

"Maybe not," I whispered. "A parlay does give me one opportunity I wouldn't otherwise have. Another gamble, my friend. That they want *me* more than the rest of you."

"Don't push it, Marius. You were right once, but this is different."

"I'll surrender to them," I said, pulling up the collar of my coat. "I'll demand they give up pursuit of the *Dangerous* in exchange for me. That will at least get you to Nowhere."

Esteban rolled his eyes and was about to mock me with a laugh, but I grabbed him by the neck and shoved him against the door to my cabin. "Listen! *If* I manage this, *if* I manage to bluff my way into captivity, using Kish as an imaginary deterrent, *you* need to make me a fucking promise." I released my grip, but he didn't struggle. "They will torture me and they will use me if they can. The Sunken God will not stand by while we flee into the void. He could twist my mind and body, perhaps even infect me with worship." I gulped, hating what I was forced to ask. "If he uses me against you on Nowhere, you must make sure my survival means *nothing* next to the survival of the Eastron. I no longer matter. Promise me!"

He shoved me away from the door and grunted. Others had seen the exchange, but no one had heard my words. Above and below us, sailors, legionnaires and Dolcinite Pilgrims waited to hear my orders. Their amazement at Kish and his Ik'thya'nym was softening their impatience, but everyone seemed to understand that we couldn't stay here forever, and that seven Dark Brethren warships and a Winterlord ironclad were still hounding us.

"It's all I've got left," I muttered. "Otherwise we all die. It'll break my daughter's heart, but it's the one choice I have left."

He nodded, but didn't look me in the eye. "I promise, though I wish Asha and Gaius were here to call you a selfish cunt – or some other cutting assessment of your character."

There was much I wanted to say, and many people I wanted to talk to, especially Marta, perhaps the only person I truly loved, but all I said was, "Signal the ironclad."

PART FOUR

Adeline Brand aboard
Halfdan's Revenge

10

W e pulled ourselves back aboard *Halfdan's Revenge*, surrounded by a hundred voices all wanting to know what happened at the parlay and why swords had been drawn. Between Rys Coldfire, Siggy Blackeye and myself, we managed to convey that the Winterlords opposing us were now our enemies. Their totem spirit, the mighty Dawn Claw, had been corrupted by the Sunken God – and their prince, Oliver Dawn Claw, had fallen to the same power.

"Are we attacking them?" asked Captain Tynian Driftwood, hobbling towards me on his crutches.

Rys Coldfire dumped Daniel's corpse on the deck and inspected the fatal cut in his neck. "No man could survive that," he said. "How does he... how does it happen?"

"Don't know," I replied. "I've only seen him die once."

"Adeline," said Driftwood, "we have a fleet waiting to see what we do."

Kieran Greenfire was below deck and shouted up to us. "Ballistae ready!"

Siggy Blackeye quickly moved to the starboard railing, ready to signal the fleet at my order. "Fleet stands ready."

Across the still sea of Blood Water, ten Winterlord ironclads were packed into a channel between two islands and ill equipped to meet any kind of attack. As Eastron, their wyrd was more powerful than ours, but as sailors they had a lot to learn. Arrogance was not a friend to those at sea.

I also had ten ships, with the High Captain closest, aboard the *Never*. His ballistae were sighted on the narrow sea channel, and with a word they'd be charged with wyrd and sent at the enemy. Seven other ballistae boats were similarly armed and ready, all waiting for the *Revenge* to start the fight. *Our* ballistae carried casks of black dust and would break across the first few Winterlord ships. Unfortunately, Daniel was in no condition to take charge of his explosive substance.

"Okay," I grumbled, "let's get this done. Someone take the man who can't die to Bjorn's cabin until he's no longer dead. Kieran! Don't blow us up while he's not here."

"I'll try not to," came the reply from below deck.

"Siggy," I continued, "signal the fleet that we're attacking those ironclads. They're to wait for our first volley."

"Aye, my lady First Fang."

"Let's kill some Winterlords," I shouted.

Somewhere on the quarterdeck, behind the cheers of the crew, I heard crying. I glanced back and saw Rys Coldfire with his arms around the sobbing form of Elizabeth Defiant. She was the only Winterlord aboard – the only one of her people who'd come to Nowhere – and it was now clear that she'd remain alone.

"*We'll* take the dead man," said Rys, shepherding Elizabeth to the stairs, before picking up the corpse of Daniel Doesn't Die. "If we get to close fighting, shout for me."

There were a few dismissive comments directed at Elizabeth, but most of the sailors ignored them and moved to their battle stations, preparing to launch death at the

Winterlords. Bells travelled across the fleet, and the other ships opened their ballistae ports and prepared to fire. Ahead of us, as Natasha Dawn Claw and her retinue were helped back aboard, it was clear that the ironclads were trying to move. Their turning circles were far too wide for a quick deployment, and the ten cumbersome ships bumped and jostled against each other as they tried to clear the narrow channel and enter the open expanse of Blood Water.

"Kieran," I shouted, "fire!"

The ship bucked, as ten engines flexed and ten huge bolts arced through the air, carrying casks of black dust towards the flailing ironclads. The Winterlords didn't know about the Sundered Wolves' dust, and they had no defence against it. The casks smashed against their railings, masts and across their decks, showering the first three or four ships in black dust. Then the High Captain loosed his own bolts, followed a moment later by the other seven ships. Their engines fired no casks, but each ballistae tip was charged with crackling, light blue wyrd.

"Wait for it," said Captain Driftwood, standing next to me at the railing.

The second and larger volley of ballistae bolts struck home, all across the most prominent ironclads. Wherever wyrd hit black dust, a huge explosion shot outwards. I stood back, shielding my eyes, mimicking every other Sea Wolf aboard *Halfdan's Revenge*. A fearsome line of fire erupted in the narrow sea channel, eclipsing the water, the land, even the sky, until muddy clouds and sharp peaks of red and yellow flame covered everything.

"Reload!" I commanded.

The deafening explosions and crackling of fire were gradually overtaken by the howls of burning men and women. Then the closest masts began to topple and wooden debris crashed into the sea. As the clouds settled and my vision cleared, I saw two stricken ironclads. The closest two were enveloped in roaring fire, with everything made of wood quickly turning black. Everyone aboard the two ships – at least everyone above deck – was either howling in pain or already dead. The metal of their hulls was turning red in places, as the fierce flames boiled the vessels from within. Hundreds of Winterlords were roasted to death, and hundreds more succumbed to the flames.

"That's a bad way to die," I muttered, suddenly convinced that the Winterlords were no threat to us at sea, and hating the cacophony of death-rattles. We'd destroyed two ships, and three more were aflame. The other five were doing their best to panic, with little room to manoeuvre.

"We won't get this chance again," replied Driftwood. "They'll find a way of coming over land next time. And we can't match them in close fighting."

"Hmm," I said. "You interrupted my doubts *just* before I had them. Very good."

I turned with conviction, addressing the crew of *Halfdan's Revenge*. "The people we kill are not Winterlords. They are servants of the Sunken God, beholden to a fallen totem and a fallen king. If we don't kill them now, they will find a way to stop us travelling through Utha's Gate. So, we *will* kill them now, where we have the advantage. We are Sea Wolves! Fire!"

Kieran Greenfire had been poised and ready, and the command barely left my mouth before our ballistae fired again. Ten more casks of black dust were launched, at a higher trajectory, towards the ironclads. They struck targets further into the assembly of vessels, scattering across as much water as wood. A second volley of charged ballistae came from the rest of the fleet, causing the entire channel to erupt in violent flames.

Across my ships, Sea Wolves and Kneeling Wolves stood in silence, watching the Winterlord fleet burn. Half were on fire and the rearguard were trying to turn, with escape on their minds. One on one, they had the most powerful wyrd of any Eastron – but at sea their arrogance had killed them.

"Looks like four of them are done," announced Siggy Blackeye, squinting through a looking-glass. "There'll be survivors, but the ships are stricken."

"And the others?" I asked.

"Two are in trouble," she replied, wiping the reticule of the looking-glass. "They're trying to save their masts, but... I think they're sinking. There are fires across three more, but they're still seaworthy. I think six will survive. Looks like they're fucking off north. Retreating. They'll remember they were spanked by the Sea Wolves."

A restrained celebration travelled across the Sea Wolf ships. It was a tremendous victory, against mighty foes, but killing so many other Eastron, especially Winterlords, had left a bad taste in every mouth. I told myself that the lines of war had been drawn, but I couldn't help but empathize with Elizabeth Defiant. The mightiest camp of Eastron had fallen to the Sunken God.

"Siggy, is the sea channel blocked?" asked Tynian Driftwood.

"Oh, yes," replied the mistress of the *Revenge*. "One of the many downsides of encasing your ship in metal. By the time the wreckage settles, no ships are getting into Blood Water that way."

"Tell the fleet to stand down," I commanded.

The entire conflict, such as it was, had taken less than ten minutes. By the time the surviving ironclads had managed to turn and flee, Daniel Doesn't Die was staggering back to the quarterdeck, with an arm slung around Rys's shoulders. Elizabeth wasn't with them, and I frowned, imagining her in tears below deck.

"Is it over?" asked the Sundered Wolf, a distinctive new rasp in his voice.

"Looks like it," answered Driftwood, nodding to the burning ships.

Rys Coldfire helped Daniel across the deck, to stand with the captain and I, looking at the smouldering sea channel opposite. The Wolf's Bastard had an obvious fascination with the man who couldn't die, and kept his dark eyes on the part of Daniel's neck that had been cut. The wound was now just an ugly, red scar and would likely disappear entirely in a few minutes.

"Two volleys," observed Daniel. "I'd have done it in one. We only have so much dust left."

"It worked," I snapped. "They're running. At the very least, this buys us more time to get people through Utha's Gate."

"Back to Duncan's Fall?" asked Driftwood.

"Back to Duncan's Fall," I confirmed. "Keep two warships here to watch the other channels, just in case the Winterlords want another spanking."

★

I stayed on deck as the fleet deployed, mostly because it was entertaining to hear Rys Coldfire's endless questions to Daniel. The Wolf's Bastard was usually a laconic man, who frequently criticized others for talking too much, but now he wouldn't shut up. I was still the only one who knew Daniel's former names and how old he was, but the man formerly called Michael of the Mountain and David Fast Claw was surprisingly open with all other information. The only thing he'd not yet told anyone, including me, was how the fuck he couldn't die. All he'd told me was that he'd arrived from across the sea with Sebastian Dawn Claw, the first Always King. Eva Rage Breaker, his former wife, had described it as a story he'd not yet told.

"And fire?" asked Rys. "A burned body part would just grow back?"

"So far," replied Daniel. "The remnant turns to ash and the limb heals. Same as if you cut my head off. The biggest part of me re-grows."

"What if you're burned to ashes?" asked Rys. "If there is no biggest part, what can re-grow?"

Daniel had found a bottle of ship grog and was taking deep swigs between answers. "Well," he slurred, "no one has yet seen fit to *burn me to ashes*... but I'm sure something would happen. Trust me, I can't die."

"But you still feel pain?"

Daniel puffed out his cheeks. "Yes, I still feel pain. Every fucking time." He was getting irritated with the interrogation, and his speech was getting increasingly slurred. "Next question."

"How did this happen to you?" asked Rys. It was not the first time he'd asked this question, and it elicited a laugh from Daniel.

"You wouldn't understand the answer," chuckled the Sundered Wolf.

"Are you drunk?" I asked, interrupting Rys.

"Almost," he replied. "I'm hoping there's no more action today. Fighting and running around... I'm ill-suited to it."

"You're fat," offered Rys. "Why not take care of yourself?"

"I prefer chubby," said Daniel, taking a deeper swig of nasty grog. "And I confess to taking naps whenever I can. It's an old habit."

I laughed, as much at Rys's reaction as Daniel's quip. The Wolf's Bastard was a legendary duellist of the Severed Hand who'd devoted his life to killing people, and he was very good at it. No matter the wyrd, the intelligence or the skill, Rys believed he had the ability to kill anyone. To meet someone who was immune to his only talent was causing him to question himself.

"Doesn't your Winterlord wife need attention?" muttered Daniel, finally fed up with having to answer questions.

Faster than I could react, Rys had his hands clasped around Daniel's throat. The Sundered Wolf gasped for air and was thrown to the deck. "Still feel pain, yes?" grunted the Wolf's Bastard.

"Rys!" I snapped. "Leave him."

"Don't fucking talk about Elizabeth," he grunted. "She just lost her people."

It was a tense moment, though Daniel seemed more concerned with his bottle of grog. It had fallen from his grasp and settled against a coiled rope. His left hand felt for it, as he largely ignored the powerful Sea Wolf pinning him to the deck. After a confused moment, Rys softened his grip.

"Okay," said the Wolf's Bastard. "Threatening you seems a little hollow."

"I've already died once today," replied Daniel, grabbing the bottle of grog. "I'm not at my best. If I offended you, I am most sincerely sorry. But if I die twice in one day, I'll probably shit myself. I'm not joking, it'll be an awful fucking mess."

It took a few seconds, but all three of us laughed. Nearby, Siggy Blackeye and Tynian Driftwood suppressed laughs of their own, having heard the exchange. A handful of sailors started chuckling on the quarterdeck, and a ripple of laughter travelled across the crew. *The Sundered Wolf's gonna shit himself* – it was not the most inspiring of chants, but served to significantly raise our spirits. As *Halfdan's Revenge* left Blood Water and entered the Red Straits, there was a wonderful moment of levity.

Charlie Vane and the *Lucretia* were ahead of us, with the rest of my warships in a narrow column behind. None of us were in a hurry to return to the earth of Nowhere. All we had to do *there* was wait, and find more ways to defend those sheltering on the island, until it was our turn to walk through Utha's Gate. We'd succeeded in closing every way an enemy could come ashore, except Duncan's Fall, and would now have to find other things to do. On land, we had to accept that Marius Cyclone's void legions and their commanders were in charge. At sea, we still held supremacy.

Then everything changed. The *Lucretia* didn't ring warning bells or shout alarm. The Kneeling Wolves just stood on deck, staring for a moment before we saw what they saw. Around the hook of Nowhere, within sight of Duncan's Fall, were burning ships. Hundreds of refugees from the Dark Harbour had built a floating settlement across dozens of small vessels, waiting their turn to come ashore. The entire structure was now blackened and sinking, with flames rippling across all wooden surfaces.

"Brethren cutters," shouted a lookout from the *Lucretia*. "A dozen of them. Some troop ships too."

It was impossible to see how many people had died across the burning ships. Certainly there was no evidence of life. They'd been simple people – the lower classes of the Dark Harbour – and someone had massacred them. The only movement along the Red Straits was at Duncan's Fall, where unfamiliar Dark Brethren ships held a perimeter. They were fast cutters, with low draft and angular sails. Two troop ships had beached and a forest of black armour was flooding ashore. Three more were poised amongst the cutters. The Brethren were a divided people, with half on our side, following Marius Cyclone, and half corrupted by Alexis Wind Claw and her like.

"It was a fucking distraction," I growled. "They used ten Winterlord ironclads as a fucking distraction."

At first, no one reacted. A fleet of Dark Brethren ships had crept up on us. They could have waited along the Red Straits, until we left to confront the Winterlords. Without the Sea Wolf warships, the landing at Duncan's Fall was vulnerable, and they'd exploited it. Slowly, the rest of the fleet cleared Blood Water and saw the same as us. Almost in unison, with no signals being relayed, my remaining eight ships unfurled more canvas and shouted for battle stations.

From our own crow's nest, there came a further shout. "They're signalling from the barricades. Looks like Death Spell's legionnaires are holding them at the beach."

"Get us closer," I commanded. "Need to see what we're up against."

I was really fucking angry, with my knuckles turning red as my one hand gripped the railing. How was this possible? Who commanded those ships? And how many Brethren would we need to kill to secure Nowhere? Their wyrd wasn't as powerful as the Winterlords, but they appeared to have at least two full void legions, plus ships and troops in reserve. It was an organized invasion force, likely from the Open Hand.

As we sped up past the burning ships, the *Never* came alongside us, with the others fanning out across the Red Straits. The *Lucretia*, the only ship amongst us with no ballistae decks, was still in the lead. Charlie Vane was at the fore, with his grubby Kneeling Wolf raiders banging weapons against the hull and shouting challenges at the Brethren.

"Tough fight," muttered the Wolf's Bastard, suddenly uninterested in the man who couldn't die. "The legionnaires inland – the Stranger's warriors – will they stand?"

I nodded. "They'll stand. Just remember, the ones on our side no longer have owls on their tabards. Don't get confused."

"Fuck off," he said, drily. "I know who our friends are."

The two of us both glanced across our eight warships, then to the stationary Brethren fleet ahead of us. As we cleared the fired ships, and the sea channel widened, the scale of the assault was revealed. Twelve cutters and three additional troop ships formed a semi-circle around Duncan's Fall. They were anchored close together, blocking the approach to the beach. Between them and land were dozens of launches and hundreds of legionnaires. Either side of them, on the high cliffs, Jessimion Death Spell's own legionnaires were loosing arrows and hurling casks of flaming pitch at any warriors that reached the sand. Further up the beach, where the sand and rocks turned into a sharp grassy rise, our barricade was under attack. The vanguard of their forces, from the first two troop ships, were in columns and methodically assaulting the defences.

"Daniel!" I shouted. "Get over here. How much black dust do we have left?"

Alcohol aside, the chubby Sundered Wolf still appeared groggy from his recent death, but he managed to haul himself up the railing. "Not enough for all of them. Maybe two and a bit casks. Could stretch it to four ballistae bolts."

"And ashore?" I asked. "What does Rage Breaker have?"

"Eva has barrels of the stuff at Cold Point," he replied. "Enough to detonate half of Nowhere."

"Doesn't help us now," offered Tynian Driftwood, approaching from the helm. "If we're gonna give 'em a broadside, Adeline, we need to deploy the fleet. There's not much room to move here." He was scratching at his bushy beard, and I saw concern flow across his rugged face. I'd never call the tough old bastard *afraid*, but he certainly displayed little confidence.

His face made me even angrier. If the enemy did not have troop ships and a huge advantage in numbers, I'd have trusted our superiority at sea to destroy them. As it was, they weren't here for a sea battle. They were here to get thousands of legionnaires ashore as quickly as possible.

"Heave to," I said. "Siggy! Signal the fleet – one broadside, then it's wood and steel. We need to get ashore. We have a better chance of defeating them from in there than out here. There are thousands of innocent people on Nowhere. Wolves *and* Brethren."

11

Before I could decide how to proceed, I heard the sound of a whistle and felt myself being pulled through the glass. Everything slowed down and no one else reacted, as if I was outside of time. Images and colours flashed across my eyes, reminding me of the spectacle I'd seen on the shadow bridge, until I once again stood on the stone balcony, looking across the Sea of Stars to the Sunken City.

My clothes were casual, my hair was clean, and my severed arm had returned. Duncan Greenfire, called Sharp Tongue, was still next to me, but now he was not alone. Perched on his shoulder was a small green creature of some kind. It was humanoid, with large eyes and pointed ears, and was sitting in a basket of thorns. It was a spirit of some kind, though strange arteries of power connected it to the young Sea Wolf.

"Twist, this is Adeline Brand, the First Fang," said Duncan. "She's leading the Sea Wolves to safety."

"What is that?" I asked.

The green imp narrowed its eyes at me, before climbing down Duncan's body on a rope of brambles. It crept towards me, until a broad smile appeared and it darted back to its perch.

"He's a pain spirit," replied Duncan. "At least he was. Now he and I are the same being. If it weren't for him, you'd have no void realm to escape to, but that is a long story. Now, tell us, why have you come back?"

"What? I don't fucking know. I didn't choose to come here. I'm actually quite busy, so if you could send me back, I'd appreciate it."

He tilted his head in confusion. "I can't send you back, nor did I bring you here. You came last time because you needed to see something. Perhaps you're back because you need to see something else."

I pinched the bridge of my nose, resisting the urge to shout curses at the boy and his imp. I'd gone from a battle commander, as tightly wound as possible, with thousands and thousands of lives depending on me, to a peaceful balcony, with a supposedly dead Sea Wolf for company. It made me light-headed. "Is the world fucking with me?" I muttered.

He considered it. "Not in the way you mean. Someone has identified you as a leader of the Eastron, equal to Marius Cyclone. It's been decided that you need to know certain truths. Shown certain things."

"The pale man," I replied. "I barely remember him."

Duncan nodded. "He prefers it like that. He's made mistakes, so he only wanted to show you the truth when he was sure your mind could deal with it. Amongst Eastron, only Marius has shown the same strength as you."

"So, what do I need to see now?" I asked, disliking the comparison with the Stranger, but gradually calming my thoughts.

"I don't know," he replied. "Take a look and see."

I stepped to the edge of the balcony and put both my hands on the black stone railing. The view was shifting away from the Sunken City and across the Sea of Stars. I saw endless miles of ocean, calm and rippling, before a harsh, dark landscape came into view. It was the island of Big Brother, a vast, unchecked wilderness. Most of this land had never known the footprint of an Eastron, with only a tiny portion of the northern coast settled. The Kneeling Wolves had paid great respect to the land when they built Four Claws Folly, and it was said that Jorralite Pure Ones had assisted them in construction of the hold. The rest of the huge landmass had been ignored by the invaders from across the sea.

"That place has a long history," said Duncan. "There's said to be a cathedral of flesh in the deepest jungle, raised in honour of a forgotten giant. Great battles were fought on ground now reclaimed by nature. But, before all that, ages past, beyond memory or written word, there were primitive humans here. They'd not yet called themselves Pure Ones, but they lived in harmony with the land. Their ancestors survived, as mighty civilizations rose and fell. Some lasted centuries, some even for millennia, but all disappeared whenever the sea rose."

As my view travelled across the endless wilderness, I was reminded of how little of the world I'd seen. Perhaps it was a trick of this realm of form, that a simple mortal woman could not look beyond the small world her people had created. "We're different to these other civilizations. The Eastron are different. Aren't we?"

"Yes," replied Duncan. "But not through might, honour or wisdom. The Eastron are different because a shadow giant arrived from the distant void and decided to save you. You're just one of countless empires and kingdoms this realm has known. Perhaps luck is the true gift of the Eastron."

The view from the balcony slowed in its movement, as we reached the northern coast of Big Brother. The Inner Sea was not as calm as the Sea of Stars, and massive waves crashed against rugged cliffs. We were hundreds of leagues from Four Claws Folly and Hook Point, where most of the Sea Wolf refugee fleet had been destroyed. Beneath the balcony, a huge forest of dark green pine trees abruptly ended at a wall of pulsing sea water. In the wash, well-spaced apart, were the three huge whips I'd seen at Hook Point and again at the Sunken City.

I gasped and pulled back from the black railing. I didn't need to ask if this was happening *now* – I knew that it was. I took a deep breath, then a single stride forwards, forcing myself to look. All three of the whips were bipedal, with arms and legs of various sorts. One of them was taller than the others, with powerful limbs and the face of a malevolent toad. Another was squat and blubbery, like an enormous upright frog, with the spines of a deep-sea fish. The third was just a titanic skeletal creature, grey and green in colour, with wide black eyes and a hunched back. Each of them was like an insane amalgamation of frog, fish, toad and my worst nightmare. The three whips tiptoed in the ocean, as if testing the water. As before, there was something about the Inner Sea that disturbed them.

"The tall one is the Vile Whip," said Duncan. "The big frog is the Bulbous Whip. The thin one, with spikes all over its body, is the Hateful Whip. They are millions of years old, and they are trying to reach Nowhere and Utha's Gate."

I gulped, desperately wanting to be back aboard *Halfdan's Revenge*, facing the simple matter of a few thousand void legionnaires. "What's stopping them?" I asked. "Nibonay is just across the Turtle Straits."

"The Inner Sea is the territory of other creatures," replied Duncan Greenfire. "The Sunken God and his minions are not the only things to have been thrown forth by the rising sea."

"They don't look afraid," I said. "Just... tentative."

"It won't last," he replied. "I think that's what you need to see. Look!"

The Bulbous Whip was first, springing from the coast to land in the shallow ocean water. The enormous bipedal frog waited, as if it expected some kind of retribution. When nothing happened, it splashed its flabby arms in the water and excitedly beckoned the other two. Suddenly, they weren't tentative. The Vile Whip dragged his pulsing, webbed hands through a mile or so of forest, casually flinging pine trees into the air, before striding over the coastline and entering the Inner Sea. Lastly, the Hateful Whip – all spikes and sinewy limbs – slid a grotesque foot into the ocean.

The sheer scale of the creatures made them hard to look at, and I needed to shield my vision against the intangible glare. Then I felt dizzy, as if I was staring too long into an endless black sky. The whips didn't make sense to my eyes, but still I forced myself to look. "What's changed?" I slurred. "What were they afraid of?"

"As you said, it wasn't fear. Strangely, it was respect. Unfortunately for us, the creatures they respected are only just waking up. They're a few years behind the servants of the Sunken God."

"So there is nothing to stop them," I stated. "They'll be coming for Utha's Gate."

"Indeed," replied Duncan. "The warriors attacking Nowhere are *nothing* compared to this."

"Ha," I exclaimed, stepping away from the balcony.

I tried to compose myself, finding it oddly easier with two arms. Suddenly there was a symmetry to my pacing, exclaiming and face rubbing. The view from the balcony was fucking terrifying, but to so quickly dismiss the ships attacking Nowhere was deeply foolish. To call it *nothing* was almost an insult.

"Marius Cyclone isn't here," said Duncan. "That means *you* are in charge. You need to defend the island... from the void legionnaires, Alexis Wind Claw's creatures, and from the Sunken God. We don't want to ask this of you, but there is no one else."

I straightened, trying to fit everything I knew into some kind of useable order. "You just said a lot of things. Is Alexis Wind Claw the one attacking us?"

He nodded. "Her brother, Lucio, is occupied with the Dark Harbour, so she gets the honour of attacking Nowhere. But you don't have long until the whips arrive."

"Fuck off," I sneered. "Do you know how many people are still on Nowhere? And do you know how many people can travel through the gate at a time? I was never skilled at mathematics, but it seems to me to be a simple equation."

The small green imp reared his head and made an odd burbling sound. From his thorny perch, he stood up and absently scratched at Duncan's neck. The young Sea Wolf didn't appear to notice, or maybe he just didn't mind. It was as if they were having some kind of conversation, of which I was clearly the subject. Duncan said nothing, but nodded or shook his head in response to Twist's burbles and scratches.

"Sorry to interrupt," I said, drily, "but could you use some actual words?"

"When we are ready," replied Duncan. "We are trying to frame our response in a way that will not make you angry."

"I'm already angry," I said. "Just speak."

"Very well. We must accept that fewer Eastron will escape than we hoped. You must close Utha's Gate before it is too late – before the great whips arrive, for the Sunken God will not be far behind."

I raised my eyebrows at him, then narrowed them at the imp. "I don't know exactly how many people are still on Nowhere, but most are simple folk of one stripe or another." I mused on the numerous camps, temporary settlements and clusters of fearful Eastron who filled the island of Nowhere. "I won't leave them behind."

"Consider this," said Duncan. "In asking this of you, we accept that Marius Cyclone will also be left behind. But *he* doesn't matter. Neither do you. You have accomplished great things and are a mighty commander of the Eastron, but only the survival of your people truly matters. Enough have already passed through the gate to ensure the Eastron will endure."

He was right, though his cold assessment proved that the lad I'd known as Duncan Greenfire was greatly changed, or perhaps gone forever.

"Are you angry?" he asked.

"Of course," I replied. "But not at you, nor your blunt conclusions. I'm angry because, one way or another, this world is going to end, and it will not end quietly."

"When the whips arrive," said Duncan, "most of you will die. When the Sunken God arrives, the rest of you will die, as will those already in Utha's realm... unless the gate is closed."

Since I'd been possessed by the Old Bitch of the Sea and met Daniel Doesn't Die, my tolerance of the bizarre and unreal was highly developed. Though we'd set aside spirits, the Eastron were still creatures of both form and void, and I was glad of Duncan's intervention, however fucking depressing it was. At least now I knew what we were truly up against. It was strange, but I smiled as I left the balcony and returned to the quarterdeck of *Halfdan's Revenge.*

Time twisted and turned for a moment, with both realms passing in front of my eyes, until I was looking up at dark blue sails. The crew showed no awareness that I'd been away and were focused on the relatively simple matter of a fleet of Dark Brethren ships, attacking the cove of Duncan's Fall.

"We could beach," said Tynian Driftwood, clearly not wanting to make the suggestion, fearful of what would happen to his ship. "All eight of our ships. Battering rams punch through and we keep going. They've got far more warriors than us, but their vessels are fucking shit. The Dark Harbour has the best ships. These tubs have never had to deal with Sea Wolf warships."

I was back on the Red Straits, facing a well-organized beach assault, with two void legions doing their best to force their way through our barricades. Having seen what was on its way, I found myself a little detached from Alexis Wind Claw and her Dark Brethren. I was still angry, but there was a veil of calmness over my thoughts. Around me, Rys

Coldfire, Siggy Blackeye and Captain Driftwood rattled off a dozen thoughts and strategies of how we could get all our people ashore.

"Good idea!" I stated, loud enough to shut everyone up. "Signal all ships to target our broadside at the nearest two cutters. We'll use what black dust we have left. Then we drop the Fair Lady, get the *Never* alongside us and ram them to pieces. We make a hole and we beach."

"We'll have to abandon ship," agreed Driftwood. "All of us. When we strike the stones of the beach, every last Wolf and Winterlord will have to get ashore as quickly as possible." He put a hand on the railing of his ship and stroked the wood, as if saying goodbye. "I suppose she can't come with us anyway."

"We'll build others," I replied.

"New ships, new seas, new tides," he mused.

"Let's get it done, captain," I said, gently.

Siggy was already signalling the other seven ships. All but the *Lucretia* had ballistae decks, and we deployed as best we could in the sea channel.

"Daniel!" I shouted below deck. "You said we could muster four bolts of black dust. Get them ready. Fire at my command."

"That's the last of it 'til we get back to Cold Point," he replied.

"Understood," I shouted. "We're beaching the *Revenge*."

Kieran Greenfire was spreading the word to everyone aboard. We were ramming the Brethren cutters and abandoning ship. A few hundred void legionnaires were between us and safety, battering against Jessimion Death Spell's barricades at the edge of the beach. Hopefully, the appearance of a mob of angry Sea Wolves would disrupt their attack.

Rys disappeared below deck, likely attending to Elizabeth Defiant. She was fit and healthy, but not a woman of action, and would need help to flee the ship with the required alacrity. I wanted to suggest that a less fearsome warrior helped her, but I thought he'd just ignore me. I wanted him with me on the beach, but I'd survived without him for months, so would have to make do.

"I'll probably stay here," said Driftwood almost absently, as the fleet quickly positioned itself.

"You'll do fucking what?" I replied.

He smoothed down the forks of his unnecessarily large beard and looked at the stump of my left arm. "A woman with one arm can still run. But a man with one leg?"

"You're pretty good with those crutches."

He screwed up his face and grunted. "Maybe, but I don't feel like just dumping her on the beach. I think this is where you and I part ways, Adeline. I'm going to stay with my ship. If she was holed at sea, I'd drown with her. Why is this any different?"

I sneered. "You can shove that up your arse, *Tynian*. I'll fucking sling you over my shoulder if I have to."

He raised his eyebrows. "Neither you, nor anyone else aboard, will make me do a fucking thing I don't want to do. You should have learned that by now, my lady First Fang. I am a Sea Wolf of Last Port, captain of *Halfdan's Revenge*, and my wyrd flows strong. If I want to die on my ship, I'll die on my ship."

I just looked at him. The warship came to a stop, as did the rest of the fleet. In the distance, the Brethren cutters made no attempt to move or oppose us. They would have been expecting our return, but had no apparent means of defending themselves. Like the Winterlord ironclads, they were not our match at sea.

"Are you going to say something?" asked Driftwood. "Everyone's waiting for your command. Those ballistae won't fire themselves."

"Fuck off," I grunted. "You timed your suicidal announcement perfectly."

"I know," he replied. "Now, give the fucking order."

I gave him a restrained punch on the shoulder. "Kieran will carry you, even if you don't let *me*." Before he could respond, I addressed the crew. "All hands, prepare to turn and ram the bastards. Daniel! Fire!"

Unlike at Blood Water, we'd not had time to properly mark our targets, but we were close enough that it didn't matter, and Daniel was highly skilled at using the black dust. Four bolts flew from the *Revenge* on a flat trajectory, striking the edge of the Dark Brethren line. Three bolts hit one cutter, and the last struck a second ship. The rest of the fleet were quick to follow up, with a barrage of wyrd-charged ballistae, aimed at the same point of the attacking line. These were not Winterlord ironclads, and their hulls were no protection against the explosive power of the dust. There were detonations from the Red Straits to their angular masts, with a wall of water and smoke eclipsing the semi-circular line of ships.

"Drop the Fair Lady," I commanded. "Bring us about."

Two heavy chains were released and the huge serrated metal battering ram was winched to the waterline. Across the fleet, canvas was unfurled and ships deployed. The High

Captain manoeuvred the *Never* alongside us, as they dropped their own ram. Off to the side, and not part of our line, was the *Lucretia*. Charlie Vane and his Kneeling Wolf raiders were already sailing for the beach. They'd follow close behind the two battering rams, and probably beat the rest of us ashore.

The smoke cleared quickly, revealing two ships aflame. The closest was stricken, with a gaping hole in its hull and a torrent of fire coating its deck. The other was still afloat, but its forecastle was destroyed and its crew were flinging themselves into the shallow water. The rest of the Dark Brethren perimeter were panicking at the explosions, though their average seamanship meant that all they could do was turn. Some turned to starboard, trying to use the encircling cliffs as cover; others turned to port and tried to move away from us into deeper water. The three troop ships, still at sea, lurched into movement, attempting to get their human cargo ashore before we could fire again. Luckily, they had no fucking clue that we'd run out of black dust, and their panic made our approach far easier.

"There's a gap," shouted Driftwood.

I took stock of the disintegrating invasion fleet. "Tell Charlie Vane to go for the gap and get his grubby bitches on that beach. We'll follow once we've skewered some Brethren ships."

"Right!" boomed Tynian Driftwood, taking charge of *Halfdan's Revenge*. "Point the Fair Lady at that ship." He reared up and pointed to the closest cutter, not on fire. "The *Never* can have that one." He threw a dismissive hand to the neighbouring ship. "We are going to give those two crews a great honour – we are gonna let them die, knowing that it was Sea Wolves who killed them."

My eight warships formed a wedge, with the *Lucretia*
keeping pace. Driftwood struck a rhythm on the quarterdeck
with his crutches. After a moment, other Sea Wolves began
striking the deck, either stamping their feet or banging their
fists, sending a raucous cacophony across the *Revenge*. Almost
the entire crew was up on deck now, ready to abandon their
home when we struck the beach, but the deafening drumbeat
of defiance kept any despair at bay. In fact, as we picked up
speed and bore down on the hapless Dark Brethren cutter,
many of the crew began to laugh. I could only imagine the
terror this would cause amongst the enemy, seeing hundreds
of angry Sea Wolves cackling at them.

"Brace!" commanded the captain.

The Fair Lady obfuscated the last ship length, with
everything tumbling together into a tapestry of sails, water,
shouting and laughter. Then we struck their hull. The *Revenge*
was almost twice the size of the cutter, and the Brethren vessel
appeared to come apart at the seams. We slowed, but we
didn't stop, with the sharp, grating sound of the metal ram
eclipsing the last vestiges of laughter. Wood, steel and flesh
flew left and right, framing our approach, as we dismissively
cut the ship in two.

The *Never* was not as fast as us, nor was her ram as
formidable, but she still made a terrible mess of the adjacent
ship. At the same time, scything through the growing gap in
their lines was the low draft of the *Lucretia*. The Kneeling
Wolves got ahead of the three troop ships, making sure my
forces would hit the beach first. In no time at all, we'd unload
close to two thousand warriors and sailors at Duncan's Fall.

For a moment, it was nice to remind ourselves that
the Sea Wolves would always be the best sailors amongst the

Eastron. Unfortunately, our elation was quickly dispelled when we saw the void legionnaires already ashore. As we plunged past the cliffs, a mass of black armour came into view. Between the beach and Death Spell's defences was a full void legion. They were divided into cohorts, half of which were attacking the barricade. The others had turned and were pointing rectangular shields and long spears in our direction.

As the broken shell of the cutter fell away, *Halfdan's Revenge* undulated forwards and backwards on a sudden bow-wave, before settling down and entering ever shallower water. The boisterous shouting was gone and the crew were braced, seeing the scale of what we were doing. Behind every set of eyes, including my own, there was a silent goodbye. We were abandoning ship. Amongst the Sea Wolves, this was a funeral. Sails were quickly trimmed and the warship slowed.

"How many warriors?" It was Daniel Doesn't Die. "How many people do we have to kill?"

I smiled at the Sundered Wolf, aware that he didn't hold the same reverence for our beloved warship. With the Wolf's Bastard occupied, Daniel was certainly the most powerful amongst us, though he was reluctant to use his wyrd.

"A void legion is two thousand Brethren," I replied. "But we don't have to kill all of them. We just need to get inland before more arrive on those troop ships."

"How many do *we* have?" he asked.

"We match them in numbers," I said, recognizing that such an engagement had never happened. Our two peoples – the Dark Brethren and the Sea Wolves – had fought at sea a hundred thousand times, with Sea Wolves holding complete dominance. But there were no stories of great land battles between us.

"They're better equipped," observed Daniel. "Spears, shields, full armour."

"Our wyrd is stronger," I replied. "And the average void legionnaire is afraid of us."

"I'll fight with you," said Daniel. "But I will only use my wyrd if I have no other choice. This is not a battle for me to unleash."

"I've never seen you fight," I replied, drily. "Just kill your share. Now, hold onto something."

We braced a second time, as the hull of the *Revenge* grated along the shallow seabed and wedged herself into the rocky beach. We were just to the left of the *Lucretia*, where grubby Kneeling Wolf raiders were already leaping into the shallows. Either side of us, the rest of my fleet hit the beach. Then the word came, echoing across all eight vessels – *abandon ship*.

12

The interior of Nowhere was filled with powerful Eastron and skilled battle commanders, but there was little cohesion. Xavyer Ice, called the Grim Wolf, had a few thousand warriors of Ice. Jessimion Death Spell and Santos Spirit Killer each lorded over a void legion. Then there was Eva Rage Breaker, called the Lady of Rust, who commanded the Wolves in my absence. I imagined they were arguing, perhaps even sitting around Death Spell's council chamber in Cold Point, endlessly debating the best way to defend Nowhere from Alexis Wind Claw's forces.

But whatever dog shit they were spouting made no difference to me. I was standing on stones, in a foot of seawater, with a dense line of Sea Wolf killers either side of me. They leapt from warships, left and right, with all eyes looking forwards. Charlie Vane's raiders were further up the beach, hefting swords, knives and all manner of sharp implements. Together, we were two thousand warriors, focused and ready. Behind us, our few non-combatants were abandoning ship, throwing anything valuable ashore, so as not to leave it to the enemy. Rys Coldfire was helping Elizabeth Defiant from the warship, but every other warrior was with me. In the confusion of abandoning ship, no one, not even Kieran Greenfire, had noticed the absence of Tynian Driftwood. I hoped we'd be well into the fighting before they did.

"Listen!" I shouted, marching along the growing column of angry Sea Wolves. "Hear me. I am Adeline Brand, your First Fang, and I will ask nothing of you that I will not give myself. Our people are ashore and need our help. *I am prepared to die to get to them.*"

I wasn't finished, but no more words were necessary. My people were already on a knife-edge of adrenaline, and they began chanting oaths of loyalty and violence as soon as I started speaking.

"Let's fucking kill 'em," said Siggy Blackeye, hefting her basket-hilted cutlass and grinning.

Alongside me, in front of our warriors, were Wilhelm Greenfire, the High Captain, and Daniel Doesn't Die, with Kieran and Siggy standing over each of my shoulders. All of us but Daniel pulsed with light blue wyrd, holding little back and presenting a formidable show of strength. Most of the sailors and duellists displayed their own spiritual power, creating a wall of crackling wyrd along the coast of Duncan's Fall. Then Rys Coldfire, called the Wolf's Bastard, marched through the ranks of Sea Wolves to join us. He'd let someone else take care of Elizabeth, and the duellist was a vibrating ball of power, looking past me and focusing on the enemy.

A void legion was in front of us, with more on the way, but those on the beach had more than just us to worry about. From Death Spell's barricades, our presence had been noted, and the defenders of Nowhere redoubled their efforts to repel the enemy.

"Charlie Vane!" I shouted. "Attack the left flank. Wilhelm, attack the right. Rys, you're with me in the centre. We will cut through them and defend this island."

"Enough talking," snarled Rys, crouching down, as if ready to start a sprint.

I pushed wyrd into my throat and made sure my words were heard by all two thousand warriors. "Once more for the Wolves!"

The line broke as one single entity, plunging from the shallows in a flash of steel and wyrd. I was front and centre, with a deafening clatter behind me. The Kneeling Wolf raiders were ahead, and Rys was keeping pace, but there was nothing else but a rocky beach between me and a line of Dark Brethren void legionnaires, pointing their rectangular shields and long spears in my direction. Suddenly, I was acutely aware that I only had one arm. I missed my spectral limb, and realized this was the first proper fight I'd had since the Old Bitch of the Sea left me.

As we neared the void legionnaires, all I could see was a wall of shields, with spears at every gap. Only half the legion had turned to receive us, with the rest keeping their focus on the barricade. Their line was only half as long as ours, but they were forming a defensive semi-circle, with no obvious gaps. *Our* tactics were more basic – we simply pumped ourselves full of wyrd and ran at them. The sound as we hit them was deafening.

Our wyrd struck first. All along our lines, Wolves lashed out, cushioning the initial impact and stopping their defensive line from holding us. In a flash of cracking, light blue energy, two hundred shields and the warriors holding them were thrown backwards. Other legionnaires flew left and right, or back over our heads, as their defensive tactics proved ineffectual against the wanton brutality of two thousand angry Sea Wolves. Between Rys and myself, five legionnaires had been thrown backwards, and the next rank were struggling to recover from the impact of our wyrd. Then it was steel on steel. Individually, Dark Brethren void legionnaires were skilled fighters – well-trained, well-equipped and fanatical in their loyalty. In contrast, Sea Wolves were fucking savages.

I parried a desperate spear thrust, knocked off the woman's helmet and rammed my forehead into her nose. With a back swing, I cut a second legionnaire's throat. Next to me, the Wolf's Bastard was still unarmed, but had tackled two Brethren to the ground and was pummelling both their faces with elbows and punches. Siggy Blackeye had jumped on the closest enemy and found an exposed piece of the man's neck to bite into. Kieran Greenfire was less brutal, but just as effective. The small Sea Wolf was extraordinarily fast, using his wyrd to flicker around spear points. The enemy were well-armoured across the chest and limbs, but up close there were gaps that a skilled fighter could exploit.

The fight quickly broke up, with the legionnaires trying to maintain some kind of order to their formation. Their wyrd was strong, but their training permitted only restrained use of their spiritual power. With an occasional mighty spear thrust, a subtle deflection of a blade, their wyrd emerged only when absolutely necessary. They couldn't cope with the sudden, explosive energy *we* were prepared to use. In the long run, their method was far more efficient, but in a short, brutal melee they were outmatched. They clattered together as we pressed forwards. Their spears were ineffectual at close range, their shields were cumbersome, and their armour did little but guide our blades to their exposed necks, thighs and underarms.

At some point, I lost all peripheral stimulus, and was focused only on killing. I couldn't see where we were, but we'd pushed forwards enough to be close to the barricades. People were dying on both sides, and corpses were becoming a serious obstacle, but Rys and I, with Kieran and Siggy alongside us, created a hole in the mass of black armour. On our left flank, I could hear the War Rat's raiders approaching us, and the High Captain's warriors were cutting through on the right. I had a few cuts, and my arm was sore, but the void legionnaires were just too predictable and limited to worry a powerful Sea Wolf duellist, let alone the First Fang. Our advantage was heightened by a barrage of arrows and flaming pitch from the barricades. Whoever commanded the Stranger's warriors was helping to clear the way for us.

Then the void legion broke. Two thousand Brethren against two thousand Wolves in an open, dirty fight, and we'd made the bastards run away. I stopped swinging my cutlass and found secure footing on the rocks. Rys was panting next to me, flexing a bloodied jaw and pulling in his formidable wyrd. All around us, Wolves roared and shouted to the sky.

"Adeline, you're hurt," said Siggy Blackeye, cleaning her cutlass.

I was about to smile at her, but looked down instead. From my left side, just above my hip, there protruded a shaft of wood. Some part of a broken spear had found its way through my ship leathers and punched a bloody hole in my side. "Oh, fuck," I grunted.

I'd been hurt before. Many, many times. I'd had my left arm bitten off, I'd been cut, battered, beaten and bloodied.

But I was still alive and no random void legionnaire was going to interrupt that. Someone – Siggy, I think – hefted me forwards, over the barricades, to rest against a wooden cart. I passed out a few times, watching the rest of my warriors join the void legionnaires and People of Ice on the interior, while Bjorn Coldfire, the spirit-master of *Halfdan's Revenge*, busily pushed healing wyrd into my wound.

Time started moving in small, ten-second chunks, as my body healed. I saw enough to know that we'd succeeded. The enemy had fled back down the beach, likely to regroup with the other troop ships. On *our* side, a thousand more warriors turned to defend the barricades, while the wounded were taken inland. We'd lost a few hundred, but killed near half of the enemy. I wanted to regain my senses and talk to those around me, but Bjorn had dulled my mind and I could do little but lay down and dribble, while passing in and out of consciousness. I still had planning to do, orders to give and a defence to mount. I couldn't afford to slump on the ground all fucking day.

"Stop trying to stand up," said the severe spirit-master.

"I need to..."

"You need to fucking sit down or you'll die," he replied. "You keep reopening the wound with your fidgeting." Bjorn was a tall, skeletal man, and his bony fingers were poking at my side.

From somewhere nearby, a man strode towards me. I had to blink and rub my eyes, before the diminutive figure of Kieran Greenfire came into focus. "Where's the captain?" he snapped at me. "He didn't come ashore with us."

"Easy," said Bjorn. "She's barely conscious."

"Tynian stayed on the fucking ship," barked Kieran. "Why the fuck would he do that? We have to go back and get him."

"No," I murmured. "He won't leave the *Revenge*. He made a decision. Leave him be. Help see to the barricades."

"You should have told me," he replied. "Even if *he* didn't want to. The mad old fool. He's too fucking sentimental. He'd rather die with his ship than leave her behind."

I felt light-headed, and may have passed out again. Certainly, when I was next aware of my surroundings, Kieran and Bjorn were nowhere to be seen. I could see open sky above me, and I could smell grass and blood. I was awake... sort of. A glance either side of me revealed a long line of similarly injured Wolves and Brethren. We were in some low ground, beyond the beach, and I couldn't see the barricades. Along the line of injured bodies walked Bjorn Coldfire, Tomas Red Fang and several People of Ice, distributing healing and wyrd where it was needed. When Tomas reached me, the old spirit-master knelt down and smiled.

"Still alive, Addie," he said.

"Just about," I grunted, sitting up with a deep intake of breath. "How do we fare?"

The old man inspected my wound. "Before we get to that, let's make sure our leader isn't going to die."

"I'm fine," I stated, instantly realizing it was a stupid thing to say.

"Adeline, stop being a child," said my spirit-master. "You got stabbed. It's healing, but don't rush to resume command. There are plenty of people here capable of defending the island in your absence."

"I don't trust any of them... and we're running out of time."

"I know, I know," murmured the old man.

"No you fucking don't," I snapped, wincing as the sudden movement made my side burn. "You can't know because I haven't told you yet. The Sunken God is awake, Tomas. He's awake and he's on his way. Someone or something showed it to me. I saw his whips entering the Turtle Straits. I don't know how long we've got, but we need to close the gate."

He stood from my side, his back cracking with the effort it took. "Adeline, there are thousands of people still on this island. We can't close the gate, not yet."

My ship leathers had been cut away and I wore only a loose, black tunic. I arched forwards and raised my legs, curling up into a pained ball on the thin bedroll I'd been allocated. Duncan Greenfire had not given me a timetable, so I was faced with a nebulous amount of days until we were all dead, including those who'd already passed through Utha's Gate.

Suddenly, I chuckled. "Why did I have to get stabbed? I wish I'd seen the legionnaire who did it... I don't even know if I killed him. I don't even know what's happening on the beach. Some fucking First Fang I am. Just tell me the rest of the island is still secure."

"I'm not the best person to answer that," said Tomas.

"Then go find me someone more up to date," I replied, as gently as I could.

The old spirit-master nodded. "Once that's done, I'll go back to Utha's Gate. I don't know how to close it, but I'll try and find a way. Just not yet."

"Keep moving people through to the void realm. But we need a way to close that gate or all this is for nothing. I'm needed here – when I can stand up without wincing."

The beach at Duncan's Fall had thick fencing from the low ground up to each of the overlooking cliffs. At its lowest point, where our defence was concentrated, the fences became a formidable barricade, graduating backwards in a series of platforms and killing grounds. Even before we'd arrived to break the siege, the barricade was holding. Defending a fortified position was perhaps the greatest skill of the Dark Brethren void legions.

I'd made my way up to the cliffs, trying to get a sense of Alexis Wind Claw's deployment. We'd given her a slap, but while I was barely conscious, she'd been planning her next move. We'd pushed her warriors off Nowhere, but she had three more troop ships and a small fleet of cutters.

"Should you be walking up here?" asked Tasha Strong. "Bjorn said you need to rest. And this is quite steep. You only got back a few hours ago."

"Jessimion Death Spell is up here," I replied. "I need to speak to him, and I need to see what our friends in the Red Straits are doing."

I was doing my best to hide the pain in my side, but Tasha knew me well enough to notice. I'd not let her accompany me aboard *Halfdan's Revenge*, but she'd quickly found me as I lay wounded in the low ground. Behind her, following at my request, were Daniel Doesn't Die and Xavyer Ice, called the Grim Wolf. Rys Coldfire was somewhere inland with Elizabeth Defiant, and Kieran was grumpily standing vigil on the inner defences. He seemed to think that Tynian Driftwood would change his mind and need rescuing when he came ashore. Most of his crewmates evidently agreed.

The gradient levelled out and I took a deep breath. The top of the cliff had only rudimentary defences, with the third void legion stationing mostly archers up here. If an attacker was stupid enough to try and climb the sheer cliffs, they'd either quickly be crushed to death by the waves or get an arrow in the face. Added to this was the forest of jagged rocks, pointing up from the ocean at the base of the cliffs. No vessel could get close enough to us to unload their warriors.

"My lady First Fang," said Jessimion Death Spell, coming to meet me along the cliffs. "You are healed?" The commander looked smug, even when he wasn't trying, but his clean-cut face and closely shaved black hair made him look just like ten thousand other void legionnaires.

"I'm fucking fantastic," I replied, eliciting a restrained giggle from Tasha.

"Nasty wound that," observed the Dark Brethren commander. "Best not to rush such things."

"I may not be able to fight, but I can still walk, I can still talk, and I can still think. If there are any other skills you feel I currently need, you're welcome to state them."

Daniel and the Grim Wolf came to join us, and we all turned to look across the bay of Duncan's Fall. I didn't want to verbally joust with Death Spell, not any more. I didn't fully trust him and his men, but I was wise enough to accept that they were certainly our allies. This feeling was only amplified when I saw those in the bay. Alexis Wind Claw's ships were now in two lines, struggling to find room in the sea channel. The closer line, reformed after our attack, was comprised of the ten remaining Brethren cutters and three troop ships. Beyond them, unable to get their massive hulls into the shallow water, were the ironclads who'd escaped our attack in Blood Water. Six Winterlord warships were at anchor beyond the cutters.

"When did they get here?" I asked.

"About two hours ago," replied Death Spell. "It took them that long to get those hulks in a line and anchored. They must have floundered around the whole island to get back here. I imagine they sailed in circles for an hour or two."

"I thought the Brethren were the worst at sea," observed Daniel, regurgitating something he'd heard from the Sea Wolves. "Sorry, I don't mean to cause offense."

Death Spell raised his eyebrows but, like everyone else on Nowhere, he felt uncomfortable around the Sundered Wolf who couldn't die, and didn't rise to the accidental insult.

"They're both quite poor sailors," I said. "But I think we can all agree that the Winterlords are the best at close fighting."

"The ironclads are too big and heavy to get close," said Death Spell. "But there are a lot of Winterlord knights aboard those ships. We've been expecting them to launch rowing boats to get ashore. So far, all they've done is row between the two fleets. Alexis Dawn Claw has definitely talked to the Winterlords."

"There is some good news," said the Grim Wolf, pointing his blue eyes and bearded face out to sea. "If they're all here, that means the rest of my island can't be breached. You did well, Adeline."

"I just blew up a few cliffs," I replied absently, keeping my narrow eyes focused on the enemy fleet. "We had to make sure they attacked at Duncan's Fall."

"Well, it worked," announced Death Spell. "And here we are. Yes, well done indeed. You must be very proud."

I looked at him. We were of similar height, though dressed very differently. He wore black steel armour, across from my leather trousers and thin shirt. I'd been honest with him at Cold Point, and he knew I didn't like him, so continued smugness was completely unnecessary. I didn't want to focus on how much he pissed me off, but he was just annoying enough to draw my attention away from the fleet.

"Has Marius Cyclone returned?" I asked.

He thrust out his chin. "We expect him and the final refugee ships to arrive in the next day or two. We can bring them ashore on the northern cliffs."

"Good," I replied with a smile. "Now, look at me. This is the face of your commander. Until the Stranger returns, there should be no doubt that I am in charge. Even when he skulks back to Nowhere, I'll probably still be in charge. So, please stop being a smug cunt, it is not helping."

"Adeline!" chided Tasha. "We're all friends. We all want the same thing. You saw the void realm... it's lovely."

I kept looking at Jessimion Death Spell. "Time," I said. "That's the enemy. Every second we hold this island, more people escape to safety. Do we agree?"

He shrank a little, perhaps agreeing with me, perhaps fighting a lifetime superiority complex, or perhaps just surprised that I'd called him a cunt. "Yes," he replied. "We agree. And you are in command."

"Look!" said Daniel. "The troop ships are moving."

In unison, Death Spell and I turned towards the high cliff top. Beneath us, from three separate points in the line of cutters, came swift landing vessels. They were huge, rectangular boxes, powered forwards by oarsmen and simply designed to contain as many void legionnaires as possible. The full legion we'd fought on the beach had come ashore in two such vessels, so three meant a significant committal of warriors.

"That's a strange move," I whispered, mostly to myself. "Jessimion, are three thousand more legionnaires a threat to our defences?"

The commander was frowning at the three troop ships. "No," he replied, "not now you and your Wolves are back. What are they thinking?"

I craned forwards, peering down at the three troop ships. Unlike the two we'd seen on the beach, these were covered, with billowing fabric tied at each corner. We'd beached eight warships at Duncan's Fall, but they were far enough apart for the low draft of the troop ships to strike the rocky beach. I could see no spears, shields or black armour. Nothing that indicated void legionnaires, other than the oarsmen, who sat on either side of the transports.

"Prepare our defences," commanded Death Spell, addressing his warriors. "Get word to the barricades – attack incoming, repel at all costs. Xavyer, we need your archers on the other cliff."

"They'll be watching this," said the Grim Wolf. "When you fire, they'll fire."

"Rage Breaker is sending more black dust," said Daniel. "Should be here soon. I can arrange a surprise for whoever comes ashore."

Everyone paused, looking at me for an order. But all I saw was the closest troop ship. "Look," I said. "What the fuck is that?"

The fabric covering was discarded and the front of the vessel hinged forwards, thudding onto the rocky beach and forming an exit ramp. The transport was intended for a thousand fully equipped void legionnaires, but it was something else that filled that space... and something else that bubbled ashore.

PART FIVE

Marius Cyclone on Kish's Island

13

How does a man prepare to die? No matter how things progressed, whether I was right or wrong, or if I was a complete fucking idiot, I was very likely to be dead soon. Certain scenarios included a prolonged period of torture, or perhaps some kind of mind control by the Sunken God. Whatever the outcome, I'd made my decision. I would meet with Santago and Oliver, with the Ik'thya'nym keeping the peace, and I would offer to surrender if they gave up their pursuit of the *Dangerous*. One life for four hundred, it was simple enough.

Signals had been sent to the encircling fleet of Brethren cutters and the single Winterlord ironclad, inviting their leaders to a parlay. As I waited on the rocky beach, I found myself engaging in a staring contest with a big, black cat. We'd erected a large table on the beach, and the remaining men of the twenty-third void legion stood in close guard, but it was Titus who drew my attention. Even beyond Esteban Hazat's stern glare and the Two Hearts twins, gossiping about what an idiot I was, there was the cat.

"I don't know what you're worried about," I whispered. "I doubt my brother will want my cat as a prisoner as well as me. I think you should probably go back to the *Dangerous* and be with Jess and Marta." I smiled at him, tickling under his chin. "This might be goodbye, old chap." I screwed up my face. "Try and stay alive, won't you? Utha's realm will need bastards like you. And look after my daughter."

"Marius!" shouted Esteban. The commander had stationed himself in the shallows of Kish's island, waiting for Luca Cyclone, my cousin, to signal from the *Revenge*.

"What?" I replied.

"We have an answer from the ironclad. They agree to a parlay."

I took a deep breath and looked across the beach. Dozens of Ik'thya'nym lurked in the shallows, conspicuous in spite of their attempts to say hidden. Kish and his creatures ranged in height from six to twelve feet, and all were gangly and expressive. I'd tried several times to explain the situation to them, but all avenues of conversation led to the same conclusion – Kish wanted peace and didn't really understand why others might not feel the same.

"They've launched a boat," relayed Esteban. "Looks like ten people coming ashore."

I stood from my rock and set aside contemplation of my imminent death, before striding down the rocky beach to greet whoever was coming ashore.

A ring of Dolcinite Pilgrims stood around the parlay table, with Esteban's few remaining legionnaires forming a wider circle around them. The majority of the four hundred people aboard my ship were non-combatants, and I'd ordered anyone who could use a sword to at least be visible. It gave a nice illusion to my brother that the *Dangerous* was filled with killers. In reality, I had forty void legionnaires, fifty sailors, and as many Pilgrims as thought they could swing a quarterstaff. Everyone else had remained aboard ship, with Luca and a skeletal crew prepared to leave in a hurry if needed.

"Two faces are known," shouted Esteban, still standing in the shallows.

"Name them," I replied.

"One moment," said Esteban, conversing with the *Dangerous*. "They recognize your brother, Santago, and... someone who looks like Prince Oliver Dawn Claw."

"Looks like?" I queried. "Is it him?"

The commander finished talking with the ship before leaving the shallows and coming to join me by the parlay table. "It's him," he said. "But... different."

I nodded. "Somehow bloated and sickly."

"All they said was *different*," replied Esteban. "But the launch displays a white flag, so we won't have to fight him."

Flanked by the void legionnaire, I strolled away from the table. Asha and Gaius Two Hearts were close by and would watch whatever happened until they were needed. In the meantime, I had to sit and talk with a couple of people I thought were essentially cunts, and treacherous cunts at that. I couldn't even gain a victory of wits over my brother, knowing that I'd be surrendering to him when the parlay was done.

We stopped just before the gently lapping ocean reached our feet, facing the oncoming launch. The boat was white, of Winterlord construction and crewed by four oarsmen. As it rowed past the bow of the *Revenge*, I saw two people. Santago Cyclone, my older brother, was wearing black armour and a blacker smile, but he was just an ornament compared to the swollen Winterlord towering over him.

There was a time when I'd had affection for Oliver Dawn Claw. He'd been a good man, strong and honourable, despite his strange world view and weak will. I'd rescued him from the Silver Dawn, saving his life when Alexis Wind Claw massacred hundreds of other Winterlords at the parliament. Then I'd made the biggest mistake of my fucking life and shown him a vision of the rising sea. I'd meant to convert him to our cause, but instead he'd clearly liked what he saw and returned from the void as a bloated, rotten servant of the Sunken God.

I gulped and suddenly wanted to change my mind. I was far too much of a coward to be this selfless. I was choosing to die when all I really wanted to do was run the fuck away. But I didn't. I just stood there.

"Try to be polite," I muttered, as much to myself as Esteban.

"You're saving four hundred more lives," said the commander of the twenty-third void legion. "Added to the thousands you've already saved. I think you've earned the right to be as rude as you want. I'd start by insulting Oliver's shitty complexion, then just swear a lot until Santago's face turns red. Insult his intelligence, I hear he hates that."

I chuckled. "He really does. Even growing up, he always thought he was the cleverest Eastron in the kingdom."

As the boats reached the beach, the oarsmen – all Winterlord warriors – threw their oars and jumped into the shallows. They wore padded armour and chainmail, suitable for sailors, and each had a heavy axe at their hip. The other two occupants didn't move until the launch had been hefted a few feet up the beach.

"Little brother!" shouted Santago. "You've made some new friends."

"As have you," I replied, pointing to the swollen man in greenish silvery armour. "Does he still talk? Or has he bitten off his own tongue?"

Prince Oliver Dawn Claw leapt from the rowing boat, making a resounding clank as his steel-shod boots struck the rocky beach. He had always been a huge man, but now he appeared almost unreal, around seven feet tall, with limbs twice as wide as a normal man. I couldn't conceive of how he'd donned his plate armour, and I suspected he didn't often remove it. He didn't shout back at me, or join my brother in a quip. The Winterlord prince just strode from the launch, until he could converse without raising his voice.

"I talk," rumbled Oliver. His head and face were completely hairless, and red veins covered his swollen white flesh. Around his mouth and nose were crusty patches, and green and red scabs covered his cheeks and neck. He looked like a decomposing corpse.

"I'm sorry, Oliver," I said. "This is my fault. I should have let you die at the Silver Dawn." I bowed my head. It occurred to me that my mistake had probably cost us the entire camp of Winterlords. "What happened to you? Did you kill Quinn and Silver Jack?"

"Enough," said Santago, coming to join us. "I don't think introductions or pleasantries are needed." He smirked at Esteban, then frowned at Titus. "Shall we sit?"

Before any of us could move, the cat turned and sauntered back towards the parlay table, showing his tail to Santago and Oliver. I smiled and followed him, taking a deep breath when I was sure the others couldn't see me. I'd not closely studied Oliver's face, nor his reactions, and I feared what I'd see if I did. He'd spoken, but the words had been hollow, as if filtered through a screen of restraint. I wasn't sure if he was even human any more. Perhaps he was just dead, and the corpse in front of me was animated by the Sunken God. Either way, I needed to compose myself before I looked him in the eyes.

Titus sat first, leaping atop the wooden table and positioning himself at the far end. I sat closest to him, with Esteban, frowning and trying not to look at Oliver, sitting next to me. Santago sat opposite, keeping his triangular smile aimed at me, and the thing that had been Oliver Dawn Claw sat last.

Even the loitering Ik'thya'nym couldn't break the tension. They'd been acknowledged with glances and frowns from the Winterlord sailors, but no extreme reactions. Even Santago had just given them a sideways glare, as if they were poisonous animals – dangerous, but safe when respected and kept at a distance. The gangly form of Kish was closest, but he was perching on a rock and appeared content to watch and listen. His huge black eyes flickered across the new faces, though I saw no particular reaction to Oliver's rotting appearance.

"You're Esteban Hazat," said Santago, still smiling. "Commander of the twenty-third. You should have accepted my offer."

I turned to stare at my friend. "Offer?"

Esteban nodded. "This slimy prick tried to recruit me and my legion against the Dark Harbour. What was it you said? Ah, yes, *Marius is a worm, soon to be squashed.*"

I laughed and rubbed my eyes. Esteban smirked, and between the two of us, we appeared to successfully convey that my brother could go and fuck himself. Then Oliver snarled and banged his fist on the parlay table. I was startled, and involuntarily locked eyes with the hulking man, before turning away.

"I care for none of this," said the Winterlord prince, the words croaking out of his mouth. "I would bury my teeth in your flesh, if Santago had not advised me otherwise. I would consume your body, raw and alive, savouring the taste of a defeated foe." He paused, smacking his crusty lips together. "But you have value to the Risen God. You lead the traitorous Eastron on Nowhere and can be used. *You* wanted a parlay, *I* just wanted to violate the bodies of your friends and family, forcing you to watch until your mind turns to mush." His teeth ground together. "So, what did you want to parlay about, Marius the Stranger?"

I bowed my head, staring down at the table. I was scared. Not of Oliver, though his words certainly made my skin crawl. I was afraid that I was a fucking idiot whose plan was the height of stupidity. And I was afraid that Jessica, Marta, Esteban and everyone else aboard the *Dangerous* would die as a result. But I had no choice.

I looked at Oliver, blinking until I could maintain the look without squinting. "That all sounded very scary," I said. "Particularly the part about violation. But you can save the creepy shit for another time. I plan to surrender to you. But I will *not* surrender my ship."

The Winterlord stood, rumbling to his feet and jolting the table. Given his size, it was a startling move, making everyone close stand ready. His green-tinged armour followed the bulky lines of his body, as if tailored for him, and I judged that he had swelled to over seven feet in height. "No conditions," he snarled. "I take you and your ship... and your people... and your fucking soul."

Santago gasped and pushed back from the table, staring in alarm behind Prince Oliver. Esteban smiled and Titus padded happily on the wood. Kish had silently appeared behind the Winterlord. He was standing at his full height, though his limbs were still gathered. His expressive face was turned down at Oliver and displayed pity and concern, as if the aggression truly bothered him.

"Enemies talking, not fighting," said the Ik'thya'nym. "Don't be angry." He smiled gently at Oliver.

The Winterlord prince turned and I studied his rotting face for any signs of fear or doubt as he looked up at the elegant sea creature. From his eyes came a subtle green glow, then a mist of fetid vapour ghosted from his mouth – but he did not appear afraid of Kish.

"I know who you are," breathed Oliver. "I have bathed in the waters of eternity and seen ages past. You know better than to stand in our way."

Kish slithered downwards, gathering his limbs until he was the same height as the Winterlord. Then his shoulders widened, doubling his width and accentuating the dexterity in his arms. When they were face to face, the Ik'thya'nym spoke. "Stand in whose way? You are Eastron, not Zul'zya'zyn. Why speak of yourself as one of them?"

Oliver's mouth twitched and he clenched both fists, causing a nauseating crack of his knuckles. "Be careful, creature. My patience is but a thin layer of fabric, apt to tear at a moment's notice."

"Sit down," I said, mustering a more commanding voice than I thought possible.

Kish balked at my tone, hopping away from Oliver and chirping to himself, as if he thought I was talking to him. The swollen Winterlord just glared at me, perhaps insulted at my tone. After a moment, he stopped his animalistic snarling and resumed his seat.

"Better," I said, leaning forwards and maintaining eye contact with Oliver. "I told you what's going to happen. I will surrender, and you will let the *Dangerous* leave in peace."

"Peace," echoed Kish, now huddled up on a rock.

"You will not pursue my ship," I continued. "But you may do whatever you wish with me." It was a horrible thing to say and I hated that Oliver might be able to discern the anguish behind my stoic glare. "Agree to it. It's all I'm prepared to give you. Say no, and endlessly sail around this island, unable to touch us, while the people on Nowhere leave this fucking realm of form." I turned to Santago, mustering a smile. "Come on, brother, you've won. I willingly surrender to you."

When not looking at the decomposing Winterlord, I found that my mind worked better. I could see my older brother's thoughts whirring, as if I'd surprised him. I imagined he was pondering questions of time and whose enemy it was. They were complicated questions, involving massacres, running battles, sea creatures, ancient gods and the destruction of the world. In the end, I hoped that victory over his youngest brother would be enough. I really, really hoped it would be enough.

Santago sat back in the chair, his dark, triangular smile disappearing as he surveyed the beach and waters of

Kish's island. He noted the void legionnaires, the Dolcinite Pilgrims and the Ik'thya'nym. Lastly, he took a long look at the *Dangerous*, as if assessing its value. A glance back at Oliver told me all I needed to know about the power dynamic between them. Santago was certainly the brains. I didn't know what Oliver contributed, aside from being a huge walking corpse.

"You have a deal," said my brother. "Your ship can leave for Nowhere. *You* will come with us."

"A day," snarled Prince Oliver. "We will not pursue for a day. For the flesh of Marius Cyclone, that is what we offer."

I tilted my head backwards and flexed my neck. I couldn't bluff my way out of this. The bizarre thing was that I was trying to bluff my way *into* this. I needed them to want me more than my ship. My success was also my death. "Ah, fuck me!" I whispered, probably loud enough for Esteban and Titus to hear. "I accept your offer. One day."

"One day," confirmed Santago. "Do you need time to say goodbye, little brother?"

I wanted to kick the smug bastard in the face, or maybe ram my forehead into the bridge of his nose. I shared a look with Esteban, and was reminded that I should be exceedingly rude to my brother, but my heart wasn't in it. My heart wasn't in anything; it had nowhere to go except to be torn from my body and probably eaten by Prince Oliver.

"No goodbyes," I replied, standing from the table. "Let the last chapter of my life begin."

"Marius," said Esteban, frowning and standing to join me. I could tell he wanted to say more, but he was a tough void legionnaire and conveyed all he needed to with a look.

I turned, not waiting for Santago or Oliver, and marched towards the Winterlord rowing boat. I thought of the people of the Dark Harbour, sheltering on Nowhere. I thought of every one of the million things I should have done differently. But most of all, I thought of my daughter, and hoped Jess would help her understand why I was gone. I hated goodbyes and was terrible at them, especially with the few people who truly mattered to me.

As my physical form moved towards its end, my mind was allowed a moment of reflection.

"Hello, Marius," said the pale man.

"Hello, Utha," I replied.

"You lost. It took some time, but you finally lost. I always knew you were a gambler, but I hoped you'd stay lucky for a while yet. At least until you knew peace. I'm sorry."

"I'm just tired," I said. "I'm tired of all of this. Since you showed me that fucking vision, I've – fuck, I don't know. Maybe I just want to die."

"I see armour around you, Marius," said the pale man. "They didn't catch you, you surrendered. They can't scare you, because you don't fear death. You are one life who has saved hundreds of thousands. What can they do to you?"

"Pain," I replied. "I've known it in many forms, from my earliest memories. I fear they'll cause me more pain than I can deal with, and force me to betray the people on Nowhere."

"Can you kill yourself?" he asked. "Say *fuck you* one last time?"

"Probably not," I replied. "Santago will want me alive, and I don't feel like ending it by smashing my head against a wall. Not yet. Though the time may come. How do you fare?"

"Nowhere is under attack," he said. "The Winterlords, then the Dark Brethren. They're trying to break through to the refugees."

"Jessimion and the Grim Wolf will stand. They'll defend the island."

"They're not really in charge," replied Utha. "Adeline Brand is the battle commander. She destroyed half the Winterlord fleet and stopped Alexis Wind Claw breaking our defences."

"Sea Wolves!" I grunted. "Why didn't she just listen to me in the first place? Because I'm the Stranger?"

"She needed to see for herself, but she is now our friend," replied the pale man. "Duncan has spoken to her. She's more thoughtful than you might think."

"Good for her," I whispered. "I hope she makes better decisions than me."

"Are you preparing for death?"

"Not really. I know they'll kill me, but I'm preparing for pain and torture. Death is like a good night's sleep at this point. Whatever they do to me, whatever bits of me they cut off, burn or eat, I'm terrified I won't endure it. If you can, tell everyone on Nowhere that I'm dead, and any trick or apparition they see isn't real. If Esteban gets there he'll make sure."

"If I can, I will," he replied. "But don't worry about that now. I'm serious – if you find an opportunity, take it out of their hands. An unsecured knife, a discarded sword. If the ironclad is big enough, throw yourself down some stairs."

"I don't want to," I replied, finding it something of a revelation. "I might not fear it, but that doesn't mean I'm ready to die. As you said, my luck just ran out."

"Where I'm from it would be an honourable death."

"Honour?" I replied. "Honour is too often used as a justification for doing something stupid... primarily by Sea Wolves. I'd rather be a good man than an honourable one. Unfortunately, I'm neither."

"Well, allow me to be stupid for a moment and say that it's been my honour to know you, Marius Cyclone."

14

I was in an empty square room of black stone bricks. The floor was cold and covered with gravel and dust. A dark vapour seeped from every angle, creating a vague cross of mist in the centre of the stone cube. I was slumped in the middle of the floor, wearing torn clothes. My feet were bare and covered in blisters, my face was thin, with a straggly beard, and my limbs were weak. I didn't know where I was or how I'd got here, but I felt as if I'd spent months as a prisoner. My skin crackled, my eyes saw only shadows, and my breath was shallow.

Then four windows appeared, one on each wall. There was sudden light, enough to make me wail and screw my eyes tight shut. Moments turned to minutes as I tried to blink enough to see. When I looked up, I saw that the windows were just open squares, with no bars, shutters or glass. The cross of vapour was now a cross of light, with each window providing a different level of brightness, as if they looked out across different places.

I adjusted my rags, scratched at a bald patch on my scalp, and managed to pull myself into a kneeling position. I blinked, coughed, rubbed my face, and tried to focus enough to look out of the closest window, where the light was darkest. I saw water first – a bay or inlet, surrounded by dark buildings, built up to the coast. It was the Dark

Harbour. It was my hold. Perhaps mid-morning, with an overcast sky. The streets were empty, filled with dust and whistling with wind.

I gripped the edge of the window, my hands shivering and frail, and peered out. It was like a painting of an enormous tomb, drawn with charcoal, in tones of black and grey. At the edge of my vision, I could see the far north of my hold, where Merlinda Night Eyes and the Tender Strike made their homes. Around the Glaring were the void legionnaires of Lucio Wind Claw. They'd secured what was left of the Dark Harbour and were now dealing with the few citizens who'd chosen to stay behind.

Sometimes I enjoyed being proven right. But not now. Merlinda had hundreds of followers, and at least half were nailed to wooden planks and set on fire. They were servants of the Sinister Black Cats, and their only crime had been to hate me. They were being tortured, mutilated and burned. I'd left them behind to die. Merlinda herself was still alive, but Lucio Wind Claw had made an example of her. She'd been chained in the square. Slowly, over hours, they'd sliced through her feet and hands, an inch at a time, until her wrists and ankles were all that remained.

I fell away from the window, vomited violently, and curled up on the dusty floor.

"Look again," gurgled an inhuman voice. "Or choose another window."

I shuffled away from the thin vomit, and curled up in the corner of the room. I didn't remember when I'd last eaten, and my stomach burned.

"Look!" echoed the voice, making me put shaking hands over my ears.

I edged along the wall to the next window, and pulled myself up the brickwork. The sun was brighter here, though the air was colder. Below was a pristine hold of white and silver, encircled by a high wall and formidable battlements. It was First Port, the seat of the Always King. I knew what I was looking at, despite never having visited. But it wasn't the *hold* I was supposed to see.

There was a man, a Winterlord spirit-master, with a burned face. He was frenzied in his devotion to the Dawn Claw, the great eagle spirit. He'd been visited by something that looked like the lord of the quarter, but somehow different, somehow changed. The spirit had rotten feathers, covered in green mould and decaying flesh. Oliver Dawn Claw had infested the mighty spirit whose name he shared, and the eagle now flew for the Sunken God. From then on, it was a swift matter to corrupt the spirit-master, then the duellists, then the hold. Their innate sense of superiority had been the door through which they'd fallen, but they'd have had little choice, like a virulent infection targeting only the ignorant. I'd failed with Oliver, and it had cost me the Winterlords.

This time I didn't vomit, or fall from the window. I managed to keep my frail legs straight and move away with a modicum of dignity. But I couldn't stand without holding onto the wall, and quickly fell back to the floor, wincing and gathering my legs. I shivered and gasped, until my back found the wall and I could sit up.

"Failure," boomed the voice.

I began to splutter, grabbing my ears and screaming. I rocked back and forth, feeling pain, weakness, and the loss of all imaginable hope. Why me? Why did I have to save the Eastron? I'd failed in almost every possible way. I was a terrible leader, who'd made bad decision upon bad decision.

I awoke, and felt wood against my naked back and chains around each of my wrists. I was a prisoner aboard Prince Oliver's ironclad, the name of which I'd not bothered to learn. I'd been given a solid beating, with a probable dislocated jaw and several broken fingers on each hand, but I was mostly whole. I'd only been here a few hours, but some twisted void-craft was assaulting my mind.

"You're awake," gurgled a deep voice.

I coughed, blinked my eyes and spat on the floor, before looking up into the small cabin. I was somewhere in the bowels of the ironclad, but the ship rolled only slowly, as if at anchor. The cabin had no portholes, and the back wall, against which I was chained, was made of black iron.

"Who are you?" I grunted.

I wasn't able to focus on the cabin's single other inhabitant. All I could make out was the outline of a portly man, standing over a table. The man made a horrid smacking sound with his lips, full of saliva and smugness. I didn't know who he was, and couldn't see him clearly, but I fucking hated him.

"My name is Hopfrog," said the man, scuttling forwards so I could see him clearly.

I wanted to rub my eyes, but all I could do was blink. After a moment, the portly man came into focus. It wasn't a man; at least, it was only part man. It had arms and legs, squeezed into bulging black fabric, though its webbed feet and membranous hands were exposed. Hopfrog was not a Sunken Man, but he had wide, black eyes, and a pouting, fishy mouth. His belly was swollen and his legs short, making him waddle as he moved. His body, like his speech, was almost human.

"You're a hybrid," I coughed. "I've heard of you. Sunken Men raping Eastron."

Hopfrog slapped me, leaving a layer of slime across my cheek. Then he returned to his table, grumbling to himself. "Do you know who was my mother?" he asked. "She was a fine, noble woman of the Winterlords."

"And your father?" I replied.

He craned his fleshy neck backwards and smiled at me, with glistening, frothy saliva pulsing from his mouth. He didn't answer my question, but there was sadistic malevolence in his eyes, as if I was some kind of toy.

Then the cabin door opened and two men entered. I had to shake my head to focus, and even then my neck was too sore to get a proper look. I saw Santago, my older brother, and Prince Oliver Dawn Claw, but I couldn't lock eyes with either of them. They stood by the door, closing it behind them and facing Hopfrog.

"Speak, creature," said Oliver.

"He has looked through two windows, my king," grunted the hybrid. "His mind is breaking. Subservience will follow."

Santago took three strides across the cabin and looked down at me. I tried to shift position and look at him, but my arms didn't bend that way, and I just hung limply from the iron wall.

"Hear some truth, Marius," said my brother. "Follow us... or we'll make you."

"No," snarled Oliver, "he does not get to choose. We don't need him."

"My king," said Santago. "He is influential. My counsel, humble as always, is that we use him against the traitors on Nowhere."

Oliver straightened, his crusty mouth twisting into a grin. "Of course. After all, there are two more windows... and he has been such a failure."

The word caused me physical pain, like a needle had been inserted into my mind. Whatever they'd done to me had weaponized the word *failure*, making it akin to a cut or a punch to the face.

Hopfrog waddled away from his table and inspected my face. His greasy hands pinched my chin and raised my head, until he could lock his bulging black eyes onto my own. "Shall I send him back, my king?" gurgled the hybrid.

"Yes," replied Oliver. "Be crueller this time."

The black stone floor was freezing cold against my naked body, and the gritty dust made me clench my fists to stop from scratching. Patches of hair and scalp were shedding from my head, and my teeth had started loosening and falling out. I'd been weak, but now I felt brittle, as if too much movement would break bones. I couldn't remember eating or sleeping, nor how I'd arrived here. Only two of the four windows were now open, and I was still compelled to look through them.

An inch at a time, I pulled my broken body to the wall. I had to move like a caterpillar, shifting my weight to not overstress any particular limb, until I was beneath the nearest opening. The last two windows were the brightest, as if a blazing sun shone beyond each, though it did not affect the temperature in the stone cube, which remained close to freezing. My rags were gone, and my naked body was covered in bruises, blisters and dead skin, almost enough that the cold was a secondary concern.

I couldn't stand, but I could gain enough leverage from the windowsill to crawl upwards and peer out. Beyond, under a bright morning sun, was a coastline. It was the northern edge of Big Brother, around the headland of Hook Point. It was called the Bone Coast, but all I could see was flesh. Hundreds of bloated Sunken Men wallowed in the shallows. Sea shells and coral were woven into their grotesque bodies, and their weapons all utilized the pincer in some fashion. They were pulling Eastron corpses from the water. Hundreds of dead Sea Wolves, perhaps a thousand or more. This was where Adeline Brand's refugee fleet had been destroyed, though all wreckage had already been pulled below the surface. Only the dead remained.

Further inland, the corpses were being piled into separate groups, perhaps five hundred Sea Wolves per pile, though there were as many chunks of severed flesh as complete bodies. Around the piled dead were other Sunken Men, though they were smaller and wielded no weapons.

I blinked, trying to process what I was looking at. They were somehow sticking the corpses together, with their own oozing excretions acting as glue. They gathered it from their mouths and gills, spreading the slime across the dead Sea Wolves, until each pile was coated and connected into a single mass of flesh. The pulpy things they created started oozing left and right, as if given purpose and mobility by the craft of the Sunken Men.

I retched, but my stomach was empty and shrivelled. These people had been refugees, fleeing the broken hold of the Severed Hand. They wouldn't have been here if I'd been more persuasive. If I'd made them realize the threat. If the Sea Wolves and I had hated each other a little less and I'd argued a little more.

"Failure!" said a raspy voice. "*That* is your legacy."

I fell back from the window and howled in pain. The feeling was deep and complete, as if every inch of my body, inside and out, was being stabbed. More than that, my mind was under assault. It hurt to think. I struggled to remember my name. I didn't know where I'd come from or where I was going. All I knew was that I'd failed, and all I saw was the cold stone room and the one remaining window.

"Wait," said the gurgling voice. "Don't look just yet. You have more pain to feel. You are paramount in the thoughts of the king, and he demands I be crueller."

I had nothing left. No fight, no energy, no strength. Even my mind was crippled. I took a slow breath and closed my eyes, hoping death would come and embrace me. My heart was still beating, but the rest of my body was limp and powerless. Still, death was nowhere to be found.

"You are so very primitive and weak. Your body, your spirit – but mostly your mind. Easy to twist, easy to mould. You form attachments and wallow in your own morality, thinking it gives you purpose. All I see is how fragile it makes you. I cannot be too cruel, or your simple mind will turn to mush before it can be used."

I wanted to stand, or more likely crawl, to the last window. I felt I had to, but I was pinned to the floor. Every second I lay there, I whimpered in unimaginable pain, as if it was all I had ever known. I was broken and worthless, though I didn't truly know who I was. I felt that I had a name, an identity, perhaps even a purpose, but they were like wisps of smoke, impossible to grasp.

"Stand and look," cackled a voice full of phlegm and bile. "And be changed. Be reborn in a new light."

My frail body was released and I rolled onto my stomach. I could feel my ribs, pressing against the gritty stone floor. I gathered my limbs and crawled to the last window. Every slight movement hurt, and I felt as if they might be the last movements I ever made. Whoever I was, whatever I wished for or loved, it was all coming to an end.

With great effort, I pulled my chin to the windowsill and looked out. What I saw was another world. That is to say, it was *our* world, but it was different. I viewed it from far above, as if gliding through the clouds. It was the past, or the future, or a mixture of the two. It felt adrift in time, as if days, months and years were petty concepts with no true meaning. The mountains didn't care; neither did the tides or the winds. Even geologically finite things, like rivers and trees, cared nothing for the progression of time. It was through this lens that I saw the land I'd once called the Kingdom of the Four Claws.

The islands of Big and Little Brother were now connected by a jagged land bridge of reefs and rocky pinnacles, forming a barrier between the Inner Sea and the Sea of Stars. Along the coasts of both landmasses were more strange formations, brightly coloured with coral and algae, as if two enormous walls had risen from the deep ocean. Further north, forming swirling patterns across the Inner Sea, were thousands of islands, where before there had been nothing but open ocean. Each island was volcanic and encircled by sharp peaks. I couldn't remember where I'd seen such islands before, only that they reminded me of the past, when my mind worked properly.

Then I saw that *life* was very much a part of this timeless land. Two separate races of immortal creatures dominated the world – one, amoral and arrogant, the other, peaceful and furtive. They kept mostly to the seas, leaving the continents to whatever primitive animals evolved. Complex apes lived mortal lives, largely ignored by the dominant creatures... unless they rose too high, or explored too far.

But everything was not in balance. There was a single point of disparity. A single entity that lorded over all others. It was not a physical being, not in any real sense, though it could summon a monstrous form when needed. It was comprised of some alien matter, brought to this world at the very beginning of its history. It was one of two such entities, though it was the only one that remained. It had fathered the Zul'zya'zyn and its long forgotten sister had birthed the Ik'thya'nym.

I shook my head, feeling the unknowable entity's power and malevolence. My eyes saw it only as a black shimmer, against which light was repelled. The closest my mind could interpret, in terms that made sense, was a titanic, thick-limbed humanoid, with a beard of writhing feelers and sharp, red eyes. But it had no true form, just a mask it wore to terrify lesser creatures. Klu'zu... the Sunken God. I'd seen him before.

I fell back from the window and roared, emptying my fragile lungs. It was primal, filled with naked emotion, as if it was the last sound I'd ever make. But it wasn't. I didn't die, nor did my mind break. A wall had been broken, or maybe a dam been breached – but something had changed. I widened my eyes and coughed. Slowly, the cough became a chuckle. Then the chuckle became a laugh. I was Marius Cyclone, called the Stranger, and they would *not* break me.

"I've seen him before," I shouted. "Remember? Ten Cuts showed all of us. He didn't drive me mad then, and he won't now. Maybe I'm just stronger than you and Oliver Dawn Claw." The laughter became manic cackling. "Fuck you all! If I am an insignificant mortal, just fucking kill me." My mouth and jaw twisted into a wide grin. "I'm a coward... I'm a failure... I've got people killed." I stopped laughing. "But I *tried*. I *tried* to save us."

Hopfrog threw a bucket of water over me and I woke up spluttering. I was still chained in the bowels of the ironclad, but each of my limbs felt significantly worse, as if I'd been here longer than I thought. There were dried tears on my cheeks, blood on my chest, and my jaw hurt. I remembered smiling, and the elation continued. Once I'd spat out the water and shaken my head clear, I grinned at the hybrid.

"That wasn't very pleasant," I grunted. "Do you have more? Or was that it?"

The half-man waddled back towards me, rubbing his membranous hands together. It was hard to read his bulging, black eyes and pouting mouth, but I sensed he was confused. "How have you done this?" he gurgled. "You are just an insect. Your mind should not be able to resist us."

I tried to roll my shoulders into some kind of comfort, but ended up just pushing back against the iron wall of the cabin. "Well, I am truly sorry for the inconvenience I've caused. Can I die now?"

He slapped me, splashing a gout of slime across my naked torso. "Silence," he spluttered.

Oliver and Santago still stood at the back of the cabin, but their presence no longer disturbed me. If gallows' humour was armour, then I was well protected indeed. Utha was right – they hadn't captured me; I had surrendered. They couldn't scare me, because I didn't fear death. And now, I'd resisted their mind tricks and mental torture. I was still fucked, but I was not broken. I started to laugh again.

"Silence!" repeated Hopfrog, this time in a screech.

He slapped me again, then a third time, then a fourth – until a tooth flew from my mouth to loudly strike the iron wall of the cabin. I flexed my jaw and spat blood onto the wooden floor.

"Creature!" snapped Prince Oliver. "What is happening?"

Santago was staring at me and muttering something to himself. Unlike the bloated Winterlord, who was clearly insane, my elder brother still appeared mostly in control of his mind.

"He's laughing," continued Oliver. "Why is he laughing?" He clenched his fists and bared his teeth at me. "I don't like him laughing."

"My king," slurred Hopfrog. "It is not my doing." The hybrid appeared to shrink before the huge Winterlord, his slimy webbed feet shuffling backwards.

The scabs at the edges of Oliver's mouth began to crack and blister as he snarled at me. When he moved forwards, it was in slow, predatory inches, with his eyes playing over every part of my restrained body. I suddenly felt like a roasted animal, done to a turn on the spit, with every morsel appearing delicious. I was no longer laughing.

"I'm going to eat you, Marius," said Oliver. "And I'm going to do it slowly."

"We still need him," said Santago, with a frown and little conviction. "He knows the secret ways ashore on Nowhere. He knows how they get refugees up to the cliffs. If Alexis can't break their defences, he's our only way onto the island." He paused, clearly unsure if Oliver was even listening. "If we've not broken through when the whips arrive... we will be punished."

"*You* will be punished," growled the Winterlord, still approaching me. "*You* are still mortal flesh. *I* am the Forever King... and I am hungry."

He loomed over me, licking his lips and rubbing his hands together. After a moment of disgusting contemplation, the huge man crouched down. I could see red veins across his thin, sickly skin, and his breath was rotten against my face. He was dead, with the Sunken God somehow animating his corpse.

"You're thin," he whispered. "You need to eat more. I hoped for some flesh and fat. Something to savour." He pinched at my sides and stomach, shaking his head at the lack of loose flesh.

"I rarely have time to eat properly," I replied, trying to hide my fear of the unreal monster Prince Oliver Dawn Claw had become. "I'd gratefully accept a few days of hearty meals... to really plump me up."

His bald head rose and a horrible smile appeared. He stroked a hand across my greasy, bloodied hair, before gripping my neck and jolting my head backwards to face him. "There is still good meat on you."

I was helpless. The one thing I had no armour against was pain. It was what I'd truly feared since I decided to surrender on Kish's island. It was the problem I couldn't think my way around. I didn't even know what my tolerance was. I'd said *fuck you* to them and their Sunken God, but I was terrified that I would never have enough armour.

Oliver knelt in front of me, his hands stroking my naked chest and stomach. His tongue flicked at the blistered corners of his mouth and green saliva dripped onto the floor. He tilted his head and looked at my left side, just above the hip, as if selecting a prime cut of meat. When he moved, it was slow. He gripped my waist and craned downwards. Then he growled, dug his teeth into my flesh, and ripped away a chunk of blood and meat.

15

The ironclad was moving. It rolled gently from left to right, occasionally lurching forwards or tilting sharply. The vessel was huge and heavy and dismissed the tides as beneath its notice. It was not fast or manoeuvrable – but it was a floating fortress, moving east with purpose and intent. Somewhere, across the Inner Sea, the last refugee fleet from the Dark Harbour was about to reach the Red Straits and the island of Nowhere. Behind them, hopefully making good time, was the *Dangerous*. They had a day's head start on ten Brethren warships and a single Winterlord ironclad. I hoped it was enough.

"He's awake. The wyrd is holding on his side."

"He must live," gurgled a familiar voice.

"He'll live. Unless the king decides to eat something he can't live without."

"His thigh needs more attention."

"Yes... that's a particularly deep bite."

Oliver had torn a chunk from my side and left Hopfrog to stop the bleeding. An hour later, the prince had returned and gorged himself on my left thigh. It required the intervention of a Winterlord spirit-master to stop me bleeding to death. After that, Oliver returned at regular intervals and chewed through two of my fingers, ate a mouthful of my right calf, and bit off one of my ears. I'd stopped howling in pain after the second visit, and fallen into a state of semi-conscious torpor. No individual wound was life-threatening, and Hopfrog and the spirit-master had closed the worst bite marks, but I was still a bloody mess, slumped against the iron wall.

Both my arms were dislocated from hanging off the chains, and my clothes had been cut away, leaving a naked, broken man, still trying to come to terms with his own death. I was numb. Somewhere in the bowels of my mind, I'd found the strength to ignore the pain. Or maybe my nerves were just overloaded by being slowly eaten alive. Eventually they'd kill me and all I needed to do was endure until they did. *Just fucking kill me*, I thought.

"He's still whole. More or less," said the spirit-master.

"If we can keep him alive, the king will be able to feast for another day."

"I will gain favour if I can stretch it to two," replied the Winterlord. "While Alexis Wind Claw massacres those on Nowhere, King Oliver can watch, dining on this man's liver."

"Which part will he take next?" mused Hopfrog. "Better for you if he avoids the torso and head."

"I will encourage the king to eat the prisoner's arms," said the spirit-master, pinching my limp bicep. "There is good meat there, and the wound will not endanger his life."

My vision cleared a little and I could now identify who was speaking. Hopfrog, the slimy hybrid, appeared in charge of my mundane medical care, applying bandages, salves and stitches. The spirit-master, a robust Winterlord with flowing silver hair, was using his potent wyrd to push energy into my mangled body and trick my arteries, nerves and muscles into thinking nothing was wrong. It was powerful wyrd-craft, and could keep me alive indefinitely... as long as I lost no major organs.

Then I heard the door open, but couldn't find an angle to see who'd entered. Hopfrog and the spirit-master moved out of my limited field of vision, going to greet the visitor. Their movements didn't suggest reverence or fear, and I hoped that Prince Oliver had not come for his next course.

"He's awake," observed Santago Cyclone, my elder brother. I wanted to hear just a tiny sliver of pity in his voice, but all I heard was spite. "You said your wyrd would lull him."

"He is unusually resistant," replied the spirit-master.

"As he was with *my* efforts," offered Hopfrog, as if trying to mitigate his failure to break my mind.

"He's awake, but can't feel the pain," grumbled my brother. "What's the point?"

"If I let him feel pain, he'll probably die of shock the next time the king takes a bite."

Santago strolled towards me, appearing sideways to my narrow field of vision. He clicked his fingers in front of my face, but I didn't react, not even a twitch. Then he slapped me – again, with no reaction. "King Oliver has finished dining for today," he said, clearly addressing the others. "You are to securely restrain Marius. Men will soon be here to bring him up to the command deck. I believe we have something much more painful for him to endure."

More painful than being slowly eaten alive? My numb senses were almost curious to know what torment he'd conjured. Being buggered to death on the quarterdeck by a hundred sweaty sailors was trivial compared to what I'd already experienced. Nevertheless, he appeared sincere as he turned and strode from the bloody cabin.

*

I fell in and out of consciousness, barely registering the two huge Winterlord knights who unchained my naked body from the iron wall. Hopfrog assisted, making sure the bandages held. My side, both my legs, my hand and my ear – all were covered in muddy white dressings. The wounds underneath were all savage bite marks, but the pain was minimal.

I didn't fully open my eyes until my skin was assaulted by bright sunlight. I couldn't feel the floor, or the hands that held me, but I could feel the sun. The warmth caressed my body, bringing life to my extremities for the first time in hours. I could wriggle my toes and move my remaining fingers. I could even blink clear my eyes. Not that I'd see anything I wanted to see.

I was a naked, bloodied body, being dragged along a wooden deck, surrounded by armoured Winterlord sailors. My remaining ear began to work again, and I heard mocking calls and swearing. These people hated me. I wasn't just the Stranger to them. I was the traitorous cunt who'd defied the Sunken God, and they made sure I knew it. I was used to being hated, but to these Eastron it was a religious matter. I couldn't believe how totally they'd fallen.

"Bring him here!" demanded a nearby voice, accompanied by much laughter.

I was dragged over wooden planking, up steps, and thrown forwards. My face hit the deck, and I tasted saltwater on my lips. Rolling onto my back, I started to feel pain flow across my nerves, as if the spirit-master's numbing wyrd was slowly losing its potency. Rough hands grasped at my hair, my neck and my arms, hefting me upwards. My legs were too damaged for me to stand unaided, but I was held upright by the same two hulking Winterlords who'd brought me up on deck.

I was at the bow of the ironclad, on a raised platform. It was wider, taller and longer than any warship I'd been on, and would be crewed by five hundred or more Winterlords. Santago and I appeared to be the only Dark Brethren aboard. The largest Winterlord was facing me, his back to the sunlight at the very front of his ship. Prince Oliver – or King Oliver, or whatever other title the decomposing man possessed – was beckoning me to the edge of the raised platform.

"Marius the Stranger," said the man who'd been eating me alive. "Come and see."

I was marched forwards by the two men who held me, until the remaining fingers on my left hand felt the wood of the railing. I flexed my arms, but I had no strength, and both my shoulders were dislocated. They flung my midsection over the wide, wooden railing, aggravating the wound in my side and causing a sharp intake of breath. Then someone grabbed a handful of my hair and raised my head.

"Look," said Oliver Dawn Claw.

I coughed and blinked, trying to focus on the horizon. The ironclad was sailing east, through the Inner Sea, but there was a ship ahead of us. A ship that shouldn't be there. I shook my head and screwed up my face, but I couldn't see clearly.

"Look!" demanded Oliver.

On the horizon, rolling under half-sail, was the *Dangerous*. It should have been well on the way to Nowhere. The cumbersome ironclad shouldn't have been able to catch up. What the fuck were Esteban and Black Dog thinking? Why was it not under full sail? Why had they not escaped?

"We gave them a day," crowed Oliver. "And yet... here they are."

The Brethren cutters flanking us had gone on ahead and were now encircling my ship, cutting off any means of escape. The horizon contained no land and I guessed we were still hours from the Red Straits.

I gritted my teeth. "No," I grunted, through a dry mouth and cracked lips. "Why are they here? Why the fuck are they here?"

Oliver laughed. "It was all for nothing. Your noble sacrifice – and you *still* get to watch me eat your wife and child."

"No!" I screamed, starting to struggle against the two men who held me. "Get the fuck off me. Get the *fuck* off me." I had no strength. My limbs didn't work properly and I had no wyrd to summon. I was naked and helpless, made to watch a fleet of ships surround the *Dangerous*, until she was forced to trim her remaining sails.

The swollen Winterlord prince grabbed a fistful of my hair and mockingly shook my head. "Looks like you get to live a little while longer."

I flailed and wriggled, trying to summon the energy to scream. I was suddenly reminded of Utha's advice, and wished that I'd found a way to kill myself. It wouldn't change what was about to happen to my ship, but at least I wouldn't have to watch.

"Just kill me," I whispered. "I lost, you won. Just end it."

Oliver laughed again. It was a rumbling sound, like he was gargling stones. "No, Marius, I will not kill you. I wonder if you remember... On our way to Snake Guard, you once laughed at my naivety. Now, I laugh at yours."

I had no response. My wits, like my mind and body, were fading into darkness. Some orders were shouted, but I struggled to hear individual words. The ironclad kept moving, and her sailors rushed back and forth, preparing for combat. Ahead, the cutters had corralled the *Dangerous*, forcing her to a complete stop in the Inner Sea. I thought I heard a command that included my name, and I was held in a tight choke-hold. They marched my limp body away from the forward railing, back to the quarterdeck and past a hundred jeering Winterlords.

Santago was waiting at the top of the downward steps, his face twisted into a triangular smile. "Back to your chains, brother. Don't worry, you won't be lonely down there. Hopfrog has hooks and chains ready for your family. The rest of your crew will have to settle for a simpler death at the edge of a blade. Then on to Nowhere, where Alexis Wind Claw should already have breached the island. This is the end, Marius."

With my feet not touching the wood of the steps, I was carried downwards, until the bright sky disappeared. Another set of steps, surrounded by shouting sailors, then my head fell limp and I didn't see the remainder of my journey. It was only a minute or two until I was back in Hopfrog's chamber at the bow of the warship. The two Winterlords remained, securing me to the iron wall. My arms felt like each bone was rattling around in my body, disconnected from each other. I barely felt the manacles tied around my wrists, or the chains securing my feet to the floor.

"Welcome back," gurgled the hybrid. "See here." He waddled left and right in front of me, displaying three additional sets of restraints on each wall of his cabin. "The

king wishes to dine in front of you. I hear there is a wife...
and a child."

I was in the middle of a nightmare, with horrific elements
forming into a single vision of pain, failure and torment.
My life was already forfeit, but now so were the lives of my
family and close friends. I was also trying to process the news
that Alexis Wind Claw was attacking Nowhere, and that the
Dangerous had somehow squandered a day's head start. If
it wasn't a nightmare, it was part of no reality I wanted.
Everything had gone wrong. Santago was right; this was the
end. Not just the end of me and my people, but the end of
the Eastron. In my vivid, blood-soaked nightmare, I imagined
this was the literal end of the world. I tried to think as if I
was already dead and this was merely a last fever dream, in
the hope it would soften the torments to come.

When my mind was clear enough to see and hear, I felt
that the ironclad was still moving, covering the last few ship
lengths to the *Dangerous*. I could hear shouted commands,
the clank of metal and the creak of wood, but little else.
Whatever strategy and formation they were using to cut off
my ship was happening beyond my sight. Neither the Dark
Brethren, nor the Winterlords, could match the Sea Wolves
aboard ship, but there would be enough skilled captains
amongst the cutters to deal with whatever Black Dog was
doing to escape. I thought my cousin was a good sailor, and
couldn't think of a reason why he'd be so easily caught by a
slower fleet.

"Oh, it's getting interesting," said Hopfrog, craning on his
flabby legs to look out of a porthole. "Your strange-looking

ship has nowhere to go. The wind favours us, and you are surrounded." He smacked his lips together and swallowed the resulting saliva, gulping with contentment.

The two large Winterlords went to a second porthole and both smiled.

"We'll be launching boats soon," said one.

"We need to get there before Santago's filthy sailors," said the other. "The glory of the massacre should be ours."

I had a diagonal view of them. It was all my restraints and dislocated limbs would allow. Then the ironclad juddered violently, displacing the minimal furniture, sending the three inhabitants flailing to the wooden floor. It was as if the huge ship had suddenly beached or struck an enormous, submerged rock. The ship had been moving quickly, and I didn't know of anything, hidden in the Inner Sea, that could cause it to stop so suddenly. Anything large enough would have been seen from miles away.

The two Winterlords struggled to their feet, as the cumbersome warship settled in place. The flabby hybrid merely pulled in his limbs and sat on the floor, next to the remnants of his table. All three of them were dazed, with the two Eastron sharing unlikely theories about what could have stopped the ironclad in such a fashion. But, before they could return to the portholes, there was a shimmer in the air.

Breaking the glass at sea was usually suicide. Few Eastron had mastered swimming in the void. The spiritual ocean didn't behave the same as normal water, and most of us would drown, pumping our arms and legs, trying to gain purchase that wasn't there. Nevertheless, either side of me, two Eastron broke the glass and entered the cabin.

"It fucking worked," said Gaius Two Hearts, wielding a pair of short swords.

"People to kill," snapped Asha, his sister, hefting a hand-axe in one hand and a large, serrated knife in the other.

They pushed away from the iron wall and leapt at the two Winterlords. They were far smaller, but had surprise and skill on their side, and they were the finest killers I'd ever known. The first sailor caught Asha in mid-air, but received two swift stabs to the neck and head as he did so. The second was too stunned to react, and stood like a massive, stupid statue, letting Gaius stick him in the ribs and the heart. A few more frenzied stabs and both Winterlords were dead, with blood rapidly leaving their bodies.

"Fuck a pig, Marius," said Asha, appearing to notice me for the first time. "What have you done to yourself?"

"*He* didn't do it, the Forever King did," gurgled Hopfrog, now sitting cross-legged in the corner of the cabin. The hybrid didn't look scared or especially alarmed by the two assassins. There remained on his bulging face an expression of delicious contentment, as if he was happy with his work.

"Is that a costume?" asked Gaius.

"Or are you some kind of monster?" added Asha. "With your big eyes and webbed feet."

I wanted to tell them to kill him. I may even have mouthed the words, but I didn't have enough breath to actually speak. Luckily, the assassins had not come here for a conversation, and struck quickly.

It was a strange fight, with Hopfrog unable to defend himself, but possessing thick skin and copious slime, making it difficult for Asha and Gaius to actually kill him. Cuts glanced off his flabby body, thrusts didn't penetrate, and he was far stronger than he looked. The hybrid flapped at the air with his membranous hands, but any deflection or block was entirely accidental. Whenever his random flails hit one of the twins, they winced, as if punched by a skilled fighter.

"Pin him down," barked Asha.

"Get the arms," grunted Gaius.

Between them, they mounted Hopfrog and trapped his limbs. Asha was closest to his head and delivered three sharp blows to his face with the hilt of her axe, before sizing him up and driving her serrated knife into his left eye. The hybrid's howl was as much phlegm as sound, and erupted from his wide mouth with a spray of greenish blood.

"Ha, that fucked you up, didn't it?" crowed Asha, stabbing him in the other eye. "Now you're blind." She dropped her axe and held the knife downwards in her dominant right hand. Then she stabbed him four, five, six times, alternating between his left and right eyes, until the creature stopped moving. "And now you're fucking dead."

"Time to go," said Gaius, jumping from Hopfrog's corpse and coming over to me. "Marius is fucked."

I wanted to smile at him, but I thought my jaw might be broken from repeated slaps, punches and backhands. All I could manage was a pained grimace. I felt something other than torment. I felt a tiny sliver of hope. It was only the pinched expression of shock on their faces that reminded me how injured I was.

Asha went to the door first. It could be barred from within and she placed a heavy plank of wood across the frame. Gaius was cradling my head and assessing the chains and manacles that secured me to the iron wall. When his sister joined him, they held me up from the floor and pushed a sharp slice of wyrd into my chains. They flexed and weakened enough that the twins could pull me from the wall, separating the steel links.

"He's a mess," said Gaius. "He can't even stand."

"We carry him," replied Asha.

"We carry him," agreed Gaius.

PART SIX

Adeline Brand on Nowhere

16

We'd turned Nowhere into a fortress. But a fortress against Eastron. Thousands of warriors could throw themselves at our defences and thousands of warriors would be repelled. Even if the Winterlords were somehow able to get ashore without drowning, I liked our chances of cutting them to pieces on the beach and driving them off at the barricades. But there were things we didn't know how to fight. We'd held our own against the Sunken Men, destroying the Temple of Dagon and driving off their depth barges at Hook Point. The frogspawn had been devastating, but fire had seen us victorious. We'd even killed the Gluttonous Whip at the Bay of Bliss. But Alexis Wind Claw had conjured something new for us to fight.

For a minute or two we just stood on the cliff and stared. Three troop ships had struck the beach and three *things* had come ashore. They folded outwards from the relative confines of the floating wooden boxes, and wriggled through the shallow water, righting themselves on the rocks of Duncan's Fall. Each one was a mass of flesh and limbs, glistening with slime. Thousands of human bodies had been fused together and somehow animated. There was a vile craft to their assembly, with legs scuttling under each mass, and groping arms creating an undulating frill. Heads and torsos completed the abominations, forming a bulky midsection to the three huge monsters.

"They're Sea Wolves," said Daniel Doesn't Die. "From the Bone Coast. Corpses from the refugee fleet we were too late to save."

"How are they moving?" I replied. "How are they stuck together and how are they fucking moving?"

"We need to defend the barricades," said Jessimion Death Spell, his pinched eyes focused on the three abominations.

Along the cliff top, dozens of void legionnaires looked down, bows hanging loosely in their hands. Opposite us, the warriors of Ice on the other cliff were similarly stationary. I couldn't see the barricades, but I imagined the stunned reaction was shared by all the defenders of Nowhere. No one knew what these things were, nor how they were even possible. Like Daniel, the astute might have recognized the fused bodies as Sea Wolves, but everyone else just saw three rumbling mounds of flesh, heads and limbs. Their legs propelled them up the beach, but they were not coordinated and appeared to roll as much as walk, flopping from one side to the other, before scuttling forwards. The flopping and scuttling moved them at no great speed, and worked in our favour, as everyone needed a moment of silence to process what they were seeing.

When that moment was over, I started shouting. "Listen to me! It's just another enemy. Death Spell, Xavyer, your archers will open fire when the *things* are in range. Give the order, then accompany me to the barricades. Daniel, go and get the black dust. Conjure that surprise for us."

"Adeline, slow down," said Tasha. "Your wound…"

I looked down at my side, where Bjorn Coldfire had sealed the puncture wound, and remembered that I couldn't fight. I'd almost forgotten. "Okay, come here," I said, "let me lean on you."

The Kneeling Wolf rushed to my side as the others shouted orders to our warriors. The orders were picked up and relayed across the coast of Duncan's Fall, gradually drawing everyone's attention away from the three abominations, and back to their duty.

Daniel left first, rushing back down to the beach, eventually followed by Tasha and me. In short order the cliffs were alive with archers, and thousands of void legionnaires pointed spears and shields from atop the barricades. Between cohorts of Brethren were mobs of Sea Wolves, far more mobile than the legionnaires, and able to move between the locked shields and plug any gaps in our defences. It was a gratifying sight, perhaps never seen before – an army of Dark Brethren fighting alongside an army of Sea Wolves. It was also possible that this was part of the single largest army ever assembled by the Eastron. Only Mathias Blood's fleet at the Battle of the Depths came close.

As we reached the level ground, I was greeted by Siggy Blackeye, Wilhelm Greenfire and Santos Spirit Killer, the commander of the second void legion. They'd organized the defenders into companies of two hundred warriors, with senior duellists and legionnaires commanding each company. They'd pulled everyone back from the first and lowest barricade, beyond a pit and killing ground, to the second and much higher barricade. It would be suicide for mortal men and women to attack us – they'd have to climb the first wall, make their way through the pit, and around the sharpened stakes it contained, before trying to climb the taller wall, all the time being shot with arrows and savaged with long spears. But we weren't being attacked by mortal men and women.

Tasha and Siggy helped me up to the nearest wooden platform, looking south across the beach. Kieran was a little way down the wall, commanding a company of sailors from *Halfdan's Revenge*. He nodded to me along the line of warriors, before pointing to the three approaching abominations and mouthing the words *what the fuck?* Of the frontline defenders, half were Sea Wolves, and each of them muttered similar things to their neighbours. The Brethren void legionnaires were more stoic, and conveyed their shock with wide eyes and deep breaths.

"Where's Daniel?" I asked Siggy. "I think we'll need him."

"He's somewhere with his dust," she replied. "Those... *things* will reach us before he's ready."

The abominations had spread out, their grotesque, undulating movements dragging them halfway up the beach. With each flop and scuttle the view got worse. They were vast, slimy creatures, stuck together with something resembling frogspawn. Chunks of legs and arms grasped at the ground and the air with equal purpose, surrounding a central fleshy mass of torsos and heads. The things had no front, back, top or bottom... but they did have faces.

A Sea Wolf close to me vomited. Another dropped his sword and turned away. Across the surface of the abominations were living faces. Their eyes stared, their jaws flexed and their mouths screamed. They filled every gap between limbs and flesh, bellowing outwards, before being subsumed by the mass and reproduced somewhere else. The closer they got, the louder the screams, until they were almost deafening. No words or meaning, just howls of pain and torment.

Two sheets of arrows were loosed from the overlooking cliffs. The void legionnaires fired first, swiftly followed by the warriors of Ice. They targeted all three of the abominations, burying hundreds of arrows in each, but there were no cries of celebration. From the moment the bows flexed there were whispered words of doubt about their effectiveness – whispers that became shouts when the creatures didn't slow down, or even appear to notice the blanket of arrows sticking in them. Another volley was launched from each cliff, this time with the arrows aflame, but the reaction on the beach was no different, and the fires were quickly extinguished by the rolling movements of the creatures.

The abominations spread out even further and reached the outer barricades, groping at the wooden construction with hands and legs. Santos Spirit Killer was nearby and commanded his warriors to hurl pitch and fire into the killing ground, quickly causing the narrow space to erupt in flame. All of our forces on the second, higher wall took a step back and shielded their eyes.

"Where the fuck are you all going?" I shouted. "Get those spears front and centre. You will cut any flesh that gets close enough to be cut. Now!"

The void legionnaires were hesitant, but they obeyed, locking rectangular shields and bracing their long spears. The Sea Wolves had less range with their cutlasses and falchions, but were quicker to respond, striding back to the defensive wall.

"Ready your wyrd!" I boomed, primarily addressing my own people. "If fire and blades don't stop them, it may be all we have."

I was at the eastern edge of our barricades, within spitting distance of the closest abomination, but I could see all three through the fire, equally spaced and bubbling across the first wall. The fire caused no more reaction than the arrows, though it produced a sickening smell and blistered the exposed flesh of a thousand slimy corpses.

"Stand firm," commanded Santos. "Ready to strike."

"Strike to sever," I added. "Not pierce. Cut off the arms and legs, slow them down. They're not alive... we can't kill them."

Santos, the commander of the second void legion, looked terrified, but no worse than any other man or woman standing on the barricades. "You heard," he shouted. "Spears aloft, strike down." He nodded at me. "Good luck to us all, Adeline Brand."

The order was relayed and thousands of void legionnaires raised their spears. The weapons had broad blades and tremendous leverage when used to cut from a high angle. It was a bad move in a conventional fight, but this was different. Simply stabbing these vast mounds of body parts seemed futile.

Our huge defensive line was suddenly filled with shouting, as if everyone had got their voices back. I heard Kieran Greenfire, positioning his warriors as close to the front as possible. I heard Siggy Blackeye, directing mobs of Sea Wolves between every company of legionnaires. At the edge of my view, at the opposite end of our defences, was Wilhelm Greenfire, the High Captain. Behind our lines, Xavyer Ice, the Grim Wolf, was directing thousands more warriors to join us on the barricades. Behind him, Jessimion Death Spell held the rear. If we broke, the commander had enough of his own legion to fall back and defend Utha's Gate, at least for a little while. I silently hoped that Tomas Red Fang was close to finding a way to shut it permanently.

Then my eyes were drawn back to the forward barricades. The three abominations were now wriggling through the killing ground, still on fire, but unconcerned, as they groped and tumbled towards the second wall. Their screams continued, making it hard to hear orders, but we managed a coordinated attack nonetheless. The best part of an entire void legion struck downwards, flexing their spears and cutting at the flailing limbs. Hands and feet, arms and legs, pieces of a hundred bodies were severed and flew into the air. Most of the limbs were on fire and sent sickening chunks of blackened flesh across our lines.

"Again!" shouted Santos Spirit Killer.

The creatures didn't react to their injuries, nor did they slow down. It was only the second wall, too high for the abominations to simply ignore, that stopped them. The second spear strike was less forceful than the first, and delivered with hesitance and fear. More limbs were severed, but dozens of void legionnaires took a backwards step, as reaching arms topped the second barricade. They couldn't roll over the sturdy, wooden wall, but they could pull it apart. For a moment, they stopped, smashing against the obstacle, but unable to move past it. The one closest to me was a ball of screaming faces, stuck together by frogspawn, with pulsing flesh and arms moving across its mass.

I wanted to draw my cutlass and advance, but the simple movement of grasping the hilt caused pain in my side and reminded me I wasn't yet able to fight. I was forced to watch as Kieran led the closest group of Sea Wolves against the abomination. Spears were of little use now, and it fell to a company of Sea Wolves to cut and slice any arm or leg that reached for the barricade.

People started to die, pulled from the barricades by a thousand arms. Some were torn apart, others caught fire and howled themselves to death, but most were simply crushed under the vast fleshy creatures, disappearing in pools of blood and slime. All across our lines, the abominations attacked wood and people with equal brutality, as if everything was simply an obstacle to be destroyed. Sea Wolf duellists, warriors of Ice, void legionnaires, sailors from *Halfdan's Revenge*, they were all treated like flies, buzzing around a superior creature.

"Wyrd!" I roared, summoning my own spiritual power and seeing every Sea Wolf close to me do the same. The Dark Brethren were not accustomed to displaying their wyrd in such an explosive fashion, but many at least tried.

A sudden line of crackling, light blue energy formed along the second wall, accompanied by a frenzied snarl from the Sea Wolves. Pockets of black and red light emerged, where the Dark Brethren surged outwards to join us, and the three abominations were suddenly flung backwards. They couldn't ignore our wyrd, as they could ignore our fire and steel. It was the only barrier we had that repelled them – but it was finite.

I turned from the wooden wall and scanned the low ground, searching for Daniel Doesn't Die. The Sundered Wolf and his black dust may be our only chance of destroying the abominations without an unacceptable loss of life. The more defenders who died, the more the balance tipped in favour of Alexis Wind Claw and the Winterlords. Sooner or later, we'd manage to hack the vast creatures apart, but if it cost hundreds of lives it would leave Nowhere vulnerable to a conventional invasion.

"Tasha, go and find Daniel," I snapped. "We need his dust now!"

The Kneeling Wolf cook had turned her back on the killing ground and was eager to accept my order, or indeed any excuse to turn from the frontline. She hopped from the platform and pushed her way through massed Sea Wolves, asking everyone if they'd seen Daniel. It appeared none had, and she quickly moved inland.

"We need to retreat," said Santos Spirit Killer. "We can't hold them here."

"Then where?" I replied. "Cold Point? They can just go around it. Utha's Gate? It's in the middle of open ground. We hold them here, or we don't hold them at all."

I scanned across to where Jessimion Death Spell loitered, behind the frontline. "Death Spell!" I shouted. "Take your legion back to the gate. Help Tomas Red Fang get it closed. But stand by."

He'd heard me and we locked eyes, but the order was relayed nonetheless. Everyone within earshot made sure the commander of the third void legion knew exactly what I'd said. It was an admission that we might lose, and it travelled swiftly across the thousands of warriors in our rearguard, letting everyone know that this might be our last battle. It was a credit to their loyalty and conviction that no one broke or retreated. Everyone here was committed, whether it be to the Eastron, the Wolves, the Brethren, the Stranger, the First Fang, or just in angry defiance of the Sunken God.

"Adeline!" shouted Tasha, waving her arms to be seen above the press of warriors. "I found him."

She was pushing through the rearguard, accompanied by Daniel Doesn't Die and Charlie Vane. Behind them was a mob of killers from the *Lucretia*, and a dozen of Eva's Sundered Wolves, pulling three barrel-laden carts.

"Get up here," I shouted, before turning back to the killing ground.

Our barrier of wyrd was holding for now, but less powerful Eastron were already beginning to back away, their spiritual energy spent. Strangely, it was the Dark Brethren void legionnaires who maintained the barrier, using their wyrd more sparingly than the Sea Wolves. The three abominations kept bashing against the crackling barrier, apparently unable to comprehend something they couldn't simply destroy.

"I'm going to get drunk after this," said Daniel, wheezing his way up to join me on the barricade. "Fuck me, look at them... all arms and legs."

"Finally, something you've never seen," I replied. "Now, do you have a surprise for them?"

He didn't answer straight away, just grinned at me. The Sundered Wolf appeared to enjoy being obtuse and annoying. After a moment, he nodded back to where Charlie Vane and his Kneeling Wolf raiders were distributing small wooden casks amongst themselves. Thirty casks in all, being swiftly distributed along our lines.

I grabbed him by the throat. Even with the wound in my side I could exert enough strength to make him splutter and grab my arm. "Listen, you fat cunt, those things could kill us all, or leave us exposed and vulnerable. If you have an answer, deliver it, or I'll strangle you out of sheer fucking frustration." I slowly released my grip and shoved him backwards.

"Trust me," he murmured, rubbing his neck. "We needed to do this anyway, to repel the whips. I suppose killing those things can be a happy by-product."

I saw our barrier of wyrd begin to falter, as exhausted men and women started to faint along the wooden wall. Close by, both Kieran Green Fire and Siggy Blackeye were still pulsing with wyrd, but even they were pushing themselves into unconsciousness. Gradually, one flailing limb at a time, the abominations crept forwards, testing the shrinking barrier and finding small gaps.

"Do it now," I said, through gritted teeth.

Daniel Doesn't Die nodded and bent forwards over the wooden wall, assessing our lines. Half the Kneeling Wolves had delivered their casks to the appointed place on the wall, and the others were swiftly following. From our position on the right-hand side of the barricade, to the High Captain, commanding the far left, they formed a broken line, preparing to throw their casks over the wall. At the midpoint, an evil grin on his face, Charlie Vane, called the War Rat, stood defiantly on the barricade.

Then Daniel raised his arm. The closest Kneeling Wolf did the same, until all of the cask-bearers had an arm in the air. Our lines were silent for a moment. Thousands of Eastron took a breath. Many fell to the wooden platform, their wyrd spent and their strength gone. When Daniel dropped his arm, so did the Kneeling Wolves, and the thirty casks were hefted from the barricade. At the same time, our barrier of wyrd spluttered and began to disappear. Suddenly, the only Eastron on the inner wall using his spiritual power was Daniel Doesn't Die.

I'd seen him use his wyrd only once before, aboard *Halfdan's Revenge*. It had been an explosion of red and gold, and far more powerful than anything I'd seen from other Eastron. On this occasion, it emerged from his body as a fiery bird, unfolding two sets of huge wings and releasing a shrill caw. It was a phoenix, a much smaller version of Anya's Friend, the vast spirit that had taken the *Revenge* through the void. With warm eyes of burning red and a noble crest of golden feathers, the phoenix soared from Daniel's body as if it were lighter than air, leaving a glittering trail behind it. Those defenders still conscious stood in awe of the bird, silently marvelling at the Sundered Wolf's bizarre spiritual power.

Then the bird's movements became a fiery blur as it plunged along the line of thrown casks like a comet, shooting through the killing ground. The first explosion was close, then the second and third struck one of the abominations. Swiftly, one by one, each of the thirty casks of black dust was struck by the phoenix, sending a wall of fierce flames outwards. Most of my warriors took cover, but Daniel had somehow made sure the fire burst outwards, leaving us unharmed.

The smoke and flames were all-encompassing, reducing my world to a few feet in each direction. There was a sharp ringing in my ears, and with only one arm to shield my eyes, I was forced to close them. Tasha was huddled next to me, and Daniel had collapsed, face-first from the wall, landing in a heap behind us. The phoenix had not returned and the Sundered Wolf had likely expended his wyrd.

As my ears cleared, I could no longer hear the maddening screams of the abominations. I stood, helping Tasha up, and tentatively walked along our line. Others did the same, with those unconscious or dying being helped backwards from the wall. We'd lost a few hundred. Hundreds more had used more wyrd than was wise and would need time to recover.

"Steady," I said, passing in front of haunted men and women. "Keep eyes front when the smoke clears."

I passed Kieran, just getting to his feet and retrieving his cutlass. Then Siggy, scraping her falchion across the wooden wall and gnashing her teeth.

"Adeline, listen," said Tasha. "I hear something. Sounds like... cheering."

We stopped on the barricade and the smoke quickly danced into mere wisps. From above the diminishing blanket of grey and black, the defenders on the near cliff top came into view. Legionnaires of the third were waving their bows in the air and shouting down at us. Their shouts were jubilant and accompanied with embraces and boisterous swearing. As the wisps turned into clear air, we all saw what they were cheering at. The three abominations were now twitching mounds of black, cracking and glowing with embers, like huge, burned trees. All around them, the top of the beach was also now black. The fire had solidified the dust, forming a wide line in front of our barricades.

I felt anger rise within me and began breathing heavily. "Fuck you!" I shouted at the now dead creatures. "Fuck you and your god!" I found a high point on the wall and stood at my full height, spreading my arm and my stump. "No gods, spirits or men hold dominion over us! Once more for the Eastron!"

17

For a time, silence reigned. It was not the kind of silence in which you could find peace or rest. It was an angry silence, during which people feared to close their eyes or breathe too slowly. There were bodies to be retrieved and wounded to be cared for. This gave us purpose, but did nothing to alleviate the silence. As hours passed, it became clear that no additional attack was imminent. The ships at anchor off Duncan's Fall didn't move. I hoped that Alexis Wind Claw was raging at her failure and not plotting another wave of aggression against our barricade – but I was probably being naive. All I could really hope for was that she had no more piles of Sea Wolf corpses to throw at us.

My own wound was healing quickly, and with each passing hour I could move more freely. Next time we needed to fight, I'd be ready. As for the rest of the defenders, the most alarming thing was that Dark Brethren, Sea Wolves, Kneeling Wolves and Sundered Wolves were all working together. The legionnaires had mostly discarded their helmets, creating a sudden humanity amongst them that their customary armour was designed to suppress. Our Eastron camps didn't seem to matter any more, and men and women mingled freely. If the silence had not been so pervasive, I imagined they'd be laughing and joking together, as warriors do when they've fought together and defeated a more powerful enemy.

Word had spread quickly, and I'd made sure to inform Jessimion Death Spell and the Grim Wolf of our victory. We were able to keep Utha's Gate open a while longer, and ferry more people through to the void realm. Of course, I still didn't know if Tomas was even able to close the doorway. There was much pressure on the old spirit-master, but I trusted him. He, like Rys Coldfire, was a reminder of the world we were leaving. We'd spent a lifetime together at the Severed Hand, and I saw in all three of us the means to keep the Sea Wolves alive.

As it began to get dark, I found a secluded corner of a temporary wooden pavilion and fell asleep. Around me, sheltering on narrow canvas beds, were Tasha, Kieran, Siggy and Daniel. Without exception we all fell asleep within moments of reclining. The void legionnaires were elsewhere, catching what rest they could in their own black tents. Wilhelm Greenfire, the High Captain, had declined sleep and was making sure the barricades remained full of warriors, while testing his diplomatic skills with Santos Spirit Killer and the second void legion. Death Spell remained at Utha's Gate, probably taking his own rest, before the sun rose and more innocent people needed to be shepherded into the far void. We needed two or three days at least. After that, it was the simple matter of closing the gate. If only it were simple.

As I slept, I felt myself gently falling through the glass. Dreams and reality mingled together in a strange soup, as if my mind had been braised for a few hours with some carrots and onions. When I opened my eyes, I felt a cool breeze, ruffling my hair and making my skin tingle. It was daytime and I wasn't in a wooden pavilion. The gentle breeze was followed by a familiar peace as I woke up in the void realm, beyond Utha's Gate. My first breath was crisp and clean, filling my lungs with a calming warmth. After the battle at Duncan's Fall, it was the nicest possible place to wake up.

I sat, rubbing my eyes and flexing my neck. I'd been reclining on the bare stone of a high gallery within the Shadow, the dark citadel at the head of the huge, green valley. I was still dressed in the thin tunic and leather trousers I'd fallen asleep in, and the wound in my side was almost fully healed.

"You are *ridiculously* tough," said an odd voice.

I turned along the gallery. Standing against a black railing, with the sun rising behind him, was a pale man with long, braided white hair. He was stocky, with large shoulders, and wore a simple black robe. He was strange looking, but otherwise appeared to be a normal man.

"Utha," I said. "That's your name?" I stood up and stalked to the railing, a little way from the pale man.

"Yes," he replied, in a precise accent.

"I think we met once," I said. "At the Severed Hand. After the chaos spawn attacked. You looked different and you tried to control my mind. The Old Bitch of the Sea protected me."

He nodded. "The shadow form was necessary to defeat the spirits. The mind control – I no longer try such things. I've learnt that your people respond to other stimulus." His white skin and pink eyes managed to convey much regret. There was even a slight vulnerability, deep within his expression.

I took a stride forwards and punched him. It was a right hook, landing on his jaw and rocking him backwards. He didn't fall, but stumbled back to the railing, clutching his jaw.

"Your reputation suggests nothing less than a punch in the face," said the pale man. "I'm sure there is nuance and thought behind your fist, but please don't do that again."

"It was deserved," I replied. I then offered him my hand.

He narrowed his eyes, but shook my hand after a moment's hesitation.

"This is deserved too," I said.

"A punch and a handshake," replied Utha. "Your people remain something of a mystery to me."

"You're the reason we'll endure," I said. "But you're also part of the reason why so many of us are dead. So, what did you want to talk about?"

He laughed. Behind his expressive eyes, oddly precise accent and white skin, I saw nothing intimidating in the man. He was Marius Cyclone's shadowy benefactor, who had first told the Eastron of the Sunken God, and started a cascade that would see one world end and another begin. That he was only now choosing to speak to me, suggested he had something to say.

"My view of the Sea Wolves has not always been especially positive," he began. "I'm sure the influence of Marius has something to do with that. He is somewhat uncertain as to why you hate him so much."

"Because he's an arrogant, slimy cunt," I replied with a smirk, aware that I didn't really believe this any more and was adhering to a Sea Wolf stereotype.

"Indeed," said Utha, returning my smirk. "As I was saying, for misjudging your people, you have my apologies. For everything you have done to help the Eastron, you have my thanks. You've done far more than Marius could have done alone."

"Okay," I replied, suspicious of his long-winded speech patterns. "Is that what you wanted to talk about?"

"No, no it isn't."

"Then kindly get to the point. I have a lot to do. There's a massive fucking fleet off Duncan's Fall, no doubt conspiring more unpleasant ways to breech our defences."

"Very well," he replied. "I want you to wait for Marius. Sooner or later you'll find a way to close the gate. When you do, I want you to wait. He of all people should not be left behind."

"Hmm," I said, surprised by this request.

I turned from the pale man and took a long look down the vibrant green and brown valley. Tens of thousands of Eastron could be seen, with tens of thousands more exploring through the virgin land.

"Duncan Greenfire and his little imp told me the Sunken God could come through the gate. I assume he was telling the truth?"

"He was," replied Utha.

"And you want me to wait?" I asked, raising an eyebrow.

"For Marius? Yes."

"Two or three days," I said. "That's how long it should take to get the last few refugees through your gate, not including the island's defenders. Depending on the ease of our retreat from Duncan's Fall, this will all be over in three days – assuming we can close the fucking gate." I kept my eyebrow raised. "You know how to close it, don't you?"

"I do," he replied, again showing me a sliver of regret. "I hoped you'd find it yourself."

I laughed, banging my fist on the railing. "Talking of arrogant, slimy cunts. You'll withhold this information for the sake of the Stranger?"

"No!" he snapped. "I withheld this information because it requires a decision I don't want to have to make a second time. My debt to Marius is separate."

"Tell me how to close the gate," I snarled, meeting him face to face. "If it's within my power to save Marius, I will do so – but not at the expense of the Eastron. You have my word."

"Your word is enough," said Utha.

"Tell me," I repeated.

The pale man bowed his head, and the regret in his eyes morphed into pain and conflict. Whatever else he was, I thought that Utha was a deeply moral individual.

"To open the gate, I had to consume the wyrd of a powerful Eastron. Duncan Greenfire. He sacrificed his power willingly, because he knew the pain spirit within him would save his life. He endures in the void. The Eastron you must sacrifice to close the gate will not have that luxury. Someone will have to die. That was the decision I didn't want to have to make. Sea Wolves have the unique ability to detonate their wyrd, and one will need to do it."

"That is unexpected," I replied. "But simpler than I'd feared."

"It matters nothing if the Sunken God reaches the gate," said Utha. "I do understand that. But if you wait for Marius, he may bring you another option. Perhaps even a way to draw the enemy's eye from Nowhere."

★

The conversation with Utha did nothing to affect my sleep. When I awoke, surrounded by friends and allies, I felt well rested and clear headed. A good thing too, as I was faced with a difficult decision. My first reaction was to sacrifice myself, safe in the knowledge that thousands of other Eastron would do the same if given the opportunity. But perhaps it wasn't that simple.

As I washed and dressed, sharing gallows humour with Siggy and Kieran, I had two questions to answer. Who would close the gate? And when would we close it? Marius and the last of his refugees were overdue, and it was easy to assume they were dead. Santago Cyclone and Oliver Dawn Claw were still loitering out there somewhere. My hunch was that, if they were not at Nowhere, they were hunting down the Stranger.

I splashed water on my face for the third time and took a deep breath. At the far end of the wooden pavilion, Wilhelm Greenfire and Charlie Vane were finally accepting that they needed some rest. They'd been on the barricades all night, making sure we didn't let our guard down. Now, with red eyes, the two of them approached to give their report, before falling into an exhausted sleep.

"Adeline," grunted the High Captain, nodding at Kieran, his only living son. "No movement off Duncan's Fall, except a bit of flailing from the Winterlords."

"They're all heavy armour and broadswords," added the War Rat. "The shiny bastards can't fit their ships into the Red Straits and they can't get ashore without getting dead. It's pretty fucking funny watching them strategize."

"They almost launched boats a few times," said Wilhelm. "But the archers on the cliffs made them behave. This is a good place, Adeline. We can defend it."

"But what does that line of black stuff do?" mused Charlie Vane. "It's turned hard on the beach."

"We may have other visitors," replied Daniel Doesn't Die, pulling on a dark green tunic and involving himself in our conversation. There was a tattoo on his chest that I'd seen once before, displaying a rampant bear, growling outwards. "Eastron aren't repelled by the dust, but Sunken Men and whips are."

The War Rat and the High Captain looked at each other. They'd bonded during the defence of the Sea Wolf refugee fleet and now appeared to share a clear understanding. Hearing the Sundered Wolf's reply, they both rolled their eyes and made for the nearest bedrolls. It was done in near perfect unison and made Kieran chuckle at his father.

"One last thing," said Wilhelm, barely able to keep his eyes open. "Word from the northern cliffs. It looks like the last refugee ships from the Dark Harbour have finally arrived."

"The platforms are bringing them ashore," added Charlie, slumping face first onto a thin mattress.

"The Stranger?" I asked.

"Not seen," replied Wilhelm. "So far all we've heard is *Dolcinite Pilgrims*, whoever they are. There's a woman called Antonia, seems to be in charge." The High Captain slurred the last few words, before closing his eyes and falling asleep on his bedroll.

I took a moment to think, shovelling down the offered breakfast of hard bread and ham. Tasha stood next to me, nodding whenever I took a bite and encouraging me to eat more, with an elaborate series of nods, raised eyebrows and happy sounds. Outside the pavilion, I could see hundreds of Wolves and Brethren, shaking themselves awake and preparing for another day defending Nowhere. Within the next few days, we'd have to start sending the defenders back to Utha's Gate. Like Marius Cyclone, each of them had earned a place in our new world, but it was a delicate balancing act to keep the barricade secure as we retreated.

"Right," I said, tossing aside the crust of my second chunk of bread. "Let's get to the northern cliffs and find out where the fuck the Stranger has got to."

Those closest to me reacted by pulling on their boots, buckling on their weapons and stuffing as much food as was possible into their mouths, before trooping out of the wooden pavilion. Kieran and Siggy had become almost as close to me as Tasha, and Kieran had even stopped blaming me for Tynian Driftwood's decision to stay behind. Together with Tasha and Daniel Doesn't Die, they formed my inner circle. Siggy generally did my shouting for me, Tasha reminded me to take care of myself, and Kieran told me when I was being an idiot. As for Daniel, his position was somewhat nebulous, but I wanted him close by from this point onwards. I would have liked Rys Coldfire to be with us, but the Wolf's Bastard was at Cold Point, with Elizabeth Defiant. Once the Winterlord scholar was secure and comfortable, I expected him to return.

We left the pavilion and commandeered a supply cart to take us north. I was used to incessant grumbling from Sea Wolves, who could generally find something to complain about in the most mundane of activities, but now there was nothing. The only chatter was light-hearted. As the cart clattered over uneven ground, moving quickly away from Duncan's Fall, I found myself laughing more than I had in days.

"I think Rys Coldfire is obsessed with you," said Kieran, grinning at Daniel Doesn't Die. "Don't be surprised if he starts sticking sharp things in your head, just to see what happens."

Siggy nodded. "I saw his eyes brighten when he asked about fire. Maybe he'll just start burning you at inopportune moments. You know... hiding behind corners with an oil lantern." She mimicked the action of the Wolf's Bastard jumping out at the Sundered Wolf. "Boo!"

"I'd keep an eye out next time you're having a piss," added Kieran.

"Fuck off," muttered Daniel, trying to look angry while chuckling to himself.

"Elizabeth will stop him hurting you," I said. "Turns out he's a bit of a softy really."

"You should see the cottage he's building," said Tasha. "It's really nice. And he likes fishing."

"It's true," I replied. "He'd retired until I went and dragged him back."

Daniel shook his head. "A man like that doesn't retire. A man like that dies. He'll keep killing until something kills *him*. I'd call it his life's work – fighting anything he can fight, angry that nothing is his match. His life will only make sense when he dies."

The rest of us looked at each other, momentarily silent at Daniel's morbid assessment of the Wolf's Bastard. The cart was jolting left and right, but only gently, as we approached the cliffs north of Cold Point.

"When you're not being annoying," I said, "you're actually quite wise. But you've kicked my good mood in the face."

"And mine," agreed Kieran.

"Anyone would think the world was ending," said Siggy, slapping Tasha on the back.

A final peal of laughter flowed over the cart as we came to a stop. Ahead of us, close to where we'd blown up a section of the cliffs to block a trail inland, stood a gathering of robed Dark Brethren. They certainly weren't void legionnaires. In fact, the only weapons I could see were quarterstaffs. Mingling amongst the robes were groups of thin, ragged people, being helped ashore. These were the homeless and downtrodden of the Dark Harbour.

We left the cart and I led the way to the cliff top. The People of Ice had erected huge gantries here to bring people up from the bottom of the sheer stone walls, with balanced platforms allowing dozens of people to travel up at once. Below us was a small fleet of Brethren ships, who'd managed to sneak their way to Nowhere without riling Alexis Wind Claw's ships at Duncan's Fall.

Andre, the young legionnaire formerly tasked with keeping an eye on me, was acting as a first point of contact for the newcomers, distributing food, blankets and what information he could give. When he saw me, he broke off from the refugees and approached, bringing a red and black robed woman with him.

"My lady First Fang," said Andre. "May I present Antonia, of the Dolcinite Pilgrims."

The woman bowed to me. "I am humble in your presence," she said, in a deep voice. I was surprised that the leader of the refugees was a young woman, still in her twenties. "I have the honourable good fortune of speaking for these people."

"Good to meet you, Antonia," I said, offering my hand.

Andre shook his head at me. "She won't shake your hand, but it's not meant as an insult."

I withdrew the gesture. "Very well. Will you at least tell me where the Stranger has disappeared to?"

Antonia was still bowing, and I noticed that her feet were bare. She placed both her hands against her chest, as if emphasizing the truth of her reply. "Lord Marius attacked Prince Oliver's fleet on his own. He enabled the rest of us to escape. Last we saw, his ship was leading the enemy north-east, away from Nowhere. He gambled that they wanted him more than us. We are truly not worthy of his sacrifice."

"Fuck," I grunted. "I thought we'd at least know if he was alive or dead."

"Sounds like he's dead," offered Kieran Greenfire. "How good is his ship? And does he have people who can sail it?"

"Is it that floating wedge?" asked Siggy. "Ugly black thing, but its hull repels ballistae almost as well as an ironclad? The *Dead Horse* fought it once, off the Emerald Coast. Cold Man wasn't happy when the Stranger managed to get away."

Antonia didn't raise her head and her curious reverence was making all of us a little uncomfortable. "His vessel is called the *Dangerous*. I speak with little authority, but it is believed to be the finest Dark Brethren warship."

"Indeed," I replied, smirking at Siggy. "I'm sure it's formidable. What chases him?"

"His brother, Santago, has ten fast cutters, and the prince has a huge ironclad."

"Hmm," I murmured. "One moment, Antonia, I need to confer with these two."

Between Siggy, Kieran and I we had much knowledge of seamanship, but all three of us were chewing our lips in thought. "What do you think?" I asked them.

"Tricky," replied Kieran.

"The ironclad won't be able to catch him," added Siggy. "But the cutters…"

"Ten cutters versus an ugly black wedge," I said.

"Can the Stranger sail?" asked Kieran. "I'm from Last Port, remember. I don't know much about Marius Cyclone."

"People have lost much betting against him," I replied. "If you pressed me, I'd say he's one of their better sailors."

"As I remember, the ship's got a good captain," offered Siggy. "I think Cold Man called him Black Dog. And they'll have legionnaires."

"North-east," I mused. "Heading into the Crown Sea. If they live, it could be weeks before they get here. Fuck!"

"Why does it vex you so much?" asked Daniel, again involving himself without being asked. "It's only one ship."

I glared at him. "I hate Marius Cyclone as much as anyone, but that shimmering doorway into the far void is here because of him. I won't just write him off until I have no choice. I gave my word to someone, someone who says the Stranger may be able to help us. We shouldn't abandon him."

"Adeline," exclaimed Tasha, smiling at me. "That was a truly honourable thing to say. I'm proud of you."

"Very well," conceded Daniel, taking a step back.

"You, Andre, get these people ashore as quickly as possible. I want them travelling through Utha's Gate with the others. Antonia, raise your fucking head."

The Dolcinite Pilgrim was reluctant, but spread her arms and looked at me. "I am humble and know of my sins," she whispered.

"I'm sure you do. Now, help your people to the gate and find an old Sea Wolf called Tomas Red Fang. You can't miss him, he's got skin like paper. Tell him I know how to close the gate."

"It will be as you say, noble First Fang," replied Antonia.

"And what are *we* doing?" asked Kieran, scratching his shaved head.

"Defending this fucking island for another few days. Until each and every Eastron on this island is safe and free."

Suddenly everyone's ears pricked up, as a galloping horse approached from the south. I waved Andre and Antonia back to the rapidly spreading mob of refugees from the Dark Harbour, and went to receive the rider. It was Hitch, formerly the lookout of *Halfdan's Revenge*. He was a small man, wearing thin clothing, on a light horse. Whatever message he had to deliver had been sent with great alacrity.

"What's so urgent?" I shouted, just as Hitch wheeled his horse to a stop in front of us.

"You won't fucking believe it," he replied, flexing his legs to relieve saddle soreness. "They shot a white arrow onto the beach. The bastards wanna parlay."

18

I didn't like having so many things in my head. I preferred life to be simple, but was struggling to remember the last time it *had* been simple. A duellist of the Severed Hand, who'd seen her friends and family die, thrust into leadership. That was me, that was Adeline Brand. I was the First Fang of the wolves who sail, the wolves who kneel, and the wolves who are sundered. It was a new title, given no ceremony or mark of office. Everyone just heard it and accepted it. There was a time when this would have caused me to doubt myself and over-think everything. Not now. Now, I was committed to a single goal – getting as many people as possible through Utha's Gate before closing it.

By mid-morning, I was back at the barricade, looking out across the beach from a raised platform in the middle of our defences. The ships in the bay had tried to deploy, forming a wide opening for a single launch to approach the rocky beach. The Red Straits bulged as the cumbersome ironclads twisted and turned into position behind the Brethren ships, attempting to provide cover for the launch. It was a laughable display of seamanship and sent a ripple of mirth across our lines. No one on the barricade was scared, not any more, and thousands of Eastron glared at the incoming boat, gliding towards the beach under a white flag.

"My lady," said Santos Spirit Killer. "I should go with you. You represent your people, and I'll represent mine."

"Very well," I replied. "Do you know Alexis Wind Claw?"

"By reputation," he said. "She and her brother are inheritors of a different era, when the Dark Brethren revelled in dominance and treachery. They're descendants of Medina Wind Claw, the first lord of the Open Hand."

"They sound fucking delightful," I replied.

The launch struck the beach, next to the abandoned monument of *Halfdan's Revenge*. The tide was higher, and all the ships we'd left were gently rolling in the shallows. The Brethren sailors had searched each of them, but no one had been dragged out and executed. I imagined Tynian Driftwood was hiding somewhere in the hold of his ship, sipping liquor and awaiting the end of the world. Either that, or he'd just been unceremoniously killed when they found him.

"They got a Winterlord with them," shouted Charlie Vane from further up the barricade. "Big guy in armour."

"Who else?" I shouted back.

"Skinny woman. Bunch of Brethren sailors. Ten in all."

I turned back to Santos. "Ten it is. You and me, four of mine, four of yours. Let's hope it goes better than our last parlay."

"Agreed," he said.

"Give me a moment," I said, hopping down from the barricades and going to find Tasha Strong.

The Kneeling Wolf cook was helping a wounded Sea Wolf change the dressing on his damaged shoulder, wrapping fresh bandages around a grisly cut. I waited for her to finish before pulling her aside. She wasn't coming with us to parlay, but there was something important I needed to tell her.

"What's up?" she asked cheerfully, washing the blood from her hands in a bucket of seawater.

"This parlay might be a trap," I said. "And I can't walk into a potential trap being the only one who knows how to close the gate."

"You should tell Siggy or Kieran," she said. "Or Tomas."

"I'm going to tell you," I stated. "And *you* need to tell Tomas Red Fang."

Her cheerfulness disappeared. "If you think it's best, Adeline."

"Listen carefully," I began, standing close to her. "Opening the gate needed an Eastron to burn all of their wyrd. Closing it requires the same. A Sea Wolf needs to detonate their power within Utha's Gate. Do you understand?"

She hesitated, her eyes flicking back and forth. "Someone has to die?"

"Someone has to die," I confirmed.

"What about Daniel?" she asked, smiling again, as if she'd thought of something terribly clever. "He could do it and stay alive."

I shook my head. "It takes training. As far as I know, the craft is unknown outside the Sea Wolves." She looked upset at the news. "Are you listening, Tasha? It's important."

"Yes, yes, I understand. So, who will it be?"

"Just tell Tomas," I replied. "I need to go and be polite to someone who wants to kill us all… again." I walked away, without giving her anything else. I heard her say *good luck*, but I didn't respond.

Back on the barricade, Santos had assembled four of his legionnaires. They'd discarded their helmets, and two of them had even replaced their black armour with Sea Wolf leather, the easier to traverse the wooden walls. On my side, Siggy stood with three grizzled sailors from the *Revenge*. The ten of us moved to the centre of our lines, where a series of planks formed a temporary route down to the beach. Opposite us, past the three burned abominations and just pulling themselves out of the shallows of Duncan's Fall, were nine Dark Brethren and a single Winterlord.

I took a slow walk south, flanked by Siggy and Santos. We were a small dot on the landscape, with thousands of defenders looking at us from the barricade and the cliff tops. As we neared the midpoint of the beach, those opposite came into view.

The skinny woman was tall and elegant, with a flowing black cloak over what looked like velvet clothing. At her side was a hulking Winterlord in silver armour. I recognized him as Gustav High Heart, the commander of Falcon's Watch, who I'd met the last time they tried to parlay with us. However, the Winterlord duellist now had cruel burn marks across his face and head, likely the result of our black dust.

"Alexis Wind Claw!" I shouted. "Welcome to Nowhere. I'd offer you a drink, but I fucking hate you."

She didn't respond until our two groups had stopped, within ten feet of each other, forming two lines of ten. With the possible exception of the Winterlord, I judged my side as being the more formidable.

"Adeline Brand," said the elegant woman, as if greeting me at a dinner party, "I find it strange that I didn't know you only had one arm. What a peculiar thing. I'd pictured you a hundred different ways, but not like this. You're just a normal Sea Wolf. When I heard the Wolf's Bastard speak of you at the Silver Parliament, I imagined you a titan of Eastron might. But you're just a woman, aren't you?"

I sensed an angry bristle from Siggy Blackeye, but she knew Alexis was just trying to bully me, and she knew I could handle the taunts in an appropriate manner.

"Just a woman, perhaps," said Gustav High Heart, thrusting his chin at me. "But she killed Natasha Dawn Claw. Her foul craft killed the king's mother."

"*My* foul craft?" I barked. "What of yours? What of your fucking craft? You sent dead Sea Wolves against us, stuck together like a fucking mass-grave." I snarled at Alexis Wind Claw. "You wanted this parlay, not me."

She smirked, though there was a twitch of annoyance at the corners of her mouth. I sensed she was accustomed to a different kind of etiquette, where enemies jousted with each other, verbally sparring to get the upper hand. Rys would just say they talk too much, and either walk away or kill them.

"You are correct," said Alexis, her eyes flashing a rotten green colour. "I must remember to whom I am speaking. A lower class of Eastron requires a more guttural vocabulary."

"I'll make it simple," I said. "You and your god have been trying to kill us, and you have thus far failed. You can't beat us in a fight and you know it. It would be simpler for you to just fuck off, but apparently you have words. Yes?"

Siggy and the Sea Wolves laughed. Even Santos and his legionnaires displayed a certain boisterous confidence at my summation. The unity we'd found defending Nowhere had become a strange new kinship, with each side influencing the other.

"I do have words," replied Alexis, the twitch in her lips increasing. "I will set aside my... revulsion at your presence, and give you this last chance to surrender." She was being sincere, acting almost as if she was doing me a favour.

I narrowed my eyes, studying the slender face of Alexis Wind Claw, looking for signs of humour, or knowledge to which I wasn't privy. "If your god's driven you mad, just let me know."

She stopped twitching and the green in her eyes flared slightly. "I was tasked with taking Nowhere before..." She left the thought unfinished and I saw fear envelop her face. "Your resistance will end, one way or another. You must surrender to *me*. I have committed myself to it. What is your answer?"

I took a step towards her, making the Winterlord flinch. Alexis came to meet me, until we were face to face. "I believe I speak for all of the faithful Eastron from across the sea, when I say... no."

"So be it," she replied.

We locked eyes. Behind the fear and madness, I saw hatred. This woman really fucking hated me. To Alexis Wind Claw, I'd been little more than an annoyance. Then I'd become an obstacle. Now, finally, I was a hated enemy, refusing to move out of her way. She was of the Open Hand, with little experience of Sea Wolves, and I was glad to be giving her an education.

"We want nothing more of this realm of form," I said. "You can have it. Now, take your fleet and fuck off."

Her fear, madness, and hatred morphed into a single expression I couldn't identify. At the edges of her eyes, where the green light festered, I saw a rotten owl spirit. The Night

Wing, totem spirit of the Dark Brethren, was as corrupt as the Dawn Claw I'd seen at my parlay with the Winterlords. Rys had told me what happened at the Silver Parliament, and I knew Alexis was a powerful enemy, able to fly on wings of mouldy green wyrd. But right now she was neutered, unable to flex any kind of power for fear of being riddled with arrows from the flanking cliffs.

"You want us to leave?" she asked, the strange expression on her face twisting unnaturally. "You will get your wish. When we return to our ships, I will order every captain to sail west, away from Duncan's Fall. We will launch no more attacks at Nowhere."

I narrowed my eyes at her. What was I missing?

"Adeline," said Siggy, pointing upwards. "Look!"

I followed her gesture, over the heads of Alexis and her delegation, beyond the forest of sails at anchor off Duncan's Fall, to the northern coast of Nibonay. Somewhere to the south, above the Plains of Tranquillity, there boiled an enormous storm cloud. It was bubbling black and grey, with green edges, and stood in sharp contrast to the clear, blue skies all around it. There was something unnatural in the cloud, as if it meant harm to the rest of the sky. It was hard to place it geographically, though it was certainly further north than the remains of the Severed Hand, and moving slowly towards us.

Suddenly, I knew what it was. I knew why Alexis was afraid, and I knew why she would order her fleet to fall back. I'd been so wrapped up in defending Nowhere from the soldiers and abominations that I'd pushed the three whips to the back of my mind. The Vile Whip, the Bulbous Whip, and the Hateful Whip... they were here, maybe two or three hours from

Duncan's Fall. I gulped down my own fear, knowing that the Sunken God was not far behind.

Without saying anything further, Alexis gave a shallow bow of the head and started backing away. Gustav High Heart and the rest of her delegation did the same. They still faced us for ten feet or more, before turning sharply and hurrying back to their launch. Siggy, Santos and I just stood on the beach, staring at the eldritch cloud. They could both tell from my reaction that I knew what it signified, and that I was afraid.

"Shall we fall back to the barricade?" asked Santos. "Before this new curse arrives?"

"Yes," I replied, "I believe we should. And quickly."

We didn't run, for each of us kept half an eye on the storm cloud, but we moved back to our barricade far more quickly than we'd left it. We rushed past the low, outer wall, the line of solidified black dust, and the three ashen abominations, before being hefted back behind the higher, second wall.

"The fleet's deploying again," shouted Kieran, coming to greet us.

"They're fucking off," replied Siggy. "Something else is coming. Alexis doesn't want to be in the way."

"Is she afraid of a bit of rain?" asked Daniel Doesn't Die, nodding up at the storm cloud. "If so, she's less dangerous than I thought."

They all looked at me. Siggy and Santos had seen my face when I first saw the cloud, but everyone else wanted to hear why the parlay had ended so suddenly.

"It's not the rain," I said. "Nor the lightning, the thunder, or our fearsome defence of Nowhere."

Daniel stood and narrowed his eyes at the clouds. "Oh, fuck," he grunted, appearing to realize what the cloud signified. "I hoped we'd have more time."

"It's the whips," I announced. "We have a few hours."

Everyone within earshot straightened. The Sea Wolf defenders had all been at Hook Point and had seen the three huge creatures. The void legionnaires, now our close comrades, were told what this meant. Across our line, a thousand warriors looked to the south, as the news spread quickly. We'd fought back against anything and everything that had been thrown at us, but no one knew how to defend against this. Could they be stabbed? Could they be cut? Would our wyrd even affect them?

I let everyone gawp, then hopped down next to Daniel. "Black dust," I said, quietly. "Will it repel them?"

"In theory," he replied. "It repelled the First Whip at the Starry Sky." He looked across our line, then up to the cliffs, encircling Duncan's Fall. "We need to get some dust up to the cliffs. From what I remember, those whips are fucking big. The cliffs aren't high enough."

"Can it be done in time?"

He nodded, assessing the casks of black dust, stored behind our barricade. "If we don't delay."

Charlie Vane led a gang of Sundered Wolves and Kneeling Wolves, acting as Daniel's beasts of burden. They'd retrieved three carts full of dust from Eva Rage Breaker, who was busy with the final evacuation of Cold Point. All of the War Rat's men and women were fitter than Daniel, and most had discarded their armour and weaponry in an attempt to be swifter of foot.

"Charlie!" shouted Daniel. "You take the eastern cliff, I'll take the west."

"Righty ho," replied the War Rat, grinning at his warriors.

"Remember," continued the Sundered Wolf, "a thick line of dust along the edge of the cliff, then take cover and burn it. And hurry up."

"Already on my way," replied Charlie.

The group split into two, with each Eastron hefting a cask on each shoulder and beginning the jog up to the cliffs. Daniel was the last to leave, taking a few deep breaths and trying not to look too unfit.

"You'll get an impressive light-show in a few minutes," he said, before trudging up to the western cliff top.

I jumped back up to the barricade and peered to the south. Slowly, the narrow sea channel was emptying, as the Brethren cutters managed to find some empty water. The Winterlord vessels were far slower and managed to bump and jostle each other. A few even scraped along the northern rocks of Nibonay before they moved off. They'd be clear of Duncan's Fall in less than an hour. On any other occasion, their flailing would cause raucous laughter from the Sea Wolves, but not now. We had other things to worry about. The evacuation wasn't finished. To abandon our defences now would leave too many people still on Nowhere. I took a second to curse Utha the Ghost for creating a doorway that functioned so fucking slowly.

I was in the middle of the wooden wall, with Kieran, Siggy and Santos. Either side of us, the long, snaking platform was packed with men and women, staring at the storm cloud. Our auxiliary forces, behind the line, were jostling for position on top of carts and barrels, all to get a look at the whips. I found it strange that such collective fear had caused no one to run, or even falter. The defenders of Nowhere were without a doubt the toughest warriors the Eastron had ever produced. Maybe not in wyrd, or martial prowess, but in conviction. For the first time, we weren't fighting amongst ourselves, or for imagined supremacy; we were fighting for survival. It appeared to concentrate the mind.

"Adeline," whispered Siggy Blackeye. "Do you remember when I asked for your permission to die?"

I nodded, keeping my eyes to the south. "Yes. You survived the loss of two warships and thought that being lucky was a curse. You've done a lot of good since then, Siggy. Rys would say: don't think too much."

She smiled. "And *you* would say, no gods, spirits or men hold dominion over me... so I'll think all I fucking want."

I laughed and put my arm around her shoulders. "I don't say it much any more. Still think it though. Sorry, Siggy, what did you want to tell me?"

She returned my laugh and gave me a light dig in the ribs, before throwing my arm from her shoulders. "I wanted to tell you that I don't want to die any more. It's funny, before I knew the world was ending, I wanted to. Now, when I'm almost certain to die, I want to live."

"You definitely talk too much," I replied, smirking at her.

Before she could swear at me again, the two of us, and everyone else on the inner barricade, turned their eyes upwards, as both cliff tops erupted in flame. The fires started closest to the beach, then stretched away in a crisp, red and yellow line, like two enormous curtains had been drawn either side of us. The black dust behaved strangely when set alight. It wasn't consumed by the fire, but rather appeared to gain life from it, changing into a different form. In combat, it coated the enemy; when burned on rock or earth, it hardened into resin.

As the flames died down, a wall of thick smoke spread outwards, rolling across Duncan's Fall and the waters of the Red Straits. It didn't reach the fleeing ships, but the eruption and the smoke must have given them a fright. Other than what they'd seen us use against the abominations, no one in Alexis Wind Claw's fleet would know anything about the black dust. It made me smile to think that we'd not needed it against mortal men and women. Steel and wyrd did for them. Daniel's strange craft was reserved for things that couldn't be killed with sword and spear.

"Not to doubt the man who can't die," said Siggy, "but is that our only defence against them?"

"A line of black stuff," said Kieran Greenfire. "It's not exactly a fleet of Sea Wolf warships."

I raised my eyebrows. "You want to go and fight them at sea?"

"No I fucking do not," he replied. "I was just saying."

"I think the man who can't die and his black dust may indeed be our only defence," I said, calmly. "Now, order everyone back from the barricade. Swords and wyrd won't help here."

"Aye," they said in unison.

On this occasion, the void legionnaires responded to the order far quicker than the Wolves. Santos Spirit Killer and his warriors appeared to have no desire to see the whips, and quickly fell back from the wall, whereas the Sea Wolves all seemed to have a morbid desire to look the enormous creatures in the eyes.

At the far end of the line, the High Captain's warriors were the first Wolves to move, as Wilhelm Greenfire screamed at them to *get the fuck off the wall*. Closer to the centre,

Siggy and Kieran began dragging people backwards, until a general retreat was underway.

I stayed for a while longer.

The storm cloud over Nibonay was far closer now, and I thought the whips would appear any moment. As I stood alone on the barricade, trying to tune out the chatter of the two thousand warriors behind me, Daniel Doesn't Die returned from the cliff top and stood next to me. He was trying to pretend he wasn't out of breath, but beads of sweat dripped from his ample nose as he leant forwards across the wall.

"You really should exercise," I said.

"I like a sedentary lifestyle," he replied, taking deep breaths. "This is far more exciting and energetic than most of my life has been."

"The benefit of living forever," I replied. "You can waste as much of it as you like."

"Indeed," he said. "We can't close the gate yet, can we?"

I shook my head. "We need at least another day. Not to mention these fuckers down here. How long will it take for us all to run back to the gate? And Marius Cyclone still hasn't appeared. A strange pale man told me the Stranger would bring us help – though of what kind I can't imagine."

From either side of us, the cliff top archers reached the low ground. People of Ice came from the west and the second void legion from the east, until every defender of Nowhere had fallen back into a vast column behind the barricades.

Daniel wiped sweat from his brow and laughed. "I'd trust the pale man. There's a reason I retrieved *that* from Cold Point." He nodded to a cart behind us and the ornate chest it carried. It was Anya's Roar, the talisman that allowed a ship to fly through the void.

"What…" I didn't finish my question, as something from the south drew my eyes and ears.

A huge section of rock had fallen from the northern coast of Nibonay, as if announcing the arrival of the cloud. Its crackling black edges appeared to cut through both the air and the earth, drawing back a veil on the ancient monstrosities that approached. It felt as if a slice was being cut out of reality. A mouldy crest had appeared over the horizon. It was the Vile Whip, the tallest of the three.

"Another benefit of living forever," said Daniel, staring south. "You rarely see something new."

Gradually, the head of an immense misshapen toad appeared. It was flat and warty, coloured a sickly green, with mottled red patches. The whip's cruel, angular eyes were covered in a milky white film, which blinked and rippled, as if the creature was scanning the horizon. I thought it was lying flat, or at the very least crawling, perhaps to get a furtive first look at Nowhere. Apparently, the creature was unaware that its head was the size of a warship.

Then all two thousand of our warriors gasped, as an enormous, bloated frog hopped from the coast of Nibonay, to land in the Red Straits. It displaced the water with a deafening crash, sending a wave across the beach of Duncan's Fall. It was the Bulbous Whip, though none of us had seen it in such detail. The sea channel was deep enough for Winterlord ironclads, but the immense frog was barely covered to the belly. Its blubbery head was as tall as the cliffs, and the gurgling sound it made was deep and filled with phlegm. From its gummy mouth there rolled a white tongue, which licked across its full lips before shooting forth and grasping one of our smaller abandoned ships. The slimy tip stuck to the wood of the deck, and the vessel was effortlessly pulled into the whip's mouth, as a normal frog would snare an insect.

Finally, as the storm cloud destroyed the sunlight, the Hateful Whip appeared. It wasn't skulking like the Vile Whip, but standing proudly opposite us, on the low northern coastline of Nibonay. It was a bipedal fish, skeletal and covered in serrated red spines. Red veins pulsed across its body, and its grey skin was translucent.

Any one of the three whips was large enough to wade through our defences, swatting away any feeble attempt at resistance, until we were totally broken. I echoed Siggy and Kieran's doubts, but knew we had no choice but to trust in Daniel's black dust.

I turned away from the whips and smiled at the chubby Sundered Wolf. "If the rest of us die, Daniel, promise me you'll remember what happened here. Promise me the Eastron won't be forgotten."

PART SEVEN

Marius Cyclone on the Inner Sea

19

I was pulled through the glass. My senses had returned and every part of my body was painful – not just the bits that Oliver Dawn Claw had eaten, but every muscle, joint and extremity. I had no strength, no wyrd, and I felt as if my body was forcing itself to pump blood through my veins and air through my lungs. If I didn't concentrate – if I wasn't aware enough – I feared that my body would just give up and I'd be dead. A part of me still wished for it, but a larger part had defiance on his mind and curses on his lips. I wasn't sure what was happening, but I knew I was alive. For now, that was enough.

Entering the void was like sticking my head in a bucket of freezing water. From the mundane torments of a bare cabin aboard the ironclad, I was plunged into a world of colours too vibrant to process and a sky too endless to understand. I disliked the void at the best of times, but being dragged through it by Asha and Gaius Two Hearts was a deeply unpleasant experience.

My feet struck something, but I couldn't tell what. It certainly wasn't the void-sea, in which we'd surely drown. Whatever it was, it arced away like a floating dome, bridging the gap between the ironclad and the *Dangerous*. The Winterlord vessel had a modest reflection beyond the glass – appearing as a solid outline, but with little spiritual presence.

The same was true for the encircling cutters. Conversely, my own ship was almost as solid as it was in the realm of form. Whatever echo of Salty Alphonse remained gave the warship clean lines and a more vibrant complexion, with black appearing dark blue, and brown shining as a warm orange.

"Pick him up," said Asha Two Hearts.

"I am picking him up," replied Gaius. "I'm carrying more weight than you."

"You won the last arm-wrestle," she snapped. "You're the strongest until we wrestle again."

"I'll be the strongest then too," he bragged.

"So you carry more weight than me," she replied. "Stop fucking complaining."

Beyond the glass, the twins had glowing arms and legs, showing that their wyrd made them extremely dextrous and nimble. Unfortunately, they were not the strongest of Eastron, and I was a dead weight, considerably larger than either of them.

"Where are we?" I coughed, using considerable energy just to speak.

"We're on the shell of a huge turtle spirit," said Asha. "Seriously. We heard a spirit-whistle and it just appeared."

"And if we don't hurry up," added Gaius, "we're all gonna die."

I blinked my eyes and tried to focus on the voidscape. As long as I didn't look up, into the glaring, blue sky, I could keep my eyes open. Ground level – if the concept truly meant anything beyond the glass – was easier to look at, though no less spectacular. Ahead of us, arcing upwards, were the raised green sections of an enormous shell. Between the two ships was a huge neck, craning upwards to an imperious head. Ten

Cuts had told me of the great turtle spirits, how he'd listened to one for decades, and how they viewed time backwards, but I never thought to see one.

"How..."

"Marius, shut up," said Asha.

"We're rescuing you," snapped Gaius. "Be grateful."

"Why am I not dead?" I wailed. "I should be dead."

"So ungrateful," said Asha, repositioning my right arm over her shoulder.

They carried me across the shell of the turtle spirit, away from the ironclad and towards the stern of the *Dangerous*. The void-sea lapped at the edges of the shell, and the spirit filled a vast section of water, somehow blocking the ironclad from approaching in the realm of form. As we reached the highest point of the shell, the spirit's enormous, leathery neck craned backwards, until its golden brown eyes were looking at me. What I saw was more than a spirit. It was a primal entity, closer in scope to a mountain or even the sea itself. If there was an expression on its timeless face, I didn't understand it any more than I understood the eruption of a volcano or the changing of the tides. It was here, now, in the Inner Sea. Perhaps it had always known it would be here and was just doing what it remembered, or perhaps it had been drawn here.

"Hurry up," said Asha.

"I'm *hurrying* up," replied Gaius. "He's heavy."

With the turtle's enormous head following our movements, we began our descent down to the *Dangerous*. I didn't know what was happening in the realm of form, but I guessed Oliver Dawn Claw and the Winterlords would be more confused than me, wondering what had stopped their ship.

The Brethren cutters had no such impediment, but would be reluctant to attack my warship without the ironclad.

Then legionnaires of the twenty-third appeared in front of us. They were Esteban Hazat's warriors and they had come to assist us. After a moment of distress at the general state of my naked body, two large men took over the carrying duties, allowing the Two Hearts twins to grumble their way ahead of us.

"He's alive," said Asha. "But he's in a bad way."

"I think someone was eating bits of him," added Gaius.

"It was Oliver Dawn Claw," I grunted. "Why the fuck did you come back for me?"

"Just get him to the spirit-master," said Asha.

With stronger arms holding me, we sped up, until the spiritual reflection of the *Dangerous* loomed above us. Then, with a flash of wyrd, I was pulled back through the glass, into the dark wood of a ship's cabin.

"We got him!" roared Gaius. "Get the fucking ship moving!"

I couldn't tell who he was shouting to, nor which cabin I'd been brought into, but the shout was echoed through the bowels of the ship, rapidly spreading word of my rescue. Then, with a robe draped around my naked shoulders, I was gently placed upon a wooden table. Faces moved across my field of vision, but I struggled to focus. The cabin tilted and the ship started to move, but all I could do was whimper in pain. Most people left the cabin, with just two or three left, inspecting my broken body. I tried to smile and be grateful, as Asha and Gaius wanted, but I was in too much pain to force the expression. I couldn't even remember which bits of me had been eaten.

★

Waking suddenly from a dream is a strange experience. Sometimes you're confused and disorientated. Other times, you're startled and afraid. On very rare occasions, you wake up smiling and content, as if a warm blanket has enveloped you while you slept. On this occasion, I experienced the latter. My dreams had been indistinct, but I pictured a smiling face of large, black eyes and a long, expressive mouth. It was the cheerful face of an Ik'thya'nym, though there weren't enough distinguishing features to tell if it was Kish or one of the others I'd seen. Either way, the inhuman smile and warm features allowed me to wake up refreshed and content.

"Father!" exclaimed Marta, seeing my eyes open. She gently wrapped her arms around my neck and I could feel her tears on my cheek. From elsewhere in the cabin, Jessica approached, adding her arms to our daughter's hug.

I managed to raise my own arms and clutch them both tightly. The pain in my body had faded into an all-encompassing numbness, and I recognized the sensation of healing wyrd.

"I'm alive," I whispered, as much to myself as my family. "Where are we? What's happening?"

"Take your time," said Jessica, kissing me on the cheek and wiping tears from her eyes. "We're... safe... for now."

"The Nym helped us," said Marta, smiling. "You don't need to rush, Father."

"Away, away," muttered another voice, ushering my wife and daughter away from me. It was Vladimir Falling Moon, my cousin's spirit-master. Few of the crew ever got to meet the old man, for he was most comfortable in his own company, but Black Dog had a soft spot for him. It was only the second time I'd met him.

"How do I look?" I asked him, in a pathetic attempt to be funny.

"Like someone has been eating you," replied Vladimir. "In order of severity – your legs. Your left thigh and your right calf will never fully heal. They were gnawed on, though the nerves are mostly intact. Constant pain and a walking stick. Maybe crutches."

I looked down at my legs. Oliver had taken a large chunk of flesh from each, but had not reached the bone. Both wounds were heavily strapped, but I still managed to wiggle the toes on each foot.

"Your left side, above the waist," continued Vladimir. "It looks nasty, but you didn't lose anything you can't live without. Constant pain and a huge scar. Must have bled a lot."

That was the first bite taken by the eagle prince and the only one I could remember clearly. Hopfrog, the hybrid, had failed to break my mind with images of horror and failure, leading Oliver to torture me out of spite. I still wasn't entirely sure how the Two Hearts twins had managed to rescue me, and why I wasn't dead.

"Two fingers and an ear," said Vladimir. "The ear is superficial. Won't affect your hearing, but you aren't as pretty. The fingers – are you left-handed?"

"No," I grunted.

"Then it's an inconvenience," he replied. "You also had a broken jaw, two broken arms, a missing tooth, severe cuts and bruises across most of your body, and you'd almost bitten through your own tongue. Wyrd – yours and mine – has dealt with the minor stuff."

I leant back against the pillow and looked up at the vaulted ceiling. I wanted to get up, find Esteban and Luca, and find out how they'd managed to rescue me, and which of them had disobeyed my orders to hasten to Nowhere. I wanted to know about the great turtle spirit and how the Ik'thya'nym had helped us. I wanted to, but I didn't have the energy. Every little element of pain and distress flowed into a single expression. "I feel completely fucked."

Vladimir nodded. "You *are* completely fucked. But you're alive. Your arms and your brain still work. What else do you need, my lord Marius?"

Marta rushed back to hug me again. I stroked her hair and held her tightly. "It's okay," I whispered. "He's right. I'm still alive and I still have my mind." I looked up at Jessica. "Please, at least tell me where we are."

She managed a smile, looking at me like she'd already processed my death and was now having to deal with me being alive. "We're at the western mouth of the Red Straits, off an island called Nug. We can just about see Nibonay to the east."

"And Santago?" I asked. "Where is Oliver? Are we safe?"

"Seven cutters and an ironclad," she replied. "They're still there, but they can't get close to us. As I said, we're safe for now."

"Ik'thya'nym?"

She nodded. "These ones seem different, not as shy. There's one up on deck with Esteban and Luca."

"And who decided to risk everyone aboard this ship to come and rescue me?"

She craned forwards and kissed me, stroking my cheek. "Everyone," she replied. "Everyone decided."

I clutched her face and cried. My defences disappeared and I broke down, exposing every nerve and emotion. I'd pushed myself beyond what I thought possible and I felt completely naked. Perhaps I wasn't going to die after all. Perhaps I could even have a life after all of this – find somewhere to be at peace with Jessica and Marta, with plenty of nooks and crannies for Titus to explore. Certainly, I was almost done with leadership. Just a few more days of being the Stranger and I could just be Marius... minus an ear and a couple of fingers.

With Jessica still holding me tightly, I turned to Vladimir. "Walking stick. Or crutches. I want to go on deck. Help me."

He pursed his lips and gave a slight shake of the head, but complied, retrieving a pair of solid, wooden crutches from the corner of the cabin.

"Jess, help me sit."

We linked arms and she pulled me up. I was alarmed at my lack of strength, but with her help, I managed to sit on the wooden table. Slowly, with much wincing, I pivoted to the side, and Jessica helped put my wounded legs down, until I was fully seated on the edge of the table. Marta rushed over with a pair of soft, leather shoes, gently placing them on my feet and guiding each one to the wooden floor.

"Well, that's a good start," I joked, smiling at them both. "I can actually feel my feet." I flexed both shoulders, strangely grateful that Oliver had left me with two functioning arms.

Vladimir positioned the crutches under my armpits, but did nothing to help me stand. He left that to my wife and daughter, before backing away to open the cabin door. "Be slow and precise, until you are healed," said the old spirit-master.

I leant forwards, keeping the weight on my arms, until some semblance of sensation came back to both legs. Jessica held my waist, taking some of the weight, and Marta made sure my feet were planted. My left leg was weakest, where my thigh had been gnawed on, and any pressure caused pain. My right was better, able to take some weight without buckling. I raised my left and made a tentative movement away from the stability of the table. Jess and Marta kept close, but I managed to stand unaided, grunting and tensing both arms. Strangely, it was the loss of two fingers that caused me the most discomfort. It made clenching my fist difficult.

"Slow and precise," repeated Vladimir.

From the doorway, Asha and Gaius Two Hearts appeared. The twin assassins gawped at me, before grinning.

"He's standing up," said Asha.

"He fucking is," replied Gaius.

"Idiots," I said, smiling. "Come help me."

Marta clapped her hands, elated that her father was still whole. Jessica gave me a final kiss, before backing away and leaving me to the Two Hearts twins. "We still have a life to lead," she said. "No more gambling, no more heroics."

"I can't promise that," I replied. "But I'll try."

She stroked her hand down my face, but said nothing more.

"If you hadn't been such a fool," said Asha, moving forwards to help me.

"You'd be able to stand on your own," added her brother.

They helped me out of the cabin. One of my legs still felt mostly intact and both my arms were slowly regaining their strength. As Vladimir had predicted, I was in constant pain

– but, with the crutches, I was able to shrug off the twins and move under my own power.

The lower decks of the *Dangerous* were filled with sailors, void legionnaires and Dolcinite Pilgrims, silently waiting for me to prove I was still alive. I wore only a robe, with my worst injuries hidden, and I was able to look each of them in the eye. Slowly, nods turned into smiles, then smiles turned into cheering.

Lord Marius lives!

The cheering travelled across the ship, telling everyone aboard that my foolishness had not resulted in my death. The Dolcinites bowed their heads in deference, the legionnaires saluted with gusto, and everyone else just cheered. It was as if a great battle had been won. I was humbled by their reaction, and felt flushed and uncomfortable. But still elated. I was at my most vulnerable and couldn't keep from crying. For the second time since I woke up, I broke down. It was only the reassuring hands of Asha and Gaius Two Hearts that kept me moving forwards.

Gripping the crutches as best as I could, I was helped to the nearest staircase. I saw blue sky above me and felt the warmth of the sun. Shrugging my shoulders, I pushed away Asha and Gaius, determined to reach the deck on my own, even though every movement caused me pain. My left leg burned, and the wound in my side felt like a chunk of me was missing. I couldn't help but lean to the left, as I wrestled with crutches, legs and stairs, pulling myself upwards through sheer will. Dozens of people watched me, with the cheers getting louder and taken up by those on deck.

When I emerged into the daylight, I was quickly gathered in Esteban Hazat's arms. The commander of the twenty-third void legion had let me struggle up the stairs, but forgot formality once I cleared the top step.

"Your luck almost ran out," said Esteban. "Almost."

"He bit my fucking ear off," I replied, returning his embrace.

Esteban laughed, before holding me at arm's length. "You look terrible. How are the legs?"

I winced, trying to find stability on the deck. "One of them sort of works. The other... maybe it'll heal."

"No more fighting for you," he said, his laugh turning into a warm smile.

"How about fishing?" I asked. "Can I do that? What about sitting down and reading a book, or playing on the floor with my cat?"

He nodded sarcastically. "Rest when you're dead, Marius. And we aren't dead yet. Come, let me help you."

I let him steady me, as we made our way to the quarterdeck amidst cheering sailors. I'd surely get the hang of the crutches, but for now I must have appeared as little more than a crippled man.

With Esteban's help, I finally had a chance to see where the *Dangerous* had ended up. We were between three small islands, with the imposing, grey coast of Nibonay a way to the east. I was unfamiliar with these waters, but I thought that the seaweed-covered pinnacles all around us were a new addition to the Red Straits. Another formation had risen from the deep ocean, this time at the edge of the Inner Sea.

Further west, keeping their distance from both the *Dangerous* and the pinnacles, were my brother's ships. There was no sign of Oliver's ironclad, and I imagined it was still trying to negotiate its way past the great turtle spirit.

"Cousin," said Luca Cyclone, called Black Dog, moving from the helm to embrace me. "You look nowhere near as grave as Asha is telling everyone. She said you'd lost both your legs."

I adjusted my robe, showing him the wounds on each of my legs. "Not exactly," I replied, smiling. "Now, Jess told me there was an Ik'thya'nym up here."

Luca nodded. "We ran into them a few hours after we left Kish's island. Believe it or not, until then we had no feasible plan to rescue you, no matter how much the Two Hearts twins insisted." He turned and gestured amidships, where a pair of large, black eyes were peering at me from around the foremast. "His name is Vil'arn'azi, but Esteban started calling him Villain and it stuck. He says his island is to the north-east of here. We'll sail past it on our way to Nowhere. Best we avoid the Red Straits."

"Come out," I said to the Ik'thya'nym. "You are already my friend."

The creature managed to hide its entire body behind the slim mast, gathering in its long limbs, much as Kish had done, creating a small profile. When it emerged, slinking outwards and upwards, it became the largest of its kind I'd seen, perhaps a slender fifteen feet tall. It had distinctive red frills around the circumference of its round face, with the colour repeated in vibrant veins across its otherwise light green body. Despite the creature's size, it caused no listing on the deck of the ship, as if it was far lighter than it appeared.

After a moment of staring, the Ik'thya'nym shot me a sudden smile, elongating its wide mouth into a huge semi-circle, bisecting its round face. Unlike Kish, this creature also smiled with its frills, creating a warm red mantle around the expression.

"You Marius," said Villain, speaking surprisingly clearly.

"I am," I replied, returning his smile. "You Villain."

As I hobbled towards the huge creature, I began to see more shapes moving in the shallow water around the *Dangerous*. The pinnacles didn't provide an actual barrier, as they had at Kish's island, and were far more chaotically placed. The deterrent this time was dozens of Ik'thya'nym, apparently less timid than those we'd previously met. They twisted and turned under the clear, blue water, before breaking the surface in dives and somersaults. It was clear they were protecting my ship.

"Hin'bak'ish likes you," said Villain, reaching down to pat me on the head, as I might do to Titus. "Says I should help you."

Esteban and Luca joined us, each receiving a similar pat from the tall creature. "It took a while to explain *torture*," said Esteban.

"Torture," repeated Villain, his smile disappearing, as if the word made him unhappy. "Making you hurt, for no reason or cause."

"That was the closest we got," said Luca.

"It's close enough," I replied. "Thank you, Villain."

His smile returned and he crossed his gangly arms in front of his sinewy chest. For the first time, I noticed retractable claws on his long, webbed fingers. Kish had no such weapons, and I judged Villain to be considerably less passive. Perhaps some kind of warrior caste amongst the Nym.

"Did they fight for us?" I asked Esteban.

"They didn't need to," he replied. "But they didn't retreat from Santago's ships, and those claws are rather nasty. A show of force was all we needed to get back here."

I took a breath and chuckled to myself in relief. Slowly, the crew of the *Dangerous* returned to work across the deck, preparing the ship to make way. We were less than a day from the northern cliffs of Nowhere, though none of us knew in what state we'd find the island or Utha's Gate. Nevertheless, we were closer to safety than we'd been since I first met Utha the Ghost and started the evacuation of the Dark Harbour.

20

The *Dangerous* would have to sail north-east, past the Mirralite land of Helion and Villain's island, to avoid the Red Straits, where there would surely be more Brethren attack ships. It added an hour or two to our final journey, but gave me more time to sleep. Villain and his Ik'thya'nym encircled us as we sailed, and provided me with a sense of peace as I slept. Their very presence was calming, and I felt much as I had when we first met the ancient sea creatures.

I heard a distant whistle and my dreaming mind sailed away on a wave of gentle serenity, until I found myself walking barefoot in the shallows of Kish's island, my wounds suddenly vanished. Everything around me was still and quiet, as if the world was at peace. And yet it was not a mortal peace, nor a mundane sensation. It was primal and absolute, as if I was experiencing the very first day of this world, before mortal creatures invented such concepts as struggle, suffering and war.

With my breath steady and my footsteps light, I strolled out of the shallows and towards the central peak of the island, where Kish had first taken us. The brightly coloured coral and sparkling formations of crystalline rock framed the cave entrance, beckoning me within. I felt an irresistible pull, sensing that the source of all this peace and tranquillity was somehow waiting for me in the cave.

Beyond the narrow slice of daylight, I entered the domed cavern. Just as I remembered, the cave was dominated by a wide pool of still water, with a strangely angled jewel protruding from the middle. Opposite me, on the far wall, was the benevolent face of Nym'zu, the mother of the Ik'thya'nym. And I knew that, above my head, scowling at the air, was the face of Klu'zu, the twisted father of the Sunken Men, whom Kish had called the Zul'zya'zyn. There was power in both carvings, but the source of peace and tranquillity lay elsewhere. It was the jewel.

I walked around the pool of water, staring at the jewel and its subtle, red surfaces. Its angles and the light they created were strange and hard to look at. I tried to find a place to view the jewel clearly, but every angle fell into the next, forming a series of impossible shapes. It reminded me of a unique grain of sand, a droplet of water, or a snowflake. But it was none of those things. I didn't know what it was.

In my dream, I crouched down at the edge of the water and reached for the jewel. It was too far to grasp, but a gentle fizz of warm, red static leapt to my fingertips. I stretched out, getting within inches of the impossible shape, but unable to touch it. The closer I got, the more the two carvings reacted. The faces were mere stone renderings, but each was infused with an ancient power I didn't understand.

Nym'zu, the closest face, reacted with warmth, much as the Ik'thya'nym did when touched. Klu'zu, on the far wall, flared outwards with anger, as if looking for me. I was committing some kind of sin against the Sunken God, and his eyes were blind to all else. Whatever the impossible shape was, it was deeply important to the enemy. More than that,

I felt that it was some kind of unknowable treasure, perhaps a way to draw the eyes of the enemy.

"Why do I need this?" I mused. "What's happening on Nowhere?"

I left the cave. My perceptions travelled away from the jewel, moving at great speed through rock and over water, until I saw a huge landmass. The dream was answering my question, and the answer was terrifying. I could see Nibonay and a chunk of the Turtle Straits. It was all covered in a black and green cloud, roiling from horizon to horizon, and moving towards the small island of Nowhere.

I'd been acting on the assumption that the island and Utha's Gate would be some kind of salvation. I'd left two void legions to defend it, and Adeline Brand's Sea Wolves were a formidable addition, but the island was still under threat. The mundane forces of Alexis Wind Claw had fallen back, awaiting the arrival of the Sunken God himself. The ancient entity wasn't just awake, he was active, and getting closer to the island with each passing hour. Everything I'd been through since leaving the Dark Harbour could still be for nothing if the cloud reached the gate.

"No peace for me," I grunted. "Not just yet."

I opened my eyes to a bare cabin aboard the *Dangerous*. A bell was being rung from the deck, interrupting my dreams and pulling me from sleep. Unfortunately, being awake also meant being in pain. I'd fought a hundred fights, killed a hundred warriors, and been cut, bruised and battered more times than I could remember, but I'd never been eaten alive before, and this pain was something new.

Pain turns to pressure when it becomes constant, and my left leg felt as if two fat men were sitting on it. My right was stronger, with mobility slowly returning, giving me hope that I'd be able to walk with a stick rather than crutches. The wound in my side certainly looked worse than it was, and only really hurt when I moved a significant amount, though it also caused me to lean to the left as I walked.

I thought about rolling over and trying to find more sleep, but the bell didn't stop ringing and my dream kept repeating through the edges of my mind, robbing me of the necessary relaxation. I rubbed my face, took a deep breath, and resolved to get up. Jess and Marta were elsewhere and I had to get dressed without their help. I considered donning the robe again, but stubbornly decided to wrestle with a pair of grey trousers and a black shirt. The shirt was fairly straightforward, but the loss of two fingers made pulling on the trousers a surprisingly complex challenge.

When I was as dressed as I was going to get, I reached for the crutches and tested my legs. As I'd hoped, the wound in my right calf was healing well, and I could feel some strength return. I couldn't put my full weight on it, but I thought I'd soon be able to. For now, I still needed both crutches to topple away from the bed and towards the door. The ship was moving, but only gently, and I managed to grasp the door handle without falling to the floor like an idiot.

Outside the cabin, a few dozen Dolcinites reclined in hammocks, with the crew moving amongst them, busy at their work. When they saw me, I was greeted by a varied mixture of gasps, smiles and whispered words. Two legionnaires were on guard outside my door and they saluted my presence, before offering to help.

"I'm fine," I said. "What's the bell for?"

"Villain's island," said one of the legionnaires. "Just off our port side."

"How far to the cliffs of Nowhere?"

"Not sure, my lord. A few hours, maybe."

"I'm going up on deck," I replied. "I'm going to try and do it unaided, but if I fall backwards, I'm trusting you two to keep me from looking like a complete fool."

"We accept your charge," replied the other legionnaire, managing to keep a straight face.

Walking up the steps was easier without a hundred people looking at me, but it still hurt like an absolute bastard. It was the little movements – a twinge here, a flex there, an occasional stab of agony. Yet, as I ascended to the deck, I still felt the residual calmness of my dream, allowing me to shut out the pain better than before I slept. By the time the morning sun hit my face, I allowed myself a smile.

The *Dangerous* was moving along a wide sea channel, north of the island of Nug and the Mirralite land of Helion. We were parallel to the Red Straits, travelling slowly towards the northern cliffs of Nowhere. Nibonay was no longer visible to the south, but the angry storm cloud signalled its location. The thing that drew my eyes, as I hobbled towards the helm, was a small, volcanic island in our path. It lacked the encircling pinnacles of Kish's island, but was otherwise remarkably similar, formed of a single peak and sandy beach, with brightly coloured coral and seaweed adorning the volcano.

"Marius, go and rest," barked Luca from the helm. "We're still a few hours out."

"As Esteban would say, I'll rest when I'm dead."

I managed to join him with just the crutches for help. Half a dozen sailors got out of my way, offering salutes and smiles, but all thought better of offering assistance. They knew I was a stubborn old bastard and wouldn't appreciate the help. Most of the crew even averted their eyes when I reached my cousin, discarded the crutches and slumped onto a nearby barrel.

"You are an absolute mess," said Luca.

"And you have a small cock," I replied, wincing and rubbing the wound in my right thigh.

He laughed, slapping me on the shoulder. "Villain's island up ahead. Everyone's feeling a bit... I don't know, calm, I suppose. Like before. The weather's fair, but a storm is rising over Nibonay, moving north. We'll reach Nowhere before it hits."

"Where's the Ik'thya'nym?" I asked.

"At the bow," replied Black Dog. "He's looking at the island like it's his mother's tit."

I grunted a few times, knowing that I'd have to trudge back along half the length of the ship to speak to Villain. I couldn't see the creature and imagined he'd gathered his limbs into a ball, skulking behind the forward capstan, while gazing at his island.

"I need to ask him something," I said.

"Well, there he is," replied Luca. "Why don't you just pop down to speak to him?"

"Fuck off."

He laughed again. "Everyone who'd help you is wise enough to be sleeping before we reach Nowhere. No one knows what'll happen when we get there, so Esteban, Asha, Gaius, Sergio, Jessica and Marta are probably fast asleep.

We're almost at Utha's Gate, Marius. We won... *You* won. We all get to live. Stop being paranoid."

"Where's my cat?" I asked.

"For all I know, he's sleeping under a Dolcinite's hammock," replied Black Dog. "And he's too small to help you walk, cousin."

"So, I'll walk on my own," I stated, gritting my teeth and retrieving the crutches.

The ship was operating on a skeletal crew, as the majority took the opportunity to sleep after a week or so of frenetic activity. Luckily for me, this meant I could keep my head down as I grumbled from the helm to the bow, only having to stop for the occasional nod or smile. When I reached the forward capstan, I again discarded the crutches, and found a coil of rope to sit on.

"Hello, Marius," said Villain, poking his round, expressive face over the capstan. "There are holes in you."

I smirked. "Yes, there are holes in me."

Skulking on all fours, the Ik'thya'nym slinked his way across the bow of the *Dangerous*, before perching in front of me. "You have question?"

"Hmm, how did you know that?"

"You look like you have question," replied the broadly smiling sea creature. "Kish says your people are made of questions."

I considered it. "I suppose humans are naturally curious, though it doesn't always work in our favour."

"What is Marius's question?" asked Villain.

I looked over the railing to the volcanic island on our port side. "Does your island have a cave with a pool of water and a strange gem? Like Kish's?"

"Yes," replied the creature, nodding.

"What is it?" I asked. "The gem? And why does it calm mortal minds?"

Villain blinked his large, black eyes and gathered his webbed hands in a display of thought. There was much going on in his head, as the ancient creature tried to fathom a response to my simple, mortal wonderings. "You understand Ya'lan'ah'loth?" he asked. "Klu'zu and Nym'zu?"

"I'm not sure I'd say I *understand*... but I know who they are, yes. I know you don't understand what a god is, but it seems to apply to them."

The creature's head rolled in a tight circle, as if he was processing my words. Much like Kish, he clearly had highly advanced senses, enabling him to understand our speech with very little exposure.

"Understood," he replied, after a moment of thought. "I will call them *gods*... as a gift to Marius." His wide mouth turned up again. The expression was almost too big to be called a smile, and it conveyed unfettered warmth and friendship.

"Thank you," I said, unable to conjure any more profound words. "Please, continue with your answer." A conversation with an Ik'thya'nym was clearly not as linear as a mortal conversation. "What is the gem in your cave?"

He shuffled towards me, until we were mere inches apart. He'd reduced his height to be at my eye level, and I tilted backwards involuntarily. He smelled of salt water and seaweed, with a faintly sweet aroma tickling the back of my throat. Slowly, so as to appear less intimidating, Villain raised a hand and exposed a retractable claw on his right index finger. It was subtly curved and the size of a large knife, with spiny, red serrations along its length. He then gently reached for my face with the claw. I flinched, until his smile returned, and I gingerly allowed him to touch my cheek. I felt slight pressure, but nothing more, until a droplet of blood fell from my face to the wooden deck.

"The gem," said Villain, pointing at the small drop of blood.

I gawped at him for a moment, then at the drop of my blood, then at the nearby island. "Fuck me," I muttered. "That's why the Sunken God reacted in my dream. The gems are droplets of his sister's blood. A god's blood."

"Yes," said Villain. "This word... blood. Nym'zu's blood. It calls to Klu'zu... Sorry, Marius, I mean *sunken god*."

"Don't apologize," I said, grasping his light green face in friendship. "You may just have told me something of great worth."

Villain chirped, closing his eyes and nuzzling into my hands. It occurred to me that I was essentially petting a creature who was millions of years old. Luckily, Titus wasn't around to get jealous.

"Please," I said. "This drop of blood could be used. If such a thing is possible. Klu'zu may care more for it than for the refugees on Nowhere." I smiled, thinking I understood what my dream meant. "How dare a mortal hand reach for the essence of a god... Sorry, Villain, I mean Ya'lan'ah'loth."

We shared a smile and I felt a strange kinship with the creature.

"You want visit my island?" asked Villain.

"I think I need to," I replied.

★

Nowhere was just about visible to the east, but I had ordered the ship to stop and drop anchor within sight of our refuge. The deck of the *Dangerous* was packed, with half the people looking to Nowhere and the other half staring at Villain's island. There were whispers, smiles and all manner of gossip. Most aboard hoped to be reunited with loved ones on Nowhere or through Utha's Gate. So many people had left the Dark Harbour ahead of us, and had no idea where we'd got to. They'd have to wait a little while longer to find out. Strangely, I had every confidence that Adeline Brand was leading well in my absence.

Asha and Gaius Two Hearts helped me down into the longboat, with Esteban grumbling along behind. The commander of the twenty-third was reluctant to delay our escape to Nowhere and accompany me to Villain's island, but the alternative was to let me go on my own, and he wouldn't allow that. He insisted that ten legionnaires came with us to the volcanic island, as if he was expecting a surprise attack. Not even Villain's contagious smile and warm welcome appeared to allay his fears. Dozens of Ik'thya'nym were visible, but all except Villain stayed in the sea, observing us from afar.

We'd dropped anchor within a few boat lengths, so I didn't have to drag my crippled body too far from the *Dangerous*. I was slowly getting used to the crutches, even with the constant commentary from Asha and Gaius. Luckily, despite their caustic observations, they helped me walk without me needing to ask.

"Do you want us to cut off your left leg?" asked Gaius. "It's fairly useless."

"We'd do that for you," added Asha. "Just say the word." She patted one of the many blades sheathed across her body.

"How truly selfless of you," I replied, wincing as the rowing boat struck the rocky beach of Villain's island. "Just help me get to the cave, you cheeky bastards."

The twins were already positioning themselves either side of me. Esteban and his legionnaires jumped from the boat and stood in awe of the central peak and the bright colours encircling it. The main difference between this and Kish's island was a curious black mineral, woven in veins through every rocky surface. It was shiny, almost reflective, and resembled no kind of mineral or rock I'd seen in the surface world.

"This island's bigger," observed Esteban.

"So is Villain," I replied, nodding to the fifteen foot sea creature standing with us.

"If times were different, this would be a perfect Sea Wolf outpost," said Esteban.

"But times aren't different," I said, wincing my way up the beach. "Times are what they are."

"Stop trying to be profound," said Asha Two Hearts, steadying my left arm against the crutch.

"Why are we here?" asked Gaius. "Do you just wanna delay our arrival to make it more dramatic?"

"No," I replied. "Villain's agreed to lend me something."

"This way," said the Ik'thya'nym, pulling in his lanky body to fit through the small cave entrance.

Esteban followed first, leaving Asha, Gaius and I to play a complicated game with my crutches and the narrow slice in the rock. We eventually found an awkward sideways shuffle, with our arms linked together. My pain had now settled into a constant throb, with little sudden discomfort, enabling me to move without wincing. Even still, I had to rely on the Two Hearts twins to get within Villain's cave.

It was larger than Kish's, but only slightly, and had all of the same elements: the pool of still water, the detailed rendering of Nym'zu's face, and the beautifully strange gem in the centre. Knowing what it was made it no easier to look at, but I looked all the same. Esteban and the twins didn't know that I intended to take the jewel and use it to draw the Sunken God away from Nowhere. I'd had the idea and I'd acted on it, telling no one but Villain. The Ik'thya'nym had offered the gem freely, with no conditions, as if giving it to me was somehow spreading its peaceful influence. The one thing I'd not yet decided was who would sacrifice themselves – the Eastron who led the Sunken God from Nowhere would surely not be able to travel through Utha's Gate, but they'd save thousands.

"Take, take," said Villain, gesturing happily to the gem.

"What's he talking about?" asked Esteban.

I shrugged off the twins and stood on my own, inches from the pool of water. "Do you know what that is?" I asked him.

He considered it. "A strange rock of some kind. Though, on balance, it's one of the least strange things I've seen since we left the Dark Harbour. What is it?"

"Blood," answered Villain, apparently very pleased with himself. "Blood of Ya'lan'ah'loth. Sorry, Marius, blood of a god. Blood of my mother."

"Okay," said Esteban. "Why do we need it?"

"Watch," I replied, wincing as I struggled downwards to take a seat at the edge of the water. "Villain, hand me the gem. Hand me the blood of Nym'zu."

The smiling sea creature dove into the pool with inhuman grace, causing barely a ripple. He disappeared under the surface, showing how deep the pool was, before poking his grinning face back into the light. Then he reached a hand towards the gem and grasped it, though it was difficult to tell where his fingers actually touched its irregular surfaces. It was roughly the size of a human head and Villain held it effortlessly, showing pleasure at its touch, before handing it to me. I slowly reached out, feeling a crackle at the end of each fingertip. Small arcs of energy leapt from the blood, making the hairs rise on my arm.

Every Eastron in the cave gasped, as a red light flared outwards from the wall above the entrance. The face of Klu'zu, invisible up to this point, was now the main source of light, glaring angrily up above. It was just as I'd seen in my dream. The Sunken God could not bear the thought of a lowly mortal touching the essence of his sister. If the ancient entity had reason, it was absent at that moment.

"You fucking hate this, don't you?" I snarled, looking up at the carving. "I'm Marius Cyclone, called the Stranger, an Eastron mortal of the Kingdom of the Four Claws... and I am about to touch a droplet of blood from your sister." I tickled my fingers in the air, millimetres from the jewel, before closing my fist and retracting my hand. "Not yet."

The red light faded, until the stone rendering of the Sunken God was again invisible. Esteban and the twins had all instinctively reached for weapons. They knew blades were of no use, but they were more tightly wound than they cared to admit.

"I think I understand," said Esteban. "It can draw the eyes of the Sunken God away from Nowhere. But you can't ask the *Dangerous* to do that. Not now. Not within sight of safety."

"I haven't decided yet," I replied. "I don't even know if I'll need to decide. But it's a weapon we didn't have before."

"Not a weapon," said Villain, clutching the gem to his chest. "Hin'bak'ish likes you... *I* like you. This will help you survive. But it can never be a weapon."

I motioned for the twins to help me stand. With the aid of my crutch I was quickly vertical again. "Fetch canvas and sacking. Wrap it up as best you can. I don't want anyone touching that thing, not until they need to. We're taking it with us."

Esteban paused, glancing around the cave and directing significant glares at both Villain and the blood of Nym'zu. "Promise me something, Marius. If this thing needs to be used, if we need to distract the Sunken God away from Utha's Gate – promise me it won't be the *Dangerous* we sacrifice."

We locked eyes for a moment, but I couldn't answer.

21

Something was happening in the Red Straits. As the *Dangerous* stopped, under the huge platforms on the northern cliffs of Nowhere, everyone on deck could hear strange noises and see a stranger cloud formation, rolling north. There was an angry atmosphere in the air, as if the pressure had changed. We had no Ik'thya'nym to calm our minds, and everyone's hackles began to rise. Vil'arn'azi had wished us well, and returned to his own world. Our excitement at reaching Utha's Gate was now struck down with a solid blow of pessimism. I'd told no one about my dream, and what the cloud was.

There were dozens of People of Ice above us, waving frantically for us to begin our ascent. Nothing in their manner, hurried though it was, conveyed any warning of what was happening at Duncan's Fall, but it was all anyone on my ship could focus on. The Dolcinite Pilgrims were the first to board the wooden platforms, but even they struggled to turn their eyes from the storm cloud. Here we were, approaching journey's end, and some new curse had come to plague us.

The blood of Nym'zu was securely wrapped in a dozen layers of thick sacking and bound with rope. It wasn't heavy, and could be carried by a single person. I'd submitted it to the care of the Dolcinites and sent it up the cliff with the first group to ascend.

"How long?" I asked Luca. "How long to abandon ship?"

My cousin winced at the word, and the prospect of leaving the ship behind. He'd offered to stay and scuttle it, but I'd insisted that the *Dangerous* and Salty Alphonse be set adrift, perhaps one day to be found by whoever was next to occupy these lands.

"Another hour," he replied, glaring at me.

"Before you complain again about leaving the ship, think of all the Sea Wolf ships they've abandoned. And then think of how much those ships meant to *their* captains."

He gritted his teeth, but quickly turned back to stare at the malevolent cloud. Elsewhere, Esteban's legionnaires were corralling everyone aboard into lines and groups, awaiting a ride up to the cliff tops. Baggage was being piled along both railings, with Jessica taking charge and Marta trying to keep Titus from leaping out of her arms. The cloud kept everyone's nerves taut and, for the most part, their mouths shut. Those above us were too distant to hold a meaningful conversation, so no one could find out what I already knew about the cloud until we reached the cliff top.

"Come on, Marius," said Asha, appearing next to me with her brother. "Time to go."

"What?"

"The Dolcinites were first," replied Gaius. "Then the elderly, the young…"

"And the infirm," said Asha. "That's you. You're really infirm."

I raised an eyebrow. "You can both fuck off. I'm staying until the end."

"No," replied Asha. "We've been given very specific orders."

"By someone that outranks *me*?"

The twins parted, pointing in unison to my wife, standing amidships and waving. She tilted her head, as if she felt she had no choice.

"She also has a message for you," said Gaius. "Apparently, you're not needed down here, but you might be needed up there."

"It's a fair point, Marius," said Luca. "Go find out why that cloud seems to hate the world."

I rolled my eyes. I pretended I didn't care about abandoning the *Dangerous*, but in reality it was a difficult parting. I wasn't sentimental by nature, but this mixture of wood, steel and canvas had kept me sane. I didn't know if it was really haunted but, unlike my daughter, I enjoyed thinking that it was. Salty Alphonse had given me a home, a refuge, a friend, and the ship had taken everything the world had thrown at it. Now I was leaving it forever.

"Okay," I said. "Let's go. I suppose I can be the Stranger a while longer. But Marta and Titus are coming with me. I won't presume to tell Jessica when she should leave."

"Righty ho," said Asha Two Hearts, positioning herself at my left shoulder.

"Off we go then," said Gaius, securing my right.

The two of them were treating me like a child and having an enormous amount of fun, but I was forced to rely on them. I was being stubborn and only using one crutch, with my left leg having to carry some weight. I had little hope that my other leg would ever heal enough to be useful, so I was investing much in the one that almost worked.

The twins helped me from the helm of the ship, down to the main deck, where a gap had been cleared for me to struggle onto the next wooden platform. The care and reverence shown to me was almost enough to distract the crew from the storm cloud, but not quite. They gave the odd salute or the odd smile, but continued their work without drawing attention to my departure. Only Jess and Marta came to meet us at the platform, with a grumpy cat being held tightly in my daughter's arms.

"I'll be right behind you," said Jess, as Marta helped the twins get me seated on the wooden platform.

"No, you won't," I replied.

"No, I won't," she conceded. "I'll be here as long as these people need help. I'll come up with Luca and Esteban."

We shared an awkward embrace, before Marta hugged her mother and joined me on the platform. Titus appeared to accept that he was also coming with us and settled into my lap with barely a hiss. Asha and Gaius sat cross-legged at the edges, dangling their feet from the platform, and giving room for other wounded members of the crew to join us. I gave them no instruction to ascend with me, but Jessica clearly had, and I was secretly glad to have them with me when I finally set foot on Nowhere.

"Heave away!" shouted Asha, to the People of Ice on the cliff top.

The Sea Wolves were not known for their skill in engineering. In fact, Adeline Brand's people were known for little but seamanship and killing. However, the wooden platforms, heavy chains, and huge gantries had been constructed with great skill and efficiency. As we rose from the deck of my ship, there was barely a creak of wood or a clank of chains. The platform swayed against the cliff face, but didn't bump against it or tilt in the air. It stayed flat and true, until the chains elevated us above the cliff top, where bearded Sea Wolves swung the platform onto solid ground.

Before us, stretched across the rugged northern plains of the island was a very strange sight indeed. The last time I'd been here, just before I left for the Silver Parliament, this entire area was like a small shanty town, filled with citizens of my hold, awaiting their turn to walk through Utha's Gate. Now, it was empty of people, with nothing but the remnants of a thousand small camps. Cold Point was visible to the south-east, but I could see no fires or plumes of smoke to indicate it was still inhabited. Maybe, just maybe, everyone had already escaped. Maybe I didn't need to use the essence of Nym'zu and condemn someone to stay behind.

"Marius the Stranger," said a woman of Ice, one of a dozen or so Sea Wolves assisting my people from the *Dangerous*. "We've been waiting for you. Your last refugee fleet arrived yesterday. That Dolcinite woman, Antonia, is organizing them." She looked me up and down, as the twins helped me to stand and leave the platform. "Where's the rest of you?"

"That's funny," said Asha, without laughing. "Because he's missing an ear and some fingers."

"Definitely," added Gaius. "Maybe the rest of him will come up on the next platform." He looked to his sister. "No one told us the Sea Wolves had a sense of humour."

"Relax," I said, securing myself on the crutch. "Where's Adeline Brand? And Jessimion Death Spell? I have something of interest for them." I glanced across at a small group of Dolcinites, clustered around the blood of Nym'zu.

"Adeline's at the beach with two thousand warriors," replied the woman. "Death Spell's at the gate with ten thousand people queuing for safety. Who do you wanna see first, Lord Stranger?"

"Ten thousand?" I exclaimed, my optimism vanishing. "Fuck, that's a lot of people."

The woman of Ice puffed out her cheeks, as if I was saying something obvious and rather stupid. I was aware that I'd arrived at the end of something... or perhaps during it. Either way, there were an awful lot of things I didn't know.

"Okay, just tell me what's happening at Duncan's Fall. How close is that cloud?"

She shared a few loaded glances with other nearby Sea Wolves. They were all afraid, as if they knew the answer to my question but didn't understand it.

"We've been fighting Winterlords, then Dark Brethren, then... some balls of Sea Wolf corpses." She took a breath, remembering what she'd seen. "Those things were fucking nasty. We had to burn them in the end."

"And now?" I asked. "What are we fighting now?"

"I think they're called whips," she replied. "Three of them. I've not seen them myself. Massive Sunken Men. But we've got the black dust."

Her words were like a punch to the face – though, given my recent treatment at the hands of Prince Oliver, I could walk through a punch to the face. "What the fuck is dust going to do against whips? Or that cloud?"

From a small rocky outcropping, another woman coughed. She'd been there, leaning against the rocks, as the crew of the *Dangerous* made their way ashore and she'd been close enough to hear my conversation. She pushed away from the rock and ambled towards us, gathering her thick, multi-coloured skirts.

"Hello," she said. "I'm Eva Rage Breaker, called the Lady of Rust, and I've heard a lot about you, Marius Cyclone. A lot of people on this island don't like you very much."

"A lot of people *off* this island don't like him either," said Asha Two Hearts.

"*No one* likes him," added Gaius.

I smiled at Eva Rage Breaker, wondering why I'd not heard of someone with such an impressive name. She didn't look like a Sea Wolf. She had light hair and pale skin, and no air of imminent violence. In fact, I felt a subtle mist of wyrd, emanating from her. Everything in her demeanour suggested a woman of peace and calm, as if conflict was impossible in her presence. It was bizarre and subtle wyrd-craft, like nothing I'd seen before, and certainly not of Sea Wolf origin.

"I don't know you," I said. "Though I feel I should. Are you coming with us through Utha's Gate?"

She was perhaps sixty years old and had a kind, motherly face. "Yes, of course. My people and I have committed ourselves to Adeline Brand and the free Eastron. The Alpha Wolf howled and we answered. Many Sundered Wolves are down on the beach, defending this island, and many more have already passed to the void realm, where they will live in peace."

"Sundered Wolves?" I queried, trying to remember the little I knew about them. "Like David Fast Claw and Michael of the Mountain?"

"Similar to them," she replied, knowingly. "But I'm younger."

"Good to have you," I said. "Do *you* know how dust can help against whips?"

"I do," she replied. "The black dust is a repellent against them. Adeline is gambling that it'll be enough."

I smiled. "Gambling has favoured me of late. Let us hope the First Fang is as lucky. Now, Eva Rage Breaker, where do you think I am most needed? For I assume Adeline is too busy to meet. Though I truly need to talk to her."

"Cyclone!" bellowed a voice from behind Eva.

Asha and Gaius twitched, as a tall, powerfully built Sea Wolf appeared from the rocky outcropping. It was Rys Coldfire, called the Wolf's Bastard. Like Eva, he'd been there the whole time, likely waiting for me. I'd not seen him since he left Snake Guard with Elizabeth Defiant.

"Rys," I said, nodding at the legendary Sea Wolf duellist. "Where's Elizabeth?"

"At our cottage in Utha's realm," he replied. "She has vegetables that need tending. You're a fucking mess."

"Oliver Dawn Claw decided to eat me," I said.

"*Your* mistake," he replied. "The Winterlords fell because you fucked up. Losing an ear and a couple of fingers? Well, it could be worse. Not worth whinging about."

The Two Hearts twins looked at each other, then burst out laughing. Rys had summarized days of teasing from the two of them, and added an extra note of bile.

"Shut up," I snapped. "Rys, I need to speak to Adeline. I have a way of drawing the eyes of the enemy away from Nowhere."

He looked past us, to the huge, wooden gantries, then across to the large mob of Dark Brethren, gathering on the cliff top. Finally, his eyes fell on the Dolcinites and the bound droplet of Nym'zu's blood.

"That thing has power," said the Wolf's Bastard. "What is it?"

"For now, just something we need to keep safe," I replied. "I want to visit Utha's Gate. Then I need to speak to Adeline. How long do we have and how long do we need?"

Eva and Rys looked at each other. Again, I was faced with knowing too little. Whatever they'd done to defend Nowhere, I'd not been part of it. I could only hope that Jessimion and Santos had commanded my legions with strength and honour.

"About nine thousand refugees are left," said Eva Rage Breaker, "not including the defenders at Duncan's Fall. The gate allows only small groups at a time and doesn't reset straight away. Another day and a half and we can close the gate."

"And the cloud?" I asked. "How long until we're all dead?"

Rys took a step forwards, until we were face to face. Ordinarily, I was only slightly shorter than him. Now, the Sea Wolf towered over my broken body. His angular face and short, spiky black hair all pointed down at me. I felt a tinge of anger that I would never again be a warrior. I'd been pretty good at fighting, though nowhere near the prowess of the Wolf's Bastard. Even so, he reminded me that I was now fairly helpless. If an enemy let me sit on a chair and hold a sword, I could still kill, but in the real world, my fighting days were over.

"How long?" I repeated, in a whisper.

"We don't know," he replied. "It depends on the black dust."

"It's half an hour walk to the gate," offered Eva. "We'll survive that long." Her wyrd made me smile at her gentle manner, mitigating my new feelings of inadequacy. "Okay, let's go," I said. "Though one of you is going to have to explain where the fuck this black dust came from."

Rys snorted. "And you, Cyclone, are going to have to explain how the fuck we lead the Sunken God from Nowhere."

The journey from the northern cliffs to Utha's Gate was a strange affair, filled with bizarre stories of Sundered Wolves who couldn't die, explosive black dust, and grotesque monsters created from Sea Wolf corpses. Adeline Brand and the defenders of Nowhere had accomplished much and suffered greatly. And I thought I'd seen some fucked up stuff in the last week. I took everything they told me on faith, considering Eva Rage Breaker and Rys Coldfire to be reliable sources. Even so, it amused me to withhold information about the Ik'thya'nym. It was like a trump card – *yeah, but I made friends with some immortal sea creatures.* I told them about the blood of Nym'zu, and what it could do, but I didn't elaborate or answer questions. Luckily, Rys was highly laconic and Eva was far too polite to press me. They knew what they needed to know and that was enough. As for what was happening at Duncan's Fall, we barely discussed it. The implication was that things would be decided, one way or the other, within the next day.

The twins accompanied me, but I left everyone else on the cliff, with instructions to follow us to the gate as soon as they were able. The blood of Nym'zu would be safe with the Dolcinites until I went to meet Adeline, assuming she was still alive.

"Marius!" shouted Jessimion Death Spell, commander of the third void legion. "You are a welcome sight, my lord." He was positioned at the top of a temporary watchtower and became visible to us before the refugees.

I smiled up at him, but my response got lost in my throat when we crested a rise and saw the flat plains of Nowhere, the shimmering monument of Utha's Gate, and the thousands of people, formed into thick lines, waiting to go through. Void legionnaires and warriors of Ice acted as gate-keepers, moving between more abandoned camps and wooden buildings. It was so different from when I'd last been here that it could have been an entirely different place. People had arrived, built temporary homes, lived in them for days or weeks, then gone through the gate – all since I left for the Silver Parliament. I'd started this evacuation, but since then it had gained a life of its own.

As I limped towards Jessimion and the watchtower, the distant gate flashed outwards in a crackle of glaring, blue light. The next group of refugees – a large family of poor Sea Wolves – were ushered forwards. They stepped into the light, just as it settled into a wall of crystalline glass, and vanished from the realm of form.

"It won't open again for five or ten minutes," said Eva Rage Breaker. "There appears to be no way of speeding up the process. It's beautiful on the other side though."

I nodded. "Yes, it is. A perfect home for the Eastron."

Jessimion slid down a ladder and came to greet us. He was wearing light, Sea Wolf armour – leather with steel plates. The armour of a void legionnaire was highly effective in combat, but a pain in the arse if you were forced to wear it for prolonged periods. The rest of his legion were similarly attired, with the odd flash of black steel to show that not everyone had completely abandoned their armour.

"Who cut you up like that?" asked Jessimion, his warm smile hardening when he saw me close up.

"He was tortured," replied Asha Two Hearts.

"But we all want him to stop whinging and get over it," added Gaius.

"Why do you let them talk to you like that?" asked the commander, wincing at the twins' disrespect. "I'd flog a legionnaire for less."

"Lucky they're not legionnaires," I replied. "And they make me laugh... sometimes."

He nodded and his smile returned. "I'm glad you're alive Marius. When Antonia told us what happened, we feared the worst. Someone's going to have to ride to the beach and tell the First Fang. She seems to think you bring something of great value."

I nodded, but my eyes narrowed. "How the fuck does she know that?"

"I'm just a soldier," he replied. "Adeline Brand does not confide in me."

"Talk to the Pure One," said Rys Coldfire, nodding to a nearby tree stump and the old man sitting on it. He'd been turned away from us, but as he swivelled around, I saw Ten Cuts smiling at me.

The Pure One was over a hundred years old, his longevity bestowed upon him by Utha the Ghost. Even so, he looked frail and ancient. He'd spent years sitting at the feet of a great turtle spirit and perhaps knew more than any other mortal. He was the pale man's closest ally, closer even than me, and had been my friend since we first met. He possessed a powerful spirit-whistle and had used it to save my life when I rescued Oliver at the Silver Parliament, and again when Snake Guard had fallen. But, before all that, it was his whistle that had first shown me a vision of the Sunken God.

"You do not look well," said Ten Cuts, looking at me through curtains of waist-length grey hair.

"I'm thinking of retiring," I replied. "Fishing, sitting down, barking at people to bring me food. I'm looking forward to it."

"Soon," he replied. "You near the end of your story, Marius, but other deeds are yet to be done." He glanced at Eva Rage Breaker and the Wolf's Bastard, nodding with respect. "Now, tell me what you found on the island. We knew to send you there, but not what you'd find."

I laughed. "You know, this would all have gone a lot more smoothly if you or Utha had told me the whole story when we first met."

"I wasn't able to," he replied. "Time doesn't work like that, nor do great turtle spirits give their wisdom all at once. The island?"

"Yes, the island." I shook my head at him, but didn't comment on his obtuse language. "I won't ask if you know what the Ik'thya'nym are, but one of their number gave me a droplet of blood. It belonged to a creature called Nym'zu, and the Sunken God cannot stand the idea of a mortal man touching it."

"It's the blood of his sister," added Asha Two Hearts, with an infuriating grin that made me want to punch her.

"The Sunken God's called Klu'zu," said Gaius. "In case you were interested."

This news didn't make Ten Cuts or Eva react, but Rys and Jessimion stared with disbelief at the twins. They'd each been fighting the Sunken God, in their own ways, for over a year, and to hear his name and of his sister was a significant development. The commander of the third void legion and a legendary duellist of the Severed Hand were not easily surprised, but to hear talk of a god's blood made even their eyes widen.

"It'll lead the Sunken God away from Nowhere," I said, when everyone had stopped staring. "We just need someone to take it."

PART EIGHT

Adeline Brand on Nowhere

22

Within the muddy, black cloud, I saw things move. Not just random wisps of wind, but solid forms and definite shapes, with the details obscured within the black mass. Impossible limbs, shifting appendages, staring eyes, crackling lights, all roiling together. It appeared to cover the entirety of Nibonay, from the shell of the Severed Hand to the Red Straits. Now it was towering over Duncan's Fall and the coast of Nowhere. The cloud radiated power and intention, as if it were more than alive – and I thought that perhaps we were all looking at some other manifestation of the Sunken God, come to view its greatest children eradicate the few remaining free Eastron.

Two thousand defenders of Nowhere were assembled in a loose column behind our barricades. We were a mishmash of Dark Brethren void legionnaires, Sea Wolf duellists and sailors, with a scattering of Kneeling Wolves, Sundered Wolves and People of Ice. At any other time and against any other foe, it would be a formidable army of battle-hardened warriors. But against the three greatest whips of the Sunken God, none of us felt formidable.

The smallest was the Bulbous Whip – an enormous frog, sitting squat in the shallows, with pulsing, blubbery legs. Then there was the Hateful Whip – a skeletal fish, walking upright on spiky limbs and wading towards us through the

Red Straits. The largest, an immense warty creature, with the head of a toad, was the Vile Whip, though the largest was also the most furtive, staying on the distant coast of Nibonay and not revealing its full form. Only its grotesque head was visible.

Below the whips, and tiny in comparison, were hundreds of Sunken Men, rising from the Red Straits in small clusters. There were no depth barges, but they'd be close, likely with hundreds more Sunken Men. They wielded staffs and pincers, with armour of sea shells, woven together with seaweed. They formed the lowest rank of a three-tier attack, with the whips above them and the malevolent cloud at the top.

"Adeline," said a voice that I ignored.

"Adeline," repeated the voice.

"Quiet for a moment," I replied. "I'm taking all of this in. I advise you and everyone else to do the same."

The speaker was Santos Spirit Killer, commander of the second void legion. He was a brave man and had proven loyal, making sure the Brethren and the Wolves melded as a single army. Nevertheless, I needed another few moments to process the enemy at our door. The Sunken Men were nasty, but skill and steel would do for them. The whips could only be truly repelled by the lines of black dust. As for the cloud, I just didn't know. I concluded, against my aggressive instincts, that the best strategy was to wait.

"Adeline," said Santos for a third time.

I turned to him, realizing that he was speaking to me so that he didn't have to look at the whips. I gave him a shallow nod, indicating that he should carry on talking.

"Everything's in place. If the Sunken Men attack, we should hold. If the whips attack, we have anchors, hooks and chains. Maybe we can bring one down and cut it up. I don't know about the cloud, but we all stand ready to die if necessary... if the black dust doesn't repel them."

"Do we have any left?" I asked.

"Daniel says he's keeping some in reserve. Maybe he's waiting for something worse than *this*."

I grinned and slapped him on the shoulder, realizing he'd discarded his black steel breastplate and donned a thick, leather tunic. If it weren't for his shaved head and clean-cut, dark features, he could pass as a Sea Wolf.

"Do you think they have tactics?" I asked.

"Probably not," replied Santos. "Which do you think will attack first?"

"I'd say... the whips. The two big ones could just wade through us. It'd be the simplest path to victory."

"So we just wait?"

"Well, we could summon our wyrd and charge them." I shook my head. "Actually, no, we should wait."

The void legionnaire smirked at me. "Whatever is about to happen, I'd like to say that it has been an honour to fight alongside you and your people."

I nodded, keeping my eyes focused on the beach. "On balance, I think we've won more than we're about to lose. We'll be remembered, Santos." I chuckled. "Hopefully, as more than a one-armed Sea Wolf and a fucking Dark Brethren."

"Funny," replied the commander. "You probably don't know this, but that was the most difficult thing for us to understand about the Sea Wolves. Void legionnaires don't talk when fighting, and they certainly don't swear and make jokes. Yesterday, I saw one of your duellists lose his left arm to an abomination. Do you know what he shouted at the thing? He shouted, *fuck you, I'm right handed!*" He hesitated. "What did you say when you lost yours?"

"Not much," I replied. "I was unconscious when Tomas cut it off. Seems a long time ago. But, if you wanna talk about swearing, I heard one of your void legionnaires call Alexis Wind Claw a *treacherous cunt* this morning. I think we're rubbing off on you."

"I don't like the facial hair, though," said Santos. "I prefer my warriors to be clean shaven."

I glanced along the barricades and saw Sea Wolves and Dark Brethren standing side by side. "If it weren't for my people wearing beards, I doubt I could tell the difference." I smiled again. "We're one people now."

We said nothing more, though there was a clear understanding between us. We'd managed to make each other smile, and that was a huge victory under the circumstances. As the moment faded, we kept our eyes focused on the assembling Sunken Men and the three huge whips, both trying not to contemplate the approaching cloud. Our immediate future would take one of two paths – the black dust would be effective and we'd live, or it wouldn't and we'd be annihilated. At least there was a simplicity to our situation.

The moments stretched out and we were forced to watch the Sunken Men form into a huge mob between our abandoned warships. The blubbery frog pulsed and gurgled behind them, as if communicating with its minions, but the army of Sunken Men held their position in the shallows, facing our barricades but not attacking.

I pushed a sliver of wyrd into my throat and raised my voice to be heard by every defender of Nowhere. "It's about to happen. Whatever it is, we will trust in the warrior at our side. And if we die, we will die well. Once more for the Eastron!"

From around the eastern cliffs, splashing through the ocean, crawled the Hateful Whip. The skeletal fish-man was on all fours and his cruel, spiny mouth was popping open and closed, with green mucous dripping from lines of curved teeth. It was as if a fuse had been lit, suddenly enraging the whip and driving it towards us. It passed over the Sunken Men, sending a powerful wave across the beach, before clutching its sinewy hands into the rock and sand of Duncan's Fall. It looked ungainly, but that might just have been its immense size, for it was hard to take in every sinewy movement as it rushed toward us, slobbering with unimaginable rage.

As it got closer, I gulped and took quick breaths. The Hateful Whip showed no awareness of the black dust, solidified on the beach before us, and we entered into a terrifying game of chicken. The monster left the Red Straits and the Sunken Men behind and dragged its way up the beach. One pulsing movement after the other, it ploughed towards the barricades, as if it thought it could simply crawl over us. I didn't turn away, not wanting to know how those behind me were reacting.

Then the Hateful Whip's right hand landed on the broad line of solidified black dust and everything changed. The reaction was instant. It had been moving quickly and with intent, but now it tumbled to a stop, as three of its fingers burst into flames. It emitted a high-pitched squeal, with a deep undertone, like the death-rattle of a whale, and grabbed at its burning hand. In doing so, its back rolled onto the black line, sending a wave of fire down the ridges of its spine. The huge creature was just beyond the low outer wall, so close we could see the veins dancing under its translucent, green skin. But it didn't want to attack any more. The line of black dust had caused it more than just pain. The effect was all-encompassing and appeared to creep across its immense body, causing it to flail wildly. It rolled and tumbled, displacing huge amounts of sand and rocks.

I glanced back at the defenders of Nowhere, and saw two thousand warriors reacting exactly the same as me, with wide eyes and quick, short breaths. No one had run, though I knew all wanted to. Instead they clung to their swords, spears and shields, pointing everything forwards, as if they wanted to be back on the high barricades. As it was, only Santos Spirit Killer and I were standing on the wooden wall, watching the Hateful Whip writhe in pain. Several cohorts of Brethren mingled in the centre of our forces, wielding heavy ship chains, hooks and anchors, hopeful that they could be used to entangle and restrain the whips. Tynian Driftwood and the crew of the *Revenge* had killed the Ravenous Whip at the Bay of Bliss, so we knew they could die, but the Hateful Whip and his brothers were far, far bigger.

"Stay sharp," commanded Santos, needing to empty his lungs to be heard above the whip's guttural bellowing.

An immense arm flailed into the barricade, crushing a section of both walls and killing a handful of Sea Wolves, before flailing elsewhere. Half the monster was now on fire and it had no control over its movements. We watched, with the column bulging backwards at the midpoint of our lines, giving the Hateful Whip some room to convulse in pain. Then, with a final bellow of phlegm and slime, the creature slumped forwards, its head landing across our lines, close enough for hundreds of warriors to see its millennia old eyes slowly close.

As it writhed, its body being consumed by the fire of the black dust, Sea Wolves ran at its head. Dark Brethren joined them, with all warriors hacking at the Hateful Whip's skull. The thing might already have been dead, but that didn't stop the defenders of Nowhere from cutting chunks out of its head to make sure. Spears were driven into its eyes, cutlasses and hooks dug into its gills.

"Look," said Santos, pointing at the whip's chest, which lay across the black line.

The fire on its back was now smouldering to a fierce red and gold, turning its flesh black and charred, until it was completely eviscerated, with a clear separation between its legs and its torso. Its innards met the same fate, turning to charcoal as soon as they bubbled from its enormous body.

"That thing might have been a million years old," I muttered.

"And now it's dead," replied Santos. "And I'm forty-two years old... I'm sure there's a parable there somewhere."

I almost laughed – it was the sort of thing Rys Coldfire would have said – but, looking at the corpse of an enormous sea creature, I couldn't find the humour in our situation. I could summon relief that the black dust worked, but it didn't extend to optimism, or even a smile. Deep within me was a slight smirk that we were still alive, but I fought against it, wanting to keep my edge for whatever happened next.

"That's enough!" I shouted, dragging a hundred blades from their frenzied attack on the whip's head. "Save your wyrd for something that's still alive."

"This isn't over," shouted Siggy Blackeye, from within the nearest mob of Sea Wolves.

"But the cunts know we mean business," roared Kieran Greenfire, further along the line.

The last Eastron to leave the Hateful Whip's twitching head was Charlie Vane. The cackling Kneeling Wolf raider finished cutting an eye from the creature's enormous skull, before dumping it on the craggy ground and kicking it repeatedly. "That's what you get," growled the War Rat, stomping on the huge, sickly white eye until it fell into mush.

Whatever the black dust was to these creatures, it caused more than just injuries. The burning, the pain – the dust made the Hateful Whip lose all reason and focus, preventing it from even trying to escape when it could have done. But it was a trick we could only play once. The Sunken Men on the beach were twisting and turning in distress, engaged in some kind of bizarre dance at the sight of the dead whip and the black dust. They waved their weapons in the air, hopping from side to side, with several groups trying to skulk back into the ocean. It was only the gargled sounds of the Bulbous Whip, towering over them, that stopped half the group retreating.

"Daniel!" I shouted, looking for the Sundered Wolf amongst Siggy's company. "Get up here."

He jostled to get back up to the barricade.

"It worked," he said, apparently as relieved as the rest of us.

"Now what?" I asked. "They saw what we've got and they're fucking terrified of it. So what will they do?"

He shrugged. "How should I know? I'm not an expert on the Sunken God and his minions; I've just seen a lot of shit and I know a lot of shit." It was hard to know when he was being sincere, and when he was just being vague.

"And you don't know this?"

"Not a clue," he replied, shaking his head. "But I don't think they're going to run away." He looked up at the malevolent cloud, which had stopped its advance in line with the enormous frog. "As long as that cloud's up there, they'll throw whatever they've got at us. We're the last free Eastron, remember. I don't think they've got anywhere else to go."

"We have more dust? We'll need to use it."

"No," he replied, surprising me. "It's with Eva, as is Rys Coldfire. There's another chapter to this story, Adeline."

"Fuck off, just speak sense," I grunted, exasperated at his obtuse manner.

"No," he repeated. "You need to concentrate on *this*." He nodded at the beach, the small army of Sunken Men, and the two remaining whips. "Let me, my former wife, and the Wolf's Bastard worry about the next thing."

"Rys should be here with me," I snapped. "He said he'd return."

"He will," said Daniel. "After Eva has finished with him. He wanted to know about me, so she's telling him a story about the Bright Lands, the Death Bear, and why a man can't die."

I was about to swear at him again, perhaps warn him that one more obtuse comment would result in a slap, or complain that he'd never told *me* the origin of his unique ability. Unfortunately, before I could do either of those things, the Bulbous Whip hopped forwards. The enormous, rancid green frog flexed its legs and left the Red Straits, landing halfway up the beach. It was far shorter than the Hateful Whip, but equal in mass, with layer upon layer of blubbery flesh. Its gummy mouth was as wide as *Halfdan's Revenge*, with a sickly pink tongue, tickling the air of Duncan's Fall.

Santos Spirit Killer rushed along our lines, until he reached the broken section where the Hateful Whip had fallen. He turned to the defenders of Nowhere, but none of them needed an order to stand ready. Every man and woman stood their ground, forming a single column in loose formation.

"If you've got any more tricks, now's the time to tell me," I said to Daniel.

"I've got plenty of tricks," he replied. "But the black dust is all I've got against that thing."

I left him, rushing along the wooden platform, towards Santos. "Time to see if you bastards have tactics," I said to myself.

It was strange to see the Sunken Men reluctant. Of all those I'd seen, fought and killed, I'd never seen them afraid or even tentative. It was only the Bulbous Whip that pulled them from the shallows. They moved singularly and in mobs, with no real cohesion, skulking up the beach towards the immense frog. The black dust terrified them, as a wall of raging fire would to an Eastron. They recoiled from the line, averting their eyes, but unable to resist the whip's commands.

I reached Santos Spirit Killer, next to the break in our barricades and the twitching corpse of the Hateful Whip.

"Looks like they're going to rush us," exclaimed the void legionnaire. "Can they do that? Across the black line?"

"I have no idea, but we need to reform on the second wall. And plug that gap."

The commander turned from the massed Sunken Men and started shouting at the warriors behind us. The closest legionnaires returned to the wall with the speed and skill of professional soldiers, pointing their shields and spears back to the beach. I saw hundreds of men and women with steely glares and complete focus, fighting against fear and exhaustion to stand their ground. Around them, led by Wilhelm and Kieran Greenfire, there assembled gangs of Wolves, many of whom had acquired legionary shields.

"Charlie Vane!" I shouted. "You get to hold the gap."

The War Rat grinned, showing me dirty teeth and blood-shot eyes. He nodded and led his raiders back to the enormous corpse, where they secured ropes and climbed up on the slimy, green body of the Hateful Whip. More than a hundred Kneeling Wolves stood on its neck and chest, with Charlie himself positioned on its head, at the new highest point of our barricades. The immense corpse was cut in two at the waist and looked as if it would form a good defensive position, if the enemy somehow managed to charge us across the line of black.

The Sunken Men amassed around the enormous frog, each a unique creature, smashed together from pieces of frogs, toads, fish and men, with the only commonality being that they were all bipedal and all at least twice the size of an Eastron. They held position, not advancing the last twenty feet towards the line of solidified black dust. Above them, the Bulbous Whip was croaking and gargling, slopping huge bubbles of phlegm onto the beach. I thought about ordering archers to fire at the thing, but had no confidence they'd even pierce its blubbery hide.

"Lock shields," commanded Santos, sending a clank of obedience down the line, as our steel formed a second barrier above the high wooden wall.

"Ready your wyrd!" I bellowed.

Then we waited. Seconds of tension flowed into minutes, with muscles kept taut and eyes kept open, but they didn't attack. It was hard to know what was happening, but I felt as if we were witnessing a negotiation. There were around five hundred Sunken Men, varying massively in size, and the largest few were hopping left and right on the beach, gesturing with their pincer-tipped spears. They made popping and sucking sounds, but I couldn't tell what emotion they were expressing.

"Err, my lady First Fang," said a timid voice from my left.

I turned and saw Hitch, a rig-rat from the *Revenge*, who'd been acting as a horse messenger between the beach and Utha's Gate. "What do you want?" I asked.

"This is a shitty time for shitty news, but the Stranger's arrived," he replied. " A few hours ago. Says he needs to talk to you."

I raised an eyebrow at the short Sea Wolf. "Look over there," I said. "What do you see?"

Hitch leant against the wooden wall and peered to the south. "Fuck me! I see some scary shit. Is that the right answer?" He turned from the Bulbous Whip and the massed Sunken Men, trying to smile at me.

"It's a good enough answer," I said. "Do you think I should take a moment from that scary shit to meet with Marius Cyclone?"

"Err, no," replied Hitch, as if searching for the right answer. "I think you should do whatever you want to do, my lady First Fang."

"Good. Glad to have your permission. Go back and tell the Stranger that, if he wants to talk to me, he should come down here... assuming I'm still alive in ten minutes."

Hitch nodded and quickly moved away, with the nearest warriors looking at him in bewilderment. For a dozen or so defenders of Nowhere, it was a strangely welcome distraction – not necessarily hearing that Marius had arrived, but that Hitch had chosen this moment to tell me. For an instant, there were ironic smiles. Then I looked back to the beach and saw that the Sunken Men had finished their negotiations with the Bulbous Whip.

23

The Vile Whip didn't approach. All we could see of the largest creature before us was its head, poking over the northern coast of Nibonay, overseeing everything beneath it. Neither it, nor the enormous frog and the Sunken Men, nor the bubbling cloud appeared to care that we'd managed to kill the Hateful Whip. I didn't know if they experienced surprise and I certainly couldn't read the expressions on their faces. Nevertheless, it was clear that they had no intention of retreating, black dust or no black dust.

The Bulbous Whip shuffled forwards until it was within ten feet of the black line, and twenty feet from our outer wall. The creature was large enough to simply hop over our barricades. It might even have been able to clear the column of defenders. But it didn't, as if there was an invisible wall rising from the solidified black dust. Either side of the frog, moving hesitantly, were five hundred Sunken Men of various sizes, wielding spikes, pincers and spears, all adorned with seaweed and reeking of rotten algae and decomposing fish.

Everyone on our side held their collective breath, wondering silently how they planned to attack across the black dust when it had so effectively killed one of the largest creatures any of us had ever seen. The Sunken Men and the huge frog assembled well away from the steaming corpse, on the right side of our barricades, close to where Kieran and

Siggy commanded. There they clustered together, sheltering within the enormous shadows cast by the whip.

Then the frog's blubbery throat contracted, its mouth popped and gargled, and it vomited forth a vile gout of glistening phlegm. There were flecks of red and white within the pale green vomit, and the creature sprayed it left and right, covering a large section of the black line and our low, outer wall. As soon as it touched the dust, it began to burn away – but, in the moment it was covered, the Sunken Men charged. Many lost arms and legs to sudden fire, many more recoiled so violently that they flung themselves back down the beach, but dozens reached the high second wall.

"Shields!" I commanded. "Don't let them breach the wall."

A man nearby had his head severed by a pincer. Further down the wall, one of the larger Sunken Men flung three legionnaires from the barricade. I drew my cutlass and stood behind the line of shields, seeing Santos do the same. Daniel furtively backed away, realizing he was of little use in a straight up fight. Then the killing began.

Two hundred Sunken Men had rushed us, with half that number dying when they reached the line of black dust. The whip's phlegm was barely effective, but the huge creature clearly cared nothing for its smaller brethren. Even so, the hundred creatures that reached our shields were challenge enough. They were manic and frenzied, as if the dust had infected their minds, flailing wildly at any shield or spear they could reach. We stabbed and cut, but little steel penetrated their bulbous flesh.

Dozens of flabby arms reached over the wall and past our shields, pummelling defenders to death with little effort. The biggest Sunken Men were taller than the barricades and could strike downwards with their pincer weapons, indiscriminately severing arms, legs, torsos and heads. They had no skill or strategy, but we were simply not their match in strength or durability, and our shield wall began to disintegrate.

"Go for their eyes!" I roared, moving along the line.

The more powerful Eastron on our wall summoned their wyrd and took key positions along the line. Kieran and his warriors managed to wrap a chain around a Sunken Man's head, and the short Sea Wolf repeatedly drove his blade into the creature's face and eyes. Siggy had found a spot between shields, and was deflecting pincer blows with dizzying flashes of wyrd. A remarkably tall void legionnaire had discarded his shield, grasped his spear in both hands and managed to drive his weapon clean through the head of one of the larger attackers. At the far end of our line, where there was no attack, Wilhelm Greenfire, the High Captain, was leading his warriors to the point of danger, where his prodigious wyrd would be more valuable.

I'd not yet committed to the fight and was trying to keep my wits, looking for an advantage. I pulled my eyes from the line of carnage and looked back down the beach, frowning when I saw that the Bulbous Whip and the other three hundred Sunken Men had retreated to the shallows. More surprisingly, the whip was killing its smaller cousins, snaring them with its huge tongue and pulling them into its mouth. It occurred to me that the rest of the Sunken Men would not attack again. The hundred creatures who had reached our barricades was intended to be enough.

"Hear me," I boomed. "Enough of this defensive line shit. Fight like fucking Sea Wolves."

336

"About time," roared Charlie Vane, standing tall on the head of the Hateful Whip. The War Rat held two short swords and let forth a guttural challenge, before diving onto the head of the nearest Sunken Man. He cackled as he locked his legs around the creature's neck and stabbed at its head maniacally.

All across our lines, swearing filled the air. The fight quickly broke up, with the line of shields disappearing and a thousand Eastron starting to fight dirty. The second wall was now broken in several places and the defenders formed mobs, surrounding any creature they could isolate. Against a defensive wall, the Sunken Men were devastating, but against a broken formation of skilled killers, they appeared cumbersome and confused.

Siggy had acquired a cohort of legionnaires with a ship anchor and chains, and she managed to corral three Sunken Men together, toppling them into a single pile, before swarming them with blades at close range. Kieran and warriors from the *Revenge* had discovered that groins and underarms were almost as vulnerable as eyes, and were sharing this knowledge with anyone close enough to listen.

Then I was forced to join the fight. Next to Santos and I, a void legionnaire was torn apart by a pincer and we were both thrown backwards, as a huge creature smashed through the wooden wall. Cutlasses and spears bounced off its slimy green skin, and its grotesque belly rippled as it moved. Three Brethren and two Wolves were dead within an instant, though I managed to roll aside, dropping my cutlass and pulling Santos with me.

"Get up," I snapped. "Move."

The huge Sunken Man was the first to step on our side of the lines, and the thing began to rampage through the loosely packed column of defenders. I was rooted to the spot for a second, remembering the creature I'd killed at Dark Wing's bone palace. They were of similar size, but that one had been entangled in wire and I'd been infused with the Old Bitch of the Sea. I had doubts and I had fear, but I picked up a Brethren straight sword, summoned my wyrd, and ran at the creature anyway.

It was wading onwards, with no apparent peripheral vision, relying on its thick hide to protect it from dozens of blades. As I approached its flank, with Santos behind me, I saw no obvious way of killing the thing, so I just jumped at one of its ankles. I kept hold of the sword, and used my legs to entangle the creature below the knee.

The Sunken Man paused, planting its pincer-tipped spear in the ground and shaking its leg, as if I were an irritant. Then Santos tackled its other leg and it came to a stop. The creature swayed above us, its huge belly and sinewy arms rippling in the air. I nodded at Santos and we both put all our weight into the creature's ankles, pulling it to the ground. It gargled and gulped, too large and ungainly to keep its footing, before toppling over to the side.

"Kill the fucking thing!" I shouted, finding my throat dry and raw.

I sat up against its leg and began sawing my Brethren straight sword across its calf. It was like drawing a blunt knife across meat, with no purchase or bite. Then I began to stab, and broke its skin with the third strike. Dark Brethren and Sea Wolves rushed to us, stabbing at any piece of green flesh they could find, until it dropped its pincer and began convulsing in a spreading pool of its own oozing blood.

When I stood from the dying monster, I saw the scene repeat behind us, as more and more of the largest Sunken Men battered their way through our walls, our wyrd and our steel. The smaller ones had mostly been killed or incapacitated, but those that remained took a dozen or more warriors to even slow them down. They weren't whips, but were probably thousands of years old, and able to casually kill any mortal that wasn't fast enough to avoid their mauling attacks.

I ran to join the nearest group, and found my world shrink down to a tight melee. After days of looking at the expansive vistas off Duncan's Fall and the high cliffs of Nowhere, it was strange to be fighting in close formation again, with no real view beyond my immediate surroundings. The sounds of shouting, dying and lumbering monsters told a distinctive story of what was happening, but I could only see the huge Sunken Man in front of me.

Santos was at my side and Kieran Greenfire was opposite, as we tried to surround the creature. Legionnaires wielded spears and kept their distance, while sailors from the *Revenge* darted in and out, stabbing at its feet and legs. Somewhere there was an archer, and three arrows hung limply from the thing's head, though they'd not penetrated far. It was flailing too much for us to tackle it, and the fight became a gruesome battle of attrition. The Sunken Man flung its torso around, striking at anyone within range in an attempt to stop us cutting it. Defenders were crushed by its huge limbs, but we slowly began to overwhelm it.

Somewhere beyond my sight, I heard Siggy Blackeye and the War Rat shouting. Evidently, they'd killed another of the larger Sunken Men. The one in front of me was now on its knees, with Sea Wolves swarming it, having to jostle for the best angle to strike at its eyes. As its movements degraded to twitching, I heard more shouting from the High Captain, indicating that another of our foes had been killed.

Slowly, one laboured breath at a time, I stood and surveyed the scene. The fight had broken up, and I could again see along our lines. The barricades were empty of defenders, with everyone on the low ground beyond the beach, in tight pockets of resistance. Each group surrounded either a faltering Sunken Man or the corpse of one, though repulsing the attack had taken a heavy toll on the defenders of Nowhere and I struggled to count the dead Eastron.

I assessed that the closest creatures would be dead before I arrived to help, and thought the best course was to return to the outer wall and see what was happening on the beach.

I grabbed Santos Spirit Killer by the top of his leather armour and pulled him to face me. "Finish the last few off," I ordered. "Then find how many we have dead and wounded."

He nodded, wiping sweat, blood and slime from his face. "I'll find you on the wall... but I think we won."

"For now," I replied, turning from him and pushing my way back to the outer barricades.

I had to step over mutilated bodies to reach the wall, and jostle past grim faces, each of which nodded at me. Even the Dark Brethren now saw me as their leader, and I found myself recognizing many of them. The freakishly tall legionnaire, who'd skewered a Sunken Man on the wall, was called Lazlo, and he bowed in respect as I walked past him. A stout woman, still wearing her legion greaves and braces, banged a fist against her chest and nodded to me. She'd been with Siggy when they'd used a chain to ensnare three of the smaller Sunken Men, and I'd heard her called Spectre. These were my people now, as much as Kieran, Siggy and Rys. I hoped that Lazlo and Spectre trusted me, and I hoped I could keep them alive.

As I reached the wall, a few more howls of victory told me that the remaining Sunken Men were being finished off. Above me, on the wooden platform, was Daniel Doesn't Die. He'd not been involved in the fight, and was quick to return to the barricade. He was looking south, across Duncan's Fall, though his face showed no alarm. I took this to be a good sign.

"How does it look?" I asked, hefting myself up to join him.

"Quiet," he replied.

I took some deep breaths and rubbed my eyes before looking. Our low, outer wall was mostly destroyed. The high barricade, upon which I stood, was now five or six separate walls, with huge, splintered sections between them. The largest Sunken Men had created massive gaps in our defences, but the black line, snaking east to west, was still intact.

Daniel chuckled. "Big tough warrior, afraid to look at the enemy."

"Fuck off," I replied, though I shared his chuckle, realizing I was looking in increments, afraid of what I might see.

I raised my head and looked south, to the beach of Duncan's Fall. The rocks and sand were churned up from the huge, webbed feet of the Bulbous Whip and the spiky limbs of the Hateful Whip, but the beach was empty. The tide was higher now and our abandoned warships rolled in the shallows, with several of the smaller vessels drifting into the Red Straits.

"They've gone," I said, seeing empty water and an empty coastline.

There were no Sunken Men, and both the remaining whips had disappeared. All that remained was the unnatural cloud, bubbling above the coast of Nibonay. I was reminded of Alexis Wind Claw, and the manner in which she'd pulled her entire fleet back from the coast. She'd tried to invade Nowhere and she'd failed. Now the whips and the Sunken Men had tried to invade Nowhere and they'd failed too. I gulped, realizing that whatever was in the cloud was their next, and possibly final, line of attack.

We'd repelled a hundred Sunken Men at the cost of five hundred Eastron. The survivors wore wounds, and expressions of cold steel, as they took their rest beyond the outer wall. No one thought it was over, but a few hours of quiet was a valuable resource and exhausted warriors were not going to waste it. Grizzled Sea Wolves lounged next to stern Dark Brethren, sharing jokes with grubby Kneeling Wolves. They ate bread and meat, drank dark beer, and told improbable stories of their battle prowess. Over the last few days, we'd done so much fighting against so many foes that any story was possible.

The massive, slimy corpses of the Sunken Men had been dragged into piles and set alight, providing our entire encampment with light and warmth. Twilight was here and the creatures were surprisingly flammable. Even more surprising was that fire burned away the smell, filling the air with a warm, smoky aroma.

I'd wanted to stay awake, but as dusk approached and the air became still and cold, I found my eyes drooping. I'd been laughing at Charlie Vane, bragging about how he'd pissed on the head of the Hateful Whip, but it wasn't enough to keep me awake. Most defenders of Nowhere eventually did the same, trying not to look at the malevolent cloud before they stole some precious hours of sleep. Whatever dwelt in the roiling black and grey, it was clearly in no rush to attack. Before I fell into a deep sleep, I even heard whispered talk of us being able to retreat to Utha's Gate in the morning.

"Wake up, Adeline," said a strange yet familiar voice.

I winced, coughed, rubbed my face, and looked up into the pink eyes of Utha the Ghost. Behind him, rose the warm sun of his void realm, and I felt that he'd once again pulled me through the glass. I coughed a second time and sat up, scratching at various places that had been languishing under leather for several days without feeling any fresh air. Sweat and blood made my skin tacky and itchy, but on balance I didn't feel too bad. I smelled fucking terrible, but I could live with that – it was no worse than every other defender of Nowhere.

"We can talk," I croaked. "But do you have any dark beer? It's good for breakfast. Takes the edge off."

"I have stout," replied the pale man. "Marius gave me the recipe. You use roasted malt. I've developed quite a taste for it."

"Yes, yes, whatever you've got."

We were on a high terrace of the Shadow, looking down at the beautiful green and brown valley of our new home. I'd been reclining on a sofa, and now felt the full wash of peace that the realm provided. It cut through the mask of concentrated aggression I'd worn for the last week and assaulted my mind with overwhelming calmness.

Utha was still wearing a simple robe, with his long white hair braided down his back. He retreated along the railing to a wooden keg placed on an ornate black table. I didn't know if it had been there a moment earlier, or if summoning alcohol was another of the pale man's abilities, but I didn't really care. He returned with two mugs and handed me one.

"To your very good health," said Utha, raising his mug.

"Okay," I replied, frowning at his toast, before taking a deep swig.

It was thicker and richer than Sea Wolf ale, but rather drinkable. I took another deep swig, reorienting myself on the sofa, before preparing for whatever the pale man wanted to tell me. Marius Cyclone was alive and safe on Nowhere, so *that* can't have been it. The beach had, so far, been defended, so he wouldn't want to talk about that. I gulped down half the mug of stout, and came fully awake.

"Talk," I said. "Just... not too long-winded, if you don't mind."

"You need to meet with Marius," he said. "You need to meet with him and you need to make a decision. Your swords, your wyrd and your skill are of no further use at Duncan's Fall. You should pull your warriors back, before they face something they can't look at, let alone fight. They're brave men and women. If it weren't for them, this island would have been overrun. They deserve more than to fall to something so primal."

"The cloud," I said. "Is it the Sunken God?"

He considered it. "It's the distortion in reality that the Sunken God causes. It has no fixed form, though it can appear when it wants to."

"Can *you* fight it?" I asked. "Assume that massive shadow form and, I don't know, do something?"

"I'm afraid not," he replied. "I could appear like that at the Severed Hand because the glass was broken. Everywhere else I am limited. Unless they're foolish enough to attack my gate directly."

"Brilliant," I replied, drily. "Go and get me some more beer. I assume any drunken effects will be gone when I wake up in the realm of form."

He nodded, taking my mostly empty mug and handing me his own mostly full one.

"Decide what?" I asked, taking regular swigs of the stout. "You said I need to meet the Stranger and make a decision. We fall back from the beach – okay. But Daniel Doesn't Die said there's another chapter to this. What did he mean?"

Utha smiled and his eyes softened. I was reminded that, beyond his striking appearance and his unknowable power, he was a man of morals. He may even have been the rarest of things – a good man.

"I sometimes forget," he said, making me feel like I was missing half the story. "There are two mighty spiritual forces at work here. The man who drank the Death Bear's eye is infused by the great phoenix, who sees all of time from the top of a lofty perch. Ten Cuts, my oldest friend in this realm, is guided by the great turtles, who see time going backwards and know the future by remembering it. Both forces have seen this moment. They've seen the end of the Eastron. But neither of them knows what happens next."

I glared at him, sipping from my mug of stout. "Fascinating. Doesn't answer my fucking question though. What do I need to decide?"

"Perhaps Daniel can answer that question better than I," he replied. "I knew to send Marius to a strange new island to the north, where he'd find something of great value. And I know it will force you to make a decision – whether or not you, Adeline Brand, can live in peace. But I don't know how you will answer. Perhaps the phoenix knows."

I grunted, finishing my second mug of stout. "I told you to not be long-winded. That was really fucking long-winded. Isn't peace what's waiting for us?" I nodded away from the Shadow, towards the lush valleys beyond.

Suddenly, his pale face rose, as if the smell of a predator had reached his nostrils. He ignored my question and took a deep breath, flaring his large shoulders. Under his robe, I saw a solid, muscular man, tensing his arms and legs. There was a poise and precision to his movements that made me think he knew how to fight, but rarely needed to. His reaction wasn't fear, but a predatory awareness of a threat.

"What is it?" I asked. "What do you see?"

"You should wake up," he growled. "Pull your warriors back to my gate. And find Marius Cyclone. The last chapter is about to begin."

24

Could I live in peace? It had never been a relevant question, for my entire life had been spent at war. At the Severed Hand, a duellist knew nothing but combat. Most were expected not to question their existence, and the few of us who rose to senior status would never think to doubt what it meant to be a Sea Wolf. It was simply the way of the world. When there were no battles close by, we'd created battles at sea. We'd made enemies of the Dark Brethren, simply to provide an antagonist to our heroic stories. We'd grown, lived and died, all at the altar of our imagined honour. We'd been so full of shit it made me sick.

When I opened my eyes, it was dawn. The beach at Duncan's Fall was bathed in sunlight, but there was little warmth. Something was sucking the heat from the air. As I rolled over on the wooden wall and found my footing, I saw hundreds of others waking up, as if we'd all been roused by the same change in pressure. As the defenders of Nowhere stood, silently looking south, there was no chatter, just the sound of people breathing and wood creaking.

Our view had changed. The coast of Nibonay, previously formed of sheer cliffs, was now a long line of earth and rock, as if the cliffs had fallen into the Red Straits. Trees, boulders, grass and dirt had been part of the island when I fell asleep; now they had tumbled down loose gravel to be swept away on the tides. Bizarrely, large chunks of earth and rock were also floating in the sky, as if falling upwards towards the cloud.

The cloud too was different. Not only did it now exert a gravitational pull on Nibonay, but its texture, colours and composition had all changed. The roiling black and grey had been replaced by crackling green and blue, fizzing across the horizon. It was no closer, but filled far more of the southern sky. The angry storm cloud and the strange shapes had become something else. Now there were thousands of eyes bulging outwards, with black pupils and rotten green cornea. They appeared and disappeared within the cloud, with fleshy growths bubbling between them, appearing to hang in the air, far above the crumbling coastline. I saw a hundred mockeries of form displayed in the sky, pulsing and changing, like none of it was real or solid. Or perhaps the Sunken God was deciding on a final shape. It was taking its time, destroying the coastline as it filled the sky with eldritch horrors.

I stepped back from the barricade and leant on the wall, taking deep breaths and composing myself. Utha was right – steel and wyrd were of no further use here.

"Fall back," I whispered. "We should fall back." No one was close enough to hear me, and a glance along our lines revealed a thousand men and women, staring in fear at this new manifestation of the Sunken God.

A few more deep breaths and shakes of the head and I screamed in the face of the nearest warrior. "Fall back!" It was a young legionnaire, suddenly forced to decide whether he was more scared of me or the cloud. Then I turned, locating Santos Spirit Killer and Wilhelm Greenfire further along the line. "Santos, we are fucking leaving. Wilhelm, we're falling back to Utha's Gate. Kieran! Siggy! Get everyone moving... now!"

"Abandon the wall!" commanded Santos, dragging his legionnaires from the barricade.

"Stop looking at that fucking cloud," barked the High Captain, slapping several Sea Wolves in the face.

"You wanna be scared of something," shouted Siggy, "be scared of the First Fang!"

"Time to go, ladies and gentlemen," added Kieran, nodding at his father before leaping back from the wall.

Enough of our warriors regained their senses to drag the rest from the barricade, and a full retreat began. The wounded had already been taken back north, and the rest were able to run. Our minimal supplies were left behind the ruined second wall, and well over a thousand defenders of Nowhere fled. I waited until the end, leaving the barricades only when I was sure I was leaving no one behind.

After weeks of holding the line, we had finally given up our position at Duncan's Fall. We'd held it against Eastron, animated corpses, Sunken Men and whips. Only an enemy we couldn't fight had pushed us into retreat.

The cloud didn't encroach further. As we ran north, past abandoned shelters and cold fire-pits, every one of us glanced back, but the view became less and less disturbing as we covered the ground. By the time we reached Cold Point, the Grim Wolf's empty fortress, the cloud had disappeared beyond the southern horizon. Our warriors had broken up into smaller groups, according to their fitness and ability to run, and most of us were now barely an hour from Utha's Gate.

"Riders ahead," came a call from the front of our column.

"Name them," I replied, wearily, relaying the instruction.

"Err, looks like the Wolf's Bastard," came the response. "And others… in a cart."

I turned to Santos and the High Captain, both trudging along next to me. "Don't stop. Get everyone to the gate."

"And you?" asked Santos.

"I think I'm about to meet with the Stranger," I replied, coming to a stop on the rugged plains of Nowhere. "After that, who knows? But these warriors deserve their chance at peace. Just keep everyone moving."

Santos banged a fist on his chest in salute and kept walking, whereas Wilhelm Greenfire stopped and faced me.

"You know, I never liked you," said the High Captain. "Lord Ulric Blood was more in line with my way of thinking. You're too young to be First Fang. Too impulsive and inexperienced." He bowed his head, before slowly offering me his hand. "But you might be the finest commander I've ever served under. And you've given the Sea Wolves a chance to endure."

I took his hand. "We are no longer the same people," I replied. "I respected Ulric, but his time had ended. He didn't get to see this, so he remains the last true First Fang of the Severed Hand."

"Goodbye, Adeline Brand. I hope to see you soon." Wilhelm released my hand and resumed his trudge to the gate. I didn't tell him that Duncan, his youngest son, was still alive in Utha's realm. They'd had a complicated relationship and it wasn't up to me to prepare him for the surprise.

I found a rock and sat on it, as hundreds of men and women marched past. Most paid their respects, but no one stopped to talk. After so much death, they were eager to reach Utha's Gate. I saw gangs of battered void legionnaires and exhausted Sea Wolves pulling themselves north in groups of ten or twenty, helping each other as best they could.

"Yeah, I'm sick of walking too," said Siggy Blackeye, reaching my rock and plonking herself down on the grass next to me. "After all this, the thing that hurts the most is the fucking blisters."

I smiled at her. "I've got sweat drying over sweat. I think there's mould growing in my arse."

"When was the last time you had a proper wash?"

I rubbed my hand down my face, feeling a layer of grime. "Unless you count sticking my head in a bucket of water, it's gotta be about a week."

She nodded. "Same."

"Lazy," said Kieran Greenfire, stopping to join us. "Get on your feet, we're almost there."

"Rys is up ahead," I replied. "I imagine he's got the Stranger with him. I thought I'd meet them here, just in case I have to turn back. Where's Daniel?"

Kieran turned, looking south. "He was at the back somewhere. The fat old fuck was wheezing."

The defenders of Nowhere began to thin out, with the groups in front of us parting to allow a single horse and a single cart to approach across the uneven ground. The rider reached us first, wheeling his horse to a stop in front of the rock. It was Rys Coldfire, called the Wolf's Bastard, and he nimbly jumped to the ground before the horse had come to a complete stop. The cart followed, containing three people who disembarked with far less alacrity than Rys.

"How flows your wyrd, Adeline?" said the Wolf's Bastard, using an old Sea Wolf greeting.

"Slowly and carefully," I replied. "I hear Eva Rage Breaker has been telling you stories."

"Just the one story," said Rys. "About why a man can't die."

"He's never told me that story," I said. "But we could have used you at the beach."

"You didn't need me then," he replied. "You need me now."

He'd always been inscrutable, but this time he had the advantage of knowing something I didn't. The importance of that knowledge was not yet clear, though I still trusted the old duellist.

Behind Rys, helped to the ground by two lithe, well-armed Dark Brethren, was Marius Cyclone. The Stranger wore a black robe, covering most of his body, but I could tell he was badly hurt. He tilted to the left, leaning sharply, almost to the point of appearing hunched. One of his legs carried no weight and the other was tentative, creeping along the ground as if he was unsure of its strength. Previously, he'd cut an imposing figure – tall for a Brethren, with a straight back and a slowly moving stare. Now he was frail, needing the man and woman either side to help him approach.

"He was captured and tortured by Oliver Dawn Claw," said Rys. "His mind still works though."

"*That's* Adeline Brand?" enquired the young woman at the Stranger's left side.

"She's only got one arm," observed the young man at his right.

"I'm not impressed," added the woman, shaking her head.

The two Dark Brethren had a similar frown on their faces, with the same coloured eyes. I guessed they were brother and sister. Kieran, Siggy and I shared a few raised eyebrows at the insolent Dark Brethren, but this wasn't the time to fight, so I gave a subtle shake of the head. I found that insults didn't bother me as much as they used to.

"You get that for free," said Siggy. "But another insult comes out of your mouth and I'll fucking close it."

Marius tried to laugh, but it ended in a retch and a painful cough. "Sorry," he spluttered, spitting on the ground and clearing his throat. "I'm not at my best. Adeline Brand, it's good to see you again. These two infuriating bastards are Asha and Gaius Two Hearts. They're twins and they don't believe in tact... or internal monologues."

I rose from my rock and approached him. In a display that surprised all present, including Marius, I put a hand on his shoulder and smiled warmly. "I'm sorry. When you and Utha saved us at the Severed Hand, I'm sorry I didn't believe you. You have to understand... I'm a Sea Wolf. I hated you before I hated anything else. It was hard to shake."

He coughed again, before shaking off the brother and sister and managing to stand on his own. With evident pain, he straightened to look me in the eye. "I was angry at you. But I reconciled it by asking myself a simple question... would I have told *you* to fuck off, if the situation had been reversed?" He nodded. "Yes, I probably would have done."

"It doesn't matter now," I replied. "Because of you and I, the Eastron will endure. You've made mistakes, and I've made some fucking big ones, but we're both alive. Anyone who wants to live in peace will get the chance to."

The Stranger looked past me, to the rearguard of our retreat. The last few dozen defenders of Nowhere were trudging north, most not noticing that the First Fang was having a casual chat with a deformed Marius Cyclone.

"You held the beach?" he asked. "I hope my legionnaires carried their weight."

"They did," I replied. "They're tough, loyal warriors. We couldn't have held our ground if it weren't for Santos, Jessimion and your void legions." I smiled, remembering the camaraderie we'd found at the beach. "We're one people now, Marius. This is an army of Eastron, not of Wolves and Brethren."

"I like her," said Asha Two Hearts.

"Me too," agreed her brother.

"But she's still only got one arm," added Asha. "I doubt she can fight."

I sized up the Two Hearts twins. Both were shorter than me, but they were dripping with weapons: short swords at their hips, knives across their chests, hatchets and throwing knives tucked into their boots. If I had to guess, I'd say they were killers, rather than fighters. I judged them good protection for a crippled man.

"You wanna be careful," I said to them. "I don't take that shit personally, but Siggy will tear your face off."

They frowned at me, before looking at the angry Sea Wolf standing by the rock. Siggy's mouth was twitching as if she was resisting a multitude of violent urges. Luckily, Kieran was more controlled, and gently shepherded her backwards, out of earshot. They quickly returned, using each other to stay composed.

"Old anger is the strongest kind," I said to Marius. "Sea Wolves still like to pick fights with Dark Brethren. Now, what did you bring? Utha gave me some cryptic bollocks about something of great worth."

The Stranger nodded back to the cart, directing the Two Hearts twins to retrieve something wrapped in sacking. "The story of how we found this... is rather complicated," said Marius. "An eldritch tale of ship battles, sea monsters, cannibalism, insane Winterlords and much, much death. Oh, and there was a great turtle spirit... and a cat, but he wasn't really involved."

I didn't try to decipher what he was saying. I kept my eyes on the item being hefted from the back of the cart. It was wrapped up tightly in canvas and sacking, and was held by Asha and Gaius as if they were afraid of it. A tingle of wyrd travelled down my spine. I glanced either side of me and saw that Siggy, Kieran and Rys had the same reaction. I didn't know what it was, but it had potent spiritual power.

"What is it?" I asked.

Marius nodded at the Wolf's Bastard before replying, "Rys suggested that he answer that question. Apparently, if I told you, it would sound like horse-shit."

Everyone turned to look at Rys Coldfire. He'd still not retrieved his falchion, nor chosen to don any armour, but this didn't disguise his intimidating aura.

"The Sunken God is called Klu'zu," said the Sea Wolf duellist. "His sister and equal was called Nym'zu. *That* is a droplet of her blood. When a mortal touches it, it will lead the enemy from Nowhere." He paused, with an edge of gallows humour intruding at the corners of his mouth and eyes. "And I will be its bearer. I will not travel through Utha's

Gate and live in peace. There are still thousands of Eastron, waiting to leave and build a new world. They deserve peace far more than me. Elizabeth will finish our cottage on her own."

I looked at him, then Marius, then the Two Hearts twins, as they placed the bound item on the ground before us. I filtered this new information and took from it the most important point – this thing could lead the Sunken God from Nowhere. I locked eyes with Rys as I asked the question I'd been trying not to think about. "How many more Eastron are waiting at the gate?"

"Including the warriors from the beach?" replied Marius. "Six or seven thousand. We need another day. What's happening at Duncan's Fall?"

"We don't have another day," I replied. "He's here."

"So you believe Rys?" asked the Stranger. "You have no questions?"

"I believe him *and* I have plenty of questions, but most can wait." I frowned at the Wolf's Bastard. "What are you going to do? Grab that thing and dive off a cliff? Maybe swim into the Red Straits? Hope you reach Yish before the Sunken God consumes you?"

"No," replied Rys.

From the south, at the very tail of our retreat, came a distinctive clatter. A cart was lumbering over the rough plains, moving slowly under the power of two oxen. It was flanked by void legionnaires, coaxing it forwards with the last of the fleeing defenders of Nowhere. Sitting at the reins, and looking rather pleased with himself, was Daniel Doesn't Die. Behind him, resting in the cart, was the remainder of his black dust, and Anya's Roar, the old talisman that enabled a warship to fly through the void on the back of a great phoenix.

"The *Revenge*," said Kieran Greenfire, having heard our conversation. "She's just sitting on the beach."

"It's almost high tide," added Siggy, having suppressed her violent impulses. "We could get it underway with a skeleton crew."

I took a breath. This was what Utha meant. I had to answer the question of whether or not I could live in peace. I'd not really thought about how I'd rebuild in Utha's realm. The thought of putting aside my cutlass and building a new life was not one I enjoyed, however much I'd been fighting for it. It was for everyone else, not necessarily for me.

"Okay," I muttered. "If we take Rys and that... thing, we're deciding not to go through Utha's Gate. Even with Anya's Roar, we probably won't survive."

The Wolf's Bastard strode past us to greet Daniel. Whatever he'd been told by Eva Rage Breaker had obviously given him increased respect for the Sundered Wolf who couldn't die. They grasped hands, and I saw complicated looks on each of their faces.

"How many do we need to retrieve *Halfdan's Revenge?*" I asked Kieran.

He considered it, looking at Siggy. "Hmm... we can get her moving with a dozen sailors," he replied. "More would be better." He looked up at the sky and appeared to be judging the wind. "We can skirt the cloud. South and east, past the Gates of the Moon. The wind will favour us."

"Assuming the depth barges have all retreated," added Siggy. "We won't be able to use the ballistae with a crew of twelve."

"Stop," I said, holding up my hand. "Just think for a moment. Think what you're giving up."

"No more than you are," replied Kieran.

I snorted. "Ah, the more I think about building a new world in the void, the more I realize it's not for me. But I won't make that decision for you two."

Kieran chuckled, but Siggy bowed her head. It wasn't so long ago she told me she wanted to live. Now she was deciding whether or not to take a final voyage and give up her life to save the last few thousand Eastron.

"I suppose," she muttered, "*Halfdan's Revenge* is the only ship I've been mistress of that didn't sink. I don't like just leaving her on the beach."

Kieran's chuckle turned to a laugh.

"And you?" I asked him.

"Well, I've got two reasons," he replied. "One – if I have to spend too much time with my father, we'll end up having a conversation about Duncan, and I'll end up killing the sadistic old cunt."

"And two?" asked Siggy.

"I want to know what happened to Tynian Driftwood," replied Kieran.

The three of us stood close together and shared a moment of reflection. We placed hands on each other's shoulders and bowed our heads. I shed a tear, remembering everything we'd already lost. Friends, family, lovers and rivals, so many were dead. Not to mention the Severed Hand, Moon Rock, Last Port and the entire Sea Wolf fleet. And that was just what *our* people had lost. The other Wolves, the Brethren, they'd suffered just as much. Then there were the Winterlords, an entire camp of Eastron, the greatest camp of Eastron, all but one of whom had fallen. Elizabeth Defiant was all that remained.

"Right," I said. "We need volunteers. I won't order anyone to come with us. Do it quickly. It's a good run back to the beach."

"Aye," they said in unison, quickly moving away, amongst the thinly spaced groups of defenders.

I then went back to Marius and the twins. "We'll lead the Sunken God away," I stated. "You take our people and go and live a long life in peace. Just one final question... who will close the gate? A Sea Wolf needs to detonate their wyrd."

The three of them looked at each other and narrowed their eyes, as if they knew the answer, but didn't fully understand it. "We were given a message about that," said the Stranger. "An old spirit-master said to tell you – *of course I'll do it, Addie. I can't live in peace any more than you can.*"

"I think his name was Tomas something," added Gaius Two Hearts. "He was really old."

"Friendly fellow though," said Asha. "For a Sea Wolf."

"Fuck me," I muttered. "Silly old fool." Then I smiled. It made sense. Much like me, Tomas Red Fang was a relic of the old world. A diehard Sea Wolf spirit-master who didn't make a lot of sense outside the Severed Hand. He'd served Halfdan Blood, called the Bloody Fang, he'd served his son, Lord Ulric, and he'd served me, even when I was at my worst.

"Thank you for the message," I said, still smiling. "He's my oldest friend. He followed me when he didn't need to and might be the wisest man I've ever known."

"It's a good death," said Marius Cyclone. "He'll be remembered. He also said that you'll know when the gate is closed, because the Maelstrom will return."

★

I sat back on the rock, waiting for things to happen. Marius and the twins disappeared back to the gate to fetch us horses, while Kieran took Rys's mount and rode through the retreating mobs of warriors, finding volunteers for our final voyage. The first two were void legionnaires who'd been assisting Daniel's cart across the uneven ground: Lazlo Darkling, a seven foot tall spearman, now clad in Sea Wolf leather, and Anastasia Hazat, called Spectre, a robust woman with shoulders wider than mine. They'd both distinguished themselves at Duncan's Fall and were formidable warriors. Luckily, they'd also served aboard the Stranger's warship, and were capable at sea, for swords and spears were now of little use.

Daniel and Rys had already begun the journey back to the beach, knowing the cart would slow us down when we were ready to move. I'd not asked what they knew that I didn't, but I'd decided to insist they tell me when we were again aboard *Halfdan's Revenge*.

Then a distant voice reached me. From the north, accompanied by the clatter of hooves and the whinny of horses, someone called my name.

"Adeline!" It was Tasha Strong. She was riding next to Hitch, the rig-rat, leading a dozen horses. I'd sent her away from the barricades before I met with Alexis Wind Claw, and was surprised by how much I'd missed her.

I stood up, smiled broadly, and went to meet the Kneeling Wolf cook.

"I had a bowl of soup about ten minutes ago," I shouted. "Lots of vegetables, no fish. Not as good as yours, but it was filling."

The horses stopped in front of my rock and Tasha dismounted, rushing forwards to greet me with a warm hug. "Are you okay? Did you get hurt? How's the wound in your side? Are you sleeping?"

The hug ended and we shared a smile. "Yes, no, it's fine, and yes," I replied. "Stop worrying about me."

"I'm a volunteer," she said. "Kieran says you need volunteers for a last voyage. Well, I'm a volunteer."

"You are not," I replied. "You are going through Utha's Gate to build a new life in peace."

She stepped away from me and frowned. "Adeline Brand, you will not tell me what to do. I'm your friend and I will remain so. I'll do what you say if I agree with it, but I'm still my own woman." Her frown turned to a smile. "I'm a volunteer. I assume you have not yet selected a cook for your new crew. Well, I will be your cook."

PART NINE

25

Adeline Brand aboard *Halfdan's Revenge*

"Keep your eyes on the man or woman either side of you," I said. "If you have to look ahead, look at the *Revenge*. Do not look up. You won't like what you see."

There were thirty Eastron with me, each one a volunteer. We'd only needed twelve to crew the *Revenge*, but the amount of volunteers demanded we take more. Siggy, Kieran and Tasha were closest to me, with Vincent Half Hitch, called Hitch, a little way ahead, skulking atop the outer barricades at Duncan's Fall and making sure the coast was clear. Two void legionnaires – an unnaturally tall man called Lazlo and a stout woman called Spectre – were carrying the essence of Nym'zu, tightly wrapped in sacking. Further back from the barricade were twenty more volunteers: eleven Sea Wolves, the former crew of *Halfdan's Revenge*, mingled with four Dark Brethren and five Kneeling Wolves, all defenders of Nowhere who'd chosen not to pass through Utha's Gate. At the rear of our small group, with Anya's Roar and the last of the black dust, were Rys Coldfire and Daniel Doesn't Die.

Hitch jumped back down from the outer wall. "The beach is empty, Adeline. Cloud's still there. Getting bigger. Don't think we've got much time."

The defences at Duncan's Fall were the same as when we'd left them, with a few dozen breaches from the largest Sunken Men, and the huge corpse of the Hateful Whip, still sprawled in two pieces across our lines. The enemy had tried no further incursions, falling back as the Sunken God took form above the Red Straits, creeping towards Nowhere.

"And *Halfdan's Revenge*?" asked Kieran Greenfire.

Hitch nodded. "Right where we left her. A few of the lighter ships have drifted off on the high tide, but the rest are still tickling the rocks in the shallows."

Siggy Blackeye stood briefly, poking her head around the closest breach in the wall. "Five minutes to get her moving." She glanced across the mismatched crew of Eastron. "If you all do exactly what me and Kieran say."

"Right, let's move," I ordered. "Quick and quiet, straight to the ship."

Our small group moved as one, keeping low as we filed through the splintered outer wall. Everyone but Tasha and Rys had seen the full horror of the malevolent cloud, and none of them needed to be told a second time to keep their eyes down. I let the Wolf's Bastard take care of himself, but kept close to Tasha, with my arm around her shoulders, encouraging her to look down at the rocky beach. I imagined a few people ignoring my advice and snatching a glance at this new and terrible manifestation of the Sunken God. Certainly, I didn't follow my *own* advice, and looked up when we were halfway down the rocky beach.

It was now only a cloud in the loosest sense, if you removed all connotations of weather, and saw a cloud as merely a huge, roiling shape in the sky. It was a green mass of millions of eyes and tentacles, with lightning flashes of red and blue, like veins beneath the skin. The eyes were glassy and unfocused, with pupils of a thousand different shapes and sizes, from tiny globes to enormous pulsing orbs. I couldn't guess at how big the cloud was, but it appeared to completely eclipse Nibonay, cutting off the natural light for a thousand leagues ahead of us. As I jerked my head away, forcing myself to focus on *Halfdan's Revenge*, I felt that I had seen the true form of the Sunken God.

I didn't look a second time, and I guessed no one else did, as we all made it to the shallows upright and moving. Salt water splashed across my face as I pumped my legs through the deepening water, with the black hull of the *Revenge* looming in front of me. The warship was lodged on the shallow seabed, but only loosely, and would move with a modest amount of canvas. It had twisted to lie parallel along the coast, with knotted ropes and sections of rigging hanging over the port railing.

Kieran and Siggy were the first to jump out of the water, grasping the ropes we'd used to abandon ship. The rest of our small crew followed, passing our strange baggage up through several sets of arms. The casks of black dust were the least awkward, with the essence of Nym'zu needing two people to heft it up on deck, and Anya's Roar needing the combined efforts of five Sea Wolves. I remained in the shallows, partially to oversee the baggage, but mostly because my one arm made climbing difficult and I preferred to do it unobserved. Even Daniel Doesn't Die and Tasha Strong climbed up before me.

Once on deck, the thirty of us paused on the quarterdeck of the warship we'd abandoned. It was an eerie feeling, as none of us expected to come back here. We'd removed anything of value from it, leaving *Halfdan's Revenge* an empty wooden shell, but she was still alive, as if her fighting spirit transcended any particular crew.

"Siggy, get crew aloft," I ordered. "Just raise the mainsail. Quiet and smooth, like we're drifting. Put us in the Red Straits, heading for Yish and the Gates of the Moon."

"Aye," she replied, before delivering my orders. She lowered her normal shouts to a deep, almost whispered rumble, conveying far more seriousness than a simple bellow.

"Hitch," I continued, "take five crew and do a quick sweep of the ship. Front to back, start in the hold. Lazlo, Spectre, go with him in case there are any surprises."

The two Brethren gave a legion salute and accompanied the Sea Wolf rig-rat down the nearest set of steps.

"Kieran, Rys, with me," I said, leaving the rest to help Siggy as best they could.

"Where we going?" asked the Wolf's Bastard.

"Driftwood's cabin," I replied, looking at Kieran. "You said you wanted to know what happened to him. Shall we go and find out?"

He gave me a slow nod, as if he was afraid of the answer. "Aye," he grunted after a moment.

Around the mainmast, men and women went aloft, clearly grateful that the canvas obscured our view of the cloud. As Rys, Kieran and I followed Hitch below deck, Siggy turned her attention to stowing our baggage, and making sure the warship was ready to make way. The ropes and rigging, dangling over the railing, were all pulled back on deck, before she moved to the helm, ready to steer us away from Duncan's Fall.

Hitch and the others disappeared down a further set of steps, past empty hammocks and bare wooden planking. I led the way aft, towards the captain's cabin. With Rys standing at my left shoulder and Kieran at my right, I put a boot to the sturdy wooden door, sending it inwards to reveal the cabin. I didn't know about Kieran, but I'd been dwelling within a comfortable fantasy that Tynian Driftwood had found a way to stay alive, and was enjoying a well-deserved bottle of rum. But that was not the reality. The three of us stepped into the cabin, just as *Halfdan's Revenge* rolled to starboard, scraping across the rocky seabed, as Siggy got her underway.

"Why did you stay behind?" muttered Kieran Greenfire. "You fucking old fool."

Opposite us, nailed to the wall of his cabin, was the mutilated body of Tynian Driftwood, formerly of Last Port, captain of *Halfdan's Revenge*, and my friend. His one remaining leg and both his arms had been cut into several pieces, before being reassembled and nailed in place next to his torso, splayed outwards like a piece of macabre art. His neck had suffered similar treatment, and his severed head was secured to the wall with a single, thin blade, driven through his forehead. His bushy, red beard was matted with blood, and his eyes were open, staring angrily.

Rys strode towards the assembled body parts, coldly ignoring Kieran's grumbled protests about just leaving the cabin and closing the door. The Wolf's Bastard grabbed one of Driftwood's hands, severed below the wrist, and pulled it from the wall. He inspected the fingers, rolling them up into a fist, before pointing it at Kieran.

"He died fighting," said Rys. "His knuckles are bruised from punching people. All of this." He waved back at Driftwood's corpse. "This was done after he was dead. He was already gone. It doesn't mean anything. It just looks nasty. It's just fucking theatre. Appearances – that's all these cunts have got."

Kieran bowed his shaved head and closed his eyes. He had been Tynian's quartermaster and friend for many years. I knew some of what they'd been through together, but could only guess at the true strength of their bond.

"Would you pull him down?" asked Kieran. "I don't want to do it."

"Of course," replied Rys.

"We'll sew him in his hammock and bury him at sea," I added.

Kieran and I quickly returned to the quarterdeck, while Rys enlisted help to assemble Driftwood's body parts in his hammock. *Halfdan's Revenge* was slowly moving east, away from Duncan's Fall and into the Red Straits. We let the wind take us, mimicking a random drift as best we could. I didn't know how aware the cloud was, or if depth barges loitered under the surface, but I'd made sure our passing was as smooth as possible. No one shouted, and we moved under minimal sail, with Siggy making only minor corrections to our course. To an untrained or unaware eye, we were just another drifting warship, slowly moving towards the island of Yish and the Gates of the Moon.

Hitch reported that the rest of the ship was empty, but it had clearly been searched by Alexis Wind Claw's legionnaires. The ship's cantankerous old captain would have been the only thing of worth they'd found.

Most of my small crew were now below deck, with only Kieran, Siggy and I monitoring our progress. When we reached the Outer Sea and touched the essence of Nym'zu, we'd need every one of the thirty sailors to harness as much wind as possible, but for now no one wanted to see the festering green cloud. It appeared to be growing, rather than moving, and sent a line of twilight, followed by utter darkness, over the beach at Duncan's Fall and the coast of Nowhere. It was impossible to tell how long it would take to reach Utha's Gate, but they'd be able to see the immense cloud of eyes and tentacles within a few hours. The *Revenge* was sailing around the perimeter of the darkness, drifting in and out of twilight, as we passed Blood Water, where I'd parlayed with the Winterlords.

Kieran was on the quarterdeck, staring blankly ahead of the ship and ruminating on the death of his captain, while Siggy and I stood at the helm, keeping us pointed in the right direction. We'd passed two smaller ships, drifting eastward from Nowhere, but the Red Straits was otherwise empty. The temporary settlement Marius had established on the water was now mostly submerged. The whole area felt like a tomb.

"I have to tack to starboard or we'll run aground on Yish," said Siggy, assessing the wind as it buffeted the mainsail.

I glanced up at the edge of the cloud, far above us. The more we moved to starboard, the further under the cloud we'd travel, until we cleared the Gates of the Moon and reached the open ocean. "Do it," I replied. "I doubt the Sunken God would recognize it as deliberate."

Siggy swung the helm to starboard, but only one notch at a time, making our change of course slow and jerky. She kept her eyes on the water, leaving me to assess the enemy's reaction. The cloud was growing faster and faster, but its spread was focused on Nowhere. Sections of bubbling green energy were elongating and creating impenetrable shadows, as if they were the fingers of an enormous hand, trying to envelop the island. But there was no indication it cared about the drifting Sea Wolf warship.

"We're clear for now," I said. "I need to go and talk to Daniel and Rys. You okay here?"

She narrowed her eyes, looking amidships. "I'm fine, but you might need to wait. Look yonder."

From below deck, Rys Coldfire emerged, with Vincent Half Hitch helping him carry what was left of Tynian Driftwood. The captain was sewn into his hammock, and it needed two people to heft him upwards. I left the helm and joined Kieran on the quarterdeck.

"He'd want *you* to say something, Adeline," said the quartermaster. "He was terrible at expressing it, but he respected the fuck out of you."

"He didn't like me much," I replied.

Kieran sneered. "That was just his way of showing respect." He looked at me, then smiled, despite his grief. "Okay, yes, he didn't like you very much. It was hard to win his trust… but you managed it."

"I'm just not sure he'd want anyone to say anything," I said. "Tynian was more cynical than *me*. He'd tell us that he was already dead, and what's left is just a pile of flesh and bones. Rys was right, he's already gone."

"You're right," said Kieran. "You're right. No words." He smiled again, running a hand along the wooden railing of *Halfdan's Revenge*. "He always said this ship was more than a home. It was part of him."

"So, as long as we keep her afloat, a bit of Captain Tynian Driftwood remains," I replied, putting my hand on his shoulder and nodding to the Wolf's Bastard.

Rys and Hitch positioned the body on the starboard railing, with Kieran and I standing either side. The Red Straits were getting deeper and it would be a good resting place for the old captain, close to Nibonay and the Severed Hand. With heads bowed, the body was tipped from the railing, to splash into the water. The sound was almost lost within the creak of the hull. It was a modest passing for a great Sea Wolf captain, but perhaps it was what he would have wanted.

"She's still afloat," I whispered. "I'll keep her safe for you."

It was rapidly getting dark, as Siggy steered us further under the cloud. The mournful look I shared with Kieran, Rys and Hitch was almost lost in the twilight. Once Driftwood was gone, Hitch quickly disappeared below deck and Kieran moved to assist Siggy at the helm, leaving Rys and I standing by the railing.

"I think it's time I talked with Daniel," I said. "Unless you want to tell me what I don't know?"

The Wolf's Bastard narrowed his eyes and looked down at me. "You should hear it from him. Let's go below deck. Just the three of us."

*

"Let me tell you a story," said Daniel Doesn't Die, Drinks the Death Bear's Eye. "It's not a long story, but it is complicated. A long, long time ago, in a world nothing like this, there were gods. You call it the Bright Lands, but it was just... another place. The mortal men and women who lived there, who travelled across the sea and fractured into the Eastron, were once dutiful worshippers of a dozen different gods. The Pale Knight, the Grave Lord, the Earth Shaker, the World Raven, others I can't remember. I wasn't well acquainted with most of them, for my people knew only the Death Bear. It is said that we closed our eyes until we forgot their names... for we killed our own gods and we stole their wyrd."

"You said it wasn't a long story," I said.

"Patience," said Rys. "It's important."

I raised an eyebrow at him. "You're telling *me* to be patient?"

"About this? Yes."

I looked up at Daniel. "Continue," I said.

He glared at me. "Very well. The short version. A million blades cut at the Death Bear's feet and I saw him topple to the ground. The god fell across a city and a wide bay, crippling an entire culture as he fell. But he wasn't dead. A few of us, called shape-takers, were in the air, pecking at the Bear's face. When he fell, we went for his eyes."

His glare became slightly hostile, and I sensed that I had genuinely angered him. For a moment, within the chubby Sundered Wolf, I saw someone of great power, being questioned in a way he didn't like.

"I won't bore you with the details of shape-shifting," he continued, "but I had taken the shape of a raven, and found myself leading a strike on the Bear's left eye." Daniel bowed his head and smiled to himself, as if remembering. "It took us three days to kill him. Working in shifts, if you can believe such a thing. The last morsel of his left eye – the last sliver of consciousness within him – well, that went to me. I drank the Bear's eye and his realm of death closed its gates to me."

"Daniel Doesn't Die, Drinks the Death Bear's Eye," I said.

"Eva gave me that name," he replied. "When I killed our god, I was just David Fast Claw. But I knew straightaway something had changed. I knew I'd not just killed him. Gods do not die like the rest of us. Each one killed leaves its essential essence behind, and each of the Claws killed a god. I can't tell you who killed which god, but I can tell you what they gained." He chewed his lip, looking around the cabin, as if he hoped to find a bottle of grog.

"I'm trying to be patient," I said, "but we're short of time."

"I'm just trying to frame things," he replied. "This was all a very long time ago." He took a breath. "Most of our people were killed when we defied the gods. The remaining few, now charged with wyrd, fell into camps behind those who had killed gods and survived. There were five of us, each empowered by what we'd done.

"Sebastian Dawn Claw gained power and nobility, so much so it was hard to look at him without kneeling. Duncan Red Claw gained rage and honour, and I only found the courage to talk to him once. Medina Wind Claw gained great wisdom, but also ambition, and he was a treacherous bastard. Mathew Lone Claw was my friend, and he gained high morals and a generous nature."

It took a lot to surprise me, especially now, but Daniel had a habit of talking casually about legendary Eastron. These were the men who'd established the Kingdom of the Four Claws, the greatest amongst us, upon which our civilization had been built.

"What about you?" I asked. "You can't die, but what else did you gain?"

Daniel locked eyes with Rys, and I was reminded that they still weren't telling me something.

"Well," he continued, "in the context of my story, I gained immortality, stubbornness and a liking for my own company. In the context of *our* situation, I gained the essential essence of a god."

"Which he can use," added Rys.

"Not exactly," said Daniel. "The Death Bear is still alive within me, and I can expel him into someone else, but it may kill them and it will certainly kill me."

"But it's a god, Adeline," said the Wolf's Bastard. "It's a true old god, from *this* realm of form. Its power will at least give me a chance against this Klu'zu."

"What the fuck are you saying?" I snapped. "You want to take the essence and start a fist fight with the Sunken God? You saw that cloud. Are you going to head butt it to save us?"

Rys glared at me, his lip curling into a snarl. "*You* will not die," he growled. "You are the First Fang of the Sea Wolves and you are not expendable. No one aboard this ship will know peace in Utha's realm, but I would slice my own throat before seeing them die. We will draw the Sunken God's eye away from Nowhere – and I will challenge him, with the might of an old god."

"Please," implored Daniel. "Rys and I have talked about this. He wants to die, Adeline. If he's strong enough to take the Death Bear's power, he'll be strong enough to defend the ship, perhaps even let you use Anya's Roar and escape."

"Why don't *you* use it?" I barked at Daniel. "You've had it for two hundred years – what's stopping you? Why does Rys have to sacrifice himself?"

He flared. A pulse of his fiery red and gold wyrd covered his body, but he kept himself in check. "It's not a fucking party trick. The Death Bear's power isn't a part of me – it *is* me, as much as my blood, my heart and my veins. I can't use it or harness it. All I can do is expel it... which will kill me."

I paused, looking him in the eyes. It was easy to forget how old and powerful he was, until he showed glimpses of his old life. I'd pestered him about it for months, wanting to know how he couldn't die. Now he'd told me in simple language, and I felt as if I was looking at an entirely different man.

"You want to die too," I stated.

"I've never had a chance like this," said Daniel, returning my stare. "And, like Master Coldfire here, I'm not asking for permission. I *will* release the Death Bear into Rys. It will kill me, but it may save you. It may even save those people still waiting at Utha's Gate."

Rys stood and cracked his neck. "We should be passing the Gates of the Moon any minute. It's time we got everyone on deck, and I touched the essence of Nym'zu." He gritted his teeth and looked up, as if his glare could travel through the wood of the *Revenge* to fix on the Sunken God. "I really hope it pisses him off."

"Am I now allowed to be impatient again?" I asked.

26

Marius Cyclone on Nowhere

Suddenly, after weeks and months of frenzied activity, I was forced to wait. Everything was reduced to a matter of minutes and hours, with a day being seen as the absolute end of everything. When I'd arrived back on Nowhere, ten thousand Eastron – mostly families – were still waiting to flee through the gate. When I'd returned from meeting Adeline Brand, we'd been hovering around the eight thousand mark. The additions of my people from the *Dangerous*, and the retreating defenders, had been like an unwelcome refill in a drunken man's cup, though no one complained or softened their focus. We were now down to just under seven thousand, but the number decreased agonisingly slowly.

Xavyer Ice, called the Grim Wolf, was already in Utha's realm, taking charge as best he could, along with Santos Spirit Killer. On this side, Jessimion Death Spell and Antonia of the Dolcinites were leading the retreat, with final authority held by Tomas Red Fang. The old Sea Wolf spirit-master made no secret that he was planning to detonate his wyrd and close the gate, and seemed almost to be looking forward to his approaching death. He directed boisterous humour at anyone who would listen, laughing and joking with the fleeing families. I'd not spoken to him since he gave me his message, and I'd made no attempts to exert authority over him or anyone else, but everyone knew who I was. The Brethren were respectful, the Sea Wolves were conflicted, and the others were confused.

I was content to sit on my own, trying to quieten my mind and accept that I had no control over what happened next. It wasn't that I didn't trust Adeline Brand, but I'd been at the sharp end for so long that sitting and waiting gave me a headache. I looked down at my crippled legs, knowing that Oliver Dawn Claw had robbed me of my vitality. Whatever I did next would involve a lot of sitting down, for I wouldn't always have the Two Hearts twins to help me walk and I'd developed a true hatred of using crutches.

I closed my eyes and took a deep breath. When I looked again, I still saw the rugged, grassy plains of Nowhere. Utha's Gate sat in the middle of a huge depression in the ground, around which a wooden shanty town had developed over the last few months. Thousands of campfires, thousands of tents and huts, and thousands of families had filled this island. I sat at the epicentre, where everyone would eventually travel, and the settlements here were thinly spaced, leaving a large circle of clear ground around the gate itself. There were no defences as such, but a mixed company of my void legionnaires patrolled a wide perimeter. No one thought we'd be attacked and every anxiety was fixed on the end of the day.

And yet... *my* anxieties were more unfocused. Much as I wanted to relax and look forward to a new life, lived in peace, I couldn't shake the feeling that, in this realm of form, we would always be in danger. My brother was still out there somewhere, as was Oliver Dawn Claw. Both were fanatics and I had no illusions that they'd simply given up their pursuit. They'd captured me to find a way onto Nowhere, and though I'd been told the island was like a fortress, my anxieties remained.

I looked around for Jess, Marta and Titus, but they were somewhere beyond my sight, amongst the press of fleeing Eastron. Then I tried to locate Esteban Hazat, but the commander of the twenty-third was helping organize the dense lines of people in front of the gate. The only people close to me were Asha and Gaius Two Hearts, sitting on adjacent rocks and endlessly bickering about which of them would be better at coping in our new world. Occasionally, they lapsed into surprisingly gentle fantasies of building a log cabin and growing onions. They were killers with few equals, but unlike Adeline Brand and Tomas Red Fang, they enjoyed the thought of starting again in a virgin land.

Then they stopped talking to each other and both stood. "Something going on at the gate," said Asha.

"What?" I replied, roused from my internal debates. "What's happening at the gate?"

Gaius climbed on top of a rock to get a better view over the heads of the refugees. He shielded his eyes and took a good look before replying. "The old man... something's got him angry, or... I don't know, he's shouting at people."

"What's he shouting?"

Gaius shook his head. "Too far to hear. Jessimion Death Spell's talking to him."

"Asha, go and find out what ails Tomas Red Fang," I ordered.

"Righty ho," she replied, jogging away from us.

Her brother kept looking towards the gate, frowning as he tried to make sense of what he was seeing. From my seat, I could see little, but the outer ranks of refugees were beginning to shift position as Death Spell's void legionnaires moved amongst them, alarmed about something.

"They're shouting about wyrd," said Gaius. "They wanna know who's using their wyrd."

I considered it. "Tomas is the only spirit-master here. Maybe he senses something."

"Why would anyone use their wyrd here?" he replied. "And why would it bother him if they did?"

The glass on Nowhere was like a brick wall and impossible to break, especially since the Maelstrom had quietened. There was no one to fight here, nor any reason for an Eastron to exert themselves. Whatever had alarmed the old spirit-master was not something I could feel myself. Nevertheless, I felt the need to be involved in whatever it was.

"Gaius, help me up. I'll use the stick."

Hopping to the ground, he assisted me in standing. He stood at my left side, where the leg was almost useless, while I put my body weight on the walking stick and my right leg. I'd soon be able to walk properly with just the stick, but my insistence on trying before I was ready had set my rehabilitation back several days. Being a stubborn bastard had taken me far, but it didn't always favour me. For now, if I wanted to move at any reasonable speed, I needed Asha or Gaius.

With his help, I shuffled away from the rock, towards the massed Eastron between us and Utha's Gate. The alarm was spreading, with void legionnaires echoing Tomas's concern and asking everyone if they were using their wyrd.

"Stop!" I said to a young legionnaire, emerging through the press of Eastron. He wore a leather coat of Sea Wolf design and was armed with only a straight sword. "Talk to me. What's the problem?"

"Lord Marius," he replied, alarmed by my appearance. "I apologize."

"Don't apologize, just tell me what's happening."

"The old Sea Wolf," said the legionnaire. "The spirit-master. He says he can feel something beyond the glass. He says the air is charged with wyrd, and wants to know if someone here is using their power. You should talk to Tomas Red Fang."

Asha returned through the massed Eastron, taking her station at my side. "Not sure what he's worried about," she said. "Everyone says the glass here is impenetrable."

"Take me to him," I replied. "Adeline says he's a wise man."

It quickly became clear that no one waiting on the low ground of Nowhere was using their wyrd. The refugees parted, allowing me to approach the central ground, where Tomas Red Fang and Jessimion Death Spell were engaged in animated discourse. Antonia of the Dolcinites was nearby and brightened at my presence, but everyone else looked afraid. The Sea Wolf spirit-master was a man to be taken seriously and his agitation had quickly infected everyone around him.

"Marius the Stranger," snapped Tomas, pointing a bent finger at me. "Do you feel that? A Brethren void path, maybe? Your Pure One friend with his spirit-whistle?"

The twins helped me to stand opposite the old man. "I don't feel anything," I replied, shaking my head. "Ten Cuts is with Utha. And our void paths can't penetrate the glass here. What do you feel?"

I could see a nimbus of light blue wyrd around Tomas's fingertips, as if he was caressing the air. "I don't know what it is. It started slowly a few minutes ago. At first, I thought it was just wyrd, but whatever it is, it's rotten – mouldy, like raw meat left out in the sun. I think we might be in danger."

I looked around, taking in the air. I was no spirit-master, and though my wyrd was powerful, I couldn't feel what Tomas felt. After a moment, I turned to Jessimion. "How many warriors do we have?"

"Depends," he replied. "About two thousand if you count those who ran from the beach, but most of them are fucked, or sleeping. There's a mad Kneeling Wolf and a few of his men who don't seem to need sleep, but otherwise I've got five hundred legionnaires."

"His name's Charlie Vane," said Tomas Red Fang, "called the War Rat. He likes fighting and thinks sleep is boring."

"We're glad to have him," I replied. "Something's happening."

"You feel it?" asked Tomas.

"No, but I'm fucking paranoid."

"He is," agreed the Two Hearts twins.

"Jessimion, push everyone to the perimeter," I ordered. "Eyes open, wyrd ready."

"Yes, my lord," replied Death Spell, leaving quickly while snapping orders at all nearby legionnaires.

The wide depression in the earth of Nowhere was now filled with alarmed people. Parents clutched their children, the young clutched the old, and thousands of helpless people fought the urge to panic. The void legionnaires who'd been organizing them into lines, disappeared to form a perimeter, leaving them to reassure each other. The Eastron thought of themselves as warriors, but a far larger percentage were just normal people, preparing to start new lives in a new world.

"Tomas, you can use wyrd to project your voice?" I asked.

He nodded. "Of course."

"Calm these people," I said. "You've agitated them; now tell them everything will be okay."

We locked eyes. The old spirit-master was powerful and wise, but he'd had longer to hate me than Adeline Brand, and he didn't know how to react to the Stranger giving him an order. After a moment, during which he was clearly trying to remind himself that our situation was now drastically different, he nodded his head. "Very well."

Tomas Red Fang stepped away from the gate, pushing more crackling wyrd into his body. At least a hundred of the closest people stopped talking when the spirit-master used his power. Most were Sea Wolves and deeply respected the old man.

"Hear me!" he boomed, his powerful wyrd deepening and lengthening both syllables, until his words travelled far across the open ground. "War is but a series of calamities that leads to either victory or defeat. We have been at war so very long. And our calamities are beyond count. But we are the lucky ones – we are already victorious. Nothing and no one can defeat us now, for the Eastron will endure. Think of the thousands upon thousands already building our new home, and take heart that you will soon be with them."

His words were powerful, but he still managed to be gentle, and the rising panic around us quickly turned to quiet resolve. I saw mothers and fathers, untrained in combat, wielding hand-axes and staffs, ready to fight if they needed to. Even children, clinging to their parents' legs, stopped crying and gulped down their fear.

I found myself looking at a young Brethren family from the Dark Harbour: a man, a woman and three boys under ten years old. I recognized the woman as a baker, who Jess and I visited most weekends. She had a particular skill with sourdough. Now, she held a small knife, brandishing it at thin air, while her husband held a wood-chopping axe in two hands. They were simple folk, with barely enough wyrd to be visible, but they summoned it anyway, preparing to defend their three sons.

I glared at Tomas, grateful for his words, but still anxious. "Use your craft, spirit-master. Tell me if we're about to be attacked."

He nodded and closed his eyes, letting the nimbus of wyrd flow to form a mantle around his head. He was far more powerful than any Dark Brethren spirit-master I'd known. We were trained to use our wyrd in slivers and flashes, never overextending our power, whereas the Sea Wolves expressed themselves freely, using far more wyrd in an instant than a void legionnaire would use in an hour of combat.

Asha and Gaius stepped away, making sure I could stand with the walking stick alone, before selecting which weapons to draw. They looked at each other, having a silent conversation formed of narrowed eyes, clenched jaws and odd tilts of the head. When they were done, each drew a pair of short swords. Of all their weapons, these were the most suited to an actual fight. Once armed, the two of them looked at me, appearing to assess how able I'd be to defend myself. I smiled back at them.

"He can still use his arms," said Gaius.

"Doesn't mean he can still use a sword," replied Asha.

They looked at each other and nodded. Then Asha, clearly volunteering to deliver me a hard truth, stepped forwards. "Marius, you are basically useless. If a fight starts, and we have to kill some people, you should waddle away as quickly as you can. Understood?"

"I thought you promised Jessica you'd keep me alive," I queried.

"We did and we will," she replied. "But don't try to help."

"You'll just get in the way."

They stayed close, but said nothing more to me. I found myself looking around for a rock or some such to sit on, but there was nothing. The closest structure was Utha's Gate itself, and it seemed wrong to simply lean against it. After a moment of trying to hide the constant pain in my legs and side, I slumped to the ground and pulled myself into a seated position on the grass. I looked at the walking stick, swirling it through the air, wondering how effective it would be as a weapon. But Asha and Gaius were right – whether with a stick or with a sword, I was basically useless in a fight.

I glanced over at Tomas and saw him slowly pull in his wyrd. His face was twitching, and the light blue glow in his eyes was the last thing to retreat, before he turned back to me. I couldn't tell what the old man was thinking. The twitching stopped and his wrinkled, papery skin was pinched into an unreadable expression.

"Tomas Red Fang!" I snapped, using the stick and my one good leg to stand up. "Speak. What do you see?"

He looked around, above the heads of a thousand people, as if assessing the air. "Something I've seen before," he replied. "At the Severed Hand."

"Tell me," I demanded.

He kept his eyes skyward as he shuffled over to me and the twins. "Since the Maelstrom quietened, the glass here is like a brick wall. You can't step through it, but with more power than we've got, you may still be able to break it. I think something's trying. It's like something's banging its head against the glass. Over and over again. It's a boom, boom, boom, like a drumbeat... or a battering ram."

"Where?" I barked. "Where are they coming through?"

"Here," he replied. "Right here, at the gate."

I took in our surroundings. Around Utha's Gate was a wide, empty circle of grass, but all the ground beyond that was filled with pensive families and other non-combatants. It occurred to me that defending the perimeter was a foolish move.

"Asha, go and find Jessimion," I ordered. "He needs to get all our warriors back to the gate. We need to protect *this* ground, not the perimeter. Hurry!"

She didn't even stop to make a sarcastic comment before sheathing her short swords and dashing after the commander. Gaius stayed with me, while Tomas used his powerful voice to widen the circle of refugees, keeping them back from the gate. We had a few minutes before it opened again, and whatever was about to happen felt imminent.

I was suddenly aware that I was standing in the middle of the open ground. I had a highly skilled killer next to me, and an old but powerful spirit-master a short distance away, but that was it. I could just about see Antonia of the Dolcinites helping a group of families move away, but no formidable warriors. I'd sent all of them to the perimeter. It would take a few minutes to assemble any kind of force at the gate.

"Gaius, give me a sword," I grunted.

"What are you gonna do with it?" he sneered.

"Just give me a fucking sword."

He rummaged around through his various weapons, until deciding on a large fighting knife, with sword-catching serrations along the back of the blade. Other than his two short swords, it was the largest weapon he had, and he passed it to me hilt first. My hands and arms still felt strong, but moving with any fluidity was almost impossible, and I needed to keep one arm free for my walking stick.

"Marius," said Tomas. "It's happening."

The air between us began to bend and distort – a small circle, just in front of the gate, as if someone was punching their fist into a deep pool of water, displacing more and more with each punch. It was the glass and it was gradually buckling. I'd stepped into the void thousands of times, and the glass had been like a thin membrane on every occasion. But here, on the island of Nowhere and within spitting distance of Utha's Gate, the barrier between worlds appeared almost infinite, with bulging layers that could resist all but the mightiest of incursions.

Then the air cracked, as if a sharp stone had struck a window, causing a tiny pinprick in reality and a spreading spider's web of fractures. When it broke, it made a hole in mid-air, sending out shards of charred wyrd to burn and disperse on the grass. Someone or something had smashed through from the realm of void to the realm of form. They'd managed to break the glass of Nowhere. As the hole got bigger, and larger chunks of wyrd fell from the glass, forms and textures appeared on the other side. I saw a spiritual wall, ten feet thick, with a diamond-shaped breach through its surface, crackling with blue and black lightning. Tightly packed together in the breach were dozens of dead bodies, bereft of wyrd, and a few living people, smashing themselves against the glass. They were fully armed Winterlords, though their eyes blazed with rotten green energy, as if they were mindless.

Gaius pushed me back and faced the breach, with Tomas coming to join him. Antonia and a handful of Dolcinites, armed with quarterstaffs, were the only other fighters close enough to react. I could hear Asha and Jessimion shouting to the legionnaires, but they were beyond the thick line of refugees, struggling to make their way back to the central ground.

When the first steel-shod foot stepped through the breach, I saw the true scope of what had been done. A column of Eastron – Winterlord knights and my brothers' void legionnaires – snaked away into the void. Where the column met the glass, piles of emaciated corpses littered the voidscape – hundreds of them, their bodies hanging limp within armour too big for them, as if both their flesh and life-force had been consumed. I couldn't see how long the column was, nor how many warriors wanted to enter the realm of form, but each and every one was infected with the corrosive green energy of the Sunken God, appearing to override their reason.

The first Winterlord, a man well over six feet and hefting a greatsword, had no awareness in his eyes, just a predatory malevolence. Gaius Two Hearts quickly assessed the knight and leapt at him, slicing down at his neck, cutting up into his groin, and smashing his forehead into the bridge of the man's nose. Two more mindless Winterlords appeared behind the first, then three more behind them. Gaius managed to pull the first one to the ground, barrelling into the others as he tried to clog the breach, while Tomas Red Fang summoned a formidable shield of wyrd and smashed it against anyone who emerged. The Dolcinites did their best, but they wore only robes and wielded only staffs. Against Winterlord knights in plate armour, we had no answer.

I looked around, fighting panic. People were going to die and I couldn't do anything about it. My knuckles turned white against the hilt of the serrated knife and I tested my legs, nearly buckling as I put too much weight on them. Before I could swear in anger at my helplessness, a huge Winterlord knight attacked me. He pushed past the breach, driving his greatsword through the chest of a Dolcinite, before focusing his mindless green eyes on me. He blocked my view of Gaius and Tomas, and hefted his blade above his head, as if to split me in two.

I had no strength in my legs, but my arms and my wyrd were still strong, and I used them to fling myself aside, losing my walking stick and my blade, and landing in a painful heap. The greatsword struck a rock and the knight growled, as the blade became stuck. I gritted my teeth as the wound in my side began to burn – but, using my arms, I managed to drag myself back to entangle the knight's legs. He let go of his greatsword and punched down at me with a gauntleted fist, striking my shoulder and chest, but I didn't let go of his legs. He growled again, flailing like a wild animal caught in a trap. Using all of the strength I had, I pulled his ankles together and toppled the huge Winterlord. I roared, dragging myself up his body, until I could pound my elbow into his face. He grabbed at me, but lying on his back in steel armour made him far less dangerous. Grunting and spluttering, I kept striking his face, breaking his nose and jaw with repeated elbows, until the rotten green wyrd left his eyes and he stopped moving.

Looking up, I saw mindless Winterlord knights and blank-faced Dark Brethren legionnaires flood through the breach. They were in no formation and had no synergy, as if each was already dead and being animated by the Sunken God. They grunted and gurgled, but killed with no actual words. Tomas was still alive, using his wyrd as a defensive globe, but I couldn't see Antonia or Gaius, and the ground before the gate was filled with dead Dolcinite Pilgrims.

At the edges of the central ground, appearing through the terrified refugees, Jessimion Death Spell's legionnaires were returning. I heard commands to surround the gate, and cohorts joined together in defensive units, facing the mindless attackers, but I couldn't see a way for us to win. The breach in the glass couldn't be closed, and I had no idea how many dead-eyed warriors waited in the void.

Then two legionnaires, encased in black steel, with owl helmets, ran straight at me. They levelled their long spears and I gulped down the certain knowledge that I was about to die.

In my last moments, as the animated corpses of two Dark Brethren ran at me, I took a deep breath, angry that I'd got so close to victory. So very fucking close. A tiny piece of me had even started to think that I might live through this. Jessica, Marta, Titus and I, we could have built a house and done all the boring, mundane, peaceful shit you do when no one is trying to kill you. It would have been fucking lovely.

27

Adeline Brand aboard *Halfdan's Revenge*

East of Nibonay was the Outer Sea. Moon Rock and the
Severed Hand faced it, our fishermen worked it, and our
crews trained in it, but we'd never explored far. We'd pointed
everything to the west, towards the Kingdom of the Four
Claws and the other Eastron camps. When we'd explored, it
had been to the far south and west, where we'd established
Last Port on the Sea of Stars. Looking east, into the endless
ocean, was hurting my eyes, but it was better than looking
behind us. Everyone was on deck, with half the small crew
in the rigging, ready to drop canvas at my word. *Halfdan's
Revenge* was the fastest of the Sea Wolf warships and, with
open ocean ahead of her and a strong wind, she was capable
of tremendous speed. But I couldn't predict how we'd fare
with the Sunken God chasing us.

We now had slight distance on the cloud and were no
longer sailing in twilight, but in exchange, we were treated
to a horrific view. Nibonay, the home of the Sea Wolves,
was falling into the sky. Enormous chunks of earth and
rock were being pulled upwards, destroying thousands of
miles of coastline. To the south, the shell of the Severed

Hand was reduced to dusty grey blocks, tumbling towards the cloud. Moon Rock had broken into a few large pieces and was crushed together with the mountains of Yish. The gravitational pull of the cloud was immense, and I could only guess at the destruction it had caused getting here. I'd been thinking about the end of the world for almost a year. Now all of us were being forced to watch it.

Klu'zu himself bubbled from horizon to horizon, his billions of eyes each glinting with a sickly green awareness. That it was a single being was alarming enough, but the malevolence and chaos infecting the air around it was maddening, making my eyes raw and itchy. I could only guess at how the simple folk at Utha's Gate would react to the spectacle.

"If you want to look at something," I bellowed, "look at the ropes in front of you or the deck beneath you. Be ready to lay on canvas. As much as we've got."

Lazlo and Spectre had taken the essence of Nym'zu to the forward platform, where the Wolf's Bastard was standing, arms behind his back and head held high. None of us knew what would happen when he touched it, but we had a strong wind and our sails were ready. Daniel Doesn't Die was a little way behind him, but even he didn't know what was about to happen. He wouldn't expel the Death Bear's power until we were far out at sea, with Klu'zu committed to following us and leaving Nowhere.

"Rys!" I shouted. "It's time. We can't wait any longer."

The two Dark Brethren void legionnaires began to carefully unwrap the essence, using fingertips to avoid touching it. When the sacking was spread, revealing the essence of Nym'zu, I narrowed my eyes, unsure what I was looking at. It was crystalline, but its angles all fell into each other, making it impossible to focus on its true size and shape. Marius said it was a droplet of a god's blood, and it was easy to believe him, but before any of us could ruminate too deeply on the impossible shape, Rys Coldfire grabbed it with both hands.

Sudden lightning cut the air all around *Halfdan's Revenge*, making the ocean churn, as if sliced by a thousand blades. The wind didn't change direction, but it greatly intensified, causing Siggy to brace the helm to keep us moving straight. The crew in the rigging held on tightly, as the boundless cloud noticed us for the first time. Everyone covered their ears, as a deafening sound echoed across the Outer Sea. It bounced off water, wood and flesh, forming into a many-layered roar of unimaginable outrage.

Rys had gotten his wish; Klu'zu was most certainly pissed off.

The bubbling cloud of eyes and tentacles flexed and flared, changing position and pulling in all its appendages. It was like we'd stuck a pin in the palm of a hand, forcing the digits to form a fist. As it pulsed, immense spirals and tornadoes appeared within its mass, stretching miles into the air. The tentacles were like hairs, twitching over every surface, looking for the source of the Sunken God's rage. When the cloud stopped pulsing, it coalesced over Nibonay, suddenly unconcerned with Nowhere and Utha's Gate. All of its unknowable power was now pointed at *Halfdan's Revenge*, as if Rys had committed the gravest of sins.

"All sail!" I roared, wincing and having to use wyrd to be heard.

The topsails fell, then the foresails, then every other piece of canvas we could muster. They were all dark blue and instantly caught the wind, billowing across the deck and pushing the warship east. Tasha stood with Siggy, and it took the two of them to wrestle the helm into place and keep us sailing straight and true.

"It's working!" shouted Tasha, looking back at me. "It's ignoring Nowhere."

"Brilliant," I replied. "So let's get fucking moving."

The *Revenge* plunged into the Outer Sea, leaving behind Nibonay and the Kingdom of the Four Claws, leaving behind our lives, our families and friends, and our very civilization. Everything that meant anything was falling into the sky.

The cloud was following us, but at no great speed. It rippled high above the ocean, crackling with green and black lightning, far more animated than before Rys touched the essence.

"That's all she's got," said Kieran Greenfire, joining us at the helm. "No ship in the kingdom could catch us."

"Here we are!" I shouted, projecting my voice across the ship and all of her small crew. "We are the last of the Eastron and this is our last voyage. Do not be scared. Do not have doubts."

I wasn't finished speaking, but my senses were suddenly overwhelmed with nausea. All around me, the crew of the *Revenge* felt the same thing, and thirty people fell to their knees, wrapped in too much pain to act normally. The cloud was spreading across the Outer Sea, filling the western horizon and sending waves of energy towards us, as if the Sunken God's spite travelled further than its physical form. Millions of eyes were focused on us, and they did far more than just look. My head throbbed in sharp pain, as if stabbed by needles. Klu'zu was assaulting our minds, showing that he was far more than a horrifying visual presence.

I was in a dusty, square room of black, stone bricks. Gravel and sharp stones covered the floor, cutting and scratching my skin, and a mist of noxious air hung above my head. I wore tattered rags, my hair was matted and greasy, and my skin was bruised and tingling, as if I'd been slapped repeatedly. I didn't know where I was or how I'd got here, and I spat and coughed, trying to remember my name. I rolled onto my back, tracing my eyes across the blocky angles and corners of the room. The vapour appeared to be seeping from every intersection, floor to ceiling, forming a misty cross in the centre of the square room. There was subdued, grey lighting, but no obvious source – no windows, no door, no features of any kind.

I tried to take deep breaths, but my chest hurt and my neck started to cramp. Grunting in pain, I fought the urge to panic. Through gritted teeth, I kept my breathing shallow until the pain abated, but my whole body remained weak and sore. Small movements hurt, so I remained still, until a window appeared on one of the walls. It was at head height and had no frame, glass or shutters.

I sat up slowly, one movement at a time, so my muscles burned only slightly. With my back off the ground, I noticed that I had two arms and I somehow knew this was strange, though I couldn't remember why. Luckily, I needed both of them to crawl to the window. I was shivering and my muscles kept twitching, but I managed to secure my back against the wall and slowly drag my body upwards.

With both hands clamped on the rough windowsill, I looked out.

My face was suddenly bathed in crisp sunlight and my nostrils filled with sea air. It was cold, with a sharp wind, and I found myself looking down at a somewhat familiar coastline. It was certainly north of Nibonay and looked somehow wrong. There were cliffs, but the waves easily crested them. There were grassy plains inland, but the sea was now flooding across them. It was as if the ocean was rising to eclipse the land.

I looked closer, rubbing my eyes as the view travelled downwards. It was the western coast of the Isle of the Setting Sun, bordering the Inner Sea, but it looked totally different. Hundreds of miles of forested hills were now mostly underwater, creating huge, flooded plains, across which Sunken Men moved. Between mobs of grotesque fish creatures trudged lines of Eastron. Thousands of Winterlords and Dark Brethren were being corralled like cattle to the coast. At the end of their grim procession skulked an immense frog. It was the Bulbous Whip, and the Eastron were being fed to it.

Then I heard a woman's screeching voice and narrowed my eyes.

"This is wrong," she squealed. "I am your friend and these are your loyal servants. We have served you faithfully. This is all so wrong."

It was Alexis Wind Claw. A huge Sunken Man was holding her by the wrist, dragging the powerful Dark Brethren towards the whip. She was helpless against the creature, who ignored her shrieking. I was reminded of a butcher, leading an animal to slaughter, immune to its distress.

"What of my place in the new world?" she wailed. "The beautiful chaos of the Waking God has infused me! What have I done wrong?" She was hysterical, unable to comprehend how she could have been so misguided.

I hated the woman, but I wasn't petty, and wished I could console her. "It's okay," I whispered. "Death isn't so bad. There's no more pain. There's no more anything."

"Who speaks?" whimpered Alexis, somehow able to hear me. "I need no more torments."

"It's... I'm Adeline Brand." I was disorientated and in great pain, but I still knew who I was.

Alexis tripped over in the soggy ground, forcing the Sunken Man to flex its blubbery arm and lift her off the ground. Either side of them, walking with their heads bowed, were dense columns of Eastron, moving to their deaths with grim acceptance. Where the flooded plains met the Inner Sea, the Bulbous Whip was gulping down a dozen bodies at a time, croaking and twitching between swallows. Its enormous gullet rippled with each mouthful. Its appetite appeared limitless.

"They're exterminating us," grunted Alexis, addressing me. "All of us. All of the Eastron who remain. Hundreds of thousands of men, women and children. We pledged to them... we pledged to the Waking God. We were to be lords of a new world."

"There is no new world," I replied. "Just the resurfacing of an old world. Perhaps the oldest world. You were tricked, Alexis. I don't blame you, but you were tricked. I wish you'd seen reason and joined Marius... joined all of us. For if a new world awaits us, it's not in this realm of form."

"I was wrong," she shrieked. "Please help me. I was wrong."

I couldn't help her, even if I'd not been a broken woman within a small, stone room. The Sunken Man delivered her to the front of the queue, casually breaking both her legs, as if he were hobbling a troublesome animal. Alexis Wind Claw was thrown into a pile of other Dark Brethren, waiting to be devoured. She howled, whimpered, looked left and right, apparently unable to comprehend what was happening. She was a noble of the Dark Brethren, a descendant of Medina Wind Claw, but the Sunken God didn't care.

"It'll be over soon," I whispered. "Close your eyes, Alexis. Let it happen. Die easy."

She responded to my words and slowly stopped wailing. She rubbed her broken legs and twitched in pain, but kept her eyes closed and her teeth gritted. After a moment, the Bulbous Whip finished swallowing its last mouthful, and let its sickly green tongue protrude from between wide, slimy lips. The coiled appendage sprang from its mouth, with a huge, sticky pad on the end. The tip of its tongue was large enough to ensnare ten or more Eastron in one go, including Alexis. The group of men and women became a ball of flailing arms and legs, pulled from the sodden plains to the enormous frog's mouth, where they were gulped down with a grotesque spasm of the whip's gullet. As terrified as she must have been, Alexis didn't cry out. She kept her eyes closed as she was eaten alive.

Everyone and everything that had been the Kingdom of the Four Claws was being devoured, and expunged from this realm of form. The window showed me the sea rising to eclipse all of our great holds, sending stone, wood, steel and flesh alike to the bottom of the Inner Sea, perhaps to be found in a thousand years, a curious relic of a forgotten world. The Silver Dawn, First Port, the Severed Hand, the Dark Harbour, the Open Hand, Four Claws Folly – all of it was gone, never to be rebuilt. This was what the Sunken God was showing me – the absolute end of my world. I feared that all of my crew were being shown the same thing, and that madness would follow if we were unable to break free.

I fell from the window and shuffled back across the dusty, stone floor. The single window disappeared, plunging the room back into a monochrome twilight, but I had no illusions that the Sunken God was finished with me. The insistent pain, the weakness in my mind and body, and the feeling that I was utterly helpless – it was his brutal way of reminding me how insignificant I was and how much I'd offended him. How much we'd all offended him.

But we could still beat him. Hundreds of thousands of Eastron were in Utha's realm and the *Revenge* had successfully drawn his eyes from the gate. I'd hoped to save my small crew, but if we were to die to save the Eastron, we'd die with a smile on our faces.

"Fuck you!" I screamed, enduring the pain I felt to use such volume. Saliva sprayed from my cracked lips and I began a pained laugh. "No gods, spirits or men hold dominion over me! There is *nothing* you can do!"

A hole appeared in the floor of the stone room, and I had to roll aside and gather my limbs. A blue column of light erupted into the room, the same size as the window, and the sound of crashing waves was near deafening. I crawled away, struggling with my lack of strength, and groaning at the sudden glare. After a moment, I rolled over and positioned myself on my belly, craning towards the hole and looking down.

Below me was a dark blue ocean, rolling vigorously, with a small shape dancing across the waves at great speed. My view drifted and fell, as if I was as dependent on the tides as any ship. I focused, having to shield my eyes, until the small shape became larger and I saw *Halfdan's Revenge*. She was under full sail, cutting straight and true across the waves, sailing east. I tried to look more closely, but the window wanted me to see something else. Back towards where Nibonay used to be, was a cloud the size of a continent. I couldn't make out fine details within its bubbling mass, but its attention was certainly fixed on the tiny warship. The millions of eyes and tentacles were just a distant texture, twisting and vibrating in the sky. As it followed the *Revenge*, the cloud began to coalesce, becoming more than just a formless mass.

I winced and pulled back from the hole in the floor. What I felt was hard to put into words. It was extreme emotion, perhaps even the emotion of a god, and it was pure and utter chaos. There was a depth to the emotion, like its expression could topple mountains and change the tides. It was a hundred times beyond anything I could feel, and it was entirely focused on the insignificant mortal who'd dared to touch the blood of a god. The blood of Nym'zu, the Sunken God's sister.

There were too many complex emotions for me to process, but some form of primal anger was certainly present. Anger that drove the cloud to slowly change shape, as if it were unable to interact with the world in its natural form. The cloud flared up and down, forming giant appendages and strange shapes, as it pulled in the edges of its mass. It went from hovering high in the air, to mounted on two immense pillars, as if legs were appearing. The waves buffeted against the new shapes, crashing around them as the reformed cloud strode through the ocean, in pursuit of *Halfdan's Revenge*. High above the water, the rest of the Sunken God's form gained a distinctive torso and enormous arms, until a giant humanoid shape was all that remained.

I managed to turn away just far enough to see the *Revenge*. It was still moving fast, but was now listing badly to port, moving north as if no one was at the helm. I wasn't close enough to see Siggy, or any of the crew, and I didn't know if they were even awake and active, or if they were experiencing the same things as me. Either way, with no one to wrestle the helm straight, the ship would continue to list, until it eventually capsized. Not to mention that a monstrous creature was pacing towards it, far faster than the warship was moving.

A sharp pain struck my neck, forcing me to look back at the Sunken God. With my head locked in place, I saw a mountainous, humanoid figure, many times larger than the greatest whips. Its limbs were muscular, coloured green and grey, with huge patches of oozing rotten flesh at its knees and elbows. Its fingers were tipped with cruel, curved talons, flexing and clicking in the air, as if finding their strength. Then I was forced to look at the head. It was the least humanoid part of the giant, with sharp, almost triangular eyes of burning red, covering most of its face. It had a beard of thick, wriggling feelers, each flexing independently and revealing a hooked mouth underneath, like the beak of a squid. The face was maddeningly expressive, showing a thousand layers of arrogance, spite and anger.

I closed my eyes and rolled away from the hole in the floor, fighting the compulsion to look. My weak body wouldn't respond as I wanted, and I had to tense my muscles and howl in pain to move to the other side of the hole and look at *Halfdan's Revenge*. I knew that Klu'zu was gaining on the warship, but I tried to shut him out and focus on the deck. My eyes watered and my head throbbed, but I pushed my vision downwards, until I could see the ship clearly.

The first thing I saw was myself, lying unconscious behind the helm. Tasha and Siggy were slumped in a pile near the wheel, and the rest of the crew were similarly torpid. Luckily everyone had left the rigging before our minds had been attacked, and no one had fallen to their death. Kieran was lying on his back, with a hand on Anya's Roar, as if he'd reached for the horn at the last moment, but been unable to move. The talisman itself was rolling between a barrel and the quartermaster's leg, striking each with force as the ship began to turn more sharply to port. The *Revenge* was now heading due north; soon she'd be pointed back towards Yish, and sail straight at the Sunken God.

"Wake the fuck up," I grunted. "We need to wake the fuck up or we're all dead."

"Adeline!" boomed a voice from the aft of the warship. "If you can hear me... this is goodbye."

Rys Coldfire was not unconscious. He was enveloped in a globe of red and gold wyrd, emanating from Daniel Doesn't Die. The two of them stood next to the aft railing, looking back towards the giant creature that approached. Neither of them were afraid, though they saw the same thing as me. Klu'zu kicked huge waves ahead of him, making the ship buck and twist on the previously calm sea. The Sunken God could crush the *Revenge* in one hand, and he would soon be able to.

"This is all I have," shouted Daniel, addressing the air. "And I no longer need it. I took this power from a god… and I give it to a mortal man."

His globe of wyrd swelled and changed colour. The red and gold of the great phoenix, the most powerful spirit in this realm of form, flowed together into a warm, brown glow. Daniel smiled and shivered, appearing to enjoy the power that infused him. "And now I die," he said, throwing back his head and spreading his arms wide.

The globe became a ball of fire. Daniel opened his mouth and let forth an immense roar, grasping Rys by the shoulders and pulling him into a tight embrace. The Wolf's Bastard clung to him, his own nimbus of light blue wyrd appearing insignificant next to the growing orb of reddish brown. Daniel's roar deepened and elongated, becoming guttural and inhuman, until he sounded like an enraged wild animal. Louder and louder, the roar drowned out both the crashing ocean and the sound of the Sunken God. It was a primal bellow, but not of pain or anguish. Within the roar, I sensed a resurgence, as if something was shrugging off the lethargy of a long hibernation.

The globe now obscured the entire ship, and was getting larger and larger, until the brightness forced me to turn away. It was more than just a glare. It was like moving from pitch black to a blazing sun, all in one instant, causing dots and lines to assault my eyes. I didn't see Daniel die, nor what happened to Rys, but I did feel the square stone room begin to crack and crumble, as if caught in the grip of an enormous hand.

But it wasn't the malevolence of the Sunken God.

PART TEN

28

Marius Cyclone on Nowhere

There was no spirit-whistle, no great turtle spirit, no intervention from Utha the Ghost. I was just to be another casualty in the war to save the Eastron. I was fumbling on top of a Winterlord corpse, with one spear aimed at my head and the other aimed at my chest. I committed my defence to the void legionnaire trying to skewer my head. Throwing both arms at the wooden shaft of his spear, I tried to pivot away, but I had no mobility and they had too much momentum.

Then someone dived across my field of vision, tackling one legionnaire into the other. My grip on the spear pushed it away from my head, and the other weapon only grazed my thigh, as Gaius Two Hearts saved my life. His face was bloody and swollen, and seams of red crept from under his ship leathers – but he was strong enough to draw a knife from his boot and cut two throats in as many seconds.

He was badly wounded, but managed to wrap an arm around my waist and help me upright. "This is all your fault, Marius," he grunted.

I leant against him, pulling myself from the dead Winterlord and trying to take in our surroundings. The open ground before the gate was filled with mindless Winterlords and Dark Brethren, facing outwards towards Death Spell's legionnaires. Huge numbers of Wolves, clearly part of Adeline's forces at Duncan's Fall, had joined the defence, fighting their exhaustion as much as the enemy. More and more animated corpses flowed from the breach, but they began to hold their ground, killing only to clear the earth around the gate. The thousands of refugees were being shepherded away, to be replaced with a mismatched force of defenders, but we would quickly become outnumbered if the flood of attackers didn't cease.

Then I saw my brother. Santago Cyclone, called the Bloodied Harp, strode through the breach, flanked by other Dark Brethren. His movements were quick and jerky, like he was getting used to his body, and his eyes smouldered with cold green flame. This was his reward for submitting to Klu'zu. His lust for power had led him to follow an entity he could never understand. There was no new world for him and Oliver to rule, no triumphant victory over his brother and the treacherous Eastron who dared to defy him. The Sunken God cared no more for them than he did for us. They were merely of more use. They'd not been able to stop us in any conventional way, so Klu'zu had taken away their free will and used them as a blunt instrument. My brother and his warriors were little more than animated dead bodies, overflowing with corrosive green wyrd.

"I'm sorry, brother," I said, louder than I intended.

"Marius, shut the fuck up," grunted Gaius, pulling me away from the enemy and towards the encircling defenders.

We were being cut off, as the mindless warriors filled the empty ground around the gate. Then everyone halted when

Santago opened his mouth and let forth a primal snarl. Perhaps something of my brother still remained within the walking corpse, for he pointed his glaring, green eyes at me. Gaius kept hefting me away, but dozens of attackers were now looking blankly at us. Gradually, responding to Santago's guttural noises, they began to converge on us, led by my brother.

"I think we're about to die, my friend," I said to Gaius, trying to carry as much of my own weight as I could.

He exhaled, gritted his teeth, and appeared to make a decision. "Your arms still work?" he asked. "Then use them! It's time to crawl, Marius." He winced in pain and let me fall from his grasp, before turning to face Santago.

As I hit the ground, I felt his blood all over my arms and chest. Gaius was bleeding from everywhere, but he'd carried me to the edge of the open ground. I pushed all the wyrd I had left into my upper body and began to crawl, though I kept an eye on Gaius, hoping he'd reconsider and simply run away.

We were quickly surrounded, though no one made a move to attack us. Even as animated corpses, it appeared their hatred of me overrode their need to simply kill everyone. Or maybe they'd thrown away too many warriors, battering through the glass. Beyond the oozing green eyes of Santago's forces, I could still hear Death Spell and a dozen other voices, frantically trying to assemble the defenders of Nowhere, but I was on my belly and unable to see how many warriors had come through the breach.

Santago held a straight sword and advanced beyond the other mindless warriors, his baleful eyes fixed on me.

"Gaius, run!" I shouted, desperate for him to live, but unable to see where he could run to.

"Fuck that," he replied, launching himself at Santago.

Most of his weapons were gone, leaving him with only a small hatchet in his right hand and a knife in his left, but he attacked like he had nothing to fear. He was smaller than my brother, but far quicker, and able to avoid the first thrust of Santago's straight sword. Despite the rotten wyrd that infected him, my elder brother was still a formidable warrior. He parried a swing of Gaius's hatchet and relied on his steel braces to deflect the knife, then rammed an armoured boot into the assassin's chest, sending him to the ground.

"Crawl, you fucking idiot!" Gaius barked at me, before rising into a predatory crouch and glaring at my brother. "Come on!" he spat, with blood oozing from his mouth.

Santago answered the challenge and advanced, his dead green eyes staring at Gaius as if he were an insect. I grasped at the earth and pulled myself away as they clashed, but I had nowhere to go. I could hear the nearby sounds of combat and knew that Jessimion and the Wolves would be fighting back, but I couldn't see any friendly faces.

I stopped crawling and turned back to where Gaius and Santago were locked together. The assassin managed to cut my brother across the face and neck, but both wounds were glancing and, in a straight fight, the smaller man simply couldn't match a fully armoured warrior with a sword. Gaius danced left and right, but his own wounds were taking their toll, and the point of Santago's blade appeared to be stalking him.

"Gaius, he just wants me. Run the fuck away!"

"Shut up, Marius," he replied, grinning at me through bloodied teeth. "You did your job, let me do mine."

He delivered a feint at Santago's neck, using his hatchet. It was a suicidal gambit, deliberately leaving himself open in exchange for the chance to drive his dagger into his enemy's exposed armpit. I knew the move. It was a last resort tactic he and his sister had devised for when they were outmatched and didn't care if they died. My brother pivoted away from the hatchet and aimed a powerful thrust at Gaius's stomach. As the straight sword cut through leather and bit into his flesh, Gaius howled and drove his knife up under Santago's arm, through a large gap in his armour. My brother grunted and lost his footing, pushing forwards until his sword emerged through the assassin's back.

Gaius Two Hearts cackled as he died, pulling Santago on top of him in a pile of limbs and blood, but my brother was still alive.

Time slowed for a moment. I was lying on my back, looking up at a ring of dead-eyed Winterlords and Dark Brethren, standing motionless. Then I looked back at the burning green eyes of Santago Cyclone. As soon as he'd killed Gaius, he turned his malevolence straight back to me. He pressed a hand against the assassin's head, using it as leverage to stand up, before pulling the knife out from his armpit. A fountain of blood followed, but my brother reacted with barely a flinch. He was clearly weakened, but just as clearly robbed of the normal human reactions to such a grievous wound. Looking into the depthless insanity of his eyes, I thought that something of my brother remained, like the twitch of a fresh corpse.

"Look at you!" I shouted. "Am *I* still the traitor? Is *this* still your new world?"

He staggered forwards, sword hanging limply in his hand. The blood still flowed from under his arm, but he had enough strength left to kill me. For the second time in as many minutes, I prepared for death.

Until a shape appeared in my peripheral vision.

To my left were ranks of mindless Winterlords, halted in their destructive advance by some command I'd not heard. The sounds of fighting were loudest there, as if the defenders of Nowhere were concentrating their efforts. They may even have created a small gap, though it was impossible to see from my vantage point. What I *did* see was Asha Two Hearts, bounding towards Santago. She appeared out of nowhere, drawing dozens of blank eyes, and leapt at him. Unlike her twin brother, she'd managed to keep hold of a short sword, and stuck it in Santago's neck in a single, fluid motion. He saw her at the last minute, but his loss of blood had robbed him of his ability to react, and all he could do was stare at me as Asha cut out his throat. She tackled him to the ground, sawing at his neck until his body started to twitch and a final, grating death-rattle left his mouth. Santago Cyclone, my oldest brother, was dead.

"Up you get," said Asha, leaving the corpse and pulling me back to my feet. She'd not looked at her dead brother, as I was trying not to look at mine, but we clung to each other and I found my feet.

"I'm sorry, Asha," I whispered.

"Fuck off, Marius," she replied.

Leaning against her, I got my first clear view of the battlefield. Around Utha's Gate, formed into a broad circle, were several hundred mindless warriors. No more came through the breach and I wondered how many Eastron had given their wyrd and their lives to break the glass. Maybe thousands. Around them, in a mismatched line, were the defenders of Nowhere – as many simple folk, wielding hammers and axes, as void legionnaires and duellists. They fought the animated corpses, while the more helpless refugees retreated to the edges of the plain.

Asha was pulling me to the only gap in their circle, where a gang of Kneeling Wolves had cut a hole – but, with Santago's death, those around us were no longer passive. They glared at us through fiery green eyes, before hefting weapons and advancing.

"Enough!" boomed a guttural, inhuman voice, echoing across the ground as if it were a sudden wind. "You will stop fighting... Now!"

I recognized the voice, though I couldn't see him. It was Prince Oliver Dawn Claw, the man who'd eaten more of me than I could spare. His words sent a nimbus of green wyrd through the air, striking both attackers and defenders. Whatever power he now wielded, it made everyone lower their weapons and take a step backwards.

Asha and I held each other tightly, standing amongst enemies, unable to fight or retreat. We were affected by the same twisted energy that stopped the defenders of Nowhere battling the mindless forces of Klu'zu. Whatever Oliver was doing, it turned us all into virtual statues.

When the prince himself appeared from the breach in the glass, he displayed more awareness than any of his infected warriors. He still looked like a swollen, bald, decomposing corpse, but not a mindless one. He oozed green wyrd from every facial orifice, with a globe of the stuff surrounding his body and sending wisps of rotten wind across the low plains. It had only been a few days since I last saw him, but his condition had advanced. There was nothing human left within the mighty Winterlord prince – not in his jerky movements, his swollen pale body, or the guttural notes of his voice. I imagined he was little more than an avatar for the Sunken God, come to finish us off – or simply to make sure Klu'zu could reach the gate.

"Marius the Stranger," he said, spreading his arms wide and tickling the air with his fingers. "I still see plenty of good meat." He licked his lips at me, with a slick of popping drool falling from his scab-covered mouth.

I tried to move – so did Asha – but neither of us were able. A thin mist was emanating from Oliver and spreading at ground level. It rooted everyone but him to the spot. The mist flowed across the defenders of Nowhere, reaching the refugees and turning the dead ground into a forest of motionless Eastron.

"This is your new world?" I asked. "I thought you were to be king."

"I *am* king," he replied. "But my subjects were never going to be Eastron." He glanced down at Santago's corpse. "Your brothers were useful, as were Alexis and Lucio Wind Claw – but it didn't benefit us to tell them the truth. No one will live, Marius. There is no new world... just the oldest one. The time of the Eastron is done. At least Santago had the good sense to serve and die willingly. You and your people will be punished for their defiance."

"How many Eastron did you kill to break the glass?"

"Thousands upon thousands," he replied, enjoying the answer. "I kept the best warriors until last, but everyone else gave themselves willingly."

I wanted to swear at him, or conjure a witty retort, but I had none left. A person can only fight for so long before he gives up and realizes he was a fucking idiot all along. I'd reached this point – and, looking at Asha Two Hearts, I saw that she had too.

As if he had all the time in the world, the creature wearing Oliver's body sauntered around the clear space in front of Utha's Gate. He was the only person moving, with the spreading green cloud flowing from him in greater and greater gouts of rotten wyrd. Whether he was an avatar or a conduit, I felt the presence of the Sunken God, as if the immense cloud to the south was sending forth a mighty tendril of its power.

Then he stopped, facing the gate. There was a ten foot circle of crackling blue energy, framed by jutting pillars of rock. It hadn't opened since before the attack, and seeing Oliver within touching distance of it made me deeply angry. Everything had been about the gate and stopping the enemy from reaching it. Now, I was forced to watch my final failure.

"I'll kill you, then myself," whispered Asha. "As soon as I can move my fucking arms."

"I don't think that's our decision any more," I replied, clinging to her shoulders. "We've lost, Asha. The Sunken God is going to reach the gate. I couldn't save us."

"Self-pity?" she replied. "Don't you fucking dare. Think how many people have died for you. Just because we're about to join them doesn't mean any of us were wrong..."

She wasn't finished speaking, but her thought processes were interrupted by a sudden change in air pressure. The breach in the glass vibrated, like a piece of torn fabric. Then Utha's Gate began to shimmer. At ground level, the green mist was displaced by a circle of shadows, seeming to come from nowhere and covering the near ground in twilight. It didn't travel far, but a small section of the plains was suddenly overcast.

Oliver backed away from the gate, flexing his enormous arms, but clearly confused. From within him, the green wyrd became a torrent of energy, coating his body from head to toe. He was a beacon of eldritch strength, able to influence or kill thousands of people, but the shadows scared him. Then the gate opened.

"My name," roared a ferocious voice, "is Utha the Ghost."

The shadows became angry and the mindless warriors of the Sunken God recoiled. The blue curtain, covering the barrier to the far void, fell in an instant and a single figure emerged, facing Oliver Dawn Claw. The gate became a mirror of depthless black, with shadowy tendrils reaching into the realm of form.

"You are no Eastron," gurgled Oliver, flaring with vibrant green energy.

"I am not," replied Utha, his voice echoing across the plains. "I once was a man, now I am a giant." The shadows formed around him, as if each tendril was part of his form. "You are an exemplar of Klu'zu and you should not test me."

Oliver's rotting face twisted and turned through a hundred different thoughts. Then his huge, bulbous body lunged at the pale man. Utha didn't flinch, but neither was he struck. He flickered from side to side, making Oliver pummel empty air. His pale face slowly fell into a frown after the fourth wild swing from the Winterlord, and he stopped flickering. Oliver aimed a straight right-hand and struck Utha on the jaw, but his fist didn't appear to strike flesh and bone. His fingers cracked, then his hand broke, as if he'd punched a steel wall. At first glance, Utha appeared to be far smaller, but the shadows accentuated his every movement, making the rotten green wyrd seem petty and insignificant.

"I know I can't defeat you," boomed Utha. "But this is my gate, and here I have strength enough to swat your little puppet."

Oliver grasped his broken hand, before a dozen tendrils of shadow lashed around his extremities and held him tightly in mid-air. From the glassy surface of the gate came hundreds more tendrils, aimed at the mindless warriors of the Sunken God. The shadows formed into humanoid shapes, each one resembling Utha and wielding a large axe. When they attacked, it was in perfect unison, chopping at the Winterlords and Dark Brethren as if they were firewood. Each was merely a black figure, made entirely of shadow, but within the globe of twilight they were devastating. Oliver's warriors began to die. They tried to defend themselves, using skill and strength, but Utha's axes didn't care for their steel.

Somewhere beyond my sight, Jessimion Death Spell was ordering his warriors to back off and allow the shadowy reflections of Utha to do their work. The break in the circle, from which Asha had emerged, was now filled with more Kneeling Wolves than Winterlords, as the defenders of Nowhere watched their enemies cut down by invulnerable shadow men. It was quick, brutal and eerily silent, with neither side of the battle able to speak or cry out. Broadswords and spears passed harmlessly through shadow, while black battle-axes sliced through flesh and bone, killing the mindless warriors with maximum efficiency. The only sounds came from the Kneeling Wolves. They jeered and spat curses, evidently enjoying the one-sided slaughter.

Still clinging to Asha, I turned back to the gate and saw Utha looking up at the restrained form of Oliver Dawn Claw. The bloated Winterlord prince was ten feet above the ground, held by immovable tendrils of shadow. For all the might bestowed upon him by Klu'zu, he appeared helpless.

The pale man had told me that he couldn't defeat the Sunken God directly, but close to the source of his power, or near a break in the glass, Utha was far more formidable than anything Oliver could conjure. He'd told me he'd soon be a god, and I didn't really understand what that meant, but I knew I was seeing something of cosmic immensity – something that, for its own reasons, had chosen to help the Eastron escape this realm of form.

The last few dozen mindless attackers were cut down by shadow men, and the perimeter of warriors became a perimeter of corpses. Oliver had used too many of his slaves to create the breach in the glass, leaving him with barely five hundred infected Eastron to actually attack us. I could barely conceive of the loss of life. The Winterlord prince I'd once tried to befriend had consumed the life-force of a hundred thousand men and women, maybe more. I wondered how many Eastron were still out there in this realm of form. I didn't even know how many were already in Utha's void realm. So many had died to get us to this point, and I was somehow not amongst them.

"Wake up, Marius," snapped Asha Two Hearts, slapping me in the face. "We're still alive. I don't know what's happening, but we're definitely still alive."

"That's Utha the Ghost," I replied. "Just be grateful he's on our side."

We were both wide-eyed, with her supporting half my weight, but we managed to share an expression that adequately conveyed our feelings – neither of us could believe we were still alive.

As quickly as they'd appeared, the shadows retreated, returning to the depthless black of Utha's Gate. Only those that held Oliver remained, leaving the rest of the ground filled with twitching corpses. There were plenty of defenders amongst the dead, but the vast majority were the forces of the Sunken God. Utha remained, but the pale man didn't look at the hundreds of people he'd just killed. He kept his pink eyes focused on the Winterlord.

"Marius!" shouted Jessimion Death Spell. "You live?"

"I live," I replied. "How fares the defence?"

"Is that a fucking joke?" he asked.

Asha threw her head back and laughed maniacally. She readjusted her arms around my shoulders, making sure I could stand, while her face rose into an hysterical smile. A tear came from her eye as she glanced over her twin brother's dead body, but she didn't stop laughing.

"Fuck you!" she screamed at Oliver. "Fuck you and your fat fucking face. Come on, make me a slave, I fucking dare you."

"Easy," I whispered.

We were holding each other up, and our mutual support became a tight embrace. She didn't stop swearing at Oliver, but returned my hug, as if she needed the comfort but wouldn't admit it. After a moment of crying against my shoulder, Asha sneered and went to shove me away, but changed her mind when it became clear I'd fall over without her help.

"Fuck off, Marius," she muttered.

Walking amongst the piled corpses came Jessimion and others – a curious mix of Eastron camps, each unsure how to react. Charlie Vane's Kneeling Wolves were the most vocal, and even they were subdued once the battle was over. A few innocents, mostly Sea Wolves who didn't want to fall back, also approached the dead ground, with several fighting back nausea at the gruesome spectacle.

Asha and I made our way over to the gate and the restrained form of Oliver Dawn Claw. Utha acknowledged us, but only with a sideways glance and a subtle nod. His attention was focused on the huge Winterlord.

"Just kill him," I said, wearily. "Any part of Oliver who would care for my words is already dead. What's left…" I looked around at the bodies. "What's left is little more than an avatar of Klu'zu. Just kill him."

"Very well," said Utha, his voice returning to normal.

The pale man wasn't out of breath or even flustered. There was nothing to indicate he'd exerted himself, let alone effortlessly killed so many powerful warriors. He was totally composed, though he now had an audience of thousands. From across the low ground of Nowhere, everyone was looking in his direction. Many were fixated on the corpses or the restrained body of Oliver, but all had seen the strange man with pale skin, pink eyes and long white hair. He couldn't hide any more, and I wondered if he'd ever been this exposed. Warriors, families, men, women and children – for the vast majority, it was their first glimpse of Utha the Ghost, and he'd announced himself in the most startling way imaginable.

Caressing the shadows before him, he raised Oliver higher into the air. The tendrils now came from Utha himself, flowing and elongating, doubling, then tripling his mass. As his form changed, he strode away from his gate, moving Oliver ahead of him. The pale man flowed into a giant, made of shimmering black shadows, with a thousand layers falling into each other. He towered over the low ground and the staring Eastron. He was still humanoid, but now with a mirror of the endless cosmos reflecting in his face.

I'd seen him like this before, at the Severed Hand, and seeing it again made me gasp for breath. I joined every other Eastron on the plains of Nowhere, looking up in silence at the unknowable creature who'd saved our lives.

"I am your friend," intoned the shadow giant, his voice deep and sincere. "Your enemies are my enemies. I can appear as a man, and be like you, but this is my true form. I show it to you in the hope you will not fear me." He kept one arm pointed at Oliver, and swept the other towards the open gate. "Through this doorway is a world I built for you. It is yours, I give it to you all."

The huge crowd was silent. There *was* fear in thousands of eyes, but it was tempered with awe and gratitude. These were the most resilient of Eastron – the lucky men, women and children who were still alive and still had a chance at a new life. Their respect was not given easily, but I saw it in every single pair of eyes.

"This man is an avatar of your enemy," said Utha, presenting the restrained body of Oliver as if he were an exhibit. "That makes him my enemy. Let his be the last death you see in this realm of form."

Oliver Dawn Claw, prince of the Winterlords, only son of the Shining Sword, and self-proclaimed Always King of the Eastron, was utterly helpless. He couldn't even speak, for a thick rope of shadow covered his mouth. His eyes sought me out, over hundreds of heads, but if he wanted to convey something more than spite, I couldn't see it. Then he was torn apart by thick tendrils of shadow. His arms, legs and head were all pulled from his torso, but there was no blood, just a subtle drip of green ichor. Everything else was smothered in impenetrable shadows. Utha left no doubt, as to his power and the finality of Oliver's death.

29

Adeline Brand aboard *Halfdan's Revenge*

I awoke on the quarterdeck, my limbs tangled in coiled ropes and my back against the starboard railing. Across the sharply tilting deck, the rest of the small crew were also waking up, shaking their heads and nursing minor bumps and bruises. Tasha and Siggy were closest, with Kieran gathering up Anya's Roar and coming to join us. No one spoke, nor addressed Daniel's corpse or the fact that Rys was nowhere to be seen. Everyone just stared at the giant creature off our port side.

Despite our new northern trajectory, I couldn't see the Maelstrom and had no idea whether or not Marius had led the last of our people to safety. Not that I'd be able to do anything if I had known. Every card had been played – every angle, every strategy, every advantage. Except one.

I felt Tasha grasp my hand. I looked at the terrified Kneeling Wolf and smiled. "Will you make that fish stew for dinner? The spicy one?"

She frowned at me. "Of course, but you hate fish."

"If we're still alive, I'll eat anything you cook and I'll fucking love it."

"Where's Rys?" whispered Siggy Blackeye, keeping her eyes on the rapidly approaching god. "Did he do it? Is Daniel dead?"

The mountainous form of Klu'zu was almost upon us. All it needed to do was reach down and crush the *Revenge*. Its legs were huge, grey and green pillars, blocking the horizon as they waded through the Outer Sea. The largest whip I'd seen would barely reach the giant's waist, though its immensity was almost a blessing, for it meant we couldn't clearly see the Sunken God's face. No one screamed or panicked. Our minds and our eyes were overloaded, forcing us to simply stand and wait for whatever happened next.

Then there was another roar – louder, clearer and closer that the one I'd heard in the stone room. It came from the starboard side of the ship, giving the crew an excuse to turn away from the giant. I rushed to the railing as *Halfdan's Revenge* continued to list, and saw a growing globe of warm reddish-brown wyrd, rising above the ocean. At its centre, with his limbs splayed as wide as they would go, was Rys Coldfire. His light blue spiritual power was gone, eclipsed by pulses of energy too immense to contain. From his eyes and mouth flowed huge gouts of light, enlarging and strengthening the globe. The Wolf's Bastard was powerful enough to accept Daniel's gift... at least for now.

"It's stopped," shouted Hitch from the mainmast. "The god, it's stopped!"

He was right. The Sunken God was no longer moving. It was within arm's reach of the *Revenge*, but held position, ankle-deep in the Outer Sea. Siggy had returned to the helm, and we were now moving north-east, but there was no way we could outrun the giant.

Another roar, and the globe rose above the surface of the water. It was now wider than the ship, and quickly became taller than the mainmast. The warm brown glow darkened, until Rys was invisible and the surface began to resemble fur. Deep within the globe, another face coalesced, with prominent rounded ears, small dark eyes, and an elongated muzzle, ending in wide black nostrils. The head shook, the eyes blinked, and the roar became a growl, like an animal emerging from hibernation. It was the head of an enormous brown bear, looking outwards at the ocean, *Halfdan's Revenge*, and the towering form of Klu'zu.

When I'd first seen Daniel, he'd been dead and half-naked, laying on a spirit-master's table. He had a tattoo of a bear, looking out from his chest, and I was struck with how similar it was to the actual Death Bear. The fur was reddish brown and a stoic warmth emanated from the eyes, projecting depthless knowledge and power. It was an ancient god, worshipped by the people who would one day become the Eastron.

Arms and legs appeared, growing the globe to immense proportions, as if a furry brown island was appearing in the Outer Sea. Waves were now hitting the *Revenge* from both directions at once, and Siggy had given up trying to wrestle the helm straight. We were going wherever the movements of the two gods dictated.

"Hold onto something!" I boomed, dragging Tasha to the nearest railing.

Hitch jumped back to the deck and everyone did as I ordered, as huge waves crashed over the ship, displacing anything that wasn't secured and tearing through the mainsail. With one arm, it was difficult to both hold on and wipe salt water from my face, so I was forced to shake my head and blink until I could focus.

Klu'zu stood on our port side – an immense humanoid creature, whose form was difficult to look at. To starboard, just shrugging off the torpor of centuries, was a growling bear, with limbs as wide and powerful as the Sunken God's.

There was no malevolence emanating from the Death Bear, just a stubborn resolve, accentuated by a cacophony of grunts, growls and slobbers. Its head craned over the *Revenge*, and its drool fell to the deck, splashing with more force than the waves. After a moment, when its eyes blinked clear and its head stopped shaking, the Death Bear noticed Daniel Doesn't Die, spread-eagled across the aft deck. An enormous paw rose from the ocean, and a single claw, the size of our foremast, prodded at the dead Sundered Wolf. It was surprisingly gentle, nudging Daniel across the deck, as if trying to wake him. When he didn't move, the Bear let forth a roar of anguish, raising its head and exposing black and red gums, surrounding huge teeth.

It had never occurred to me that Daniel and the Death Bear would have bonded. In the year I'd carried the Old Bitch of the Sea, she and I had almost become one. I could only imagine the connection that would develop over two hundred years, no matter how their symbiosis began. In my case, Eva Rage Breaker had dispelled the spirit from within me, leaving us both alive – whereas Daniel had died to separate himself from the ancient entity.

As I looked up at the titanic brown bear, I saw three faces within. Rys Coldfire was undeniably at the centre of the spirit, anchoring it to this realm of form, but its consciousness and power had belonged equally to the ancient god of death and the chubby Sundered Wolf. Now one of them was dead and the other confused, patting at the ocean like a dog missing its master.

The *Revenge* levelled out, gliding a little way from the two gods. Her sails were torn and the mainmast was cracked at the midpoint, but the hull was intact. Klu'zu was stationary, and the Death Bear was merely shuffling back and forth, causing only small waves.

"Steady!" I shouted, finally able to stand unaided. "Anyone hurt?"

"Just my eyes," quipped Kieran Greenfire.

"Bumps and bruises," replied Lazlo Darkling from along the port railing.

It occurred to me that our defence of Duncan's Fall and the things we'd seen had hardened our minds. A year ago, the sight of a Sunken Man had almost been enough to cripple me. Now, not even Klu'zu himself could break us. We may not get to travel through Utha's Gate, but we were far from finished.

"Siggy, is the helm responding?" I asked.

"Yes, but the mainsail's gone."

"Just turn us back east. I need to see the Maelstrom."

Klu'zu's left leg was still obscuring my vision. We were close enough that any small movement from the Sunken God could capsize us, but without the blood of Nym'zu aboard, it didn't care about *Halfdan's Revenge*. We still couldn't see its face, far above us, but I imagined it was just as confused as the Death Bear.

"Kieran, Hitch, we need some kind of sail or we're finished."

Almost before I'd stopped speaking, the mainmast fell. The top half creaked, swayed, and toppled over, sending a mess of canvas and rigging to the deck. In time we'd be able to rig something with the remaining mast but, for now, we were just drifting.

"Fuck!" I shouted.

"I was about to say that," replied Kieran Greenfire.

I ran along the port railing, off the quarterdeck, past the wreckage of the mainsail, to the bow of the *Revenge*. The ocean churned around the enormous grey and green leg, like waves against a cliff face, obscuring much of the horizon. I still couldn't see the fucking Maelstrom. For all I knew there were still thousands of Eastron before Utha's Gate. We'd gained the attention of the Sunken God, but its monstrous form could return to Nowhere in an hour or two, if Rys and the Death Bear didn't hold its attention. As for *Halfdan's Revenge* – we still had Anya's Roar to escape into the void, but I wouldn't use it until the Maelstrom returned and the gate was closed.

Klu'zu moved his leg and the ship was flung away – rolling and bucking on a sudden tsunami, but remaining upright. The rest of our rigging was now hanging by two or three ropes, and a small slick of barrels, splintered decking and broken ballistae floated in our wake.

"That's it," shouted Siggy, with grim finality. "No helm, no sails. All we've got left is the hull."

"She's not finished yet," replied Kieran, making sure he had a good hold of Anya's Roar.

The *Revenge* stopped twisting and turning on the sudden tide, and settled north-east, a dozen ship lengths from the Sunken God. I scanned the western horizon, but couldn't see the Maelstrom. Most of Yish and Nibonay had fallen into the sky, but there was no boiling black storm cloud to signify the closure of the gate.

Then the Death Bear reared up onto its back legs. It wasn't as tall or bulky as Klu'zu, but showed no fear as the two gods came face to face. The Bear opened one of its enormous hairy paws, revealing the droplet of Nym'zu's blood. It was tiny against the creature's palm, but shone with a hundred different refractions of white and blue light. Within the Bear I saw Rys again – this time he was grinning wickedly, as if relishing this final challenge. For a legendary Sea Wolf duellist, who'd spent his entire life searching for something that could best him, it was the perfect end. I only wished I could hear some last words of angry defiance from the Wolf's Bastard, instead of the guttural growls of the Death Bear.

Opposite, the beard of tentacles around Klu'zu's mouth began to wriggle and vibrate in the air, just as his triangular red eyes started to glow. The Sunken God took another step and reached out with its immeasurable power, sending waves of chaos and cosmic insanity towards the Bear, as if to exert its dominance over the old god of death. The Bear just shrugged, much as Rys would have done, and continued growling.

The crew of the *Revenge* could do nothing but watch. All of us clung to the railings, our eyes turned upwards, no more than ants to the two gods facing off above us, but defiant nonetheless. We'd seen too much to feel fear now. Not a single Eastron who'd volunteered was afraid of dying. When the two creatures closed on each other, we were thrown even further away, but Kieran's confidence was well-placed and the hull remained intact.

The Death Bear attacked first, leaping clear of the ocean and wrapping its huge front legs around Klu'zu's midriff. The Sunken God stumbled backwards, emitting a grotesque gurgling sound, but it didn't fall, and grabbed its attacker in mid-air. The Bear mauled Klu'zu's back and gnawed at his chest, growling and snarling, as if unconcerned by the size difference. It seemed to take a moment for the Sunken God to process that this big, hairy animal was immune to its aura, and would deign to attack it. I doubted its alien consciousness would ever have experienced such defiance. Would it even recognize that the thing attacking it was also a god?

Fur, slime and sea water flew in every direction as Klu'zu tried to free himself from the Bear's savage embrace. The beard of tentacles flailed outwards, hooking into the Bear's flesh and tearing huge chunks from its face and neck. Deep within the Death Bear's form, I saw Rys narrow his eyes, assessing his opponent, as if it were any other fight.

"Adeline," screamed Hitch. "Depth barges! Fuck me, there's a lot of depth barges. From the west."

"What?" I shouted back. "Are you fucking joking?"

He wasn't. A dense column of coral- and seaweed-encrusted vessels was bearing down on us, just emerging from beneath the Outer Sea. There were thousands of them. Behind the depth barges, wading through the water, was the Vile Whip and dozens of other monstrous Sunken Men. They'd been drawn from Nowhere, the Inner Sea, and all over the kingdom, to answer the summons of their master.

Kieran Greenfire flailed his way along the deck to join me at the bow. He dragged Anya's Roar behind him and the ornate horn was now dented and scratched. "It's time," he said.

"Not yet," I replied, peering west, but still not seeing the Maelstrom.

The armada of depth barges, now fully emerged, deployed into a semi-circle, moving quickly towards us. The Vile Whip, small in comparison to the Death Bear and Klu'zu, stayed at the rear, marshalling the lesser whips.

The Bear, now almost moving like Rys Coldfire, hooked one of Klu'zu's arms, planted his feet back on the seabed, and pulled his entire weight into a throw. The Wolf's Bastard was an accomplished grappler, and managed to leverage the Sunken God off its feet and out of the water, before bending his back and dumping the immense, slimy body onto its arse in the Outer Sea.

Celebratory roars of defiance flowed across the small crew of *Halfdan's Revenge*. We were now far enough away that the resulting waves just pushed us further from the battle.

"Fuck him up, Rys!" screamed Siggy Blackeye.

"Once more for the Eastron!" boomed Kieran Greenfire.

The Death Bear, with half its face torn off, let forth a ferocious challenge and dived at the Sunken God. It was almost euphoric to revel in so powerful a victory, but it was short-lived. Klu'zu seemed to have finally processed what was happening, and stood to greet the charging bear. It grasped the old god around the throat with both hands, before violently shaking it. Then its tentacles lashed out, scourging the Death Bear's muzzle. Two of its tentacles were longer than the others and wrapped tightly around the Bear's head, pulling the old god towards Klu'zu's beak-like mouth.

Rys was gaining more control over his monstrous new form and didn't stop fighting. With all four limbs, he savagely clawed the Sunken God across its chest, back and arms, but the wounds were shallow and seemed to close almost as quickly as they appeared. Then the Bear howled, as one of its eyes was ripped from its skull and thrown into the ocean. But this didn't stop the Wolf's Bastard. The Bear twisted in Klu'zu's grasp and bit off two tentacles with a single mighty snap of its jaws. The Sunken God released its grip, flinging the Bear away and flailing with its arms and remaining tentacles, as if pain was something it couldn't truly comprehend.

For a moment, everything shrank. There was too much to look at, and my mortal eyes could only see so much. Sunken Men, whips, depth barges, a giant bear with more exposed flesh and bone than fur, and the enraged form of Klu'zu. It spread out like a madman's painting, covering the horizon. The only thing that anchored me in place – the only thing that remained of the land we'd called the Kingdom of the Four Claws – was the sudden emergence of a huge black and grey storm cloud. Somewhere to the west, above what remained of the island of Nowhere, the Maelstrom had returned. A huge funnel of angry void energy split the distant sky, charging the air for thousands of miles and drawing even the attention of the Sunken God.

"Goodbye, Tomas Red Fang," I whispered, knowing that the old man had succeeded in detonating his wyrd to close Utha's Gate.

"Adeline," said Tasha Strong, wiping salt water from her eyes and holding my hand. "We need to leave. They're safe... they're all safe."

Halfdan's Revenge was now level, and her small crew clustered on the quarterdeck. Kieran and Spectre, the void legionnaire, cradled Anya's Roar. Siggy, Hitch and Lazlo Darkling linked arms and shepherded me from the bow, and everyone else just clung to each other, helpless against what they were seeing.

"It's time!" I shouted. "If you want to say goodbye to this realm of form, say it now, for we're not coming back."

"Fuck this realm of form," said Siggy.

"I was never that fond of it," added Kieran.

"Lift the horn to my mouth," I said, holding onto Tasha. "We're leaving."

The last thing I saw, before pushing all of my wyrd into Anya's Roar, was Rys Coldfire. I felt that the Wolf's Bastard was happier than he'd ever been, as if attacking a god completed his existence. I didn't know how his union with the Death Bear would progress – whether or not he could even die – but he'd certainly saved us, and shown the Sunken God something new. I enjoyed the thought of an immortal bear, with Rys's mind, plaguing Klu'zu for centuries to come.

Then I blew the horn and summoned Anya's Friend. Our vast array of enemies were too focused on the emergence of the distant void storm to notice the phoenix spirit. It appeared around our hull, with the *Revenge* nestling on its back, between its four wings. Feathers of red and gold bristled around every railing, and a huge head rose above the bow. When I'd first blown the horn and seen the spirit, I'd experienced wonder – now, all I felt was relief. Anya's Friend was a mighty spirit, small and weak compared to the Sunken God and the Death Bear, but she would fly us to safety in the void.

Halfdan's Revenge juddered forwards, quickly rising from the ocean as the phoenix began to flap her two pairs of wings. The remnants of our sails fell away and a fiery circle

435

took shape in front of us, leading through the glass. I rushed back to the bow, where the phoenix was craning its neck to turn and look at me. There was an innocent warmth in the huge bird's eyes, as if it was glad to be of use.

"Take us away from here," I said. "Far, far away."

Anya's Friend cawed, turned its enormous beak forwards, and plunged towards the growing circle of fire. Behind, still not acknowledging us, the Sunken God raged. It appeared to know what the Maelstrom meant and that it had been denied. The Eastron would *not* be annihilated. They would endure in the distant void and there wasn't a fucking thing Klu'zu could do about it.

"No gods, spirits or men hold dominion over us!" I shouted. "We won. We denied you. We are the Eastron from across the sea, and you will remember us!"

The *Revenge* was now moving as fast as if she were under full sail, rising higher and higher above the Outer Sea. Just before we reached the swirling circle of red and gold, Anya's Friend gathered its wings and swooped through the hole in the glass and into the void. All of us looked back one last time as we left the realm of form. Then the fiery circle closed behind us.

Halfdan's Revenge flew through the void on the back of a giant phoenix, with twenty-eight Eastron aboard. Our elation at escaping Klu'zu was now tempered with the reality of our situation. We were beyond the glass, safe from immediate harm, but lost in the immensity of the void sky, with no obvious safe haven. Even still, the first thing on everyone's mind was getting some sleep.

With Kieran's insistence, I'd taken Tynian Driftwood's cabin, and closed my eyes within seconds of laying down. Peace was a strange thing, rarely found and often confusing. I'd been thinking about it for weeks and come to no useful conclusions. The irony was that, in choosing to stay behind and not live in peace through Utha's Gate, I'd somehow found peace all the same. I thought of it as a victory. I was the leader of this small crew, and I hoped each of them slept soundly, feeling the same peace as me.

I didn't know how long I was asleep, for day and night were irrelevant in the void, but I awoke gently, feeling better than I had in months. My world had shrunk to the size of a single ship, and I found that comforting.

Rising from bed, I went to the wide bay window at the back of the cabin and looked out on the spectacular void sky. Within the infinite colours and shapes, I saw faces, like finding meaning in the clouds on an overcast day. First, was a young man with hard, brown eyes. It was Arthur, my younger brother, glaring at me like he wanted a fight. Then I saw the sparkling smile of Jaxon Ice, called the Wisp, my closest friend until his death. The two of them, Sea Wolf duellists like me, glided slowly away, to be replaced by the intractable, bearded face of Lord Ulric Blood, First Fang of the Severed Hand. I'd killed him in a duel and taken his station, but the face I saw smiled at me, as if to say I'd done well. Then there was Tomas Red Fang, appearing next to Ulric, and representing all that it meant to be a Sea Wolf. Lastly, I saw Young Green Eyes, the only man I'd ever truly loved.

"I'm still alive," I whispered, wishing I could talk to him. "And you were right – the Eastron didn't belong in the Pure Lands. The Kingdom of the Four Claws was nothing but a few holds and the seas in between. Then the seas turned against us and the holds offered no sanctuary. I wish I'd listened to you."

I turned away from the window, sat on the narrow bed, and allowed myself a slight smile. I had new challenges and a life still to lead, but this felt like an ending. I could accept it, perhaps even enjoy it, as long as the Eastron endured in peace.

30

Marius Cyclone beyond Utha's Gate

I looked south, over the rugged, grassy plains of Nowhere. The island was empty, with nothing but a few piles of burning corpses to remind me that we'd ever been here. I leant into my crutch and frowned. Other than Adeline and her crew, I thought that Tomas Red Fang and I were the last two free Eastron in this realm of form. The final group to pass through the gate had been made up of severely wounded defenders, most of whom would be lucky to survive the journey along the shadow bridge.

"Just me and you then," said the old Sea Wolf spirit-master. "I have to say, I didn't think my last conversation would be with the Stranger."

The cloud had disappeared, and the two of us were standing at the base of the gate, with a wall of shimmering blue energy a few feet from us. I would walk through it, and Tomas would detonate his wyrd to close it. Everyone else was already in Utha's realm. My wife, my daughter, and two hundred thousand Eastron. Enough for us to survive and prosper.

"I think we did okay," I replied. "Don't you think?"

He considered it. "It's the one hundred and sixty ninth year of the dark age. We did a lot in that time. Some good, but mostly bad. Do you want to know what I've been wondering since all this began?"

I nodded.

"How we would have changed, if allowed to grow for a thousand years? Would we have stopped fighting and started learning? Or would we still be obsessed with the same petty bullshit?" The old man smiled at me. "That's your real task, Marius the Stranger – finding a new way for us to live. All of this is only the beginning for you."

I took a deep breath, suddenly exhausted. "Fuck that. I'm retiring to a small house and becoming a committed alcoholic."

The old man's papery skin wrinkled up. "What I mean to say is... it's a beginning for you, but an ending for me."

"How old are you?" I asked.

The wrinkles became a broad smile. "Sea Wolves find that question impolite. It carries implications of being weak. But I'm ninety-four. I've been spirit-master of the Severed Hand for fifty years, and served three First Fangs – Halfdan Blood, his son Ulric, and Adeline Brand. It occurs to me that our kingdom isn't even twice my age."

I glanced around the empty plains of Nowhere, considering that Tomas was just dragging out his last moments. "It's time for me to go."

"I know," he replied. "Good luck to you, Marius."

We shook hands.

"Yours is a fine death, Tomas. If there is such a thing."

I turned to face the crackling wall of blue energy, positioning my crutch and my useless left leg so I could step through the gate in one go. I thought I should be sentimental about leaving this realm of form for the last time, but I wasn't. I'd always been pragmatic, but the last few months had refined my lack of sentiment about a world that was trying to kill us. I just closed my eyes and stepped through Utha's Gate... the last Eastron to do so.

After an acute surge of dislocation, I found myself stumbling forwards onto the crystalline black surface of the shadow bridge. My face was about to smash into the floor, but Asha Two Hearts grabbed me and pulled me upright.

"You took your fucking time," she said. "Is that old Sea Wolf terribly interesting?"

"Language," said Marta, retrieving my crutch and rushing to hug me.

Beyond Asha and my daughter, stood Jessica and a cantankerous black cat.

"We should move away from the gate," I said. "I don't know what's about to happen, but I don't want to be near it."

They helped me stand, with Marta trying to hide her tears, until we were a good distance from the gate.

"Hey, it's okay," I said, gently stroking her hair. "We won!"

"Yeah, cheer up," added Asha. "Your dad's not a complete idiot after all."

Before I could deliver a witty retort, the shimmering wall of energy pulsed and imploded. It was sudden, with the pale blue wyrd of a Sea Wolf at its centre. Utha's Gate, the doorway to our new home, flared outwards, then gathered into a single point of light and disappeared. On the other side, an infinite distance away on the island of Nowhere, Tomas Red Fang had detonated his wyrd and the Maelstrom had returned. To my perceptions, the shadow bridge now continued into the depthless layers of the void, with no further connection to the realm of form.

I laughed. All of my nerves and muscles relaxed at once, as if unnecessary tension was suddenly relieved. Physically, I was still a mess, but emotionally, I felt free for the first time in years. I could barely believe that I'd succeeded. It wasn't a complete victory, but it was enough. The fact that I was still alive was the biggest surprise. What the fuck did I do now?

"Let's walk," said Jessica. "They're waiting for us beyond the other gate."

"Who's waiting?" I asked.

"Everyone," replied my wife.

Asha helped me walk, with Marta staying close by and Jessica a few strides ahead. Titus loitered around my feet, keeping his tail high as he pranced next to me. We moved along the shadow bridge, approaching the gateway to Utha's realm. I'd only been through the second doorway once, over a year ago, and though my memories of the realm were crystal clear, I'd spent little time imagining what life in our new home would be like.

The second door was much like the one we'd just closed, though it was framed in black wood rather than stone pillars. Titus went through first, followed by Jessica. Marta and Asha stayed either side of me, and we were the last to enter Utha's realm. We emerged onto a high terrace, near the top of the black citadel at the head of the valley – called the Shadow by the first few Brethren who'd arrived. In front of us, arrayed across the vast, black terraces, were hundreds of Eastron. Over the railings, where the lush green landscape stretched away, were hundreds more.

Waterwheels churned next to the river and wooden structures of all different shapes and sizes filled the valley. Further away were pastures filled with livestock, and freshly ploughed fields. Much work had been done, though all of it stopped when we arrived, and all sets of eyes looked up at us.

"Go on," said Marta, smiling up at me. "You can walk the last few feet yourself."

Asha and Jess stepped back, and I hobbled to look out over the railing. The hundreds I'd first seen gradually became thousands – Eastron of every kind, mingling together as a single people, all staring at me. I gulped, and felt a droplet of nervous sweat trickle down my face. I'd never stood before so many people.

Standing at the top of the largest set of downward steps, was a rugged Sea Wolf. He was a large man, wearing a loose sleeveless shirt and heavy boots. His hands and face were muddy, as if he'd been working the fields and he, like everyone else in view, was unarmed. With his eyes fixed on me, the Sea Wolf started to clap. Others nearby joined him, then the clap spread across the terraces. Slowly, as the sound rose, I saw a hundred people clapping, then two hundred, then five hundred. Then cheers erupted and spread, until the entire valley was filled with roaring Eastron. Friends and family hugged each other, children jumped up and down, and tears of victory and relief were shed. It was beautiful.

I rubbed my eyes and felt light-headed. It was an overwhelming spectacle. For months I'd defined my existence by my mistakes – by all I'd done wrong, or done too late. Now, with the gate closed behind me and my people safe, I was faced with all I'd done right. I heard my name within the cheering and started to cry, though they were tears of joy and filtered through a grateful smile.

Marius! Marius!

Even Adeline Brand's Wolves were calling my name, though a significant portion still called me the Stranger. The barriers between us would endure, but they had softened and would continue to soften, until the barriers were irrelevant and we were simply the Eastron. For just the second time in my life, I actually thought I'd achieved something of worth.

Marta appeared and clung to my free arm. "This is for you, Father. It's all for you. Everyone wants to thank you. You were really brave, when no one else was."

I wished I was strong enough to pick her up, but I had to settle for a tearful hug. "Your dad did something good," I said.

"This way," said Duncan Greenfire. "Best we do this away from everyone else."

"Everyone else is getting drunk," I replied. "As I should be doing."

The bottom level of the Shadow had been converted into a brewery, with Sea Wolf ale and Dark Brethren stout fermenting next to whisky stills and wine vats. The booze was being distributed down the valley, as the largest celebration in Eastron history got underway. Unfortunately, I was required elsewhere.

Duncan led me down two flights of stairs, under the black citadel. He didn't offer to help me walk, but was patient with my stumbling and swearing. The pain was getting tolerable, but my frustration at being a cripple was only getting worse.

Luckily, I had every hope of a boring life from this point onwards.

"Can't this wait?" I asked. "What's so important?"

The stairs ended and Duncan stopped. We were in a black stone room – one of hundreds, criss-crossing the lower levels of the Shadow. Many were occupied, or being used as store-rooms, but many more had yet to be discovered.

"What's so important is that Adeline Brand and her crew are still alive," replied Duncan.

I straightened and my eyes widened. "How is that possible?"

"I'm not sure," replied the diminutive Sea Wolf. "But they escaped to the void."

"That talisman," I said, grinning. "I thought that was just optimism. Flying through the glass on the back of a phoenix. But I'd never bet against Adeline Brand and the Wolf's Bastard. Can we help them?"

"Maybe," said Duncan. "Come with me."

He walked into darkness and I followed. On level ground, I was surer of foot and able to walk without wincing. Asha Two Hearts had appointed herself my keeper, but she was off getting drunk with everyone else, forcing me to get better at using my crutch.

A wooden door emerged through the darkness, and Duncan stopped next to it. "I was going to speak to her alone, but now I think you should join me."

"Lead the way," I replied.

Duncan opened the door. Beyond was crisp daylight, but it didn't penetrate the dark room, as if the doorway led somewhere far away. Through the door was an ornate stone balcony, upon which stood a tall woman. I didn't recognize her at first, for both her arms were intact, but it was Adeline Brand.

"After you," said Duncan.

I hobbled through the door and gasped. Suddenly, with no warning, my body was whole again. Neither of my legs hurt, my side no longer had a dent in it – even the two fingers I'd lost had grown back. The balcony existed between worlds, but I disliked the illusion. If I was now a cripple, that was what I was, and pretending I was anything else was a lie.

Adeline turned. I'd never seen her with her long black hair down and her face clean. She wasn't conventionally attractive, but there was a magnetism to her that demanded attention. She seemed more comfortable with temporarily getting her arm back than I was with my own illusion.

"Hello," I said, smiling awkwardly.

"Yeah," she replied, narrowing her eyes. "Hello. You are well?"

I nodded, slowly becoming accustomed to the balcony's strange effects. "We all made it through. Oliver attacked us, but Utha dealt with him. It's done. It's all done."

"Good," she said. "How many did we save?"

"More than two hundred thousand," I replied. "Everyone's getting drunk, so an exact count will have to wait. Half of those are Wolves. Those who sail, those who kneel and those who are sundered. We have a single Winterlord and the rest are Dark Brethren. Men, women and children – a whole civilization, with many lives left to live."

She turned, and leant against the balcony. "You did well, Cyclone."

"As did you, Brand."

Duncan Greenfire joined us on the balcony, with his small pain spirit perched upon his shoulder. The green imp mimicked the young man's movements, glancing between Adeline and myself, as if assessing us. "Are you safe?" he asked Adeline.

She nodded. "Beyond the grasp of the Sunken God. Aboard the strongest of warships, protected by a mighty phoenix spirit, flying through the void. Twenty-eight of us. Rys and Daniel gave their lives."

I wanted to give her a hug, but doubted she'd appreciate it, so just put a friendly hand on her shoulder. "I know he hated me, but I liked Rys."

"He didn't hate you," she replied. "Maybe he did once, but he'd changed, just like the rest of us. His vocabulary just hadn't caught up."

"What will you do?" I asked. "You have provisions?"

"Aye. When we first abandoned the *Revenge*, she was well-stocked. For such a small crew it'll last a while."

Duncan walked around us and peered over the balcony. He swept his arm from left to right, as if drawing a curtain, and the bright daylight was replaced by a glinting void sky. Adeline and I joined him by the railing, just as a fiery red and gold bird with two sets of wings soared past. On the back of the huge phoenix spirit, gently held behind its neck and within a globe of protective wyrd, was a Sea Wolf warship. *Halfdan's Revenge* had lost her masts and was scarred from bow to stern, but she was intact.

"Look closely," said Duncan, pointing ahead of the glorious bird. "This is all the help we can give you."

I had to blink and allow my eyes to focus on the infinite black sky of the void. After a moment, it became clear that the phoenix was not flying in a random direction. It was barely visible to mortal eyes, but there was a subtle tunnel of shadowy mist, giving the spirit a direction of travel.

"Can't see that from the deck," said Adeline. "Where does it lead?"

"Utha's realm," replied Duncan. "It leads to the rest of the Eastron. I can't tell you how long it will take. Distance doesn't work the same in the void. It could be months, it could be a hundred years, but your phoenix will eventually bring you here."

Adeline chuckled, largely to herself. "That's better news than we had an hour ago."

She looked at me. Her brown eyes were calm, yet thoughtful, and I felt that she'd endured just as much as me, or perhaps even more. I didn't know all that had happened to the Sea Wolves before they joined our efforts to flee, but I knew some of what had taken place on Nowhere. She'd held Duncan's Fall against things I could barely imagine, and pulled together a ragtag bunch of men and women into a single army. She'd brought an entire camp of Eastron to our cause and, if it wasn't for her, Klu'zu would have reached Utha's Gate.

"We'll be waiting for you," I said. "And, if you don't arrive, we'll remember you."

"Is it peaceful?" she asked. "Our new home, is it peaceful?"

We locked eyes. "It is," I replied. "No one carries weapons – except to chop wood. We managed something special. Now, all we have to do is build and live in peace. A peace you made possible, Adeline Brand, First Fang of the Wolves."

She smiled. It was the most open and honest expression I'd ever seen from a Sea Wolf. "Then that's enough. I can accept an ending, as long as there's peace. And this is most certainly an ending."

"And there is peace," I added. "The kind that lasts."

Duncan turned back to face Adeline and I, and the First Fang's smile spread across all three of us. Between us, we'd somehow managed to find a way to thwart an ancient god and ensure the survival of the Eastron. I didn't know what to say, and I could tell the others felt the same. We needed to say goodbye, but the word was so small and inadequate, as if language couldn't encompass this kind of farewell. I didn't know if I'd see either of them ever again. Duncan appeared when he needed to, but that need had now vanished. He and his imp were more spirit than man, and I doubted he'd be of much use in rebuilding a civilization. As for Adeline, she had a journey ahead of her. A journey she probably wouldn't see the end of.

The smiles slowly faded, and a tear appeared in Adeline's eye. "Just fuck off," she said. "No goodbyes, no hugs, just fuck off." She turned away, leaning on the railing.

I backed away. "Live well, Adeline."

"You too, Marius."

Duncan and I walked back through the door and, once again, I was a crippled man with a world to rebuild. But my heart and mind were at peace.

EPILOGUE

U tha the Ghost sat in a dark corner of an otherwise lively tavern, nursing a flagon of rich, brown ale. It was his fourth flagon, and far better than anything he'd found in the Kingdom of the Four Claws. It reminded him that he still had earthly pleasures, and also that it was very difficult for him to get drunk. Elsewhere in the tavern, ordinary men and women were enjoying their evening. They drank, ate, told jokes, and went about the normal things that normal people did. He enjoyed watching them, for he envied the simplicity of a mortal life, and struggled to remember a time when he was like them.

The tavern had an open doorway, framed in a wooden arch, and letting in the warm evening breeze. Utha kept an eye on the door, awaiting the arrival of an old friend, while sipping from his flagon. The Ghost had arrived two hours early, and was using the time to reacclimatize to the realm of his birth. It was nothing like the realm of the Eastron, with far more diversity and a longer, much more complicated, history. Utha didn't know how long he'd been away, but was gratified that some things hadn't changed. Taverns were still taverns, and beer was still beer. More than that, he couldn't judge, not until he spoke to his friend.

"How many of those have you had?" asked a soft, lyrical voice.

Utha smiled. "Of course you wouldn't come through the front door. Still paranoid, I see."

"Paranoia is a human condition," replied his friend. "I'm just careful."

He sat down opposite, making sure the hood of his dark green cloak shielded his face from the locals.

"This is my fourth," said Utha. "I'd hoped to have a couple more before you got here. Apparently I'm not the only one who likes to be early."

"People are looking for me," replied his friend. "I can't stay long, or I may have to kill some clerics just to leave town."

"They still have clerics? Of what god?"

His friend reached across the table and helped himself to a swig of Utha's ale. "Of the Twisted Tree. You've been away a long time, Utha the Shadow, and you are not the same man I remember."

Utha smiled again, and snatched back his flagon. "It's good to see you, Nanon."

"And you," replied the ancient Dokkalfar. "It's been a little over two hundred years. I don't have many people to talk to these days. So, how does a god spend his time?"

It was a simple question with a complicated answer, but Nanon was one of the very few individuals who might understand Utha's journey. "Well, Ryuthula and I rebuilt the shadow halls beyond the world. That took time. Then I dreamt of an old one... far, far away."

"Were you strong enough to defeat it?" asked Nanon.

"No," replied Utha, "but I helped some mortals of the realm to escape. A few hundred thousand of them. They're called Eastron."

"So, you're a benevolent god?" Nanon leant back in his chair, showing an angular, grey face, black eyes and sharply pointed ears. "Are these escapees your worshippers?"

"If they choose to be," replied Utha. "Some are most of the way there, but I don't like being worshipped."

Nanon tilted his head. His people didn't express emotions in the same way as humans, and a simple twist of the neck could convey worlds of implied meaning. "A god who doesn't like to be worshipped. That's interesting. Where did you leave your few hundred thousand proto-worshippers?"

"I tailored the shadow halls for them," said Utha. "It's got a sun and everything."

"Are they like the humans here?" asked Nanon.

Utha shook his head. "Not even close. An average Eastron could tackle a knight of Ro with ease. A tough Eastron could kill five of them while unarmed. They channel energy from the void. They call it wyrd. They'd give you a good fight, my knife-eared friend."

Nanon drummed his slender fingers on the wooden table. He was one of the oldest Dokkalfar, and far older than Utha. Despite this, he was strangely grounded, with a kind heart and an eternal curiosity about the lands of men.

"You really are different," said Nanon. "Calmer... and your eyes move slower."

Utha knew he'd changed since he walked these lands as a mortal, but hearing it from someone who actually knew him was jarring. "So, the Twisted Tree is still in ascendance here?"

"The Tyrants are in ascendance," replied Nanon. "The Twisted Tree is just the divine cudgel they beat people with. North of Sisters' Reach, the Ranen are still free, but the Ro and the Karesians... it's all a very careful dance of dominance. Worship of other gods has been forbidden for a century."

Utha nodded, slowly formulating a plan. "And the lands east of here? Are they settled?"

Another head tilt, this time signifying confusion. "East of here are the Wastes of Jekka. No, of course they're not settled. What are you thinking?"

He waved at the barman, requesting two more flagons of ale. "I'm not sure, but the Eastron can't stay in the shadow halls forever. I've not told them, but within a few generations, they'll become creatures of the void and not be able to return to the realms of form."

"And you plan to find them another home before that?" queried Nanon, evidently guessing Utha's ultimate plan.

The beer was delivered and they both drank, without breaking eye contact.

"Is that possible?" asked Nanon. "Bringing them here?"

Utha nodded. "To them, this is just another realm of form. They're human, like the peoples of Ro, Ranen and Karesia. Their spiritual power aside, their anatomy is the same."

Suddenly, Nanon laughed. It was a human expression that appeared strange coming from the Dokkalfar, but he'd clearly practised it, and the sound was natural, with genuine humour.

"That's funny?" asked Utha.

"Yes, yes it is." Nanon took another deep drink of ale. "I haven't seen you in two hundred years. You ask to meet in Ro Leith, and I arrive to find a god within the man I once knew. Now, you say you have two hundred thousand followers you intend to relocate here... east of Tor Funweir. And, to make things even more interesting, these followers are mighty. You don't find that funny?"

Utha leant back in his chair. "We have many drinks ahead of us, my friend. You need to tell me everything that has happened since I left. Shub-Nillurath and his lands of the Twisted Tree may be in ascendance, but the Eastron *are* coming here and I'll be coming with them."

APPENDIX

SEA WOLVES

Formerly of the Severed Hand, Moon Rock and Last Port. One of the three camps of Wolves. Followers of the First Fang.

Adeline Brand	First Fang
Rys Coldfire, called the Wolf's Bastard	duellist
Siggy Blackeye	mistress of *Halfdan's Revenge*
Kieran Greenfire	master of *Halfdan's Revenge*
Xavyer Ice, called the Grim Wolf	elder of Nowhere
Duncan Greenfire	
Tynian Driftwood	captain of *Halfdan's Revenge*
Wilhelm Greenfire	the High Captain
Bjorn Coldfire	spirit-master of *Halfdan's Revenge*
Tomas Red Fang	spirit-master
Brindon Grief	fisherman
Vincent Half Hitch, called Hitch	lookout of *Halfdan's Revenge*

SUNDERED WOLVES

Formerly of the Hidden Claw, latterly of the Starry Sky. One of the three camps of Wolves. Followers of the First Fang.

Daniel Doesn't Die, Drinks the Death Bear's Eye
Eva Rage Breaker, called the Lady of Rust

KNEELING WOLVES

Formerly of Four Claws Folly. One of the three camps of Wolves. Followers of the First Fang.

Charlie Vane, called the War Rat	captain of the *Lucretia*
Oswald Leaf	elder of Four Claws Folly
Tasha Strong	cook

APPENDIX

DARK BRETHREN

Formerly of the Open Hand and the Dark Harbour. A
divided people.

Marius Cyclone, called the Stranger	elder of the Dark Harbour
Jessica Cyclone	wife of Marius
Marta Cyclone	daughter of Marius
Esteban Hazat	commander of the twenty-third void legion
Luca Cyclone, called Black Dog	captain of the *Dangerous*
Sergio Eclipse, called Anvil	quartermaster of the *Dangerous*
Asha Two Hearts	assassin
Gaius Two Hearts	assassin
Vladimir Falling Moon	spirit-master
Antonia No Moon	Dolcinite Pilgrim
Merlinda Night Eyes	leader of the Tender Strike
Jessimion Death Spell	commander of the second void legion
Santos Spirit Killer	commander of the third void legion
Santago Cyclone, called the Bloodied Harp	elder of the Open Hand
Lucio Wind Claw	noble Dark Brethren
Alexis Wind Claw	noble Dark Brethren
Lazlo Darkling	void legionnaire
Anastasia Hazat, called Spectre	void legionnaire

WINTERLORDS

Formerly of the Silver Dawn, latterly of First Port. Followers of the Always King.

Oliver Dawn Claw	the Forever King
Natasha Dawn Claw	the king's mother
Elizabeth Defiant	defiant of First Port
Alaric Sees the Setting Sun	spirit-master
James Silver Born, called Silver Jack	duellist of First Port
Tristan Sky	captain of the *Blade of Dawn*
Gustav High Heart	commander of Falcon's Watch

OTHERS

Utha the Ghost	a god of shadows
Titus	a cat
Hin'bak'ish, called Kish	Ik'thya'nym
Vil'arn'azi, called Villain	Ik'thya'nym
Ten Cuts	speaker of the Pure Ones
Hopfrog	hybrid

ACKNOWLEDGMENTS

I enjoyed writing this one. There's a simplicity to everything ending that made it a joy to think about. It was the one thing I could retreat to when the world decided to kick me in the head. Actually, that's a bit selfish – the world has kicked everyone in the head. At least I have the luxury of this writing thing to keep me sane. The following people have also helped.

Terry and Cathy Smith, Liz, Ralph and Rowan Lovegrove, Simon and Carrie Hall, Marcus Holland, Scott Ilnicki, Aaron Ward, Jessica Collett, Mark Allen, Benjamin Hesford, Emma Cook, Alex Wallis, Martin Cubberley, Tony Carew, Robert Dinsdale, Nigel Jones.

Things remain and things break.

AJS

ABOUT THE AUTHOR

A.J. SMITH is the author of *The Black Guard*, *The Dark Blood*, *The Red Prince*, *The World Raven* and *The Glass Breaks*. When not writing fiction, he works in secondary education as a youth worker.